CROWNED
IN
SHATTERED
STARS

BOOK IV

ELORA MORGAN

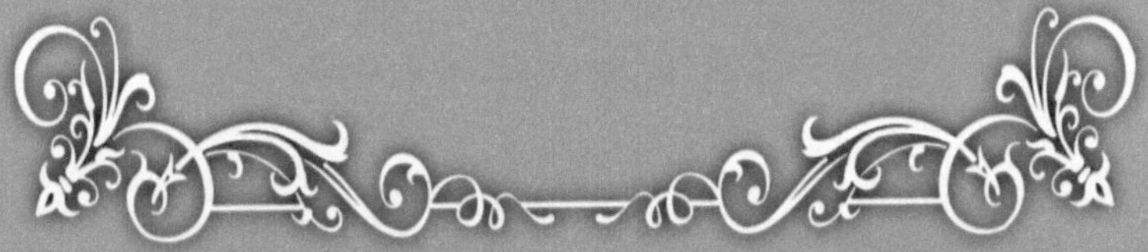

Crowned in Shattered Stars © 2024 Elora Morgan

ISBN: 979-8-9882794-3-3

Published by: Bound & Crowned Press

Content Expectations including Triggers

This book contains open door content including some dark romance and dark spice. These scenes explore aggression, manipulation, and dubious consent.

War, death, slavery, torture, fertility/infertility, trauma, the threat of violence against children, and the implication of rape are present in this book. While not all of this content is detailed or in-depth, some may be, and the mention of these sensitive subjects may be triggering for some readers.

While the circumstances involving the love triangle and the efforts to conceive an heir might not strictly qualify as infidelity within this world/series, the cloudy nature of the situation and the feelings of the characters involved could be upsetting to some individuals. Therefore, I would advise readers with a female-cheating trigger to proceed with some caution.

If you have any questions about material not covered, please do not hesitate to email me at eloramorganauthor@gmail.com

PROLOGUE

Zaria

"This is dehumanizing," Lazlian grumbled, arm pumping beneath the half-screen as he, presumably, wanked.

Lying on my back in one of High Spire's spare bedrooms, a broodmare awaiting insemination, I couldn't muster sympathy.

"Poor baby has to work for nine minutes while I'll endure for nine months," I pointed out. "Let's not forget your efforts culminate in pleasure, and mine, pain."

"Pleasure isn't the word I'd use to describe three people staring at me," Lazlian growled, indicating Lida, Kirwyn, and myself. "Not my kink, little queen."

Despite no longer being queen, Lazlian refused to call me by my name or my actual title. Perhaps admitting that I was now a princess would require acknowledging that I was *Kirwyn's* princess.

One whom, for the good of the kingdom, we'd agreed he could impregnate.

With Lida as witness.

God, this was messed up, even by royal standards.

Heat rose to my cheeks as I wondered, *but was it more or less awkward than if we'd done it the natural way? Lazlian inserting himself between my legs and thrusting hard inside me, again and again...*

Stealing my attention, a scrape echoed throughout the bedroom as the chamber door was thrown wide and Jesi burst into the room.

"I brought bubbly," she announced, smiling and tossing back her dark curls. Seeing Laz already behind the half-screen, she asked, "Oh, am I late?"

Lazlian threw an angry look at Lida as Jesi plopped onto a sofa, working the cork on her bottle.

"You said we needed a guard," Lida shrugged.

"Outside the door, not *in*," Lazlian grunted.

Jesi looked up wincing, "More witnesses would be useful, you said so yourself. So actually... I told Tomé that tonight's the night. I thought it might be helpful to have another man in the room. You know, to offer pointers or whatever." Eyeing Kirwyn, she clarified, "A man who isn't debating wringing your neck once you're done."

Kirwyn casually lifted his shoulder to indicate regicide wasn't out of the question. I supposed one misdeed was easy to speak of when we were already engaged in another.

"You're not making this any easier," Lazlian complained.

Sweating nervously on the bed, I felt the same.

The door swung wide again and Tomé strode into the room. Everyone turned to face him, and, noting the obvious tension, it only took him a beat before he rocked back on his heels and easily joked, "Ready for basting, turkey?"

Trying to divert attention from my blushes as well as to

muster some dignity while laying on my back, I stammered, "You'd do well to remember it's a - a royal baster and I'm your royal-"

"Turkey?" Tomé cut me off, laughing.

"Highness," I corrected, red-faced and cringing at my own awkward ability to make a situation worse.

"If everyone doesn't shut the fuck up, there'll be no material for your bloody baster," Lazlian gritted between clenched teeth. "Does my kingly authority hold no weight with you all? I need a new Assembly of Elites. You're useless and there are too many of you in this room."

"We're not your Assembly nor are you yet king," Lida pointed out, crossing her arms. "Besides, I only told Jesi."

"I only told Tomé," Jesi said.

On cue, the door opened a third time and Marcin stepped into the room.

"Of course I told Marcin," Tomé said, making a sound between a snort and a suppressed chuckle. Jesi finally worked the cork on the bottle and it opened with a loud *pop.* Our four witnesses broke into laughter while I covered my face with my hands, groaning.

"Hey," Kirwyn said, gently grabbing my wrists to lower them and brushing the hair from my forehead. "Don't stress. This is supposed to be the easy part."

"Give me the damn bubbly," Lazlian ordered Jesi, and she hurried to his side. Lazlian took an astoundingly long, one-handed swig from the bottle before shoving it back in her direction.

I heard Tomé and Marcin attempt to stifle their laughter, then Marcin cleared his throat. "Thank you for trusting me to be a part of this historic event," he told Lida, trying to sound serious and smoothing stray hairs back into his short goat's tail.

She nodded and calmly instructed, "Remember, no one must know. For now, we want only the barest of whispers. When the princess starts to show, we can help spread the rumor."

I felt dizzy hearing Lida talk about pregnancy in such a business-like manner. *Potential pregnancy,* I clarified. We had no idea if it would be successful right away. Or ever.

"Once it's confirmed, Juls is going to name the babe as his heir or relinquish the crown and name Lazlian king. Juls has been discreetly garnering support with some of the nobles and they're prepared to back him," Lida announced. "At the same time, we'll further spread the rumor of Zaria taking a secret position as His Royal Mistress. After she gives birth, Zaria will come to court and lay the babe at Lazlian's feet. Male or female, Lazlian is prepared to declare the newborn not only his offspring, but his heir," Lida said, nodding in Laz's direction. "Children born outside of wedlock must be claimed in the ancient manner, whereas the father publicly acknowledges the child as his by picking it up for witnesses to see."

Ridiculous sexism, I thought, *just like so much in this world.* A father could effectively deny his own blood, simply by refusing to bend down.

At least that wouldn't be the case here. Lazlian had grown increasingly fixated on me bearing his heir and was quite displeased to be thwarted in his plan to do it... naturally. I didn't doubt he'd force me to divorce Kirwyn and marry him if he could figure out a way.

A truth not lost on Kirwyn, and not helping smooth the tense process between the three of us.

On the other hand, somewhere in the darker parts of Kirwyn's mind, I suspected he debated assassinating Lazlian after a child was firmly installed on the throne -- an outcome that could potentially lead Kirwyn to rule beside me as dual-regent.

Because if the worry had crossed my mind, I knew the idea had crossed his.

I sighed, and it turned into another groan. Admittedly, my schemes alone always carried great risk. Combining all three of us cross-plotting with the stakes so high seemed to catapult the danger into the stratosphere.

While Lida continued speaking, Lazlian's eyes drifted to me, prone on the bed. *Awaiting his seed.* The half-screen covered what he was doing below the waist, but I could see the rhythm of his arm. His hot stare seared my skin as he pumped. I imagined he imagined... well, I didn't truly know what Lazlian fantasized about.

Heat spread all over my body and I swallowed thickly. Did he picture bedding me now as I lay, naked from the waist down and covered only by a sheet? Or bent over the balcony as he'd nearly taken me five years ago? Did he imagine punishing me first, as he'd spanked me that night?

Lazlian's arm moved faster, and his chest rose and fell with quickened breathing.

Maybe he thought of whipping me as he so often threatened.

If being watched isn't one of Lazlian's kinks, I wondered, *what is?*

I remembered the firm press of his fingers against my throat and guessed.

I'd... liked the feel of his hands on me that night.

Was it wrong that I wished I could see what he was doing beneath that screen? *Is he big? He felt big, pressed against my stomach, all those years ago.*

Despite ungodly amounts of fear at what we were doing, wetness grew between my legs. I knew Lazlian blocked out everyone else in the room as our gazes locked.

We breathed in unison, as if... we did other things in unison. Bringing himself to climax, Lazlian released a groan of pleasure he struggled to stifle from everyone's ears.

Not that anyone was paying attention as they passed around the bottle of alcohol. Lazlian's scorched-earth eyes were focused on me as he came into the tube provided. Meanwhile, Kirwyn stroked my hair, returning my gaze back to him.

Of all the things to ever happen to me, I thought, *this is the most bizarre.*

Closing his eyes, Lazlian took a moment to recover before calling out for Lida. She hurried to her feet, assisting with preparing the... material.

"Zaria," Kirwyn's voice pulled me from my musing, "don't spiral." He studied my face as Lida readied Lazlian's sample.

To insert.

Inside me.

God, this was nuts.

When Kirwyn and I made Teddy, it had been magical, beautiful. This was so mechanical.

But at least... not as much of a betrayal.

"Are we doing the right thing?" I asked Kirwyn, my voice barely a whisper. "This is crazy. And you're both acting like I'm stupid and don't know that you're plotting something. Stop it. I don't trust that you're not going to try to kill him, and if you get caught, I'll lose you. I can't lose you, Kirwyn. Are you okay?"

"Zaria, if you worry about me, I'll only worry more about you, so I need you not to do it," he said, not addressing the question of murderous intentions, I noticed. In fact, from the gleam in his eye, Kirwyn practically confirmed he was up to something I wouldn't approve of. I wanted to scold him, but my stomach sank at his next words.

"I'm not the one who has to go through a life-threatening process," Kirwyn said, forehead creased with worry. "Remember how sick you were the last time?"

I nodded, not wanting to think about it and hoping this time might be different, even though the odds were low.

"I can deal with my feelings about our... decisions," he said, wryly. Of course he'd *say* that. He was always solid earth underfoot, always a rock in a stormy sea. *So damn sexy.* That power turned me on, even as I worried that underneath, this was eating away at him or going to make him do something we'd both regret.

"But remaining calm isn't your strong suit -- don't argue with me," Kirwyn ordered, before I could object. "And I need you as relaxed as possible," he said in his instructor-voice, the one I liked. His thumb grazed my lips, stroking. Maybe the excitement of watching Lazlian made me do it or maybe it was the intensity of Kirwyn's gaze, but I took his thumb into my mouth, briefly sucking before anyone could see. "Because what I *can't* deal with is if something were to happen to you," he concluded.

I wish I'd known at the time how prophetic his words would be.

PART I
CLAIM THE DESIRE

MINOR SETBACK
Lazlian

Several Months Prior

I could make her come so fast on my fingers alone.

That wasn't the problem.

The problem was, thanks to Merie's intervening, we'd taken two giant steps back.

The little queen stood alone in the king's hall, gazing at the throne so intently, she didn't even notice me. The sun shone through the windows, casting a golden gleam on both her and the oaken chair, like she summoned the goddamn beams to her will the way she summoned everyone else to it. I hated her dress. Short, airy, and pale blue. Around her waist hung a gold corset-belt. It wasn't that the outfit didn't flatter her -- she was Elowan, every-thing looked good on her.

It was that I knew she wore it to please *him*. Or to please herself. But not to please me.

That was another problem... not just that she didn't wear things to please me, that she didn't *want* to.

A woman of her station belonged in traditional, backless attire. She had no need to move about so freely at court in such a short dress, revealing her legs... but her back should be exposed as a sign of submission.

On the plus side, it would be nothing to lift the short dress, bend her over, and make the heir to the kingdom right on the throne itself.

Now wouldn't that be a princeling destined for greatness?

I gritted my teeth against the growing desire below, now threatening to show, and wondered what made the little queen's brow crease as she stared. Did she think about how the throne could have been hers, with the support of Mal's army? How it would soon be mine? How much trouble it had caused her since the day my father decided he desired her for his golden son?

As much as I wanted to know, there was something else I wanted more.

"Do you know how many times I thought about taking you on that throne?"

I whispered the question from behind and against her ear, watching her stiffen and hearing her soft gasp -- the reaction out of her I desired.

Predictable yet satisfying.

"As your brother's throne or did you conveniently rid yourself of him in this daydream?"

I frowned. She knew how to ruin a fantasy.

The little queen stepped away and I was forced to grab her bicep to keep her. Not a power move and one I resented resorting to.

She looked up at me haughtily with those impossibly

blue eyes -- the same blue as the sea beneath the castle. It made me want to blindfold her.

"You can't touch me so freely," she warned.

It made me want to gag her.

She pulled her arm from my grasp.

It made me want to tie her hands behind her back.

"You wanted it," I said, studying her face. "I could see it in your eyes when we decided. *You wanted it.* What happened? Him?"

Merie, ever-helpful, had piped up with the suggestion that we simply insert my sperm into the little queen, clinical-style. Separate from me. We hadn't done the same with Merie because it wasn't known to be as effective and Merie was willing to do whatever was best -- including sleeping with her husband's brother, an event so awkward we'd only managed it twice, heavily inebriated, and that was still enough to scar the both of us for life.

But for *her*, of course exceptions were being made, as usual. And once the idea had been thrown out on the table, her boy jumped all over it. I suspected he was merely waiting for someone else to suggest it.

"Always blaming other people when you don't get what you want," she chided, scowling. "What are you not telling me? Because I know you now, Lazlian. There's something in your eyes... and I think you're lying about mutually beneficial alliances. Or, you only mean them for a time," she tried.

"I told you," I cut her off with a dismissive wave, "your boy provides value."

Him and his goddamn trees for example. I felt the sneer twitch my lips before I could stop it. I had to improve upon concealing things as she'd improved upon revealing them.

The little queen gave me a look. "I think you might be scheming to kill Kirwyn as soon as I bear you an heir." She lifted her chin. "I'm not sharing a bed with a man who plans to murder my husband, that's insanity. And there's no good reason *not* to try Merie's method..."

She trailed off and I wondered if I heard something like hope in her voice. *Give me a reason.*

I hadn't one ready. Yet.

Frustrated, I rolled my neck. "And if her method doesn't work?"

The little queen averted her eyes. A pretty blush colored her cheeks. Her breathy reply told me she *did* still want it, only thoughts of him were stopping her.

You can remember, can't you? How it felt when I made you come, right into the palm of my hand? That was only my hand. *Let me show you what I can do with my tongue, my cock...*

"We'll cross that bridge when -- if -- we come to it."

"You do realize what you're condemning me to, don't you?" I asked. The ready defiance in her eyes told me she knew I referred to yet another exception being made for her -- that we not marry.

"The people will embrace a child of ours, bastard or not," she repeated impatiently, as we'd discussed at the table. "You provide the legitimacy of the crown, I provide likability."

So she hadn't thought it out. Unsurprising.

"Yes, as long as that child remains unchallenged. But if I were to marry and have offspring with another, *in wedlock?*" I held her eyes, forcing her to understand. "If I had a *legitimate* child, he or she would supplant ours. And even if I had another bastard elsewhere, that babe might someday grow to be an equal threat. Especially if we have a daughter and I later had a son."

Do you understand now?

"It's not unheard of for a woman to take a position as

His Royal Mistress before a queen is chosen, but it's assumed the king *will* one day take a queen, a wife," I explained.

She blinked, comprehension dawning.

"To do this your way means I can never marry. It means even having sex with someone else carries risk."

Inhaling, I let the expanse of my chest reveal from beneath my shirt the scar and the tips of the star tattoos I'd gotten *for her*.

Five years of trying to move on and I'm tied tighter than ever. While you can fuck your husband -- fuck anyone you choose -- at any time.

Oh, how it had flipped from the roles destiny had carved out for men and women, kings and queens.

For me and her.

I'll be the only king in history with a Royal Mistress he's not actually fucking.

I nearly laughed out loud at the irony.

The little queen feared a life of subjugation to a king's whim, and *I*, the future king, was the one subject to her will, her whims. Without even being allowed to touch her.

I wanted to touch her so badly, my hands tingled from palm to fingertip.

Unless... I thought, making sure not to let my eyes spark at the delectable idea taking shape. *She'd wanted it,* but something I'd done at the table in her sunroom had caused this frustrating setback. It made the little queen believe I held onto one secret.

I didn't need to give her cause to suspect another.

KEEPING FIRE AT BAY
Kirwyn

"I want to show you something," I said, taking Zaria's hand.

She broke into a wide grin, the one that was like the sun shining on a lucky receiver. After all these years it still went straight to my heart, causing a pang. Zaria turned and reached up, winding her arms tightly around my neck. That was something else that hadn't changed, she still sought, reached, clung -- as if she was afraid that I would disappear once more, afraid to be left alone.

No one will steal you again, I'd swear into her ear when her eyes glazed and I sensed she was lost somewhere in the past. *You're safe.*

But the truth was, no one could ever be completely safe in this world, especially outside of Rythas... and even this island-kingdom increasingly had the feeling of being built upon shifting sands.

"You know you're the only one in the world I'll allow to

surprise me," Zaria teased as she wove her fingers in my hair.

My chest swelled with pride at the same time I frowned to know that she wouldn't -- couldn't -- fully trust anyone, to the point where she didn't even like letting go of control for things that would be pleasant. Pleasurable.

It was why we played the games we played.

Well, I thought, grinning at the memory of her bare and bent and waiting as instructed, *it's one of the reasons.*

The only area where she didn't trust me was the one where *he* was concerned, believing I planned on murdering the insolent future king.

Too simple. There were deaths more delicious than mortal ones to savor.

Disgrace, for starters.

But I didn't want to think about the prick today. I'd agreed to an heir. How could I not? But that didn't mean I fucking enjoyed it and I certainly didn't plan on letting it go unanswered.

I took Zaria's hand again and led her down the wooded trail. The afternoon heat made the moment ideal. If I could hear the water, could she? Maybe not, but I bet she could scent it. Zaria possessed a sense of smell akin to a *beast of the forest,* as she'd say.

Giving me a sly look, Zaria tried to work it out, and when she came to a conclusion that delighted her, she yanked my hand to run.

We broke through the trees and my first gift sprawled.

The waterfall was a single cascade about three stories high, draining into an enchanting pool in the middle of the forest. Gasping, Zaria twirled, her eyes unsure where to land amidst the beauty. White butterflies played with each other above soft pink flowers to one side of the shore, while a wild mare and her foal wove through the trees on the far side of the pool, presumably having stopped for a drink before our arrival.

"I thought this place was privately owned," she gushed, kicking off her sandals and splashing in the shallow water by the bank.

"It was. It is. It doesn't have to be."

Zaria paused. "What are you saying?"

"I'm saying it was Navere's. And now it's ours," I told her, sliding off my own shoes and crossing to the pool of water. "Once we restore some of the vegetation, we can open it up to the public, make it a part of the camp, whatever we want. Whatever *you* want. It's yours."

Her face lit with understanding.

"I bought it for you. It's the first of your three birthday gifts."

"Oh, Kirwyn, it's stunning," she said, laughing as she shimmied out of her dress and tossed it carelessly onto the bank. Wading into deeper waters, she cooed, "It's like a dream." Zaria dove and resurfaced a few times, giving me time to catch up in the cool lagoon.

Swimming to me she said, "I want it, but oh, you're right, we can't keep it all to ourselves."

I lifted one shoulder and agreed, "Even Navere didn't. He used it to entertain the soldiers." Nodding my head in the direction of the worst devastation, I said, "You can see the damage their partying did over there. Effective though. I'll give credit where credit is due. He knows how to buy their loyalty."

Zaria froze enough to sink a little, then started kicking again to stay afloat. "This land belonged to Navere... you... paid him?"

I nodded.

Splashing, she covered her mouth with her hand. "Kirwyn, no! Don't you see? Didn't you think this through?" she scolded. Her scowl was adorable. She might have stomped her foot if we were on land. "This must have cost a fortune. Navere might use the money for something dangerous, I don't know, like secretly buying guns to stockpile for his own use."

That's my clever girl. Grinning, I brought her body close against mine. "I hope so. Mal-Yin forged those gold coins I used to pay Navere."

Zaria's eyes narrowed. "They're counterfeit?"

I shrugged. "It's a gray area. They're real gold, but they're not of the crown's making and they're marked. We've identified the suppliers we think the Commander will contact if he's looking to secretly buy his own weapons."

"So, it's a set-up." Zaria smiled on one side of her mouth. She loved a good scheme.

I used her rapt attention to draw her legs up around my waist and hook them behind me. "Mal's been able to infiltrate the operations for two of the three dealers. Then we'll have enough proof to bring to Juls so that he can go after the Commander."

Zaria nodded her approval. "What about the third dealer?"

I slipped my hand down the neck of her sea suit, cupping one pert, wet breast. Zaria's responding arch was immediate; being in or near the water usually aroused her. I was already hard; being near her wet body *always* aroused me.

"That scenario is less ideal," I admitted.

Zaria crinkled her brow. She knew me, knew I was about to say something she didn't like.

This is where I lose her.

Anticipating an abrupt end to my exploration, I pinched her nipple just a little too hard and it was like working a string toy, the responding jerk of her hips into my cock came as sure as if I'd pulled the line on a puppet. It was a dirty trick, but her little whimper melted into a sigh of pleasure against my cheek.

"It might lead to bloodshed," I admitted, kissing her neck. "Mal may have no choice but to take down their entire organization before Navere gets his hands on any weapons, essentially storming their business to annihilate it."

Zaria froze and blinked a few times. "Annihilate it?" she repeated. "Then you left out the part where Mal's men slaughter innocent people who are just doing their job. You left out killing all those people in the wrong place at the wrong time. *Kirwyn.*" She said my name in a scolding tone, smacking my hand from her breast and ending hope for something more delicious.

I knew this lecture was coming.

"Zaria, they're selling to Rythas *and* men more dangerous than Navere, so they're not entirely innocent. This is how it works on the mainland. I do these things to keep us safe. Our family."

"So it's kill or be killed, just like always?" she asked rhetorically, splashing away from me.

I swam over and grabbed her. She pouted but didn't fight me.

"We said no lies between us," I reminded her. "Would you prefer I didn't tell you these things?"

Zaria didn't have to reply. We both knew that she preferred a world where these choices didn't need to be made. And we both knew that it was not the world we lived in.

Worst of all, we both knew these dangers from the mainland had begun creeping ever closer to our shores.

WHEN WE RETURNED to our estate that evening, I had two more gifts for Zaria. Mazriah had already put Teddy to sleep, so I retrieved Finley without any interference on our son's part.

Retrieved wasn't the right word -- I opened the door where I was hiding our new dog and she bounded out of the room, ran straight for Zaria, and nearly knocked her over with exuberance.

"She's ours?" Zaria asked, breathless. "Where did you find her? What is she?"

"How did you know she's female?" I asked but didn't wait for an answer. "I named her Finley but we can change it to whatever you like. I picked her up not far from the Low Spire docks. She's a mutt, but I definitely see some Shepherd and Husky in there."

Zaria tumbled on the floor with our new dog, cooing and petting her for a long time. When she finally tired, I didn't try dissuading Zaria from letting Finley fall asleep on the couch, knowing a losing battle when I saw one.

As a heavy moon rose Zaria sat on the sofa as well, sipping a glass of red wine I poured in anticipation of her third gift. I slid the garden doors wide, letting the ocean breeze carry the sound of the sea and the scent of night-blooming jasmine into the parlor.

There was no denying Rythas was an enchanting island,

more modern and connected than Elowa, but wholly distinct from anywhere. It had been created as a dream, a refuge, an oasis in a burning world. I'd have been contented here, even without the title. My only wish was that my uncle could have lived to see me, see us. I thought our lives would have made him proud. And the only thing I truly missed from the mainland were the showers -- hot, pounding water on sore muscles. We rigged an outdoor version in our home, but the pressure was light and the temperature tepid.

"By the time the Fae Fête arrives, the trees will be ready," I said, sliding onto the cushion beside Zaria. "The science of it -- engineering the bioluminescence from other creatures and grafting it into the DNA of trees -- was only just beginning before The Great Decline."

"What you and Mal accomplish together is frightening," Zaria remarked, sipping her wine. "I'm just glad you're on our side. Though the Spades would happily let you join their ranks to access your talents."

"Speaking of," I said, grinning, "the best part is the Spades can't say it violates the TORR. No modern technology was used, past the initial creation. It's all natural."

White lie, I thought. The best part was that it would burn the keylord. For years he'd been trying to find a way around the treaty, a power source that didn't violate it.

"It must have cost the Dorestes a fortune," Zaria mused, staring out into our own dark gardens.

Studying the changes in her face, I asked, "Where is your head?"

"It makes me happy to know we're leaving the world a little bit better than we found it." Zaria said vaguely. She chewed her lip and looked around the room.

"But?"

"But I can't stop thinking that it might all be for

nothing if the Spades invade Rythas, if they take Elowans captive... that emissary is coming soon and-"

"Stop," I cut her off, taking her chin in my hand. She was rambling and breathing faster, headed for a spiral.

"Take a deep breath," I instructed. "I want you to do it for me. Because I told you to. Can you do that for me, Zaria? I would like to see you do it because I told you."

I watched the emotions flit across her face. She was already diverted, given a task and trying to decide whether to fight me or please me.

Zaria inhaled. Exhaled.

"That's good," I whispered in her ear. I held her as she leaned back on the pillows, the weight of me making her feel safe -- like she wasn't going to float away, as she'd once told me. "The lies of Elowa are over. You're not alone in the world any longer."

The right tone made her breathing deepen and in the dimness I saw gullflesh rise along her arms.

"No one is making you marry someone you don't want to," I said, despising the Dorestes with every word. Didn't they see what they'd done to her? I kissed her neck. Zaria shivered, gasped, and her legs fell wider in invitation. I pressed my erection against her, eager for the thwarted exploration at the waterfall to recommence.

"I won't let anyone hurt you. Steal you. Force you to do anything you don't want."

"Just you," she joked softly, cracking a small smile with her eyes still closed.

"Just me," I agreed, grinning.

Sitting up slowly, I said, "I want to show you something. You're right, the price we set for the bioluminescent trees was steep. Juls and I couldn't come to an agreement on payment. He had to offer gems to close the deal."

Reaching down, I retrieved the box from its hiding place under the sofa.

"Only these gems were attached to a piece of royal jewelry."

I slid the box to Zaria as she sat up, a tentative smile playing on her lips.

"Your third and final gift. It was made for a queen, but, well, you'll see. It's not something Merie would ever wear. Unfortunately for the Dorestes, finding a buyer who could afford such a piece presented a problem. As soon as I saw it, I thought of you, of wanting to see you in it."

Her spiraling thoroughly diverted, Zaria pulled the ribbon, opened the box, and revealed the near priceless pearl-and-diamond body chain.

She instantly paled, as if she'd seen a ghost.

A second later, I saw red.

That bastard. I fisted my hands, unsure which brother I wanted to punch more. The king had brokered the deal, but I was sure the keylord was behind it.

"Merie wasn't the queen this was made for, was she?" I asked through gritted teeth. "This isn't the first time you've seen this jewelry, is it?"

Zaria shook her head, eyes wide with some memory I didn't know. She reached into the box and lifted a small piece of paper I hadn't seen before, nor had I any idea how it made its way in there. Zaria held the note flat so that I could read it at the same time.

WEAR THIS ON YOUR BIRTHDAY AND THINK OF ME. I'LL THINK OF YOU IN IT, ON MINE.

I closed my eyes and took a deep breath. It didn't help in the slightest.

I was going to *fucking* kill the keylord.

A FEW WEEKS later I sat, surveying our gardens from the second story window and ruminating on how to proceed -- not just with Lazlian, but with Navere, my other problem. I tossed back a swig of dark rum. In my other hand I held the crumpled-up letter from Mal-Yin.

What the hell was I supposed to do?

If the Dorestes didn't make an heir somehow, Navere would take the throne. I could practically see him salivating for it whenever he stroked the hilt of his sword. It would jeopardize all our lives and, without a doubt, end Zaria's. Which would as good as kill me and leave Theo an orphan. The bronzed war hero had many supporters, but Zaria was *adored.* Her popularity was too much of a threat for Navere to let her live.

Lazlian understood this. It was the only thing we agreed on. It was why the keylord knew about my plan with Mal-Yin in the first place. But Juls, Merie, and Jesi were too close to the Commander, and it blinded them to the extent of how far he'd go.

Our family could flee, should Navere seize the throne. But to what? A life on the run with Teddy? We'd be risking his safety in the backlands the same way I'd been endangered growing up, only it would be even more dangerous this time because we'd have a target on our backs. That scenario was the second worst outcome to all of us being put to the sword by Navere.

Those were our two options -- a babe or the blade. The

way I saw it playing out, Zaria had to give the Dorestes an heir, or she'd die.

Maybe we should have left all those years ago.

I fisted the letter telling me that Navere had slipped through our fingers. The alcohol did not wash away the bitter taste in my mouth.

Mal's setup had turned into a massacre and the Commander was nowhere to be found. The few marked coins Mal recovered weren't enough to link the attempted weapons deal back to Navere. We needed to capture him *directly* participating in a treasonous act for Juls to make a case against him.

I took another sip, relishing the burn of alcohol down my throat. It was way too early in the morning to drink and I didn't even like rum, but I needed something to take the edge off the sting of failure, the danger in this defeat. Laz would call a royal meeting to try to intimidate Navere, but without proof, we could do little more than posture and imply.

Maybe it was time to shift strategies. Maybe if Navere and the Dorestes were focused on each other, they wouldn't see me coming.

The decision to execute a long-awaited plan sent a thrill up my spine. I was still smiling when I heard a horse gallop across our lawn as a messenger rode wildly onto the grass. Zaria, darting from the kindery below, beat me outside.

"Fire!" the mounted man announced, pointing in the direction of Low Spire. "There's been a fire at one of the estates."

I turned to see a plume of black smoke, hidden from my view in the house but unmistakable in the garden.

I blinked. *How much bad news could we receive in one day?*

"Possibly arson," the messenger hastened to add.

Zaria was already running toward the stables before the messenger finished speaking, forcing him to follow. She quickly readied Nixie, her mare, and I loved her for her urgency... though I often wished Zaria would ride *away from,* and not *toward* trouble.

"Find a guard named Breer back at the house," I instructed the messenger as we led our horses out of the barn. "Ask him to bring a few men with water, blankets, and medical aid from the cabinet."

I'd barely finished speaking before Zaria steered Nix toward the front of the house and was off, Finley running alongside her. I took the time to thank the messenger and give him a few more clarifications on where to find what was needed. I knew I'd catch up to Zaria in seconds, and I did.

Without medical training, there wasn't much she could do to help. There was also little combative advantage she offered, should enemies linger. Zaria was a mediocre fighter, at best, yet she never hesitated to charge into battle. I always thought it meant more that she wasn't particularly skilled, and yet she did what she had to anyway.

But god, I often wished she wouldn't.

Following the trail of dark smoke, we rode from Mid-Spire to Low Spire. I heard the crackle of burning wood and felt the heat when we rounded a corner, revealing one of the grandest estates in the flatlands wildly ablaze.

My god... I'd never seen anything like the inferno and this was only one house -- albeit, a large one. I wiped the sweat from my brow and fought the urge to strip my shirt.

Piland's manor, I think. A rich and non-threatening nobleman; he had no obvious enemies at court. Could it have been an accident?

Unlikely. I didn't believe in accidents. Not like this.

Zaria's presence attracted attention and we learned that no one had been using the second home when the fire began. Luckily, the large expanse of brick pathways between the houses helped mitigate the spread. An assembly line of people had already formed, carrying buckets of sea water to the gardens and soaking anything they could around the perimeter to douse potentially reaching flames.

Zaria clasped my hand as we stared wide-eyed at the blaze.

"This wasn't an accident?" she asked, but the question seemed to be only to herself, to make herself believe it. "Do you think it was-"

"Spades," I answered, not taking my eyes from the mesmerizing flames. I hadn't even realized I thought it until I said the word aloud. They loved playing with fire -- I'd seen them strike out against lesser mainland clans in a similar manner, just for the thrill of it. This was a warning and a threat. *See how easily we can burn your kingdom to ash?*

Or... another enemy? After the downfall of Oxholde, various smaller clans had moved to the island and petty warlords rose up. They mostly fought amongst themselves and, even united, weren't large enough to take on Rythas directly. But they pestered our ships with piracy if we sailed too close.

I weighed the odds. Zaria's people were a tantalizing commodity for frustrated Spade scientists. There were even those in Rythas who thought we should toss the Elowans to them, like a bone to a dog. As if it would stop or stall the Spades from attacking us.

I wanted to shout at those people, *do you see now that there are those in Spade City who want to destroy both kingdoms?*

This felt like a first blow, fully sanctioned or not. The Spades were taunting us, baiting us. I couldn't explain how I knew, but I could *feel* it in my bones, my flesh, as real as the sweat dripping from my body as we gawked at the giant blaze.

War was on the horizon, and all the pomp and pageantry of the forthcoming emissarial visit couldn't stop it.

This is how it always begins. First, they arrive with gifts, and then, guns.

It was just a question of when everyone stopped pretending and the first shot would fire.

JOKER, QUEEN, KING... ACE
Lazlian

It didn't matter how many times the mainland rat sauntered into the war tower, the wrongness of his presence never faded. A freeborn nobody had no place in our castle, let alone this room, where the Assembly of Elites conducted royal business of the utmost secrecy.

I didn't care that he'd taken our mark. He'd sworn no vow that long-ago afternoon, Juls choosing peace over pressure. Perhaps there'd come a day I'd cut the tattoo from Kirwyn's back myself, rendering him one of the clanless. Perhaps I'd spare him if *she* knelt and swore, seeing as how my good-natured brother also failed to demand her oath.

Either outcome delighted me.

Regrettably, Kirwyn wasn't sweating. Never having fully acclimated to our heat, it wasn't necessarily a sign of nerves if he did, but it would have been amusing for the proceedings to intimidate him a little. However, the breezy height of the war tower and its many windows generally mitigated any perspiration.

A smile tugged at my lips, considering the open windows. They always reminded me of the time my great-great-grandfather tossed a would-be traitor out the second to the south, then simply carried on leading the Assembly as if nothing had happened.

Indulging in the fantasy of listening to Kirwyn's screams if I could serve him the same fate, I quickly grew distracted as the obnoxious upstart moved to his seat. *Did I detect an extra spring in his step?* Narrowing my eyes, I got the irritating feeling that it wasn't just for ambushing Navere. After all, we didn't have anything solid on the Commander. So what was the cause of his jaunty little step?

Navere entered last, all bronzed hair and brass attitude. He was accompanied by many high-ranking soldiers, possibly meant to intimidate in an attempt that affected neither my brother nor myself. His men would have to return to the base of the stairs before we began; I was only bored by the delay.

Before departing, the only soldier who caught my attention was Jesi, failing to meet my eyes in favor of the floor. *Was she anxious? Guilty?* Interesting.

Once alone, we listened for the echo of footsteps as the soldiers descended the tower stairs, then Juls stood, calling the meeting to order. "Let me remind you of your oaths," he announced. "Nothing we speak of within these walls may carry without. Do you vow not to discuss the proceedings with anyone outside this room?"

"I vow," Kirwyn said, and I knew that he meant it. The little queen liked him honorable and for her, he tried to remain so.

Something to exploit either way. It served as chinked

armor, allowing me to poke through the holes -- or, should he deign patch it, a mistake upon which to capitalize. Zaria didn't like his shining values compromised. It really was a disadvantage that the little queen placed him so high on his pedestal because it would devastate her when I pushed him off.

How pliable she'd be then, weeping at my door.

There now, let's get you cleaned up in a nice bath. Shh... you look an absolute fright and it's nothing I haven't seen before...

"I vow," Navere echoed boldly, jarring me from a pleasant fantasy with his tone. *And what was the cause of such cocky assurance in his voice? What did that mean?*

Well, fuck. I straightened in my seat. Both Kirwyn and Navere had tricks up their sleeves. I had nothing and would have to wing it.

Alright. I mentally cracked my knuckles and rolled my neck. *Let's see who can fly best.*

"I vow," I said lastly, when all heads turned in my direction, "and I always keep my vows."

Juls sat, folding his hands with formality, and a tension settled around the table like a fog we couldn't see but could certainly feel.

"I've called this meeting because we'd like to benefit from your wisdom and combat experience," Juls began, addressing Navere. Then he hit hard with an open-ended, "What are your thoughts on the thwarted weapons deal outside Shreelos?"

"I think it should have been handled by the army and not your personal guard," Navere replied, too quickly. "With all due respect, of course," he added, without sounding very respectful at all.

"Perhaps we erred in not sending our top man to do the

job," Kirwyn piped up. "Just as whoever is behind this subterfuge erred in not sending his."

At the veiled insult, Navere flashed a false smile of small, square teeth. "Their mistake is our gain. But whoever this leader is, perhaps he's learned in the future not to send an underling for what a master himself must execute."

For fuck's sake. The double-talk was so blatant it was painful. I noted Juls's furrowed brow. *Do you believe now brother?* Juls was far from stupid, but in rapid succession he'd lost his father, his wife, and the absolute power and stability over the kingdom Grahar once held. He'd lost Singen and now Navere. We'd been raised to look up to these men, to rely on them as Father's most trusted. Juls didn't *want* to believe, and I couldn't blame him.

"You know it's lucky you're here to protect the crown," Navere drawled, leaning in Kirwyn's direction. "I suppose you've been lucky since you were near enough Princess Zaria to hear her cries and rescue her on the mainland. Tell me, did you track her party for days? Was it difficult to overcome so many men?"

I tensed at the masked taunting and kept my gaze glued to Kirwyn. *Don't rise to the bait and endanger us all.*

"I've faced more difficult adversaries." Kirwyn replied unblinking, forcing me to exhale with begrudging relief.

Navere rubbed the scruff on his cheeks with feigned consideration. "Speaking of faces, yours looks so familiar. I feel like I've seen it somewhere... in a painting or a poster or..."

I gritted my teeth. The implication was so thinly veiled, Navere might as well have spoken plainly. Our Commander did not forget Kirwyn's likeness from the posters I created all those years ago, attempting to capture the rat on the day of my brother's wedding.

Navere shrugged and concluded, "Well, who knows? Such is the life of the Commander, I'm afraid. Too many blows to the head have affected my memory."

I licked my lips, watching the volley of double-talk between the little upstart and our would-be traitor. Seeing the silver lining, I wondered if they could take each other out and do the work for me.

"Maybe it's time to retire," Kirwyn suggested with a shrug.

"I *have* been thinking about seeking a new role," Navere replied, tossing his bronzed hair away from his eyes. "Yet I must remain close to protect the king in these troubled times. Without an heir, the people are starting to wonder what will become of the Doreste reign."

I snapped my gaze to my brother. *Do you see? He all but declared his intentions. He's so confident, he's playing with you. With us.*

Through the minute slumping of his shoulders, I could tell that Juls finally let go of his last shred of hope.

I hated that the world around my brother repeatedly disappointed him and that I couldn't protect him from it. But I had to give Juls credit for playing the simpleton when he smiled jovially at Navere and said, "We'd never want to see you step away from your position but you'd have my support in any future role you wish to seek. Now, however, if you'd excuse us," Juls said in an ominous voice, "I have some royal business to discuss with the Prince of Mid-Spire that's long overdue."

Navere's grin widened, revealing more of those small, square teeth, crammed behind thin lips.

"Of course," the Commander said, rising. He bowed and exited the room at a quick pace. The door closed heavily behind him and before Juls spoke, we waited in silence for a few moments, listening to the retreating footsteps down the stairs.

"Don't insult me by saying what I already know you're going to say," Juls ordered tiredly, holding his head in his hands. "What do you propose I do about it? He is Merie's brother, I still have no proof, and he has many soldiers who are loyal to the point they'd lay down and die for him. Plenty may already be on his side for whatever he's promised them under some new reign."

"What's better than a promise?" Kirwyn asked, too theatrically for my taste. After a smug pause he said, "A deliverance."

Oh, that little bastard was up to something.

"What do you propose I deliver?" Juls asked with a scoff.

I inwardly groaned, wishing my brother hadn't walked into whatever triumph Kirwyn set up for himself, although there really wasn't a better option than to let it play out.

"A big, shiny pile of gold for each soldier," Kirwyn suggested, a smirk at his lips. "Fortunes buy favor. It is the oldest and simplest solution."

He couldn't have anything left, could he? I wondered, running calculations in my head. The cost of running his estate, the camp, the waterfall... it was already a small fortune.

Juls gave Kirwyn a hard stare, quickly catching up but not having a way out. "Overflowing coffers are never simple, especially in times like these."

Kirwyn shrugged with ill-concealed arrogance. "I suppose acquiring such coin *was* rather advanced." He leaned back, letting my brother and I soak in the implication of his words.

The little fucker.

Somehow, Kirwyn had accumulated the wealth necessary to give the soldiers a handsome bonus to buy their loyalty and he was dangling it over our heads. *I'll give you the coin and you give me...* I couldn't imagine what he'd ask in return.

Juls did the best thing we could in this situation -- the same that I would have done -- and stalled.

"Gold is an interesting option," my brother hedged. "But a sum of that quantity would take a proportional amount of time to consider."

"Take your time," Kirwyn lazily permitted, as his smugness grew so big it practically filled the room, making me choke on it. The idea of my family's power further slipping away and sliding right into his hands made my stomach sick.

I looked away in disgust and a shadow underneath the door caught my eye -- there and gone. My first instinct was to grab whoever cast it and toss them from the second southern-facing window.

What the-

Oh.

Oh.

Oh, this was fun. Someone was eavesdropping... and I relaxed because I *knew* it was Jesi.

Kirwyn was in rare form, gloating too much to notice what might have caught his attention. It had to be Jesi because she was quick on her feet and the shadow was gone. I suspected maybe clouds had parted, creating it before Jesi could move to correct its casting, but she'd now swiftly adjusted her position.

I leaned back into my chair and stifled a smirk. It all made sense now. My guess was that when all the soldiers left at once, Navere had ordered Jesi to stay and listen. He didn't have the balls to eavesdrop himself, or the ability. We didn't notice the absence of Jesi's departing footfalls amongst the many, but we would have noticed if Navere had failed to leave.

I rubbed my lips, considering. If I confronted Jesi now, I'd probably gain nothing. Navere likely armed her with some flimsy excuse for lingering, something like claiming she'd lost an earring and had simply returned to search for it. The fucking traitor.

The fucking fool. Navere had seriously miscalculated Jesi's allegiance. She might do as her commander bid and remain behind, but I didn't believe she would go so far as to report royal business and betray us -- or more importantly, her best friend. Any schemes of Navere's were a threat to Zaria, and above all, Jesi's loyalty lay with Zaria.

Meaning everything she heard, she'd relay to the little queen. I didn't have to do a thing.

Well, I could hand her boy a shovel to help him dig.

I gave my brother a look only he could understand -- *I'll take it from here* -- and rubbed my chin apprehensively.

"Don't you think Zaria should be at this meeting?" I asked, trouble hinting my voice.

Kirwyn snapped his gaze to me. "This doesn't concern her."

"Her own coin doesn't concern her? Are you not married?"

Kirwyn's eyes narrowed and I had to give him credit for not taking the bait. I'd probably mis-stepped a little in mentioning it so directly when I usually avoided acknowledging their union.

"Yes." Kirwyn supplied the one-word answer dryly, refusing to give me a lot to work with. Smart. But he didn't know what I knew.

"So the gold is half hers. Don't you think she'd want to know your plans for it when they're this significant?"

"My wife is talented at many things," the prick said with a grin, and I wondered if he implied skills in the bedroom. I wanted to punch him for the images passing through my mind. "But handling money isn't one of them. She prefers that I manage it, and I do."

Oh, do you? I blinked and instead of allowing the smile I wanted to spread across my face, I let my mouth drop.

"Does she not even know of the existence of such a sum?" I asked with pained disbelief, making sure my voice carried beneath the crack in the door.

Kirwyn paused and said carefully, "I don't trouble her with what I can handle on my own, what she is happy that I handle for her."

"I think she'd want to be troubled to learn that you've accumulated enough wealth to blackmail -- I mean negotiate -- with the sovereign she serves," I mused with mock concern.

Though I didn't love my position in this game, at least I'd moved back into playing. I was hacking at their union as one would to fell a tree, and the mainland rat was moving to claim an entire forest. It was time to start scheming bigger plays.

Apparently, my brother thought so too.

"Enough talk of gold." Juls held up his hands, silencing us. "The quickest way to quell the unrest is *to have an heir.*"

I noted, with pleasure, Kirwyn clenching his jaw.

"I don't care how it's done, but I want it done," Juls ordered.

I cocked my head at my brother. In that moment, he sounded like our father. Not that I was complaining.

"Figure it out and get on with it," he demanded. Juls

stood and gave Kirwyn a dismissive wave. "You can see yourself out."

I watched the door as Kirwyn left, amused at how Jesi managed to disappear before getting caught. I wondered how long it would take before she'd run to Zaria and repeat everything she'd just heard.

More importantly, I hoped my risk paid off and she told *only* Zaria. Information was passing through our war tower more freely than messages flowed through The Exchange, and I'd allowed it. Lines were being drawn and Jesi needed to affirm her allegiance to us over her commander. Especially as Navere's moves were getting bolder.

Either he'd stumble and we'd catch him, or one of his schemes would pay off and he'd end our reign.

My brother was right -- the sooner the little queen laid back and let me plant the heir inside her, the greater stability it would bring to everything.

Well, everything but her marriage.

What a shame.

THE LAST OF THE GOOD DAYS
Zaria

That fluttery feeling in my stomach deepened as we saddled the horses. I knew how to stop it, only, I wasn't sure if something more uncomfortable would follow.

I needed to tell Jesi about the plan with Lazlian, and I feared her judgement.

Nobles might engage in any number of indiscretions behind closed doors, but this was different. It was personal, and personally, I wanted Jesi with me for my part.

"It's low tide, we can make it to Tomé's through the beach," Kirwyn called out, steering his horse, Dante, to face me.

Tomé lived at the other end of Mid-Spire, but the path was easier when the tide receded and we could take the horses around some of the rockier coves that would otherwise block the route. Unlike me, Kirwyn rode with the barest of saddles. Teddy was strapped to Kirwyn's chest and tucked safely within his father's lap as they trotted toward the sand.

Watching Kirwyn move as one with a horse always riveted me. Adding it with the total confidence I had in him to keep our son safe as they rode together, spurred the rise of arousal. He didn't face me, but I could see a half smirk from Kirwyn's sexy profile.

He knew exactly what he was doing. And that teasing turned me on as well. And he knew that too.

Finley barked, Teddy laughed, and we took off down the beach, riding past the field of giant Elephant Ears marking one side of our property. Swimming far out at sea it was always easy for me to find our land from the leafy perimeter, or by our gardens themselves. Years ago, Kirwyn and I had planted yellow hibiscus shrubs and Golden Chalice vines supported by dramatic arches. I always associated the vibrant yellow with our home, as it was the most abundant in our cheerful garden and the easiest to pick out.

Directly in the surf, the horses kicked up sand and spray as we galloped. Theo's giggles carried on the breeze and my heart thumped with happiness. Moments like this were my favorite. Riding, much like swimming, made me feel as if I were flying. Kirwyn stayed close so that I was able to steal glances at Theo's giddy face, and Finley raced in the gently lapping waves alongside us, already a part of our small family. Behind us, the sun climbed, and before us a whole day of revelry stretched.

I was glad for the distraction of a party. We all needed something to take the edge off of recent events.

It wasn't long before we reached Tomé and Marcin's house, finding it overflowing with more people than art. We left Theo with the other small children, under the supervision of caregivers hired for the occasion, and he was delighted to abandon us for the promise of play.

Outside, I bit a jagged nail as I scanned the revelers dotting Tomé's wide lawn, but I didn't see Jesi before a woman approached Kirwyn and me. She made idle conversation and suggested to Kirwyn that he might like to explore a nearby cave. I thought perhaps she was drunk, as I hadn't heard of any recently discovered geological points of interest, until another woman sauntered over and casually brought it up as well.

Jesi spied us and when she neared, the second woman quickly mumbled excuses and disappeared.

Leaning close to Jesi, Kirwyn's face lit with interest as he asked, "There's a cave nearby?"

Jesi rolled her eyes and scoffed. "There's a hole in the ground from some recent erosion. I'd hardly call it a cave. They're trying to lure you away from Zaria for a dalliance."

At our look of shared disbelief, Jesi shrugged. "You did your noble duty, married, *and* you've given Kirwyn an heir, so…"

"Well, how dutiful of me," I deadpanned and reminded, "We married for love, not obligation."

"Some nobles would say you're under no obligation not to share the love," Jesi quipped. *"If* you keep it quiet."

Kirwyn scrubbed a hand down his face. "I need another drink. Can I get you anything?"

With glasses half-full, Jesi and I shook our heads. Kirwyn disappeared into the manor, hopes of a cave now dashed, and Jesi and I headed toward the beach. Finley, having wandered up and down the sand, came to rest beside us as we spread out on towels by the waves. The jittery fish in my stomach picked up speed as I ran out of time to stall.

"I'd say he's the most desired conquest right now," Jesi remarked, interrupting my thoughts. She idly tucked stray curls back into her bun and re-tightened it. "Your husband."

"Why him? The keylord is unwed," I pointed out, "and it doesn't get any higher than that, save the king."

"Oh, Lazlian's a close number two and definitely number one for those seeking marriage."

Guilt surged through me at her words because if what Laz said was true, he never intended on marrying anyone... because of me. Yet suspicion quickly tempered my sympathy -- it was like one wave ebbing and smacking against another, flowing. *Because what was Lazlian hiding?* Something in his deceptive gaze that day at my table gave him away. My best guess was that he planned on harming Kirwyn somehow, but with Lazlian the possibilities were limitless.

"But Kirwyn is hot and rich and he's fucking you," Jesi continued cheerfully. "Which makes him very attractive, especially when the goal is less bridal and more carnal."

"That's... difficult to believe," I said, shifting uncomfortably. But I supposed it made sense. My status helped secure the throne for a Doreste heir. Why wouldn't it add to Kirwyn's desirability, in a twisted way?

"Navere is coming in a close third," Jesi announced, counting off on her fingers as casually as if she was ticking off horses in a race. Perhaps it *was* like a game to the noblewomen. "But because he beds most any girl who offers herself, he's not as much of a challenge, and the scheming ones are holding out for a ring anyway. Navere, however, won't pledge himself to anyone until..." It was Jesi's turn to shift uncomfortably. "Well, I don't know for sure what

Navere's motives are. But I think he's saving that position for someone he can leverage."

Leverage into what? I thought, stomach sinking. Jesi already suspected that Navere secretly eyed the throne. Was she starting to believe that her commander wanted the crown enough to kill for it?

"Juls, of course, would easily outrank them all," Jesi said, shrugging and sipping her drink, "but everyone knows he's too well-behaved and focused on making an heir with Merie."

I sucked in a long breath and let it out slowly.

"Jesi, there's something I'm going to tell you and it's of the utmost secrecy. Whatever you do, you can't tell Navere."

Having her vow, I related the events of Juls and Merie's recent visit and how *I'd* agreed to make the heir... with Prince Lazlian. Jesi wasn't the least bit shocked at the request, but her eyebrows reached her hairline when I told her I'd accepted it.

"I'd been wondering what that meant..." she mused, almost to herself. I didn't know what she referred to but before I could ask she looked at the sea and murmured, "So all that time, you never could have made an heir with Juls."

"No," I agreed, thinking back upon the fruitlessness of Grahar having ordered me into his son's bedchambers. "I needed you to know because I trust you and I want you to tell me if I made the right decision."

Jesi barked a laugh, toned abs shaking with the movement. "You needed me to know because you want me to validate that decision."

"Maybe," I admitted, squirming in the sand. "But you're my best friend and I would want you to know either way."

Jesi leaned back on her elbows, gazing at the sea again.

Despite her efforts, another pretty curl had fallen out of her bun, blowing in the breeze.

"I suppose you're in luck," she sighed. Sand glittered on Jesi's hands as she played with the grains. "Because I've always believed in Rythas and in doing whatever we can to support our kingdom. I'm just surprised you're agreeing to do it with Lazlian, of all people," she remarked, side-eyeing me.

"We wouldn't be doing anything together, *physically*," I qualified, quickly explaining the basting process.

"Well, I don't have any advice, but I can tell you two things," Jesi said, wagging her finger. "One, you need to hurry if this is the plan. *Everyone* is wondering why there's no heir yet and some of the more disgruntled nobles have been scheming. And two, there is no way Lazlian isn't going to try to pull something. You better stay one step ahead of him," her eyebrows rose, this time in warning, "and keep an eye on your husband, too. I wouldn't blame him if he arranged for the keylord to have a little accident."

"That's three things," I said, scowling.

"How much coin do you have, Zaria?" Jesi asked, surprising me with the subject change. She didn't meet my eyes and for the first time I realized Jesi was nervous about something too. "Enough to buy an army?"

"Why?" I asked, confused at the direction of conversation.

"Let's just say that I've heard that your husband has been hoarding gold like a dragon. Enough to purchase a sizable company of men, if he so chose."

I frowned. That didn't seem likely… but I couldn't be sure when I'd never counted coins myself.

Thanking Jesi, I made a mental note to peek inside our safe the next chance I got.

~

I CAUGHT up with Tomé in the early evening, watching from the sidelines as everyone played shoulder-war in the surf, a game where girls sat atop the shoulders of boys and tried to knock one another into the sea. Nearby, Kirwyn tossed a stick into the water and Finley retrieved it, never seeming to tire.

"You and Marcin attract so many others to orbit around you," I told Tomé, clearly in his element with the many guests encircling his home. "You know, I always thought of you two as twin suns, and the funny thing is, Kirwyn showed me in a book that such a thing exists."

"I know," Tomé replied, "I've read it."

I rolled my eyes. "That's exactly what I'm talking about. You're both good-looking and talented and athletic and smart. It's positively greedy. I bet you and Marcin also never fight and can't keep your hands off each other after all these years."

Tomé flashed that brilliant sun-grin and laughed. "Well, I doubt we'd have problems in the bedroom, we're Elowan."

Frowning, I asked, "What's that got to do with anything?"

"It's just a theory I'm working on," he said, running a hand through his short, blonde hair. "It stands to reason that if our ancestors were created to be optimal in all areas," Tomé held my eyes to convey his meaning, "that drive and stamina both without and *within* the bedroom would be included."

I blinked rapidly, then narrowed my eyes. "Are you saying your sex is better than everyone else's? That you were designed to be some kind of prodigy in bed?"

Tomé laughed again. "Neither Marcin nor I have enough experience with others to be sure. I'm just saying," he shrugged and continued, "I think we might be extraordinarily well-equipped to handle uncommonly high drives."

"I wouldn't know either," I said, drawing swirls in the sand as I considered his words. "I haven't had much experience outside of Kirwyn."

Tomé cocked a brow. His blue eyes twinkled. "Not even with the king?"

"You know that marriage was unconsummated," I said, blushing. "It's public knowledge."

"I also know that what the royals say and what they do are two different things."

Fair point.

"No," I said, shaking my head. "I've never been with anyone besides Kirwyn." *Not really,* I thought. The cocktail made me confess in a low voice, "And he's as enthusiastic in bed as he is on his horse, and just as skilled. So I don't know if your theory is true."

Tomé laughed and it was so casually cool that it made my heart swell. It was the laugh of the boy I knew in Elowa, the one I'd lost for a time when he'd first come to Rythas.

"I'm not saying everyone else can't be great in bed or just as horny," he replied, half rolling his eyes. "Or that all Elowans are. I'm just saying -- what would be the point of altering our DNA to make us as desirable as possible, without also giving us the desire to do something about it?"

"So we're hot, horny, sex gods. Got it."

Still chuckling, Tomé clarified, "I'm just saying I don't think we're *generally* bad in bed, not if we were *generally* designed to be good at things."

Laughing, I covered my flushed face and excused myself to find Kirwyn.

"Wait," Tomé said, grabbing my hand before I could depart. "I have a favor to ask. A friend of mine is a jewelry designer and her shop hasn't been doing well since the Spades stopped visiting as often. I was wondering if you could wear something of hers to the next big royal event?"

My stomach sank. *More and more businesses are struggling lately,* I thought. Looming war tended to tighten purse strings and stall trade.

"Of course," I replied, understanding Tomé's request. If I wore his friend's designs, it would inspire others to purchase. "If you trust her talent, that's good enough for me. Send over whatever piece she'd like me to wear."

Dusting the sand from my legs, I found Kirwyn on the lawn, but I'd only reconnected with him for a moment before another girl with flowing, strawberry-blonde hair sauntered up to us.

"Hi," she began, nervously addressing Kirwyn. "I hope this doesn't seem too forward but I was wondering if-"

Huffing, Kirwyn cut her off sharply. "No, I don't want to check out the cave and your boldness isn't admirable, it's rude. If you haven't noticed, my wife is standing *right here.*"

The girl blinked. "I can see that?" she said, furring her brow with annoyance. "And why would I want to go to that hole in the ground when the party's here? It's just, I heard you're friends with Mal-Yin," she continued, shyly tucking her lovely hair behind her ear and biting her lip. "I'm just really interested in everything he does, and I was wondering if you might be able to introduce me sometime..."

Oh. Mal.

Kirwyn stammered as his face reddened adorably. I laughed so hard I snorted a little. The girl's jade eyes snapped to me and I realized I'd given the wrong impression, *again.*

"I'm sorry," I quickly gushed. "I'm not laughing at you, I'm laughing at *him.* At us." I turned to Kirwyn and said pointedly, "You can make that happen, can't you? The next time Mal's in Rythas, you can make an introduction?"

"Of course," he eagerly agreed, flashing a charming grin to repair the damage.

The girl eyed us warily, as if we attempted to trick or mock her, before departing with a quick *thank-you.*

Once she was out of reach, I scrunched up my face and tsked, "That's not going to help Mal and Aewna's situation."

But it couldn't make it much worse. Their stalemate had been going on for years with no resolution in sight.

As the sky darkened with the last vestiges of a bright orange sunset fading to indigo, Kirwyn and I took a seat on Tomé's grassy lawn to watch the show. It was such a simple occurrence, yet most people in Rythas never failed to enjoy it, and today the setting sun reflected on the sea prettier than ever before. Whenever the waves ebbed, an opalescence shimmered on the wet sand nearest the shore and just beyond, a stretch of seafoam churned with a glimmering pearlescence. Further back, beyond the softly crashing waves, a ribbon of iridescence glistened.

I sighed with happiness. It had been a perfect day, and just what I needed to forget that war seemed inevitable... and imminent.

We still have time, I soothed myself. *No one is coming to attack tomorrow. Probably.*

"Last sip," Kirwyn said, grabbing a wine glass I wasn't sure was originally his, or mine.

"Hey," I protested as he gulped it down. But when he

leaned in to kiss me and I parted my lips, Kirwyn surprised me by playfully transferring the wine into my mouth, tongue swirling with the act.

I squealed and heard Jesi's laughter join in behind me.

"Come on," she cried, pulling my hand. "We're lighting bonfires on the beach."

Kirwyn and I pulled apart, hearing the sing-along begin. Laughing and stumbling in the dim light over the uneven sand, we joined everyone gathering around the fires. Finley barked as she raced back to us and, pressing her wet and sandy fur against our legs, curled up to rest.

War might come to our shores, I thought, looking over the revelers, *but it's worth the fight to protect all this.*

Beneath an endless sky of bright stars, I snuggled against Kirwyn and sung the songs of Rythas that I now knew by heart. Songs I *felt,* deep in my heart.

CHAPTER 5

A ROYAL'S WORK IS NEVER DONE
Merie

I took a moment to rest after fluttering about the castle all morning, ensuring everything was perfectly in place for the Spade emissary's visit. Smoothing my hair, I confirmed no strands had fallen from the neat twist my maid had artfully worked onto the back of my head, and I traced my fingers over my silver-and-pearl crown to triple-check that it hadn't moved.

Not that rising unrest could be eased by all the flowers I'd arranged and the sophisticated dinner I'd orchestrated, but it didn't hurt to remind the emissary what the Spades loved so much about Rythas.

Unfortunately, I'd learned many disappointing things about the emissary from his last visit, nearly six years ago when he traveled here for the Ceremony of Gifts.

Technically, that had been his *second* Ceremony of Gifts in a short time, as he'd journeyed once for Juls's wedding to Zaria and once for his wedding to me. It was a fact that the impolite ambassador would rudely remind anyone who'd listen. Brekett was an unpleasant man and didn't seem to have our same aims of continued peace close to his heart. Even I could see that.

Zaria wisely decided to steer clear from the path of the emissary's cold eyes. Considering how Brekett looked at Elowan the last time, I didn't blame her. Rumors spread of strange ongoings at secret locations -- satellite compounds ringing Spade City. It was hard to know what was true, but the oft repeated whisperings told tales of research on fertility and genetics with human participants... willing or not.

Brekett arrived behind a parade of announcers, late enough that our brief ceremony was cut even shorter to make time for our scheduled luncheon. After a meal filled with posturing and tiresome courtly games, we escorted Brekett back to the hallway, and the small talk turned shockingly weighty.

"The Dorestes have been lucky to have so many male heirs in your line," Brekett remarked, reaching over to rudely pick an imaginary speck of dirt from Juls's jacket. With exaggeration, he flicked it from his fingers onto the floor. "Back in Spade City, we've all been wondering why the two of you haven't gotten started on continuing your dynasty by now."

"As king," Juls said, tightly, "I don't need to inconvenience myself to meet anyone else's schedule or expectations."

I didn't like Brekett's lips, they shone, either with saliva from his repeated licking or the grease from whatever he'd eaten at lunch. It made his smile literally oily as he pushed the matter, asking Juls, "But surely your own people are wondering? Surely the stability of an heir would only help *strengthen* your kingdom. Why not assuage the people's concerns and fill her with the next princeling?" Brekett asked, jutting his weak chin in my direction. "She'd look lovely with a round belly and make a doting mother, I'm sure."

To see if he'd struck a nerve, Brekett studied me keenly with those cold blue eyes, and for Juls and for the kingdom, I did not cry. I would save it for later, back in our bedroom. *No, the bathing room.* I wouldn't want to further stress Juls on an important day like this.

"There is nothing that could make my wife lovelier than she already is," Juls said, using that regal voice I adored. "And why don't you let me concern myself with what is necessary to strengthen my kingdom?"

Warmth spread through me for Juls's valor, but my stomach continued sinking at Brekett's thinly veiled probing. I didn't want to be here, the point where we passed pretending. If no one even tried to be civil, it meant war was inevitable.

The prospect frightened me more than I could say.

"Of course," Brekett replied, bowing with false humility. "Forgive me if I overstepped."

The ambassador took his leave and Juls and I listened until his footsteps receded. I thought he was going to comfort me, but instead Juls announced to the near-empty room, "You can come out now. I'm aware that you're hiding behind the door."

I blinked, startled, as a moment later Kirwyn sauntered into view, completely shameless at having been caught eavesdropping. If anything, he looked annoyed as he said, "I wasn't hiding from *you.*"

"I'm aware of that as well," Juls replied. "Which is why I let you listen."

I frowned. It would have been nice if Juls had clued me into our witness.

"You're very good at inserting yourself into situations you haven't been invited to join," Juls remarked.

I chewed my lip, wishing he would have attempted to butter up Kirwyn for the task we'd discussed the night before, and not open with an insult. Sometimes... Juls could be a little prickly lately. Well, maybe more than occasionally.

"I'm just trying to emulate the royal behavior your family exhibits," Kirwyn returned with an insolent smirk.

"Let's put it to good use then, shall we?" Juls asked tightly. "I'd like you to travel as the return ambassador to Spade City. When your official visit concludes, perhaps you could stay for a while in a less *conspicuous* manner."

Kirwyn took his time to reply. I watched a muscle in his cheek feather.

"I'm much more useful there, aren't I?" he said. "Wouldn't be in anyone's way."

My eyes widened as it occurred to me that Juls had more than one motive in sending Kirwyn to Spade City. *He wants to clear the path for his brother to make a move of some kind.*

A frown again threatened my lips, wishing Juls would have shared that information with me.

"Do you want the opportunity or not?" Juls asked, unbothered.

"I'll think about it," Kirwyn replied. But he didn't sound like he'd be doing much thinking.

When no one spoke for several uncomfortable seconds, I diffused the tension by asking Kirwyn, "Would you like a tour of the royal tower? We've been remodeling it for years. I think you'll find it much improved."

"I'm sure that if you had a hand in the design, it will be nothing less than perfect," he replied, smiling warmly. I believed it to be genuine, but it was hard to tell. I hated these court games.

Before I gave Kirwyn my arm, I leaned into Juls. "Please don't make an enemy of him, my love," I whispered, covering my words with a quick kiss.

I wasn't trying to enflame more competition in Kirwyn when I gave him the tour, I simply wanted to show him that we too valued reform, inside and out. And perhaps to charm him with some polite conversation.

Most of the tower remodeling was complete, leading to expanded quarters for Juls and Laz, comprising two sides of the tower. The third side hosted a possible kindery and the fourth, across from Lazlian's, was still under massive construction.

For each of the four main chambers, one balcony faced the stunning inner courtyard and the other, either the city or the sea. Our beautiful courtyard was a dream of fruit-bearing trees and flowering plants, a wonder of color during the day or aglow with faerie orbs at night. Raised high above the ground, I'd often marveled at how the architects managed to design not just a heavy garden so many stories in the air, but a small pool as well.

"Please ignore the mess," I said apologetically, when Kirwyn and I reached the fourth side of the tower. "It's still under construction, but I can show you my vision."

"I'd like that," Kirwyn replied, amiably. When he flashed his beguiling grin, it was easy to see why the ladies at court fawned over him. He wasn't as handsome as Juls though, and I personally found Kirwyn's sharp jawline and cheekbones rather severe-looking.

A little embarrassed, I led him through the dark maze of

building supplies and half-built walls. When my tour concluded, we found Zaria waiting for us in the throne room. Of course, I didn't want her made uncomfortable by being subjected to Brekett's scrutiny, but it irked me that exceptions were always being made for her.

I did what I had to for the good of the kingdom while she drags her feet like she's above the duty, I thought, returning Kirwyn to his wife. *And it's even worse because* she's *the one who clearly wants to spend the night in Lazlian's bed, while it was unbearable for me.*

I'd tried to help her when I suggested we use the plunger. I'd said it because I thought she and Laz hated one another. But now their attraction was so obvious, even *I* could see it. Not just because Lazlian was always looking at her, but because Zaria would *never* look at him. She'd float about, enchanting everyone at our royal gatherings with her wide, beautiful smile and easy laughter, but never did she fail to stiffen and tense around Lazlian, never did she willingly seek his eyes.

It took me awhile to pick up on that, but I was very proud that I did. The brave Savior of the Bloody Shoals went rigid with fear when my husband's brother entered the room.

Making the heir with Lazlian was the least Zaria could do to reverse the damage she'd caused the monarchy. *And who didn't want a baby?* My gosh, I could see why Juls was often frustrated with her when they'd been married. It had been months since we all agreed to proceed, and nothing had yet proceeded!

Enemies from without our borders, men like Brekett, I had nothing in my power to fight. But I could help strengthen our kingdom from within.

Tonight, after the welcome feast concluded, I'd speak to

Juls about the delay and insist we plan a first formal meeting to discuss making the heir.

Publicly, Lazlian could be intimidating and difficult. He often caused Juls a headache. But privately, with me, the keylord had been as gentle as my husband. While the ordeal was too awkward to think about, it wasn't rough or painful. I was sure Lazlian would be just as tender with Zaria, if she'd only stop being so obstinate and get on with the situation like an adult.

Like a royal, with a *duty*.

GILDED DECEPTION
Zaria

Fortified with defenses old and new, three locks protected our gold room. Staring at the door, Jesi's words rang in my head.

He's hoarding gold like a dragon.

With determination, I snatched the first key from Kirwyn's secret hiding spot, eying the dreaded senorok board on his desk. Kirwyn tried to teach me the game, but it was even more difficult than chess. I hated trying to memorize the complex rules, and he always won anyway. Senorok was played on tiered boards to accommodate all the battles and engagements and could last for long, tedious days. With the ocean right outside our door, I'd much rather swim.

Making my way to our gold room, I used the key for the first lock, entered a numeric code on a spinning dial for the second, and punched the correct numbers into the third, modern device for the final lock. Our advanced fortifications weren't permissible per the TORR, but neither was the technology reinforcing the royal treasury or the gates of High Spire.

For the first time ever, I pulled the safe door wide, sucking in a breath of awe as my eyes feasted on the piles of gold coins, Spade tokens, and other currency I didn't even recognize. Jesi was right. It was a fortune beyond what I'd imagined and a bounty surpassing anything we'd ever need. Mesmerized, I walked into the small, secure room and scooped up a handful of coins. In a trance-like state, I let them fall through my fingers, making a *plink, plink, plink* sound back on the pile.

"Zaria?" Kirwyn's voice came from behind me and I jumped as I turned to face him. He'd changed into clean clothes and slicked back his hair, wet from bathing after a long ride.

"Why do we have so much gold?" I whispered.

I could tell from the way he stiffened that my accusatory tone made Kirwyn cautious. He replied, "For our family."

I separated one of the coins in my hand and threw it at his chest.

"Ow," he protested, his hand flying to the spot where I'd hit him.

"Try again," I said, holding up my hands in a *stop* motion to let him know I didn't want him to come near me.

"For you and me and Teddy and our camp," Kirwyn replied. "To protect us. It costs a lot to run our household and the programs you like providing."

I chewed on that. I didn't know exactly how much money went where and I did tend to underestimate the expense of larger endeavors. But the gold around me looked like the fortune of a small *kingdom*.

I threw another coin. It hit Kirwyn in his thigh and he cursed. I'd been aiming for his torso, but it sufficed.

"Better," I said. "Not quite the whole truth though."

Kirwyn sighed, running his hand through his wet hair. "Don't get mad," he said, voice rising at the end in a plea. "You're the one who said you didn't want to be involved in all this." He rocked back on his heels. "I've amassed what I was able for leverage against the Dorestes. The more I can outspend them, the more they're beholden to us."

"To you," I corrected.

"To *us*," he insisted.

I chewed my lip, again considering. I *had* asked to be kept from royal affairs, years ago. I'd earned a rest, but now... maybe it had been enough. I didn't like being in the dark; it felt like the past all over again. It felt like something fraying between Kirwyn and I, and I liked that even less.

"Well, I appreciate the truth," I snapped. "But next time don't make me pry it from you."

I threw the last coin at Kirwyn and he attempted to catch it in one suave move. It might have been slick if he'd succeeded, but instead it nicked his fingers and he cursed again. I couldn't help but laugh, and, tension broken, Kirwyn smirked and stalked toward me. But I still felt adversarial enough to quickly draw the dagger I often kept strapped to my waist and raise it to his neck.

"You'd be dead before you tried anything," I gloated.

Kirwyn looked down at me with mischief in his eyes. Then he moved so suddenly, I squealed. Somehow, he'd taken the dagger from my hand, knocked me onto my back, and the blade was pressed against my own throat before I could blink.

"I can feel that you don't want to do it," Kirwyn said,

cocking that diabolical grin that made me want to bare my breasts and beg him to kiss them.

God, he's beautiful.

"You can't hesitate in real combat. And you're aiming too low." He moved the blade higher on my neck. "Cut here."

"Okay," I said, a bit breathlessly.

What is he looking for? I wondered, as Kirwyn scrutinized my face. I blinked in surprise when he leaned down and kissed me.

Pulling back, Kirwyn shifted his gaze to the blade. "Okay?" he asked quietly.

Shyly averting my eyes, I nodded, although I wasn't certain what we were doing until Kirwyn pulled down his pants while keeping the threat at my throat.

"Don't speak a word," he rasped, lifting my dress and removing my undergarments to find me ready. "Look at how you want me," he teased, almost as if he were a stranger running his fingers around my wetness. It was a very naughty thought. Was he thinking it too?

The embarrassment made me protest weakly, "No."

"You sure?" he taunted.

I whimpered, thankful Kirwyn didn't delay too long before sinking into me. The entire time we coupled, he kept the weapon at my throat and the hint of danger made me climax hard against him.

My anger subdued in the afterglow and we lingered, naked amongst the gold. With my head on Kirwyn's chest, I stroked his flaccid cock with fascination.

"It's like a swordfish," I mused. "Not aggressive, but a powerful fighter when it needs to be. And then it tucks away here," I said, indicating the foreskin. "It's like it goes back into its little packaging, its little fish sack."

"Dear god, Zaria, a fish sack?" Kirwyn choked as he laughed. I reddened and tucked my head into his shoulder. "I love you but leave the dirty talk up to me. And thank you for that image I will now never clear."

Calmed and connected through our sex and laughter, I confessed to Kirwyn what Jesi told me that had brought me to our safe in the first place.

"It's half my coin too, Kirwyn. I don't want you to use it to blackmail the Dorestes and I don't want you hiding things from me ever again."

"I didn't hide it from you," he insisted defensively, still holding me in arms. "You've always known the codes."

"But you knew I wouldn't use them so it's still a lie by omission," I retorted, just as defensive because he wasn't entirely wrong. "I especially don't like that all the times you've left with Mal to acquire this, that it was for revenge against the Dorestes and not for us."

"They're one in the same," Kirwyn argued. "And can't you see Lazlian is behind this somehow? He's trying to drive a wedge between us. Don't let him."

I licked my lips and whispered, "And what of the plan, Kirwyn? Juls has called a meeting at High Spire to discuss the... process."

My head spun just saying these things. Maybe the Dorestes were used to complicated, clandestine arrangements, but I wasn't.

"I know. Juls wants you to... start. And once you do, we have to... stop." Kirwyn let out a long exhale and his fingers tightened on my bicep, either to fist in frustration or to grasp me possessively. "We can't have sex once you start the procedures," he bit out through gritted teeth. "Lazlian is going to use that time to try something, I know it. Don't let him."

"Kirwyn," I breathed, hugging him tighter, "Please know that I'm yours. I swear it."

I heard another exhale as he said, "But by doing this, you're a little bit his too."

Guilty, I didn't reply. The truth was, there was nothing *little* about what we were going to do, and the infinite, unknown possibilities caused nervous little minnows to swim in my stomach.

I want you in my bed, Lazlian had declared boldly, just a few months prior. *Willing,* he'd stipulated, that day at my table. *I want you to come to me willing.*

So he couldn't be planning anything too sinister.

Could he?

CHAPTER 7

STOKING FIRES
Lazlian

The day began beautifully when the First knocked on my bedroom door and Jesi confessed to eavesdropping, as I knew she would. Eventually. I did not apply punishment for the treasonous offense, instead stunning her with an offer.

Jesi's very reluctance to snitch on Navere proved her loyalty.

I wanted it for myself.

"I know Zaria already told you about our plan -- don't waste time denying it," I said, cutting her off with a wave of my hand as we sat at my table. "How would you like to be a part of the witness team for Zaria's conception, and later, to have a place on the Assembly of Elites?"

In one swoop, the position served to reward Jesi for her confession, to buy her future loyalty, and best of all, to take Zaria's closest companion for my side. I wouldn't have done it if it wasn't useful, but I was happy to because I liked Jesi.

Her utter devotion to Rythas was unquestioned, it had simply been channeled incorrectly.

She had that in common with Zaria and I'd rectify it for them both.

Visibly relieved and grateful for my mercy, Jesi vowed to let me know if the Commander did anything suspicious in the future. In return, I assured her that we shared the same priority -- keeping Zaria safe. After I dismissed the First, I too made my way down the royal tower, enthused for what was about to happen.

MY DAY IMPROVED AGAIN when I caught a glimpse of Zaria's hair as she strode into the parlor beneath the royal tower. She'd arrived early to our meeting, and more importantly, without Kirwyn.

Perhaps he'd been forced to remain home to care for their son after Mazriah suddenly fell ill, and Kirwyn wanted to ensure that Teddy didn't catch the sickness.

Not that the child could, unless he drank too much of Mazriah's favorite soursop tea. Strange how the very cup she made that morning turned her stomach, when it never had before.

No matter. She'll sleep it off without any lasting damage.

It had to be done.

Quietly, I followed behind Zaria. The room she'd entered was a favored spot for entertaining guests after dinner; a large space consisting of three walls with the fourth side open to a sunny veranda. Elegantly placed plants decorated the area and flowers of every color climbed the arched doorways and spilled over the balcony. Statues of my ancestors, placed atop tables and pillars, lined the room. One wall contained a large fresco of an unnamed battle. With prolonged exposure to the elements, however, many of the weapons had disappeared, having been fashioned from a silver paint that didn't fare well in our moist heat. It gave the effect of men and women charging at one another unarmed, or dancing instead of fighting.

I'd found it interesting as a child, because paintings were to be static things, yet the more time passed, the more this one changed. It was the opposite of Rythas... a fact now under threat.

A temporary blip. Once Zaria is pregnant, it will all fall back into place.

I came up behind her and Zaria turned, hearing my footsteps. She was nervous, so I said nothing, wondering what her discomfort would prompt her to say.

"When he was alive, did your father have an HRM? During his marriage to your mother?" Zaria asked, tentatively.

I was a little taken aback but liked this direction of conversation.

"No, he loved my mother very much," I told her. "Well, he had one *before* he married her. The story is that he took the royal mistress as a way to incite jealousy in my mother and to have her agree to marry sooner, since she was dragging her feet. Obviously, a smart move by Grahar because it worked out happily for everyone, in the end."

Zaria shot me a look of wide-eyed shock and disbelief. I shrugged.

"Well, maybe not for the mistress. She was promptly dismissed and a bit put out by it, I've heard. I don't see why it mattered; she was never going to be queen. But I supposed she thought to ensnare my father's heart, or at least, milk her position a bit longer."

Zaria continued staring.

"As you can see it worked out well for us too. There's a precedent to have an HRM before a queen," I told her.

"Your father... took a mistress... to bait your mother into matrimony?" Zaria asked, incredulous.

"Yes, and it worked out very well," I reiterated, raising my brows. "If I had any inkling the same would work with you, I'd fill the position."

"Lucky me I get to fill it instead."

There were many things about filling her I wanted to throw back, but instead I said, "Indeed, most girls would consider themselves lucky. Aside from being queen, there's no higher position to aspire to."

Zaria rolled her eyes and it irked me. Not *most* girls, I mentally corrected, *every* other girl in the kingdom would be thrilled if I'd give them so much as a glance. Why couldn't she be more enthusiastic about the honor I was bestowing upon her?

Because of him. He ruled her mind.

Kirwyn had done everything with her, taken all her firsts. There was no undiscovered territory to conquer, to claim, to imprint upon her memory the shape of my hand in cultivating a particular desire.

The prick.

Well then, perhaps I'd simply raze that land, scorch it; so that it could grow anew with whatever I planted.

"That night on your balcony," I began, and watched Zaria's cheeks pink at the memory. "Had your boy never spanked you before?"

"That's none of your business," she replied, primly.

"I take that as a no."

Zaria huffed. "Of course he had, but," she lifted one shoulder, "more playfully."

Meaning he never pushed beyond her boundaries.

So there is uncharted territory to explore with the little queen. Darker places he dare not tread. Places I'd lead where she'd stumble, lost and searching, and only I could see, only I could guide her out. To supplant those memories, I'd lay new tracks and push her into those dark lands. Forget fantasy. Ideas for reality shuffled through my mind, each more satisfying than the last. Buoyed as if an actual weight lifted from my shoulders, I smiled with the assurance of an actionable plan.

For what she needed me to do, Zaria really had no one to blame but herself.

HEIR INAPPARENT
Zaria

"I know you're hiding something," I said, searching Lazlian's face and growing impatient as our meeting was soon to begin. Part of me wanted to stalk past him when he started talking about the night on the balcony, but I feared he'd only block me. Laz was bigger now than he was five years ago, the span of his chest more muscled, more masculine. I supposed spending five years ingratiating oneself with mainland clans would do that. Riding through the wild forests, fighting, hunting, *sweating...*

I shook my head and ordered, "I want you to promise me you're not going to try to kill Kirwyn. I made him promise the same."

"Did you now?" Lazlian asked, cocking a half-grin. "You made him promise not to kill himself? Shame."

"You know what I mean," I snapped, exasperated.

"Swear that you won't make attempts to murder him if we do this."

"I swear it," Lazlian easily replied, eyes twinkling either because he lied or just to spite me.

"And you always keep your vows," I reminded, folding my arms.

"I told you, your boy provides value," Lazlian mocked. "Maybe I'll be generous and name him keylord after I'm made king."

I searched Laz's face for the truth. "Keep your friends close and your enemies closer?"

He gave a shrug of feigned indifference. I groaned and stalked out of the room.

Juls, Lida, and Merie were already waiting for us in the small antechamber. With its sunny windows and potted Hibiscus plants, the choice was likely Merie's. She seemed to believe that beautiful decorations paved the way for beautiful discussions. I sat next to Laz, vowing not to turn red at any point of this uncomfortable meeting and knowing I probably would anyway. As chilled strawberry and mint tea and little passionfruit cakes were served, I grew positive that Merie was designing this discussion.

Sweet treats to sweeten the proceedings. Sure, Merie.

"Zaria," Juls began, giving me a hard stare and not touching the cakes laid before him. "You wanted Elowa protected, we protected it. You wanted her exposed, we exposed her. You wanted a divorce, I granted it. You wanted Kirwyn, I gave him to you. You wanted to live safely in Rythas, I assigned you a royal title and supplied coin to start a new life. Everything you have wanted I have given to you, and it has come at significant cost to the monarchy. So I do not think offering you the chance to install *your* child as the next king or queen is too much to ask in return."

I lifted my glass of tea and drank a long, perhaps insolent, sip.

Juls didn't mention the threat Navere posed to my continued existence, probably because he didn't believe it. I also loved how conveniently he ignored all the strain this would place on my life, and the laughable irony of having escaped a forced marriage only to wind up carrying the heir with rather dubious choice in the matter.

Finishing my drink I replied curtly, "I said I would do it."

With those simple but weighty words, plans were made and a schedule laid forth. Everyone discussed my cycles as casually as if they discussed a mare for breeding, and ignoring Lazlian was as impossible as ignoring a stallion sitting in the chair next to me. It might have been less surreal, had a horse wandered into the room and casually taken a seat, than me participating in this nonchalant conversation about *bearing Lazlian's child.* The skin on the side of my body closest to Laz grew hot.

"Male or female, my brother is prepared to claim the child as his heir," Juls said.

Lazlian drummed his fingers on the table. "Male is better."

I could barely choke out my words. "Are you serious? That's revolting."

"That's the truth. Would you prefer I lie to you?"

Juls looked at me sympathetically. "He's not wrong. This is dicey enough as is. It's happened, but it's rare for Rythas to have a queen."

"Fine. I'll admit that a boy is easier to slide onto the throne than a girl," I huffed, making no attempt to conceal my disgust. "But I'm not a vendor in the markets where you can order your preferred cut of beefsteak. Whatever happens is beyond my control."

Talk of the potential outcomes made it impossible to keep worrisome thoughts at bay. They docked like conquering warships and spilled infinite possibilities into my head, invading soldiers overrunning the shores of my mind.

Kirwyn. Teddy. The sovereignty of the crown. The sovereignty of my body.

I felt the heat of Lazlian's eyes on me as our meeting concluded and he absentmindedly toyed with the silver cuff he still wore. Beneath the table, my thighs seemed to squeeze together of their own accord.

Alarmed, I realized my nipples had stiffened and shown beneath my silken dress.

From the corner of my eye I saw Lazlian's lips twitch.

THE NEXT MOON CYCLE, we began.

And we failed. Repeatedly.

Months passed and the unexpected inability to conceive an heir sent me into a downward spiral. I grew more stressed, which only decreased our chances of success. Throughout the kingdom, I heard the questions.

Where is the heir? It's been half a decade and yet, where is news of that little prince or princess?

Perhaps out of guilt, I involved myself more in royal affairs. Much to Merie's astonishment and Juls's chagrin, I used my reputation as best I could and I threw Kirwyn an ostentatious birthday soirée in the brothel district, hoping to re-draw Spade visits. But tensions still mounted so high I felt like I could climb them, and, were they an actual mountain, see all the way to Spade City.

To my shock I caught the tail-end of an argument between Juls and Laz one day, and I watched, stunned, as Juls slammed a fist right into Laz's cheek. They quickly pulled apart when they saw me, but I swore I caught a look of guilt on both their faces.

Later that day, Laz waltzed into a meeting with a black eye and Juls barely acknowledged his brother's existence.

"Where'd you get that shiner?" a portly nobleman named Haros asked. I perked up, paying attention in case Lazlian gave anything away.

"Your daughter gave it to me when my head was between her legs," Laz replied lazily. "Bit of a thrasher, that one. But then, I don't think she's ever hit such a peak before."

Haros sputtered angrily and I closed my eyes and clenched my teeth. *My god, Lazlian. You can't possibly wonder why you don't win friends like Juls.*

If Juls and Laz's relationship was a casualty of the increasing stress in the kingdom, it wasn't the only one. Kirwyn did his best, but as weeks turned into months, being unable to engage intimately frayed our connection. I swam little and ate less. Tension built and I felt increasingly responsible for letting everyone down. No one had forced me to do this, but I'd agreed, believing I could. The crown's hopes were pinned on me and I was failing the kingdom.

Finally, Juls called another meeting before my next cycle, set to coincide with the Fae Fête. The room where we gathered was a gray, indescript antechamber. There was no tea or cakes this time. Juls and Kirwyn silently fumed and pretended they didn't. Merie looked unusually irritated.

Lazlian wore an impenetrable mask. But Lida and Jesi attended this time, and they seemed eager to help.

"I know this is a difficult topic," Lida said gently, addressing Lazlian. "But I have to know. Were there any issues when your son was born? Was he healthy?"

My heart ached for Lazlian at the painful question about his son's birth. He discussed it easier than his son's death, however, an event which Lazlian never spoke of in any detail. I couldn't bear to imagine it. The raid that claimed his baby's life must have been excruciating for Laz to even think about.

For a moment, I wondered what would have happened if the boy had lived, and Lazlian took the throne.

"No issues," Lazlian replied, evenly, interrupting my thoughts. "His mother went into labor in the morning and he was born healthy a few hours later."

He'd had the luck of the high sun at his birth and it hadn't mattered, I thought sadly. *A fortuitous time to be born and he'd still died young.*

"And you?" Lida asked me.

"No complications," I said, shaking my head. "The pregnancy was difficult but the labor itself was relatively smooth."

I'd birthed Theo right on the beach and in less than an hour. The pain was intense, but it wasn't unbearable. Rythasian nobles had been quietly scandalized by my Elowan behavior. Lazlian, when he found out, had louder and less polite words to say about it.

"There's another option we can try," Jesi piped up, and I could tell she'd been eagerly waiting to voice her suggestion. "Eroska is a fertility drug that boosts the odds of conception. If you take it leading up to your window, you'll have an enhanced ovulation. Like, tenfold."

"Like twentyfold," Lida interjected, brow creased. "And it must be used with caution as it increases the chances of multiple births."

"We could give Zaria a half-dose," Jesi said, tossing back her curls. "It would cut the odds of effectiveness but also the risk."

My face heated as Jesi proceeded to explain, with total nonchalance, how taking the drug would increase my arousal during that cycle, and how the subtle changes in my body would be enhanced, as if hyper-signaling to the men around me that a fertile partner had entered the room.

It made me, and the men, sound as if we'd been reduced to animals. And at that point, I was desperate enough to consider it.

"I gave it to Merie," Jesi announced. "It's safe."

Lazlian winced. Merie looked ready to cry. I felt terrible that whatever happened between them required the addition of the drug and had *still* progressed in a disastrous fashion.

Not that we were having any more success, but I never imagined sex between Lazlian and I to want for... enthusiasm. I licked my lips and swallowed because I knew from experience, from a sampling, that he certainly didn't lack passion. Or skill.

Glancing at Merie's wet eyes, a wave of guilt washed over me. I was never sure what she disliked about me more -- the fact that I had married Juls or that I had rejected him.

But now our situation caused animosity to flare, because Merie resented that I wasn't behaving as she felt I should. Not when the stakes were this high. Not when *she'd* done her duty without complaint.

"Alright," I agreed, without consulting Kirwyn. I could

tell by his hard stare that he didn't like it. "I'll take a half dose before the fête."

CHAPTER 9

EGO SUM MARIS
Zaria

I blamed the Eroska for everything that happened that night. I was a beacon, a lighthouse -- but the saboteur sort that tricked sailors, luring them to wreck on the rocks instead of guiding them safely to harbor. My body hummed with desire; hot, heady, and turning my every thought lust-filled.

It started before we even left the house, with my choice of costume. Or rather, lack thereof. I wore the wisp of an iridescent skirt, barely covering my rear, and a bra-top consisting of little more than sheer silk and netting. I used the same netting to paint a scale-like pattern on parts of my neck and the side of my face. My eyes were heavily lined and my skin glistened to resemble a siren emerging straight from the sea. I wore a crown of dark shells, encrusted with barnacles and black pearls. More black pearls dangled from my wrist and ankle bracelets. I left my hair long and loose.

Everything about my makeup and sparse attire was sleek, gleaming and shimmering like the moon on dark waves.

I'd taken too long to dress and Kirwyn waited, but it was worth the effort.

Once a mermaid princess, now a siren queen.

I felt powerful, desirable, wanton and wild. I could hardly imagine a thrill beyond seeing Kirwyn's wide eyes and his open-mouthed stare when I met him in our parlor.

Except his hands on me. In me. Getting me off on that glorious cock of his. That would be a bigger thrill, I thought, swallowing thickly.

When he recovered from shock, he ordered, "Turn around."

Grinning and flattered, I turned and quickly met his hand grabbing my rear.

"I don't think I can let you leave the house like this," he groaned in my ear. Pressed against the small of my back, I could feel he'd already hardened from my unusual attire.

"I don't think you can stop me," I retorted.

"I can try," he said, his strong hand kneading my bottom. "Pin you to the ground and handcuff you here like you once did to me."

I spun around and smacked him playfully on his chest. "Don't you dare make me fight you," I chided. "You'll ruin my makeup and it took hours to complete. Where is your costume?" I asked, distracting him.

Kirwyn fetched an object he'd placed on the sofa and I realized it was a burgundy, demonic-looking mask.

"Oh," I breathed when he slid it over his head. I enjoyed looking at Kirwyn's angular face, but this was... interesting. "We're both a little evil tonight."

I could only wonder what expression Kirwyn made

beneath the mask as he took my hand, leading us out the door and into the night.

I HEARD the music and saw the fairy orbs hovering as we approached. No longer the terrified prisoner of Rythas that I was at seventeen, the excited, infectious air hit me even harder than it had in the past; breathing it in was like inhaling elation. With war looming and the increasing tension of not having a royal heir, I'd thought the festivities might be subdued, but that was not the Rythasian way.

The way? *My* way. *I'd taken the title, were their ways not my own now?*

As we turned to the main celebration, I saw the glowing gardens with bioluminescent turquoise, fuchsia, and electric greens.

"Oh, Kirwyn, it's amazing," I gushed, pride swelling my chest. Though we'd lost some of the more mature trees in the Oxholde attack six years ago, the magical light of the bioluminescent gardens made up for it. It would be wonderous to look out the castle windows and see this marvel nightly, complementing the cascading glory of the Water Stairs. I wondered what the keylord thought of the sight and if he would be serving drinks in the crypt, as he'd done years ago. Perhaps he'd outgrown it. *We were so young then.*

"Yeah," Kirwyn mused, surveying his work. "And the Spades can't say a word about it, as it skirts their sanctions."

"Maybe we should just use prohibited technology anyway," I said, feeling frisky from the drug. "If they're going to annihilate us, we might as well go out with a bang."

Kirwyn whipped his head in my direction and admonished, "You don't mean that."

"No," I admitted, sighing. "I'll go down fighting. But will you?"

"I'm not afraid to fight," he hedged.

I snorted. "You just don't think this is a cause worth fighting for."

"You are," he replied, evading again. To distract me, he grabbed two cocktails from a passing tray. I didn't know what they were, but I loved the marine blue color and effervescence, causing bubbles to float upwards, like the sea. Each drink was garnished with a stick of tiny shells clustered together so there could be no mistaking the oceanic design, and my sip proved it had a refreshing, mineral taste.

Eyes followed me everywhere Kirwyn and I walked, and I thought what Jesi said was true. If, when a woman passed through her fertile window, subtle body changes alerted men to the opportunity and increased her appeal, then being on the medication made it tenfold, like I was the most desirable being those leering noblemen had ever seen.

At the very least I *felt* like the most desirable version of myself I'd ever been. And I was definitely the most desir*ing*. I couldn't take my eyes off Kirwyn; stealing glances at his hands and wishing he'd put them upon me, despite the crowd. His eyes flashed every time; he knew me so well.

But we couldn't... could we?

I noticed a theme of the affair when a forest green cocktail, served in a cup fashioned from banana leaves, was unmistakably a tribute to the earth. The charming drink for that element was sprinkled with floating violets and tasted like herbs and flowers. Delighted, I wanted to try all the elemental drinks... which was a bad idea on a good day, but was especially dangerous now, given that I wasn't supposed to mix spirits with the medicine I'd taken.

Wisely, I had but a sip of the air cocktail. It was nearly flavorless, containing only the barest hint of melon. It was colorless too, yet smoked with a magic neither Kirwyn nor I could source. I wondered if it was a creation of Lazlian's.

But there was no mistaking his hand in the last drink.

The fire cocktail glowed a deep red, of course, but what made it the hit of the fête was the flame stick in each. Either a trick of the keylord's or borne of some Spade invention, once lit, the thin rod shot tiny sparkles into the air, burning for at least a minute yet leaving the liquid safe to consume.

I didn't know what flavored the drink. Rich, tangy, and sharp, it tasted like nothing I could name. I pictured rocky crags in northern, faraway places, with impatient magma writhing beneath the crust, readying to burst forth.

But by then it could have been my wild imagination, stoked by the spirits I'd consumed.

Perhaps... over-consumed.

Kirwyn and I edged our way to the grassy square crowded with couples rhythmically spinning in the Sea of Flames, and oh, how I yearned to dance. The drug loosened my limbs, made them move as if under an enchantment and I, in turn, rolled and writhed like a siren beckoning with her body.

I am as beautiful and alluring as the ocean.

Or I was a clumsy drunk, thinking she enticed as she twirled. It was hard to tell.

Like a skilled captain knowing his way around a ship at sea, Kirwyn took my hand and my waist and swept me onto the dance area. It was as if I moved with a monster or a stranger, yet I felt safe, because I knew who he truly was underneath the mask.

No longer destined to be queen, the dancing was much different this time. I'd been demoted in my proximity to power, but I was no less desirable as a partner. It made a nobleman bold enough to risk taking my hand, and Kirwyn graciously allowed it, spinning away to collect the spare woman. Once the first brave dancer started the trend, others joined, so that I was able to share in the exhilaration like anyone else. Drunk on the alcohol and the revelry, I threw my head back with laughter as one man, then another, spun me around the floor.

On a particularly far spin, my left arm flew outward while the other remained tethered to my partner. I was preparing for the second half of the spin -- the part where I'd be snapped back into my partner's arms -- but before I made it, a strong hand clamped my free wrist. With a yank, another man spun me in the opposite direction. The move culminated in me slamming against a hard body.

Lazlian.

Instantly enveloping me.

I fought to catch my breath while he seamlessly moved us in time with the music. As before, he didn't dance like a proper partner. But this time he banded one hand tightly around the back of my neck and the other dipped low on my rear, squeezing.

"Lazli-"

He brought his leg up sharply, pressing into my core so that I was forced to ride his thigh as we rocked. Laz's flinty scent filled my nose, stronger for the light sheen of sweat. Swaying with the music, the fingers on his one hand stroked my neck sensually, while the other cupped my backside, pressing me higher on his leg and toward his cock. Our rhythmic thrusts in tight lockstep were fierce, urgent. The last time we were together on this night, we danced like we fought. This time, we danced like we fucked.

"Stop. People will see," I breathed in his ear, though my hands didn't push him away. Instead, they found a place around his back.

"It's dark and they're drunk," Lazlian countered. "Besides, if anyone sees it will only validate the rumors. Let them see. Let them suspect you're my mistress."

Fair point.

"I'd tell you to play along and look like you're enjoying it," Lazlian said, close to my ear. "But there's so much lust in your eyes right now I bet if I slipped my hand underneath your skirt, I'd find your undergarments soaked."

I felt the blush spread upon my cheeks. He was always trying to embarrass me, just like when we were younger. Now I resolved, *two can play this game.*

I brought my lips to Lazlian's ear and pressed myself tighter against his body.

"Who said I'm wearing undergarments?"

Lazlian's groan was pure, guttural desire. "Are you telling me that your bare cunt is against-"

He was cut off by my being yanked from his arms. Before I could blink, Kirwyn's demon mask appeared before my eyes. In front of everyone, he abruptly tossed me over his shoulder.

"Stop! You'll make a scene!" I cried as loud as I dared, clamping my legs shut tight.

"No one cares, they're all drunk," Kirwyn replied, echoing Lazlian's decree as he stormed off the dance floor and into the woods.

"Where are you taking me?" I whisper-shouted as I kicked. "Kirwyn, put me down."

"You're not wearing anything under that skirt and I can smell that you're wet," he said, chuckling. "I think we should take care of it."

Unceremoniously, Kirwyn dumped me on my feet and I staggered, but he grabbed my elbow to steady me. We were alone, though near enough the revelry that I could still hear the music through the trees. I reached up to remove Kirwyn's mask, but he caught my wrist.

I guess it stays on.

"Were you jealous?" I asked, arching a brow.

"You have no idea how much," he admitted with ease. Kirwyn unhooked my mermaid bra, exposing me to the open air.

"Are you going to fuck me to show me who I belong to?" I teased, temporarily ignoring what I knew couldn't be.

Kirwyn spun me around, pressed me tight against him, and brought his lips to my ear.

"You have no idea how hard."

I wanted him to but...

"We can't," I panted. "You know we can't."

"Not there..." his hand slid to my backside and wedged between my cheeks. "Here."

Oh.

I flushed and my heart hammered. This wasn't the place, but if ever there was a time to try again, it was now. I was so aroused from the drug and the drink, I thought I could climax just from Kirwyn's hands on my breasts alone. Without undergarments I could feel my wetness slicking my thighs. Copious amounts of it.

I could also feel Kirwyn's love for me as he didn't immediately back up his words with action -- and he wouldn't until I'd said something to confirm or deny that I was of the same mind. His pause made me want him even more.

"I'm scared," I whispered, knowing he'd take the omittance of a refusal as my answer.

"I'll go slow," he promised, and my frown turned into a grin when he qualified, "at first."

I choked out a gasp when Kirwyn swept me off my feet and onto all fours. Even with the delicious thrill racing through my blood, I braced, knowing how much it hurt the only other time we'd tried to do this.

Carefully, Kirwyn used the considerable lubrication I'd produced to ready me. His fingers back there had me volleying from one emotion to the next. Under other circumstances, without being hyper-aroused, I might have backed down. I had in the past.

I gulped when I felt the tip of his cock against me.

"Breathe out," Kirwyn whispered, and I obeyed, squealing when I felt the pain of him passing the threshold.

I froze. He froze.

"Relax and breathe out once more for me," he said, running his fingers through my hair to calm me.

It took a few seconds -- during which I remained frozen like a frightened rabbit -- but eventually, I exhaled and Kirwyn used my untensing to push deeper.

Inch by inch Kirwyn sank into me. I couldn't help my short, fast breaths, despite his tenderness. The stab of a sword isn't soft no matter the speed. But it wasn't entirely uncomfortable. I had the oddest sensation of both being torn but having the split give way to new pleasures with each movement. I danced on the edge of a blade -- *his,* I thought with irony -- and leaning to one side stirred my discomfort, the other, my desire.

"Are you ready?" he asked, when fully seated inside me.

I gave the slightest nod and tried not to tense.

He pulled back and, as expected, one deep thrust took my breath away.

"Kirwyn," I gasped, digging my nails into the forest floor. He drew out and pushed again, until the world disappeared and my mind melted, my passage into the world of pleasure eased by the number of drinks I'd consumed. Kirwyn's hands grabbed my hips, pulling me back with as much force as he pushed forward. I struggled not to collapse my torso into the springy grass.

Yet I came back to earth at the feel of it, and then I couldn't get out of my head, in awe of what was actually happening.

"I can't come," I panted. I desperately wanted to, but there wasn't enough stimulation to break through my thoughts.

"I'll help," Kirwyn answered, leaning down to stroke my clit.

"Stop!" I cried. His movement changed his angle inside me and what was feeling good suddenly hurt. "I'll do it."

I lifted one hand to stroke myself and Kirwyn moved his arm to bear more of my weight, since I now only supported my torso with one hand. Slowly, he began pumping into me again and when he heard my moans, he picked up speed.

The dual sensation was so new, so naughty, that I felt a powerful climax build and I rubbed faster. Once more, the drug and the alcohol released my inhibitions about the scandalous place in which we coupled and the act itself. Those very circumstances might have turned me even more... the idea of doing something I'd never done before, and so nearby the festivities... How naughty we were, coupling like wild creatures in the dark wood.

I released a loud orgasm into the trees, crying and clenching. When I tossed my head back at its power --

when I was in the throes of passion and could do nothing to stop the erotic display of my climax -- I saw him watching us.

He wasn't even trying to hide himself.

My eyes met Lazlian's as I cried out.

For a moment, I wasn't sure he was real and maybe... seeing him made me come even harder. I caught Laz's wild, hungry eyes and the slack-jawed lust on his face as Kirwyn fucked me and I fucked myself. For a few seconds, the dirty scenario was so unbelievably hot. My eyes fluttered back into my head and the world faded away as I was wrapped in a mind-numbing cocoon of ecstasy.

When I felt the cool, pebbly earth beneath my hands and when I heard the distant sounds of the revelry grounding me back to reality, it dawned on me that Kirwyn must have seen Lazlian too, and he'd said nothing.

He'd neither stopped pistoning inside me nor had Lazlian stop watching.

The notion of how sexy it might have been quickly dissipated as I realized Kirwyn and Lazlian had continued challenging each other as if they played some kind of game of chicken. I'd been the unknowing fool between them, putting on an astoundingly lewd show without consenting to my audience, without even being privy to its existence.

What had been one of the most insanely erotic moments of my life at its height, morphed into one of my most rage-filled.

How dare they?

Ignoring my soreness, I let Kirwyn fall out of me with a slick *pop* and scrambled to my feet.

One look at his guilty eyes through the mask and I knew I was right -- he'd continued despite having seen Lazlian watching us, like some twisted dick-measuring contest between the two of them.

Standing above Kirwyn, I knocked the mask from his head and slapped him hard across his cheek.

He hissed, struggling to quickly pull up his trousers.

Hastily covering my breasts with my discarded bra, I marched over to a dazed Lazlian. He had to know what was coming. Laz was too aroused to look apologetic but at least he stood and took it as I drew my hand back and slapped him even harder than I had Kirwyn.

I watched Lazlian wince in pain, but it wasn't enough. He'd watched me, *violated* me. Hot tears pricked my eyes and I slapped him again, earning a *"shit,"* from his lips. I couldn't see it in the dark, but I hoped his cheek bloomed with bruises. My own hand smarted, but I ignored it. Backing away, I threw a furious look at both men.

"How dare you?" I whispered. The scene was so surreal, I had trouble believing I was standing in it. I shook my head and blinked, wondering if the medicine made me hallucinate the entire ordeal.

Neither Kirwyn nor Laz answered my accusation. Neither followed me as I re-tied my mermaid bra and stormed back in what I thought was the direction of the dancing. I wondered if they would yell at one another, come to blows, or say nothing and walk away.

I couldn't think about it.

How dare they?

But a pesky, pesky thought buzzed about me, like a fly refusing to depart.

Do you really have a right to be angry? the nagging, unwanted voice asked. *What do you expect them to do?*

I saw a fountain through the trees, headed straight for

it, and collapsed onto the edge. Only after I sat did I realize it was the same one where I'd first met Mal-Yin.

Lazlian had secretly watched me before. That certainly didn't make it right, but it made it so I shouldn't be surprised. He could have hidden as he'd once done, but he was either too aroused to bother or had some shred of honor preventing him from insulting me further. And Kirwyn... I'd put him in an impossible position for months. If the tables were turned and I was in the throes of passion in front of another woman who wanted him, would I have stopped when we were both seconds away from finishing? Especially during an act I'd always wanted and had always been denied? Or would I rub the other girl's face in it?

I didn't have a right to be angry, not really.

I sat on the edge of the fountain until Kirwyn found me. We left the fête without speaking and rode home in the same silence. To be fair, it wasn't all from tension as we were both a little drunk. Perhaps that was why, back in our house, words came out the way they did.

Before going to sleep, Kirwyn paused at our bedroom door.

"I think you like it. The man who would be king wants one thing and it's you," he said.

"I think *you* like it. The man who would be king wants one thing and you have it," I shot back, still a little angry.

"You've always been a royalist," Kirwyn said, searching my face. "You're not just doing this because you feel you owe the kingdom or even to keep anyone safe. I think you *want* to have your child sit the throne and rule the kingdom."

"So what if I do? You like power too, don't deny it. Would you prefer I lie to you, to myself, to everyone, and act like it's something undesirable?"

Kirwyn filled the doorway, not moving in either direction. He took a breath, nostrils flaring. "I can't protect you from him if you don't want to be protected," he murmured. "We said no lies between us. So tell me the truth. Do you want to fuck him?"

It took me a second to form the right response. As my mouth worked silently, Kirwyn closed his eyes and shook his head. Then he quickly spun on his heel and left the bedroom without another word. I sat on the bed for a while before I realized he wasn't planning on returning.

I sought him out instead.

Creeping down the stairs, I found Kirwyn on the couch, pretending to be asleep. Still in my siren outfit and with smudged makeup, I climbed onto the cushions beside him. Snuggling tight with my back to his chest, there was little room left over, but it was enough. For a moment, Kirwyn continued feigning sleep. Then I heard his sigh, and he wrapped his arm around my torso.

I sighed too and finally fell asleep.

The next day, I awoke with a pounding head and an aching heart.

For the first time, Kirwyn didn't accompany me to High Spire, nor did I see Lazlian arrive or depart. But the keylord did his duty because Lida came into the room, holding the dreaded plunger.

"I can do it myself," I said quietly, waving her off. Lida didn't protest, smart enough to know from everyone's unusual behavior that something was going on. She simply nodded and left the room.

Alone, I stared at the plastic tube filled with Lazlian's sperm. After a few moments, I realized I was wincing.

When Kirwyn and I made Teddy it had been one of the most beautiful experiences of my life. Our passion those nights had been blissful, Theo was a delight, and everything about his creation just felt *right.* But this... conceiving a child under these circumstances and in this emotional state... it felt *awful.* Perhaps the royals of Rythas didn't have any beliefs about these matters -- superstitions, Laz would say -- but Elowans did. Deep inside me, I had a nagging sensation of wrongness at the idea of making a baby when I felt like *this.*

I spread my hand and, without emptying it inside me, I let the unused plunger roll into the waste bin.

CHAPTER 10

STALEMATE
Aewna

The gazing glass had been cloudy and muted from its inception. A relic of an outdated process, the craftmanship also led to early tarnishing, now creeping around the mirror's edges. We could import newer, shinier versions into Elowa, but the antique look fit, and I kept the mirror above my dressing table.

Over the years, it had served to remind me to proceed slowly. Only so many modern shocks could be absorbed at once.

Elowa had become an amalgamation of old and new, not too unlike Rythas and yet very different. Coming from my father's manor and stepping onto the island was like stepping back in time. But I adjusted. It felt good to be where I could *do* good. Besides, as long as I had my books and my letters, I could live almost anywhere.

Happily, Mal saw to it that I was continually provided

new books, and that my letters to Merie, my mother, and other contacts on the mainland were safely delivered.

What more could a girl ask for? I thought, brushing my hair. *Yet he offers so much more than that.* I didn't like drinking wine to excess the way everyone else seemed to enjoy it, but each time Mal-Yin kissed me I felt like I was tipsy.

In the passage outside my room, I heard the approach of footsteps and the click of a magazine as it was disengaged from a gun. The accompanying *thud* followed as Mal dropped the clip into the basket, abiding by my *no loaded weapons in my chambers* rule.

I smiled, watching Mal-Yin approach from the reflection in the dimmed mirror. It gave him an even darker look that made my heart beat a bit faster. I remained seated, letting him come to me, and at once he ran his hands through my hair.

"Where is the hairpin I gave you?" Mal asked, frowning. "You were wearing it at the ceremony today."

Of course he'd noticed, he'd looked at me so often I worried that someone would catch on about our relationship. The Fire Maidens knew since the beginning, I was sure. Little escaped them. But the Mystics were too busy locked in their own power struggles to pay much attention, and Mal and I usually kept our public personas in place well enough for everyone else. Sometimes, it suited me, because I didn't want speculation about my personal life hindering any of the work I did bringing Elowa into the future and keeping her safe.

"I'm preparing for sleep," I replied. "You wouldn't want me to stab myself in the night, would you?"

Mal had ordered the creation of several beautiful hairpins, each decorated with pearls or tortoise shells for an Elowan look, but ending in a sharp blade, concealed by whatever hairstyle I wove around the object. They matched the many necklaces and rings he'd given me, crafted to hold poison. But I'd put my foot down when he tried to get me to wear sandals with spring-loaded blades embedded in the soles.

"Let's try the new dagger then," he announced. "The strap has been re-sized."

Mal proffered the dagger-and-belt creation he'd had made, to be secured around my thigh, concealed.

"May I?" he asked. I nodded and he knelt between my legs.

Mal slid my dress upwards and I broke out in gullflesh all over my body as his fingers moved against the sensitive skin of my inner thighs. Once my tunic was as far up as it could go while I remained seated, Mal wrapped the contraption around my leg and slid the dagger high. His hand rose until he nearly reached a part of my body he'd only barely explored, and that had been but a mere stroking above my undergarments. Candlelight from my dressing table reflected in his eyes, dark pools of desire he tried to temper. Carefully, he strapped the belt around my thigh and gave it several little tugs, reluctant to rise.

"It fits," he said, and I blushed because I immediately thought, *you would.*

You *will.* Someday soon.

"These nightly visits are too brief," Mal murmured. "Your guards can only come to one conclusion and I'm sorry that they believe I... dishonor you." His fingers gently stroked my skin. It was so slight that I didn't even know if Mal was aware he was doing it.

I laughed. "Dishonor me?"

Mal-Yin cocked a charming, self-effacing grin. "Well,

what would you call it, bedding the queen regent out of wedlock?"

"What they believe is not my concern," I replied, perhaps a bit waspishly. "They are smart enough not to gossip."

Mal continued stroking me with his fingers. "When are we going to stop sneaking around like naughty children?" he mused.

"When you overcome this constant worry and relax enough to be seen at my side," I replied, giving a slight shrug.

Perhaps my guards did think Mal bedded me each time they heard him enter my room, especially as he'd crafted such a lascivious reputation for himself. Yet I remained possibly the oldest virgin in Elowa. Sometimes, amongst the people, I heard whispers of that nature.

Aewna, the Virgin Queen.

"You're the first target they'll go for if they know you can be used to hurt me," Mal protested, as he had done many times before.

He wasn't wrong. Mal-Yin had made many enemies.

"At least you have the dignity of a passageway," I said, stroking those sharp cheekbones I loved. "Zaria told me she used to sneak in and out of the palace by climbing a tree outside her window."

"I'd climb a tree for you," he said, lifting my chin.

"Lie to whoever you wish, my darling, but not to me," I said, laughing again. "You'd order your men to bring a ladder then spend the next hour trying not to show me your annoyance, but I'd see right through you." I tucked a stray hair behind Mal's ear, but I knew it would fall forward again in seconds. I liked the way his hair did that because everything else about him remained so immaculately in place.

Mal rose and crossed to the window. He withdrew a case of Verdnal cigarettes from his pocket and lit one, blowing the smoke out my open window. Even though I still didn't like the smell, I had to admit I'd grown a little fond of the herbal scent on *him.*

"I'd feel a lot better if you'd wear the bracelet," Mal said, leaning against the window frame.

In addition to hidden defense weapons Mal wanted me to keep on my body at all times, he'd been asking that I wear a tracker, too.

"I shall not be tagged like an animal," I said, returning to brushing my hair. "You can't have everything your way."

"Yet," he qualified. Narrowing his eyes and pointing at me with his cigarette, he said, "You're more stubborn than your sister, you know. You're just quieter about it."

"Well it's good that she's both loud and tractable. How else would you have made her into such a sweet songbird?" I asked, with unconcealed sarcasm. Mal and I did not see eye-to-eye on the way he worked against Rythas and their royals.

Mal took a drag on his cigarette, then another, equally timed. A warning sensation spread over my skin, somehow both hot and cold at once. I replaced my hairbrush on the dresser and turned to Mal slowly.

"What is it? Your movements are too measured, I can tell you're trying to hide something."

"I did some business with the Spades you're not going to like," he admitted.

I stared until he was forced to continue, "I sold them a line of long-range weapons they wanted designed to certain specifications. It's usually referred to as a first line of *defense*, but the Spades being Spades, call them FLO weapons, First Line of Offense.”

I sucked in a breath, a barrage of admonishments on the tip of my tongue. Mal never made the progress he’d hoped in Rythas, but I hadn’t thought he’d go so far as to play both sides. We needed Rythas to stand with Elowa, to keep our people safe. Or had he given up hope and, in an effort to salvage whatever power he could, thrown support to the Spades?

I stood, ready to release my rapid-fire questions, when an insistent knock upon my door stopped me.

“Queen Aewna,” one of my guards called, urgently. “There’s been an incident. You’re needed in the orchard.”

The guard’s tone worsened that uneasy feeling I already had from Mal’s confession. As I tied a light robe around me, I could tell Mal shared it when he insisted, “I’m coming with you.”

I didn’t argue, although having us both appear so boldly from my bedroom wasn’t ideal. We were joined by Aric, Mal-Yin’s most trusted guard, who rarely left his leader’s side. The short, dark-haired man was both good with a weapon and a clever schemer who engaged easily with everyone. It was that disarming manner that made him useful for Mal in learning other people’s business. Together, we hurried down the backstairs of the palace and out into the rear orchards. Following four guards through a dense row of trees, we were taken to a patch of dirt where torchlights had been staked, illuminating the earth.

Mal shoved me behind him, as if to protect me from words.

THEY'RE COMING FOR ELOWA

The message had been written in the blood of rabbits, unmistakable from the furry, mutilated corpses discarded nearby, already swarming with flies.

My guards were all talking at once, trying to be helpful, but I wished they'd stop. I needed to think, and also, to not allow my dizziness to worsen.

This message couldn't mean my father or Zaria's mother. They'd been neutralized, contained on the mainland. The little ones divided their time between there and here, but that was all the power Pama or Volmar could hope for -- whispering in the ear of children. But I kept in touch with my mother to know that wasn't the case. Moreover, no true allies remained in Elowa to welcome Pama or my father's return as some kind of god.

And no one else was as concerned with our existence...

...except the Spades.

Whether this was to scare us or warn us -- or both -- this message *had* to refer to their ambitions, seeming to grow in magnitude.

Under dark skies, two of my guards set up a perimeter to study the area more carefully in the morning while the rest of us returned to the palace. Reaching my chambers with Aric and another guard, I waited to speak until Mal and I were alone.

Once the door was firmly shut, I said accusingly, "You know who's behind this. They employ these sick games. You know they won't stop at Rythas, they want Elowans for unspeakable use. And by supplying these FLO weapons, you've *helped* them."

Mal had been silent and pensive until this point, but he now relaxed into the windowsill and lit another cigarette.

"In my head," he replied, "I might have added another letter to that acronym, based off their design."

I cocked my own head. A letter? What did that mean?

A smile played at his lips. "You're so clever, my darling, can you guess which?"

CHAPTER 11

ANGUISH
Kirwyn

Intolerable days passed. I wanted this agony to end, wanted to touch my wife. Freely, without needing to stop before we went any further. The constant denial drove me mad, and, increasingly irate, I was failing to be a good husband, a good father, a good person.

Lazlian wants this. Me, driven to insanity.

I felt stretched so thin by the demands on my patience and my restraint that I was sure I'd snap any day now. She thought of me as her rock, but even a rock breaks under enough pressure.

Exactly what the insolent prince wants.

I hated that I was forced to think about him as much as Zaria, hated giving him any space in my mind and our marriage.

Strained as they were, I didn't trust my own actions. Once my weapons, I worried over words. What if I played right into Lazlian's trap and said or did exactly what he wanted?

A few weeks after the fête it was clear that Zaria had failed to get pregnant again and I could no longer sort out if I felt relief or despair when she bled, as usual. I imagined killing Lazlian a hundred times a day, but I knew I wouldn't. I'd sworn it to Zaria, and his death only endangered her life. The powerlessness to protect her and my own family ate away at me. As the days passed, I shut down, waiting for an opportunity I could seize, though I was unable to conceive of what it looked like.

Whatever we were doing now had to end, or it would end us.

"Kɪʀwʏɴ, ᴛᴀʟᴋ ᴛᴏ ᴍᴇ," Zaria said, twisting her hands. Forcing a smile, she reminded, "You used to talk so much sometimes I couldn't get a word in myself."

What did she want me to say?

It's okay?

It's not.

I'm okay?

I'm not.

I have a solution?

I don't.

With another unsuccessful conception, I'd played out the probabilities in my head and I knew what would happen. Juls would nudge me to travel as the emissary to Spade City. Using my absence, Lazlian would seduce Zaria into his bed.

The only thing I wasn't sure of is if the Dorestes would arrange for me to have a fatal accident abroad, or if they wanted the information I could glean from spying more than they wanted me gone forever.

Everything was out of my control and the only power I had left was in how it happened. *Which is preferable to letting Lazlian think he'd orchestrated anything.* I could allow myself to be ordered on an errand, like a servant to the crown, or I could claim the role for myself and perform it beyond anyone's expectations. I could tear Zaria to pieces with guilt for something I knew she felt she had to do, or I could reduce that pain... by taking it myself instead.

Which I didn't fucking want. I wasn't a martyr or a goddamn masochist. But I could see what was going to happen, and the only thing I could do was salvage power and mitigate pain.

Wait for the opportunity of a better play.

"I've arranged a trip to Spade City," I told Zaria, fixing a mask on my face she'd never see through. "Juls has been informed. If I can manage it, which I believe I can, I'll be extending the stay to spy after the official visit has concluded."

Lies. But I would make it true by sending a message to the king as soon as I could.

I watched the confusion, then the hurt, pass over Zaria's face. She'd been fluttering about our bedroom, but she froze at my words.

"No, you haven't. Since when?"

"Last month. I didn't want to tell you and spoil the fête. I'm leaving in a few weeks."

I could tell from Zaria's wounded eyes that I'd hurt her doubly now, first by deciding to leave and then by lying about it.

"You'll miss the Divine Slumber if you leave now," Zaria said, reluctant to believe I'd be absent at that time. Typically, a week of solstice festivities led up to the slumber itself, the night when the gods slept.

"I think it's for the best," I said, trying to dispel her suspicions by matter-of-factly adding a grain of truth to it. "We can barely touch each other anyway, not until it's done. So just," I gritted my teeth and forced the lie out, "get it done. I'll return and we can put all this past us and move on with our lives."

However irreversibly changed they will be.

"Get it done." Zaria whispered so softly I barely heard the words as I watched her mouth form them. Her voice rose and trailed off at the end, like a question. Several.

What does that mean? Sleep with him? Don't you want me? Want me not to?

I couldn't suppress my scoff in disbelief at the whole goddamn situation. Remaining stoic on the surface was one thing, but providing comfort and assurance for her to do it was beyond my ability. Yet there was nothing to say, as telling her not to do it didn't do any good either.

I shrugged and walked away.

UNLESS THEO WAS WITH US, I stayed away from Zaria as much as possible before my departure to Spade City. I didn't trust myself alone with her and every day only made it worse. The night before I was scheduled to leave, Zaria crawled into bed wearing a little white negligée, and I inwardly groaned as I turned my back to her.

I heard Zaria suck in a breath, perhaps hurt at my action, but I was too busy fighting a losing battle against my growing erection.

She thought it was her plainest sleepwear, I knew. But

the color flattered her and exposed the curves of her body. All I could think about was the last time she'd worn that slip and I'd shoved it to her waist and --

Not helping, I tried to tell my brain at the images passing through. The only thing worse than the mess we were in is if we had sex now and she got pregnant. All our lives would be in jeopardy and not knowing whose child it was would surely drive me mad, and perhaps Zaria as well.

I might actually be a heartbeat away from madness at the moment, I thought. *She's your wife. You should be able to have sex anytime you want. Anytime she wants.*

I felt Zaria's hand tentatively reach for my shoulder. As if she did want it, right now. I gritted my teeth and tried to take inventory of the tack we had on hand in the stables and what needed replacement.

It wasn't working. I was rock hard. Even if she only touched me because she wanted simple affection, *I* struggled not to want more.

She's your wife. You won't see her again for more than a month.

The scent of saltwater on bare skin drifted into my nose, which always turned me on because I paired it with her. Worse, it meant she'd come straight from the sea to bed. Zaria often swam to soothe herself and I knew it meant that inside right now she felt confused, vulnerable, *needing.*

Her questioning fingers tensed softly on my shoulder.

She wouldn't protest. If I pushed up that slip and buried myself inside her, she'd moan and welcome me. Even if she hesitated, I could easily override her objections. It would only take a few well-placed caresses to make her melt in my arms.

How fucked up is it that I'm *the one who has to deny myself -- deny us both -- so that she's saved for* another man?

Goddammit.

Teetering on madness, I leapt from the bed and heard Zaria's sharp intake of breath.

"I need a shower," I quickly explained. "I'm hot. Can't sleep."

That was all I could get out before I stormed out of the room, because if I didn't, I was going do something we'd all regret.

I stumbled to the outdoor shower I'd rigged, stripping my clothes as I walked and tossing them onto the grass behind me. Tepid water sluiced down my overheated skin, but it was all we had. I pictured snow, ice, and the mainland cold, but I couldn't cool down or soften my goddamn erection.

I grabbed it and pumped, giving myself over to the fantasy that didn't need to be imagined. It could be real -- Zaria was upstairs, likely hurt and waiting for me to return and to hold her.

I could flip her over and fuck her so hard, I thought, taking care of myself as I imagined her squeals and groans. *In and out...*

Spending my seed into the sodden earth underfoot, I came in an embarrassingly short time, but I felt only relief that I'd taken the edge off the urge.

It wasn't gone completely though.

Seriously considering storming back into our bedroom, pinning Zaria to the bed and never letting her leave, I forced myself to redress and head to the stables. The horses were startled and I wondered if Zaria would hear the commotion or hear me ride out. I almost didn't bother saddling Dante, preferring the wildness of riding bareback right now, but I also planned to ride until dawn and thought better of it.

Out on the lawn, I paused once more.

Everything could be different if I stopped. Nudged Dante back to the stables.

Dismounted him and mounted her.

Dammit. Go.

I squeezed my heels more sharply than I'd intended, and Dante took off.

From the house, I heard Finley bark -- either for my return or to join me. As I continued, I wondered if he watched from the windows.

I wondered, with a pang in my heart, if Zaria did too.

IT WAS BETTER THIS WAY, I told myself, feeling the wind on my face as we sailed to the mainland. I trusted myself completely in the role as ambassador. I didn't trust myself at all not to fuck my wife.

The sheer ridiculousness of the notion made me laugh out loud and resolve to get good and drunk later.

I travelled with a small party including servants, guards, and most importantly, my duplicate -- or as near a man that could be found. The plan was to arrive in Spade City with all the pomp and pageantry of a royal visit, but to depart a little more quietly. Or rather, everyone else in my entourage would be departing, including my decoy, hooded on horseback. I'd shave the short beard I'd grown as well as all the hair on my head and spend the next few weeks covertly gleaning what I couldn't overtly learn.

It worked out just fine for the Dorestes either way. If I succeeded, they'd gather intel. If I failed, they could claim I'd gone rogue and throw me to the wolves. Let the Spades do with me as they liked.

Hell, maybe the Spades would take me hostage the

moment I arrived. Pretending we all weren't gearing up for war, pretending my visit could soothe tensions, was a tiresome farce.

As we sailed, I worked with Clive, the man attempting to pass as me. While his face wasn't an ideal likeness, his frame matched mine and he was a quick study, learning my speech and my mannerisms. If everything went smoothly, it wouldn't be too much of an act. All Clive really had to do was sit on a horse and ride out the gates, and Clive was a skilled rider.

A later rendezvous on the coast had been arranged for me, where a small company would wait until I sneaked out of Spade City, alone. If I succeeded, we'd all sail back to High Spire.

In my bones I knew that war was coming either way. I just hoped I learned something useful to give us a chance at winning.

TRICKY KEYLORD
Zaria

Before leaving for Spade City, Kirwyn returned home briefly to collect a few things and to say goodbye to Teddy. When he kissed me, it hit me that I'd been worried he wouldn't. I melted into that kiss, tension ebbing from my body while at the same time, my pulse raced. I hoped Kirwyn could pick up on it, but moments later he turned cold again, his farewell to me as strained as if I were a stranger. The mixed signals reminded me of the Kirwyn I'd first met when we were younger, and I couldn't sort through them any better now than I had then, because despite having grown, the circumstances were infinitely more complicated this time.

The only thing I knew for certain was that Kirwyn wanted this purgatory of dread to end, and so did I. Anything was preferable to the constant feeling that I'd let everyone down.

Worse, the truth I didn't want to admit -- the one

Kirwyn tried to hide from me -- was that not having an heir endangered my life. If Navere took power, he would try to kill me again, and surely succeed this time with the weight of the throne behind him. The Commander might spare Juls and Merie, since she was his sister and they couldn't make an heir anyway, but if he claimed the crown it would be a death sentence for myself and possibly Kirwyn, Lazlian, and Teddy, as well.

Days turned into weeks and I expended energy by distracting myself as best I could -- riding, swimming, and running on the beach. Silent, dark nights were particularly difficult without Kirwyn in bed beside me. Finley provided some comfort, coming to fill the space Kirwyn left by nudging up against me to sleep. As I read stories to Teddy each evening, my mind wandered into fearful places, imagining what might happen to our kingdoms and how much of it was my fault. If Rythas fell, Elowa fell. Everything I'd done would have been for nothing.

Whenever Theo giggled and brought me back to reality, I'd curse myself because on top of everything I was failing at -- being a royal and being a wife -- the stress of our situation was making me fail at being a good mother, as well.

Something had to change.

I plucked up my courage and resolved not to miss my next opportunity. Alone on the beach one sunrise, I scoured the sand until I found the most beautiful shell available. Holding it in my hand, I made a wish to Keroe that the next insemination would be successful, then I tossed the shell as far as I could back into the waves.

When my fertile window came again, I left Theo in Mazriah's care and rode to High Spire. The Divine Slumber was the following day, but I'd failed to make any elaborate preparations this year, reasoning that we could go to Saos and Alette's.

When I reached the castle, to my surprise, the guards didn't escort me to the usual room. Instead, I was led to Lazlian's chambers, high up in the royal tower.

Swallowing hard, I didn't know where to let my eyes fall first -- to the large, canopy bed or to the strange man standing beside it. My alarm spiked when the door closed behind me and the guards hadn't departed. The most comforting part of the situation was Erisio's presence amongst Laz's men. Second in the army and friend to both Laz and Jesi, Erisio looked abashed and apologetic; not malicious. Not that Erisio ever looked mean.

"You can speak freely," Lazlian permitted. "My guards are sworn to secrecy."

"Lazlian," I began, my eyes darting back and forth between him and the strange man. He was short, soft, and not particularly threatening-looking. "Why am I here? Who is this?"

"He's a doctor."

"And why is he here?"

Lazlian drew a heavy breath in and let it out before replying.

"To examine you."

"What's that supposed to mean?"

"Zaria," he began, and in that moment, I hated that he'd started using my name more frequently. He had the ability to make it sound so condescending. "You cannot carry a royal baby of High Spire the same way you bear children in Elowa. There will be visits from the doctor throughout. He'll be present at the birth. You're not laboring my heir into the goddamn surf like an animal."

I wanted to dive under the covers and hide. My cheeks

flushed to be in a room full of men listening to those private details about me.

"I can and have done," I spat, seething. "And what do you mean, examine me?"

Lazlian's eyes flicked to the guards behind me and I braced for some unknown fight, some unimaginable terror.

"Zaria. He's a doctor with specialized knowledge of female anatomy."

"Yet he does not possess any," I returned. The creeping knowledge came over me of what in particular this man wanted to examine. I was sure I'd turned as red as a berry now. In my panic, I wasn't stealthy about eying the door.

"Don't make this difficult," Lazlian warned.

"Don't make this happen," I said, backing away from everyone, even though there was nowhere to escape. "Whatever it is."

The feeling in the air reminded me of the first night I'd met Lazlian. His father had arranged a dinner for the family, including me. But he'd spoken bluntly of my cycles and I'd wondered if he'd purposefully tried to intimidate me by throwing me into a roomful of strange men, or if it was just the natural result of his family being all male. I wondered the same of Lazlian now, the son who took after his father. Did he mean to coerce me by surprising me with this demand and to frighten me with a show of strength?

I weighed my options. If I refused, he could force me, and my pride be wounded even worse than if I'd acquiesced. But if I submitted, I could muster some dignity. Or would I feel more dignified by not going down without a fight?

"Lida will be assured to know the results," Lazlian said, studying me too intensely.

I snapped my eyes back to the keylord. "Lida believes I should do this?"

"She wants you to be healthy."

I chewed my lip, considering. I respected Lida's opinion, especially as she was Elowan, and saw things as I did. If Lida thought this examination wise, perhaps it was the smart, healthy thing to do.

"Alright," I agreed with a sigh, then pointed to the guards. "But they leave."

After a pause, Lazlian cocked his head toward the door -- a curt dismissal for the men to depart.

"You too," I said, folding my arms.

"You cannot be alone in such a state with another man."

"He's a healer and can be trusted."

Lazlian folded his own arms. "This is the way it's done."

Was it? I narrowed my eyes, having no way of knowing and at this point, just wanting to get it over with.

"Whatever," I huffed, and climbed on Lazlian's huge, luxurious bed. I didn't want to admit that Laz's presence had a strange, dual effect. I was infinitely more self-conscious, but also, a little soothed by it. By him. Because besides Kirwyn, Lazlian, and the healer present at Teddy's birth, no one -- man or woman -- had been between my legs before.

Beneath the modesty of Lazlian's sheet, I removed my undergarments and lifted my dress. The doctor brought me to the edge of the bed and guided my knees up. I was already wincing and breathing rapidly. To both my mortification and relief, Lazlian stood beside me and took my hand in his.

When the doctor touched me, I shut my eyes and squeezed Lazlian's hand. The whole thing was so embarrassing I yearned to disappear. On the plus side, it was over rather quickly. In less than a minute, the healer had done whatever he needed to do, and I was able lower my dress and sit up.

I watched as the doctor mixed a cotton swab containing my fluid with some kind of solution. Lulled into a false sense of security at my humiliation having passed, I was doubly mortified when the doctor locked eyes with Lazlian -- who'd been staring at the solution all the while -- and with stunning casualness he declared, "She's ovulating now."

Something between a choking sound and a squeak escaped my lips.

"We had to be sure," Lazlian said in a rush, though I barely heard him through my attempt not to hyperventilate from embarrassment. "You haven't gotten pregnant, Zaria. I had to be sure you were even calculating your days correctly."

"And she doesn't have any impediments, at least not that I can tell from this test," the doctor added, swirling his vial. "The Spades use it regularly, it's pretty accurate."

I tried focusing on the good news as the healer gathered his belongings and Lazlian escorted him out the door, but my overheated skin itched everywhere.

All those guards... the doctor... Lazlian... they were all probably picturing lewd things... And how casually and openly the doctor just declared me fertile.

Dear *god,* the whole ordeal was horribly awkward. I didn't want to think about it. In my race to depart, I grabbed my undergarments and stuffed them in my bag.

"Where are you going?" Lazlian asked, gripping my bicep.

"To tell Lida," I replied. "She'll want the good news and we need her to set up the... your... you know."

Lazlian shifted his weight and made a strange face, like a grimace but not quite. "She doesn't know you've been examined."

"You said she wanted me to see the doctor," I replied, frowning. "She'll want to know it's been completed."

"I said she'd be pleased to know the results, and she will. I never said she wanted you to see the doctor."

"What do you mean?" I asked, stomach knotting as I thought back on Lazlian's previous words. "Are you saying Lida wasn't in agreement with this? That you lied to me?"

"Rest assured, she will find the news of your health encouraging."

I yanked my arm from Lazlian's grip, heat creeping up my neck and stomach lurching.

"Are you saying you just tricked me into doing something I didn't want to do by making me believe it was Lida's counsel?"

Lazlian met my increasingly sharp tone as he snapped, "I said what I said. It's your fault if you read more into it."

Sometimes, a moment can grow from absolute peace to a complete explosion within the fraction of a second, like the shake of an earthquake or the eruption of a volcano. The signs are subtle, only noticed in hindsight, and once it begins there's no stopping it.

Just like that, one moment I was calm, and the next I was burning. I'd been tricked, and the knowledge of it came out in a hideous scream. And another.

Nothing has changed. You've always been my enemy.

Objects were in my hands, things I didn't remember grabbing. But I became aware as I hurled them across the room and they crashed into walls, splitting as they hit the floor. Vaguely, I aimed at Lazlian's head, but he easily side-stepped my throws. The more it seemed I had no effect, the greater I raged, wanting to hurt him as he'd hurt me.

Liar. Trickster. Manipulator.

Lazlian watched cautiously until my fingers clasped around a silver crown from his shelf. This made him stiffen with alarm, but by now I was across the room and he couldn't reach me in time.

Holding out his hands, he ordered, "Don't throw that. I swear if you break it, I'll break you."

It was glorious, the way he'd revealed himself in those words. I swallowed and savored them as one would a delicacy, closing my eyes for full enjoyment.

Poor baby liked this crown, did he? I grinned with the satisfaction of an imminent win. Nothing mattered beyond inflicting the pain I now knew I could, meting it out in equal measure for what he'd done to me. And hopefully, giving better than I got.

Perhaps... perhaps I did glimpse beyond my action, knowing it would spur a counteraction in Lazlian, one raising the stakes yet again as he made good on his vow and gave greater in return. Yet the euphoric pleasure of vengeance rolled down my spine as I cocked my arm and threw the silver crown into the wall.

It didn't even have time to splatter onto the floor before Lazlian had stormed across the room and grabbed me. For one ecstatic moment I bathed luxuriously in his anger, before a sensible fear seized me. Lazlian and I became a tangle of fists and fury as he carried me to a chair by his dining table.

I knew what he was doing... and maybe I'd known before I'd thrown the crown... but I thrashed with all the strength in my body and felt the responding power in his overwhelm me. My adrenaline rose, mixing with arousal in a whorl of uneasy anticipation.

When Lazlian tossed me over his thighs and flipped up my dress, he smacked me on my bottom so much harder than he did five years ago. Perhaps because he was bigger and stronger now. It stole my breath and shocked me into temporary stillness. I thought I knew the moves, but he struck me again with such force that I realized this was more than retaliation, this was course correction.

Lazlian wanted me to stop fighting him, and sensibly, I did. The alternative was I'd suffer more pain, and I wasn't going to give him that enjoyment. My rear smarted enough from the two smacks I knew had left a mark. My heart thumped against my chest like it pounded to escape my body. The only sound in the room was my heavy breathing.

What happens next?

Lazlian's hand fell upon my thigh, and I jumped from the warm intimacy before anticipation stilled me again. After a pause, he slowly slid his hand upward and it was as if he'd expertly pulled some secret lever, because as that hand rose, my legs opened in response to his movement. The higher he moved, the wider I spread.

Lazlian stopped before reaching the apex of my thighs and I squeezed my eyes shut, as if it mattered. Thrust over his knees, I couldn't see Lazlian's expression. I couldn't see what he saw, though I could imagine. I'd spread for him, revealing all of my most private areas. Lazlian's long ago words from the night we first danced rang in my ears.

I find you revolting.

Had he humiliated me into baring this view, utterly revolting to his gaze?

My shoulders tensed, curling inward. My face burned with shame for a multitude of conflicting reasons. I squirmed, unsure what I wanted as the self-consciousness became more than I could bear. Either the room held no noise or I'd lost my ability to hear it. All I knew was this intolerable tension threatening to splinter my mind.

Lazlian plunged his fingers into me and all fight left my body, along with any thought beyond desire.

I remember those fingers. Pleasure hit my brain like a potent cocktail, but instead of gradual intoxication, the change was immediate. One second I was sober, the next, soaked.

Lazlian withdrew, quickly pushing inside again and coaxing a corresponding moan with each thrust. My god, how he stroked me with his long, expert fingers. Those nimble digits, skilled at designing explosives, curled into my depths and struck places of intense pleasure as if I was a device he knew how to set to shattering.

Lazlian broke me, as promised, and it took embarrassingly little effort. Was there anything more humiliating than squirming over Laz's thighs, having been spanked and now pleasured toward orgasm, face-down and in the most submissive and humbling position possible?

Suddenly, Lazlian withdrew his fingers and I bellowed a wretched cry of frustration.

Oh god, I was so very wrong.

There was one thing more mortifying than coming over Lazlian's lap -- being brought to such a state and then being cruelly denied the release my whole body had desperately confessed I wanted.

Lazlian broke me not by fulfilling me but by making me admit I desired it, then denying me.

CHAPTER 13

HER
Lazlian

Never let it be said I don't learn from my mistakes.

You can't come, little queen. Not without my cock inside you.

That had been my misstep before -- getting her off on my fingers and quenching her desire to continue on to better activities. That night I'd recklessly satisfied her, like some common stableboy seeking a dalliance with a noblewoman, one who'd only deign to give him an offhand opportunity behind the barn some evening. This time I'd conquer like a king, or she'd have nothing at all.

The sight of Zaria spread bare and ineffectively wiggling her hips against my thighs like a desperate whore was nearly enough to unman me. I wanted to prolong it, to soak in her lust-filled anguish, but I couldn't spare more than a glance I hoped to sear into my brain for future use.

Not this time. You want to come? So do I. So fucking deep inside you.

I moved faster than I ever had before as yanked her off my lap and threw her onto the bed, unfortunately jarring her out of her haze. Zaria's eyes refocused and she stilled. I wedged myself between her splayed legs and went right for her clit, rubbing and distracting her.

I inched us forward in this manner, halting to remove a piece of our clothing or to position myself, and when doubt passed through her eyes I'd quickly pause and stroke her soaked slit, releasing the tension and eliminating the fight from her body. When she was subdued once more, I'd spare another moment to strip again.

My heart pounded like I'd run a race and hadn't yet crossed the finish line -- and nothing could stop me from doing so. I didn't care if my guards entered to investigate the ruckus, I didn't care if I had to keep Zaria on edge for hours. Nothing would distract me from taking her this time.

Splayed on the bed, she writhed with indecision and shook with unmet need. I would have pitied her, so out of her mind, if I hadn't been elated out of mine. Her nipples strained, tight with want, and she was so aroused it scented the air. Zaria's mouth opened and closed in silent gasps, as if it begged for me to stuff it with something -- my tongue, my fingers, my cock.

It took a second longer than I liked to grab the right pillow and push it beneath her hips, but I needed it there to angle her. I was fairly certain I could reach as deep as her cervix if I positioned her just right, and I wanted to hit that wall. Zaria came out of her daze again, probably wondering what I was doing. She curled her hands into fists and beat half-hearted punches on my chest.

I plunged two fingers back into her hot cunt, instantly making her body bow and sink back into the bed. Her fists unfurled, becoming needy fingers again. She grasped at me for more, frantic with desire as she tugged me toward her body.

When I pulled back to enter her, there was a tense moment on the precipice. Zaria looked up at me with round eyes and a wide, open mouth, neither pulling me toward her nor pushing me away. She had stilled with uncertainty, needing me to make the decision for her.

I obliged and --

Home. Her. Mine.

HIM
Zaria

My breath left my body and I threw my head back, mouth open in a silent scream meant to be his name but I couldn't form it. I scrambled to understand why and how Lazlian felt so deep, pushing against the walls of my womb and shoving me onto a tightrope walk between pain and pleasure. Lazlian moaned and it reverberated in my chest and echoed in every cell in my body, compelling me to him. I curled my fingers around his shoulders, letting my nails dig into his skin, unaware if they drew blood.

Lazlian moved his hips but stayed close, drawing back just enough to gather force and plunge into me again at this newfound depth.

"Take it, Zaria," he rasped, breath hot against my ear. "Take me like you were meant to."

His desire was so bare and bold, I shuddered, marveling at the wonder of Lazlian, fully seated inside me with his cock stretching and filling me. The way he'd angled my hips and legs granted him access to my innermost regions as he thrust.

I hate you, I thought. *You tricked me. You're my enemy.*

But he invaded me, conquered me, devoured me. Lazlian's hands roamed my body, his tongue swept my mouth, and his cock rammed me relentlessly. This was Lazlian at his most raw. I didn't give him what he always wanted; he took it.

My surrender.

Hot ripples of lust seized my body again and again, each stronger than the last. Lazlian stayed deep, moving back just enough for me to feel the push of his cock against my cervix. Those nerve-endings felt connected to my whole body and something unknown deep within me as well. Unexpectedly, I burst into tears, thrashing as if I needed to climb out of my own skin or climb into Lazlian's. The place he hit inside seemed to unlock a feeling I couldn't explain, something that bonded the physical and the psychological.

Lazlian enveloped me, refusing to let me go, and the pleasure was beyond my ability to handle. Yet I couldn't escape it; it demanded to be experienced. I could only weep some more and squeeze my legs around his hard body, surrendering to the sensation. But ecstasy of such acute intensity reduced me to a quivering, helpless mess beneath Lazlian. My face was as soaked as my thighs, warm and wet. Through watery lashes I locked onto Lazlian's dark eyes, desperate for connection. I didn't understand why I wept, but I couldn't stop.

I cried as I came, clinging to his shoulders.

Oh god, I came so hard for my enemy.

Lost to delirium, I knew I had blacked out for a few moments by the time I refocused. The first thing I realized was that Lazlian had come too, and though he softened inside me, his arms only caged me harder.

My god. I just had sex with Lazlian.

I couldn't bear to think about what kind of person that made me. A wretched cry echoed in my throat from the crushing guilt.

With considerable effort, I pushed Laz off my body, scrambled out of bed, and shot to my feet. Lazlian jumped to match my moves. His arms were slightly raised, as if he tensed to grab me, hands spread in a cautionary manner. His hair was tousled, as wild as his eyes. He spoke calmly but I could hear the edge of panic in his voice.

"There's nothing you can do that will undo what we've done. I've had you, Zaria, right there," he said, pointing, "on this bed. And it was good and you know it. Will you deny it? I've never known you to be a liar."

I flinched at his cold and defensive words. Deny what and to whom? What was Lazlian more concerned about at that moment -- wanting me to acknowledge it, or rather, wanting Kirwyn to know?

Angry and unsure, I spat, "I deny nothing! You wanted me beneath you, you took it. You wanted me to enjoy it, I did. You want my confession, fine. I'll admit it all to whomever you like. Happy?" I asked, rhetorically. "You see Lazlian? This is why not you. You take more than you give."

The unspoken words being *he doesn't. Kirwyn gives more than he takes.*

My god, Kirwyn, I'm sorry, I thought, closing my eyes. *Unless, I don't know! Is this what you meant, what you wanted?*

"Then make a deal with me," Laz said in a rush. "An even exchange."

Ignoring him, I found my undergarments and pulled them on, but they didn't fully stop the drip of his seed down my legs. Lazlian quickly yanked his pants back onto his body and I suspected the only reason he redressed was in case he had to chase me out the door and drag me back.

I had sex with Lazlian. Oh my god.

I needed to be alone, to process what just happened. And that *feeling* when he rammed my cervix. *What was that?*

"It's not working the other way and you know it." Lazlian reached out, hand clasping my wrist. "Stay here for the three days of your cycle and have sex with me. Do it this way, for this one window, and if you don't get pregnant we go back to the goddamn baster. Give me these three days and I swear I won't ever ask you to try it this way again."

Ask? I shot Lazlian a look. "You mean pressure."

"Whatever." He gave a dismissive wave with the hand not gripping my wrist. "I vow it. One cycle. Everyone is miserable and you have the power to end it. I'm not known to fail and I'm seldom wrong. This *will* work."

I looked at the bed. The door. The bare expanse of Lazlian's muscled chest, marked by the line of a scar near his heart and the smattering of stars surrounding it. I didn't remember when he'd removed his key necklace, but he must have done so when he'd undressed.

He still wore the silver cuff with my hair.

"More sex is the wisest course," Lazlian said, speaking rapidly. "I'm not asking you to do anything you haven't already done. Think about it, it increases the odds. By *not* doing it multiple times throughout your fertile window, what we just did might be for nothing."

"Nothing?" I whispered.

Lazlian blinked and his grip tightened. "That's not what I meant. I was just trying to explain-"

I raised my protective walls. "No, you're right. We

simply have a successful conception or we do not. But I've compromised my values enough."

Lazlian's canines weren't as sharp as Kirwyn's, but I saw the wolf in that smile.

"So you've compromised values, according to you, and yet there's no guarantee you'll get pregnant. In fact, it's unlikely you conceived from one try. But the odds increase considerably the more we have sex," Lazlian said. "So if you think about it, at this point, it's really rather an awful thing to do to all parties if you don't have sex with me again, and quite a lot. In fact, it's the worst thing for everyone."

"Wha - what the fuck?" I stammered.

"You've risked *a lot* with *little* odds of success," Lazlian pointed out. "So the more we have sex, the less harmful it actually is."

Wrenching my wrist from his grip, I held my head in my hands and nearly screamed, "What the fuck kind of manipulative reasoning is that?"

"It's just logic. Think about it."

"Stop talking. Stop talking right now with your reptilian tongue."

Dammit, I hated the idea that we might never be successful. I loathed the vision of my moon cycles stretching on and Kirwyn and I not being able to touch each other. I dreaded the anxiety each time my fertile window came around and the accompanying disappointment when I inevitably bled -- making me sick, making Kirwyn sick, making the royal family sick with the stress of it all.

The pressure made me want to burst into screams or sobs or both and I couldn't blame anyone but myself. I'd agreed to take the role at which I failed...

Or...

...or with a few short days in Lazlian's bed, I might be able to end everyone's despair.

"If you agree to stay here for three days, I vow that I won't ever again ask for this arrangement," Lazlian said quickly. "I won't allow Juls to interfere, I won't pressure you. I vow that if you don't get pregnant, we'll find some way other than the monthly basting sessions. It's over. That's how confident I am. If this doesn't make you pregnant, we'll find another way."

"Three days..." I trailed off, not agreeing. Not that Laz cared.

"But we do it my way," Lazlian said, eyes blazing as if we'd already come to terms. "Anything I want. Everything I want. No protests."

"Define anything."

"No."

"Then no. Why in the world would I agree to that?"

"Because you're too stressed and you can't get pregnant like that. We take your decisions out of it and we take your worry too. Just give me three days, Zaria," Lazlian said. He rarely used my name, and I didn't know how to feel about the funny sensation it caused in my chest. "*Everyone* is miserable and you can change that with nothing more than this little blip of time."

"Don't you dare lay all this at my feet!" I cried.

"Would you rather have no power in the decision?" Lazlian asked, eyebrow cocked, and I worried he was seriously considering taking it from me.

"No," I quickly protested.

Silence fell and I looked at the door again. I knew what was out there; more of the same. But with three days... I didn't even need to think of it that way... two moons, and I could leave upon the sun's rise on the third day.

I could end the despair of a kingdom and the misery of us all.

Is this what Kirwyn thought was the best solution, what he wanted me to do? To just get it done and over with?

"I'd need to send a messenger to Mazriah. For her to take Teddy to Saos and Alette's," I murmured, more to myself.

"Done," Lazlian said.

I licked my dry lips and swallowed. Oh god. What was I doing?

What I have to. What's best for everyone.

Get it done, he'd said.

Unable to speak my agreement, I closed my eyes, clamped my lips, and gave Lazlian one tight nod. I didn't want to see the look of triumph on his face.

"The deal is that you do everything I say," Lazlian reminded, making my eyes pop open. "Not a word of protest. If you want it to work, you can't go halfway."

Of course he pushed for everything.

"Fine," I whispered, relieved and terrified in equal measure at the idea of proceeding. "But you agree that if it doesn't work, you and Juls figure out something else. Spade technologies, another girl, I don't care."

"Done," Lazlian said, waving his hand, and then he actually *licked his teeth* as he eyed me. "Lower the sheet and remove your undergarments. Rule number one is no clothing for the next three days, unless I tell you otherwise. Rule number two is that I will only come inside you and you will come as well. It gives us the best chance for success."

Lightheadedness coursed through me as Lazlian spoke. I didn't remember when I'd done it, but at some point in our arguing I'd covered my body with his sheet.

I was pretty sure that over the next three days, Laz had

three missions. One, obviously, to get me pregnant. But I suspected he had two other intentions that he didn't admit.

Lazlian wanted to do everything to me he'd always fantasized about and, at the same time, to show me what I'd been missing. This wasn't three days of mechanical, regimented sex to make the heir. It was Lazlian's fantasy-fulfillment.

The worst part to admit was that his argument held a kernel of truth. I knew that being stressed made it difficult to conceive and had likely contributed to the lack of success thus far.

Liar, said a nagging voice in my head.

The worst part to admit is that his intentions are causing a throb between your legs.

CHAPTER 15

SEDUCTION
Zaria

Lazlian crossed his arms, displeased at my continued clutching of the sheet. With a hard swallow, I returned it to the bed and removed my undergarments once more. Burning with self-consciousness, I instinctively moved away from Laz and looked about his room for something to distract myself, or him.

A laughably fruitless endeavor.

On his shelf I spied a senorok board with artfully carved pieces. As I walked to it, I felt Lazlian follow me with his eyes.

"You play," he said, voice rising at the end with the hint of question. Before I could reply, he sneered as he corrected, "No. *He* does. Of course he does. You haven't the patience."

"Are you any good at it?" I asked, ignoring the insult.

"What do you think?"

"I'd say you're unmatched." I cocked my head and ran my fingertips over the sleek edge of the board, planning to give as good as I got. *Better.* I'd go for the jugular. "Except... I wonder about your father. Maybe he taught you. Maybe Raoul did. But I'd wager you couldn't beat Grahar, back then. Now that you're older..." I gave a half-shrug. It was cruel, but so was he. "But you don't have the chance to prove it."

Lazlian flashed a carefree smirk but his hard, reptilian eyes gave him away. *Something* I'd said was accurate. I'd often wondered if Laz was angry that his father had died before he'd had the chance to stand up to him. Grahar having sacrificed his own life to protect his golden son couldn't have helped Lazlian's feelings of inadequacy.

The keylord leaned back on his heels and cocked an eyebrow.

"Why bother discussing my daddy issues when yours are far more entertaining and lead you into the most obliging positions."

Bastard.

Lazlian stalked forward and I sucked in a deep breath, mind scrambling to guess what he'd do. The air in the room grew hotter and more stifling. The sky would break with heavy afternoon rains, but they couldn't come soon enough. *This isn't for the crown, it's for you,* I thought. *For seduction, not succession.*

"We're not children anymore, Lazlian," I said, jutting my chin. "You can't frighten me now the way you did then."

"No, I can frighten you in much better ways now."

Despite having walked right into that one, I shivered. The look on Lazlian's self-satisfied face made me want to lunge at him and scratch it off. Naked, I thought better of it.

"We're not children anymore, are we?" he asked rhetorically, crossing the room. "I can see what you try to hide from me now. You're so easy to excite with words. Yet I don't know why I bother speaking at all," he remarked, with a smug curve to his mouth. "Not when your body already begs for my attention."

I half-rolled my eyes but I wasn't sure it was believable when my flaming face muted the effect.

"Deny it. I dare you," Lazlian challenged. "I'd love to list your pleas. Were I your inquisitor, each would be a damning confession."

He took another step forward.

"Your dilated pupils," Laz said, and I blinked as if to clear my eyes.

"The blush of your cheeks," he declared, drawing closer until he stood above me.

"Your swollen lips."

I swallowed, sure he noticed my throat dip.

"Those short, quick breaths. Shall I continue below your neck?" Lazlian's eyes made pointed contact with my hardened nipples.

I shook my head rapidly and whispered, "No."

"Good. I hate wasting time with foolishness. When your body is screaming for me to touch it, why don't you use your mouth to implore?"

It's not fair, I thought. How was I supposed to feel, naked under his gaze and in these circumstances? Lazlian set up games where there was no way to win. I was sure he'd find some means to mock me if my body *didn't* respond to him, dismissing me as defective or inadequate somehow. But he shamed me just the same for the way I *did* react to his nearness. His scent. His thick, dark head of touchable hair. The knowing gleam in his eye and the sardonic tilt to those crooked lips.

I couldn't talk my way right into some kind of trap, so I

said nothing and pretended I didn't feel the ache between my legs from his close proximity.

Tugging his lip in thought, the keylord ordered darkly, "Onto the bed. Hands up, over your head."

Laz had issued a statement, no raised voice at the end as a subtle question. Kirwyn would have, in the games we played where we'd communicate wordlessly, where it was understood I could refuse.

I supposed having agreed to Lazlian's terms, he didn't consider refusal an option on the table. With my heart thumping out of control, I moved to his large poster bed and laid back, keeping my hands on the pillow. Lazlian removed his pants and my heart galloped even more ferociously as he loomed above me. Too much history existed between us for me to trust him. There were infinite ways this could proceed and all of them terrified me. Even the good ones. Especially the good ones.

"Don't." Lazlian gave my inner thigh a light, corrective slap -- or as best as he could since I'd clamped my legs shut. His voice was thick and husky. "Don't ever close your legs in my presence. Rule number three."

Long fingers encircled my thighs and he pried them apart, staring at what lay between, entranced, reverent. I couldn't seem to find air.

"I don't see how this gets me pregnant," I pointed out, rather breathy though I scowled. I knew Laz wasn't going to proceed with making the heir more mechanically, reducing it to the act itself, but the limitless possibilities for foreplay made my head spin.

"Then why are you so wet?" he mocked. "Anything that makes you wet helps get you pregnant. Anything that distracts your mind."

I deadpanned, "Oh, so you're doing this for my own good?"

"For yours, mine, and the kingdom's," he rasped, quickly moving up my body and nipping my bottom lip. "It's all one and the same."

Lazlian cocked a diabolical grin and I barely had time to feel him at my entrance before he shoved inside me to the hilt, bending one of my knees half-up as he pushed. When I tried to speak, Laz seized my throat just hard enough that I stopped.

"I'm going to spit in your mouth," Lazlian said, his dark eyes brimming with excitement. "I want you hold it in until I come. Don't cry out when you come, don't swallow it. Or I'll spit in every cup and every morsel of food you eat and drink for the next three days."

"You wouldn't."

"I would."

Narrowing my eyes, I murmured, "I hate that I can never tell when you're serious."

Lazlian smiled and commanded, "Open."

I debated for a few moments, huffed, then opened. Lazlian spit into my mouth and I held it, grimacing.

"Hold it in," he declared hoarsely, never breaking his rhythm and watching me intensely. "Don't swallow. Let it coat your tongue."

As if I had a choice. His spit moved around my mouth, mixing with my own saliva.

"That's it, little queen," Lazlian said, voice raw with desire. "You can come now."

He reinforced his words by moving faster and deeper. It took several moments but eventually, my pleasure rose as he drove into me, and my climax was better than I wanted to admit.

Lazlian let me ride it out, but as the waves subsided, he rasped, "I'm going to come... swallow when I do. Take me inside you both ways. Nod if you understand me."

I must have looked dazed. I nodded. When I felt his short, deep thrusts and Lazlian groaned, I knew he was releasing ribbons of come inside me and I swallowed.

~

IF HAVING sex with Lazlian was so surreal I could hardly comprehend it, laying with him after, like casual, long-time lovers, was even stranger.

It was either late morning or early afternoon. I had trouble telling time as clouds covered the sky and seemed to fill my head in a similar haze. I lay to Lazlian's left, my cheek pressed against the small black stars tattooed over his heart. He smelled masculine, flinty. The scent invaded my nostrils and further messed with my head.

"Your boy doesn't hit the depths I do, does he?" Lazlian said. His tone was far too casual to be genuine indifference.

"Stop calling him that and are you seriously fishing around to find out if you're bigger than Kirwyn?" I didn't wait for Lazlian to deny it. I huffed and said, "If pressed, I guess I'd say by looking you're a smidge longer and he's a smidge wider, okay? But inside it feels the same, I'm just... full. It matters more the time of my moon cycle and the position we're in. You keep contorting me." Wanting to steer the conversation away from Kirwyn, I added, "And neither of you are as big as Juls, if we're going to play that game."

"No one is as blessed as my brother," Lazlian said, with a laugh that rumbled his chest. "Totally unfair that the gods favored him like that on top of everything else."

"You've seen his..." I trailed off, surprised.

"Of course I have, he's my brother. You can't miss that thing. And even if I hadn't, Merie was generous enough to tell me."

Frowning, I asked, "What do you mean?"

"She intended it to be helpful," Laz replied, wryly. "In our two drunken and awkward encounters, Merie tried to make me feel better by telling me how sometimes sex with Juls hurt, and at least we didn't have that problem."

I covered my mouth to stifle my laughter.

"She meant well," Lazlian shrugged. "No pain for her, just for my ego."

"I'm sorry," I said, still laughing but feeling bad about it. "If it makes you feel any better, there's absolutely no reason for any girl to be unsatisfied. You're *big*. It's just Juls is..."

"A monster. I know. Wasted on a man who doesn't properly use it to his advantage, but that's life."

Poor Merie. She and Juls were so compatible, but that one area had to be... tricky. It must have been terribly difficult for someone like Merie, who adored her husband and had likely never even kissed another man, to sleep with his brother for the good of the kingdom. And Lazlian loved Juls just as much as Merie, in a different way. Perhaps after their conception attempts, Juls could never look at Laz the same. Perhaps he pictured his brother's hands all over his wife every time he saw him.

Perhaps that's what Kirwyn pictured when he looked at Lazlian, and what Lazlian imagined right back.

"How many girls have you-" I began.

"Not as many as you'd think," Laz cut me off. "At least, not to full penetration. Juls and I have done plenty of other things, but Father warned us not to grace the girl-"

"What?" I blurted.

"Not to grace a girl unless we were prepared to enthrone or entomb her, should unintended consequences arise."

I blinked, stunned at his bluntness, though it didn't surprise me that Grahar said such things.

"So how many girls have you-"

"Graced?"

"God, you're such an ass. Never mind." I pouted then added, "But what about Juls? I know for a fact you sent him two women at once."

"They were of good, noble breeding. I could trust them," Laz said with a shrug. "Plus, I gave them each the birth control shot by my own hands and examined them myself. I couldn't have anyone carrying some mainland disease to my brother, now could I?"

My face burned as I imagined what he implied. "Is that why you-"

"No," Lazlian cut me off in a deep voice. He slid a hand to my belly and laid it there, meaningfully. "I told you. Counting moon days or whatever savage method you're applying isn't as reliable as a doctor's test."

Desperately wanting to change the subject, I said, "Juls is different. He seems quieter now. Sad and sometimes angry."

"It's been an adjustment," Laz agreed. "He lost his father, his first wife, and unquestioned power over the kingdom. All related to you I might add."

And his brother? I wondered. *Did Juls lose you because of me somehow?* But I couldn't shake the feeling that only something involving Merie would make Juls that angry.

"So why is Juls cold with you now? What have you done, Lazlian?"

"That's rather rude. Though I suppose it's to be expected, considering the vulgar manner in which you were reared. Why assume I'm to blame?"

I released something between a scoff and a huff. "Because I've met you." After a pause I added thoughtfully, "And I saw you take the hit from Juls like you deserved it."

"Enough talk," Lazlian said, sliding two fingers into my mouth and cupping my breast with his free hand.

It *was* distracting, but the abrupt diversion only confirmed what I suspected. Lazlian had done something to make Juls furious.

I silently vowed to pry the truth from his lips before I left his chambers.

CHAPTER 16

BRICKS AND CIRCUSES
Kirwyn

As our company approached Spade City on horseback, I rode solo and spoke to no one, trying to imprint upon my brain as much as I could about the surrounding terrain. The forest nearest the shining, walled city had been cleared ages ago to make way for farms. The gently-sloping land provided two or three inclines. It would be too generous to call them hills, but they were the only advantage I could see. Perhaps, if one stood at the highest points and the city walls could be blown or battered down, an army might view the secrets within?

In all the dreams of my youth, never did I imagine riding into Spade City as a prince of a kingdom I hadn't even known existed at the time. Brushing aside self-consciousness, as it did nothing to serve me, I still couldn't shake the odd feeling. Had they lived, what would my mother, father, or my uncle have thought of me?

They'd each given their lives for mine, and I hoped they were proud.

Zaria had put her life in my hands and trusted me to make it a good one, a safe one, but all the gold in Rythas couldn't protect us if we went to war with the Spades. I had to make sure that if it came to that, we won.

Impossible.

Yet here I was. Hope was like the last lifeboat floating in the middle of the ocean... but one where the base might be riddled with holes, and you never knew for sure until you climbed inside and it was too late.

One thing was certain as I rode through the checkpoints and guarded stations -- a man could possibly sneak out of Spade City, but not *in*. I wouldn't squander this opportunity I was lucky to have.

Officials and their accompanying servants, or slaves, met my party inside the city to escort us. The roads, architecture, and general design of Spade City didn't match what I'd seen in books -- which wasn't too surprising as the pictures copied never closely resembled each other.

It was trickier to invade a city if you couldn't even know its layout, after all.

The city itself was a loosely shaped circle, protected by exceedingly solid, steel walls. My hopes to batter or bomb them diminished a mile for every foot thicker they appeared. Homes and businesses within the barrier were constructed from a mix of sleek and shining metals -- some of it reclaimed and refurbished and some of it newly-fashioned. Others were brick and stone. Most had been designed for efficiency over beauty. *And defense,* I thought, wryly.

But as we rode, I could tell from the increasing lavishness that the wealthier lived toward the city's center. Before

I was shown to an extravagant house of my own, I glimpsed what looked to be a central, municipal district and the curve of a large, armored building that piqued my interest.

Our party was separated into individual manors to make it difficult for us to coordinate anything, I was sure, and we were given servants to attend our every need... who'd been instructed to spy, I'd bet.

Before being left alone, I was told that I had a meeting with the High Twelve of the Aureum, the leaders of Spade City, that afternoon. I used the short time to take a shower I couldn't pretend I didn't love, and to eat a quick meal of the pears and bread we'd packed.

I didn't yet trust the Spades not to poison me.

The families of the highest rank were known as the Aureum, or the Golden Twelve, as only twelve families were ever permitted such rank. If one bloodline wanted to rise, they had to overthrow another, by any means necessary. It was no better within the households themselves as only one man or woman was allowed a designation as one of the High Twelve, meaning the hostility and skirmishes within a house could be just as deadly.

Meaning not a single person ascended without being a formidable player.

While the city itself wasn't divvied into physical slices, power between the Aureum was. Each member of the High Twelve kept his or her own small army and shared a voice in clan decisions from wages to war.

I spent the remainder of my morning scouring the house for listening devices, though I admittedly didn't know exactly what I was looking for. An hour later, I was escorted to a nearby building and the gold plates embellishing the façade made it clear to whom it belonged... but my curiosity was again piqued by that strange, circular structure, not far from where I walked. *What did it house? Technology of some kind? A shelter in case of attack? Something else entirely?*

I made a note to get as close to it as I could when my official visit ended and my real one began.

The High Twelve, comprised of ten men and two women, sat at a long table in a round room. I quickly gleaned that the nearer one sat to its center, the higher in rank. Their clothing varied but each leader wore a long chain with a gold medallion. One of the two women sat at the furthest end of the table, and at the other end sat a man who looked to be in his fifties. He had a headful of short, gray hair, and a beard to match. While he wasn't especially physically fit, he considered me with keen eyes that made me believe his mind was in sharp condition.

As the High Twelve were introduced to me by a designated speaker, Corine and Banya stood out, being the only females, as did the gray-haired man at the end of the table, Jori. As twelfth, he was the lowest of the highest. Larius Mikaster, centrally positioned and the leader of the Aureum, counted himself number one.

"Kirwyn," Larius greeted me.

"Oh, but it's *Prince* Kirwyn," Corine immediately interrupted in a mocking tone.

"We don't have royal titles here," Larius said, with dismissiveness and scorn.

"I see little difference when you have hereditary designations anyway. A prince by any other name..." I trailed off, shrugging.

"Am I a prince?" Larius asked, grinning. I wondered if they'd rehearsed this or if having a joke at my expense was a spontaneous game.

"I think you'd be a king, by equivalency to Rythas," Corine teased, leaning down the table.

"I'm happy to call you whatever you like," I told Larius. "Prince, King, High One of the Golden Twelve, Most Gilded of the Aureum, just please, let me know which you prefer so that we can proceed. By whatever name, I have a feeling you're a man who doesn't enjoy his time being wasted, and I will do my best to accommodate that need, as I share it. I was sent here on behalf of the Dorestes because I'm not known to squander the opportunities I'm given."

"No," Larius said, tightly, suddenly considering me more seriously. I wasn't sure if that was a good thing. "I can see that you don't. Please, sit."

While I was thankful Larius no longer bid me stand, as if for his amusement, I didn't feel winning his favor was ever in the cards for me. As our initial meeting unfolded, I shifted my strategy more to passivity, resolving to keep my head down and to slip off at my visit's official conclusion.

After the meeting I was given an itinerary and in the following weeks I stuck to it, touring facilities to show off Spade advancements or dining with the Aureum. Lavishness, efficiency, and formality were the emerging themes, but it was all incredibly surface level. Any hints I made to explore -- even something as simple as a walk -- were gently redirected with suggestions of another, more controlled activity.

One morning, after several uneventful days, I heard a knock on the door of my designated manor. I hadn't expected anything unusual until I answered it to find Jori, standing alone. Whenever one of the High Twelve had arrangements for me, they sent their servants.

Jori asked about my journey and my accommodations. I responded amiably, trying not to show too much impatience for him to get to the point, which, I was increasingly convinced would be interesting. I did not invite Jori inside and he did not seem offended by the slight. I thought the odds of avoiding the servants' ears were better if we remained where we were. If he was as clever as he seemed, Jori felt the same.

"You arrived sooner than we anticipated and there's quite a celebration planned in the Bowl this afternoon," he said, finally.

"Mm," I mused, wary of both his intentions and those of anyone who might be listening. "Who doesn't love a good celebration?"

"Indeed. You were scheduled to tour the far fields today, but I've arranged for you to have a seat in my box, if you'd like to join me," he offered. Jori feathered his fingers in a waving motion as he examined the glint of his ring before turning his attention back to me. "I think you'll find the celebrations more enlightening than our irrigation systems."

"Thank you," I said. "I've always been partial to enlightenment."

"Yes, I thought you might," Jori replied, nodding his head with more of a bow to himself than to me. "I'll send my man to collect you in about an hour."

Jori departed and I spent the rest of the hour reading. His man came promptly, as promised, and we walked to the so-called Bowl together. The arena wasn't as large as those before The Great Decline; I estimated it to be only a few stories high and maybe fifty yards long. It looked to be the size of an open-air theatre. I climbed the stairs to Jori's box and found him alone, though the private seating was large enough to accommodate ten or fifteen guests. Trays of food and refreshments had been set for as many.

"We're alone," I stated, though it was half-question.

"I thought you might enjoy some privacy for your first celebration. Jori spread his hand, indicating I should take the seat of my choosing. I moved to the center of the box and claimed one near the rail. Jori sat beside me and outside our box, other spectators did the same. I assumed the Spade elites took seats beside us as well, but with walls between the boxes I couldn't tell.

Below, the arena floor was empty, save a rather plain-looking stage at one end.

The idea that Jori might try to kill me or that I was a part of this celebration, briefly passed through my mind. It wasn't logical, but I considered it, just to eliminate all possibilities. Nothing in Jori's demeanor communicated any threat. But he was clearly planning *something*. I watched the Spade sip his wine and only felt comfortable enough to drink after he finished half a glass. It was likely paranoia. If the Spades wanted to kill me, they didn't need to go through all this -- an assassin could have easily met with our party along the way.

"What is this celebration for?" I asked Jori, warily.

"Victory," he replied. Knowing I'd press for more, Jori added, "I wouldn't want to spoil the surprise by elaborating."

It didn't take long for the show to begin. A thin man draped in a luxurious, silken cape of deep purple sauntered onto the stage and the crowd lost their minds.

"Castrato!" they called, "Castrato!"

Castrato? Was that... They couldn't mean...

The chanting reached feverish heights as both men and women threw flowers and petals at the performer's feet. One woman fainted and her friends seemed torn between helping to revive her and not missing a second of the man's entrance. With a flick of his hands, the performer tossed his cape from his shoulders. Beneath it, he wore no shirt and the view of his bare, oiled torso sent the crowd into such a frenzy it pained my ears. When the performer turned and preened, I glimpsed the large, black "x" on the man's back.

"Is he a slave?" I asked, confused at the duality of his obvious prestige and his mark. "Or has he been freed?"

"He is an Adornment, or an Adorned One," Jori said, reclining in his chair and eating a candied nut of some kind. "A special designation for a slave with a gift to please its owner."

"So he's still a slave," I said, snarling.

"With a better life than an unadorned," Jori replied.

The performer, smiling and bowing, held up his hands and the crowd immediately fell silent. He dipped his head in the direction of another man, with long hair and a moustache, standing on the side of the stage.

The mustached man announced loudly, "As a gift from the Family Mikaster, their Adornment will now sing for you."

The crowd broke out into another hysteria and the Adorned One let it die naturally, which took several minutes. When silence fell and he began singing, my fears were confirmed.

Castrato.

Holy shit. At some point in his youth, the performer must have exhibited an exceptional vocal talent... for which his balls were cut off to maintain indefinitely. I shifted in my chair, resisting the urge to cover my own because I knew Jori was watching me. The unfortunate boy had been castrated to keep this unnaturally high singing voice, gorgeous and grotesque. I'd read about it happening, long ago and far away. Never did I think such a horror was brought here. *Celebrated.*

For nearly half an hour the Adorned One performed several songs, each more remarkable than the last. Like the rest of the crowd, I did not speak as I listened, enraptured. It was the most hideous beauty I'd ever witnessed.

Throughout the performance, my mind returned to Zaria, again and again. What would she say or do, if she sat where I sat? This atrocity was only the opening act. I clutched the armrest, knowing worse was to come... understanding that Jori brought me here with the intention that I witness it. Why?

This *Adornment,* this mutilated man, was a prelude to... what?

More acts followed -- extravagant in display, though, I calculated, minimal in cost. The expense of so many entertainers, costumes, and sets only cost a fraction of what they would in Rythas because slaves performed, sewed, constructed, farmed. Dancers followed the singers, lithe beyond naturalness. I couldn't help but wonder if all were forced into performing, intentionally half-starved and beaten if they refused to dance.

The spectacles of grotesque beauty gave way to outright brutality as backdrops were cleared and two men, clearly pumped to fight one another, marched into the arena. One wore gray face paint and a horned helmet. The other, a pelt of brown fur with claws strapped to his hands.

"Make way for the Beasts of the Bowl!" the mustached announcer called.

This is no ordinary fight, I thought, alert but not surprised. I had expected something like this as everyone knew the Spades liked their sport. *Someone is about to die.*

"The Rhino and the Bear," Jori said, leaning over to

confirm my suspicions. "The Rhino will win again, and live."

I watched as the two men went at one another, and sure enough, the Bear was able to slash the Rhino's chest with deep scratches that drew blood, but ultimately, the Rhino succeeded in backing the Bear against the arena's wall. He bent his head and charged, spearing the Bear through his torso with that lethal horn.

Similar matches followed, including women fighting to the death as well. I drank the wine that was set before me and let my eyes glaze, counting five matches in total. I wondered how many participants had been born into slavery and how many had been captured from other clans. I wondered if their lives in the backlands were any less brutal.

Instead of focusing on the fight, my mind drifted to the relative safety my uncle had provided me as a freeborn in hiding. We faced deadly threats, especially moving around later in life, and we fought when we needed to. But it could have been so much worse. Life wasn't constant loss and warfare.

The most depressing thought I had was that for some who died in the bowl below me, their end may have been a release from a life a pain, of a fate *worse* than death, even as they bled out in the dirt to the cheers of a city.

I knew whatever was to come next would be worse, but I couldn't decide on any particular horror when the possibilities were infinite. I sipped my wine, waiting, bracing.

Once the dead bodies had been cleared, the wide, double doors at one end of the arena swung open and the long-haired, mustached man sauntered back onto the stage.

"Behold!" he announced. "The moment you've all been waiting for... Spade victory!"

A cluster of chained prisoners appeared in the doorway and a parade of captives began. Strong warriors, male and female, were marched or dragged into the arena. I didn't know their clan of origin and couldn't make out the shape of their mark from where I sat. I supposed the Spades didn't find it worth mentioning as the individuals now only existed as slaves and would soon bear the tattoo across their backs.

"The spoils of war!" the mustached man announced. "Although you may find those who are yet *unspoiled.*"

The crowd laughed at his cheap joke. Jori flashed an automatic smile and returned to pretending he wasn't watching me as I continued pretending that I wasn't watching him.

Neither of us was fooled.

I wondered what had become of the clan's less-valued members. Perhaps they were captured but unworthy of display. Perhaps they'd been killed. I wasn't sure which was the preferable outcome. That this clan consisted entirely of able-bodied men and women was unlikely.

"This is Mikaster's win. He values strength above all," Jori said, leaning toward me and offering a rare bit of insight, though it still didn't answer what became of the physically weak. Right now, I wasn't in the mood to ask.

The fighters were followed by what I gleaned to be clan leaders, stripped naked. Feeling Jori's eyes on me, I forced myself to look and gritted my teeth in silence. Below and beside me, the crowd shouted and jeered.

"Dibs!" I heard several cry.

"I want that one!" many shouted, pointing.

The luckiest of those captured were able to walk.

Chained, but with the dignity of their own feet. The unlucky had been equally stripped but were lewdly tied on their hands and knees, like horses or dogs. They were dragged into the arena on wheeled, raised platforms behind actual horses.

Those few, who I guessed to have been the clan's highest in rank, had been given the greatest degradation. And this was only their entrance. I almost wished I hadn't the ability, but I could easily imagine the horrors that would befall them next. Repulsive images shuffled through my mind and my face twitched as I tried not to show my disgust. Consuming any wine at all had been a bad idea; it roiled in my stomach. As my blood pressure rose, I knew I sweated.

Jori wasn't watching the show, he was watching me. I was his show.

He'd brought me here to give me a message, and I received it loud and clear.

CARNAL HAZE
Zaria

That afternoon a dark storm rolled in an early night and we had no desire to leave Lazlian's chambers with the pounding rain. Instead, servants brought trays of food for a decadent meal I wasn't sure whether to call lunch or supper.

Always my thoughts returned to Kirwyn. It was as if the steady thump of my heart beat his name.

Kir - wyn.

Kir - wyn.

But when my heart raced it sounded different; there was an extra *thump* amidst the beating. Another name, with a third syllable.

Lazlian, I swore, could somehow see my mind drifting across the ocean. His eyes narrowed and he jarred me by abruptly ordering, "Onto the table. On all fours. Remember our deal. If we do this, we do it right."

The table? Inwardly, I groaned. But despite beginning to

sweat a little, I crawled out of bed and onto the tabletop where he pointed.

"Spread wider," Lazlian instructed. "Don't move."

I spread, burning so hot with mortification and arousal, I wouldn't have protested if Laz dripped ice water onto my overheated flesh.

The keylord sat, right where my most private regions were exposed, and began casually dining while I died a thousand times over. I suspected he was misdirecting me, but it was hard to hold onto the thought when the heat of my self-consciousness made me weak, feverish. Pounding the veranda, cool rain beckoned for me to dart outside, just for a minute. Every twitch, every swallow, and every breath I took felt magnified under the heat of Lazlian's stare. Yet, perversely, the obsessive way he fixated on my body electrified me.

"If you don't stop wetting yourself, you're going to sully my dining table," Laz chided, and I felt myself redden. The scrape of his chair announced he'd risen. Standing beside me, Lazlian fisted my hair and yanked my head back with one hand. With the other, he ran a finger slowly down my spine. "Look at how you respond when I degrade you," he mocked.

To emphasize his point and humiliate me further, Lazlian's finger ran up and down my slit, making me shiver and, I was sure, increase my lubrication.

"This is why you need to be locked away," he decreed.

I was annoyed at the statement -- at everything he'd just said -- but willing to ignore it for satisfaction. I failed to stop the twitch of my hips, making that obvious.

"Do you wet yourself this much for every man or is it just for me?" Lazlian asked.

I knew he didn't ask the question because he cared

about the answer. It was a trap. If I said there were other men who could stimulate me to the same level, he'd use it to justify his belief about keeping me under lock and key. And if I said it was only him, I'd gratify his egotistical conviction that I was made to be his.

Lazlian hadn't stopped the stroking of his finger *up and down* my soaked sex, making it difficult to think my way out.

"I...this is different. You're new," I breathed. "It's affecting me because of the newness."

"Oh?" Lazlian said. "Well I wouldn't call myself a man of science, but I dabble. So we'll test your theory."

I didn't like where this was going. My skin prickled in anticipation of his maneuver, whatever it was.

Lazlian finally dipped two fingers inside me, shoving them as deep as he could go. But he quickly withdrew them and I whimpered in frustration.

"Once a day we'll dine like this and see how you react each time. See if you soak yourself any less."

Much remained unsaid in Lazlian's statement. He could easily up the ante to increase my discomfort with new humiliations if I failed to sufficiently embarrass myself for his pleasure. More importantly, I had but two days remaining, and little could be learned in such a short time. Did he plan on making me stay?

He couldn't. Kirwyn would kill him. The people would riot. Juls would never permit it.

Oddly, however, what gave me the most comfort was Lazlian's own vow. I knew he'd lie and deceive a hundred different ways. But he'd struck that agreement in earnest and Lazlian possessed a singular, though twisted, sense of honor to his *vow*. It took nothing short of a war for him to release himself from the previous oath that Kirwyn *was as good as dead and I was going to wish I was.* Lazlian wielded that vow like a weapon, so if he were to go back on his oath, he'd render his own tool useless.

I didn't believe Lazlian would ever blunt his own sword.

The keylord re-sat and calmly ate a meal that lasted an eternity while I remained displayed like the evening's entertainment. Trapped in my own head, my mind raced, and I wondered what would have happened if I'd been sent to marry Lazlian instead of Juls. Would he have ordered me onto the table like this on our first night as husband and wife? Perhaps on the first day I'd arrived at High Spire? Had he fantasized about this or was it a spur of the moment decision?

I'd never know; Lazlian's mind was shrouded in shadows. I could ask. But his mouth was a fortress of lies and his tongue a bejeweled drawbridge, beckoning and permitting passage before snapping shut and trapping a victim inside forever.

As I thought of that very organ, Lazlian used it.

I nearly jumped off the table when he touched the tip of his tongue to my wet center and drew one long, hot lick upwards. Time seemed to slow as he continued that searing path, not even stopping when - *oh my god* - he passed boldly over my other opening and ended on the small of my back.

Delirious from shame and arousal, I bolted, scurrying across the table on my hands and knees like an animal.

"Get back here now," Lazlian said sharply. "I won't play games with you. You made a deal."

I couldn't clear my dizzy head and I needed to. Lazlian and I played a game whether he admitted it or not. There was always some leeway, some leverage.

God, his tongue felt so good. My *god.*

What was I thinking about? Oh, right. My advantage.

With a plan and a steadying breath, I crawled back to Lazlian as seductively as I could -- though it might not have mattered if I'd used little effort at all. I was naked on his table and maintaining eye contact, serving myself up like the dish he'd desired his entire life. Sitting in his high-backed chair awaiting my arrival, Lazlian was enraptured. I could see it in his dark eyes and the pronounced rise and fall of his chest.

When I reached the keylord, I slid down from the table and dropped between his legs. With Lazlian's dazed assistance, I made quick work of lowering his pants. I doubted he would have noticed if the castle caught fire at that moment.

He had to come inside me each time? We'll see about that.

With wide, humble eyes, I swallowed his erection until the tip hit the back of my throat, permitting me to go no further. Lazlian groaned as I backed up, lapping with my tongue and sucking his cock like a woman starved for it.

It was less than a minute before Lazlian declared, "Enough."

I sucked harder. I'd win if he came in my mouth.

"Enough," Lazlian commanded.

I doubled my efforts.

"I said enough!" he roared, fisting my hair and yanking me back. As I panted, we were connected by a lewd string of saliva between my lips and the tip of his cock. A challenge passed between us in that second, and I wanted to gloat that I'd gotten far enough to nearly make him break one of his rules. But Lazlian was already pulling me up and swinging me around by my hair. I had no choice but to follow or meet pain. Not letting go, Laz shoved me against the table and yanked my torso down so that my face pressed into the wood.

I couldn't overpower him with strength, but I could win with words. I raised my head as much as I could and turned to meet his gaze.

"Lazlian," I breathed. "I want you to grace me."

His eyes darkened and he pushed my head back down. There was nothing gentle about it.

"Grace me," I repeated.

Lazlian leaned down by my ear.

"Once more. Beg for it," he commanded, but the raspy timbre of his voice made it sound like he was the one begging.

I bit back my smirk and whispered, "Please. Grace me, Lazlian."

He groaned and obliged, spearing me. Lazlian hadn't taken me from behind before and the new pleasure had me bucking obscenely. Even though he used me like a vessel for his seed, I'd brought him to the brink by my mouth, and I considered that some kind of perverse win.

"I want you to come hard now," he ordered.

My stomach tightened and heat raced over my skin. I closed my eyes and gave myself over to the sensation of his cock filling me. To the fiery scent of Lazlian, above me, and the smell of rain floating through the open windows. It took a few seconds but to my surprise, my pleasure rose in response to his desire and my orgasm built in time to his. Lazlian's delicious hardness hit me so deep, I couldn't help but shatter on it.

I was coming and, *god,* it was good.

"I - yes, I-"

"Harder," he growled.

His one command, in *that* voice, swept me into the maelstrom.

Oh god, I came so hard, much to his sardonic exaltation.

I barely had time to catch my breath, before Lazlian ordered, "On your back."

As I complied, Laz elevated and bent my legs to keep everything inside me from spilling out.

"Look at you," he rasped. But I was looking at him. His dark hair fell wild about his face and a light sheen of sweat covered his skin. "You'll be pregnant by the time you leave my chambers," he vowed.

Would I?

As I laid on the smooth wood, sweaty and parched, I wondered if Lazlian would look at his table in the future and think of me. I wondered if he'd pleasured other girls on it.

I eyed the keylord suspiciously. He kept secrets. Maybe he kept other women too.

Not that it was any of my business.

Not that I cared.

THE SKY WAS dark when I emerged from a bath, and I was startled and confused to find myself alone. Everything jumbled together and I was losing my concept of time. Why had Lazlian left?

Spying a sheet of paper on his table, I scurried over to examine it.

MEET ME IN THE THRONE ROOM WEARING ONLY A ROBE. WHEN YOU ENTER, STRIP AND CRAWL TO ME.

Well, then. I'd never expected Lazlian to be subtle, but I hadn't anticipated such blunt and potentially public directives either.

I'd be a liar if I said I didn't seriously consider just leaving. Fleeing the castle entirely. But I couldn't bear the idea of failing and wondering if it was my fault. Besides, if I played along now, I'd never have to do this again. And so, barefoot, I crept down the stairs of the royal tower and toward the throne room, not meeting the eyes of guards I passed along the way. My arrival was announced, no doubt, by the deep echoing noise the door made as I opened and shut it tightly behind me.

Lazlian sat the throne as if it was his. My heart thumped wildly and for more than one reason. Bare-chested, Laz wore only black sleep pants, a thin silver crown, and the silver cuff with my hair in it. A pathway made of candles had been laid, leading directly from the door to the throne.

With a shaky breath, I let the robe fall to the floor and stood naked in the hall where hundreds of people passed by on any given day. As I crawled through the candlelit path, I wasn't sure what game we played but I knew it was designed for me to be pointedly subservient. When I reached the keylord, he extended his foot as if he were the king. Trying not to roll my eyes, I obediently kissed it, sat back on my heels, and awaited instruction.

It didn't take long. Lazlian pushed down his pants and I understood the order. Wedging myself between his legs, I hesitated only a moment, then bent to take him in my mouth. Again, I wondered if I fulfilled a fantasy of his -- to sit on the throne while I serviced him.

But Lazlian's hands, once stroking my hair, quickly tugged my head off his cock. Still sitting, Laz positioned me on top of him but backwards, as if we faced a gathering of courtiers. It was a little awkward -- the throne wasn't made for coupling -- but I forgot about my discomfort when he filled me.

The air in the hall felt weighty as we moved. Empty, our breaths and moans echoed lewdly off the walls. Holding my hips, Lazlian helped me to brace my body from the hard arms of the chair. With his hands occupied, he ordered, "Touch yourself. I want you to come when I do. I want us to make the heir here, now, like this."

It was impossible to know if or when we'd make an heir, but I was in no position to argue. I did as he asked and Lazlian picked up his pace.

Since it was safely tucked inside my imagination where no one could judge... I did picture a crowd of courtiers watching. Even in the privacy of my mind, however, it was hard to feel free, to give myself permission to think such things. Yet the images came. I thought of this as our first time... of having been sent to marry Lazlian... and of having him claim me like this, in front of the nobles on our wedding day.

It's just fantasy, I told myself, and thus there was no harm in it. No shame. If I couldn't be free in the privacy of my own mind, then where could I be?

As I came, I cried Lazlian's name to the imagined onlookers. I let them see the pleasure he gave me, knowing Lazlian loved such power.

Immediately when Laz finished, he swept me up in his arms and switched our positions, tucking me into the throne with my knees bent to my face, keeping as much of his seed in me as possible.

As I came down, guilt crashed over me. The fantasy wasn't even what I truly wanted, not in my heart, and I struggled to reconcile the daydreams in my head with my actual desires for reality. At the same time, Lazlian cupped my pussy with his hand, preventing as much of his come from escaping as possible. Staring at me darkly, I knew he was thinking about what was happening inside me.

THE NEXT MORNING, I awoke before Lazlian and crept out of bed and onto the sea-facing veranda. It was the soft, casual moments that made me the most uneasy. Assuming servants would soon knock, I'd donned a robe I hoped didn't count as a violation and entertained the idea of leaving the castle completely. Surely, we'd had enough sex already? But I wasn't positive and I knew we had the best chance of success by spreading it out over the next few days.

The further I went down the path, the harder it was to leave, and the greater the loss. My predicament felt like trick rope, the kind where the more a person struggled, the tighter it tied. Each step forward made it more of a risk if I stepped back. Because if I did and we failed, I'd always wonder if we would have been successful if I'd just given it one more day.

Beneath me, I watched the castle awaken, courtiers popping out on balconies to stretch in the morning sun, sip tea, or simply to check on their plants. After a few minutes, Lazlian joined me on the veranda, wearing his loose black sleep pants.

"You're sad," he remarked, the word rolling off his tongue as if he'd tasted that one tart berry amongst the sweet. "Why are you sad? Don't you want to have a baby?"

I barked a laugh. Lazlian said it like it like the idea was

abnormal, when, in reality, *we* were the atypical ones. Royals and nobles might hurry to secure heirs, but none of my *commoner friends*, as Lazlian would call them, were in any rush.

I stopped myself before rolling my eyes. "I do and thanks for finally asking after all these months."

Lazlian ignored my sarcasm. A muscle in his cheek feathered. "What then?"

I looked back to the turquoise sea, picturing the threats that lay across it, beyond our paradise but not out of reach. "It's this world. We had little to fear in Elowa." I shrugged one shoulder. "Relatively. The sting of a Black Titan or a Goodnight Fish. But now that I know the truth and now that it feels like war is coming, I can't help but wonder what I'm bringing another child into."

With ease Lazlian insisted, "I'll protect you. You and our baby. One of the benefits of being a Doreste."

I gave him a sad smile. "You cannot. And I fear the closer one is to power, the more in danger one may be." Before he could refute that, I diverted by adding, "And I've never been away from Teddy this long."

"It's mere days," Lazlian remarked.

"He's never spent more than the night with Saos and Alette."

"Does he cry and miss you?"

"No," I laughed. "They adore each other. He has a wonderful time and doesn't always want to come home right away. *I* miss *him* too much."

"He shouldn't be with you so often," Lazlian declared, waving a dismissive hand. "It's unhealthy. He should be raised with the other noble children. It is our way."

"I'm Elowan. It is not my way."

"You're not in Elowa any longer."

"It's still in me."

Lazlian shot me a look and I sighed, explaining, "I don't want to be like my parents, Laz, there, but not there. Can't you understand that?"

Before he could reply, we heard a knock on the chamber door. Disappearing into the bedroom, he announced, "You may enter. We'll eat on the veranda."

Last night's storm had pushed away the clouds and the air had a pleasant crispness. Under skies clear and bright, I watched as the servant set the day's special breakfast onto the small, sunlit table.

I'd never celebrated the Divine Slumber at High Spire. In the one year I'd spent within the castle walls, Grahar hadn't made any elaborate preparations. Traditionally, the holiday began with a breakfast like the servant now arranged. Mead and honeycakes were provided to welcome a sweet life in the coming year, and figs were served for fertility -- always a concerning issue in a world with low birth rates. A honeycomb dripped luxuriously onto the central pastry, and, if the coffers overflowed, shaved flecks of gold were sprinkled atop. Sometimes they were added to the mead itself as well, symbolizing prosperity.

Indeed, the gold glinting from the miniature feast before me proclaimed that talismans for good fortune would not go amiss in the Doreste household.

Once the servant departed, Lazlian quickly ordered, "Remove your robe. Come. Sit on my lap."

"Just because you can see my body at your leisure doesn't mean you can see into my mind," I said, sliding the robe from my shoulders.

And today, the gods can't see us, I reminded myself.

Naked, I sat self-consciously in Lazlian's lap. We ate our breakfast and polished off two glasses of mead. The slight buzz helped keep my thoughts from straying to places that wouldn't be helpful.

As we stood to leave, Lazlian surveyed the table and remarked with satisfaction, "By next year's Divine Slumber, I may be king."

I frowned at his continual pushing for a transfer of power, instead of having Juls simply name his kin, his heir.

"Well then, to your health," I mocked, raising my glass, *"your majesty."*

Lazlian's eyes nearly rolled back in his head. He groaned, then seized me. The sudden move made me drop my glass, spilling the mead. I wrapped my legs around Laz's waist and clung to his muscles as he dropped me onto the table.

"Say it again," he ordered, voice thick with lust.

"Your majesty," I cried out, not from the words themselves but from Lazlian inserting two fingers inside me at the same time. His pants were down in an instant.

"Again," he commanded.

"Your-" I was cut off by my squeal as he rammed his cock inside me, "majesty."

I hadn't known my words would excite him, hadn't intended it. Lazlian moved slower this time, giving me long, languorous thrusts until we both came, right under the morning sky. After, I laid on my back for several required minutes, cleaned what dripped out of me, and returned to the balustrade, now naked.

I watched the waves, trying to force my mind to stay focused on the task of getting pregnant instead of... thoughts that would hinder success. Those that agonized my aching heart.

For Kirwyn, somewhere across this ocean.

It was a curious thing, Lazlian choosing the sea-facing

suites. He came up behind me and I found it impossible not to remember that night, five years ago. That evening had been dark and clouded, and today the skies were clear and bright. *Which had to be a good sign, right?*

Lazlian enveloped me, caging me with his arms on either side of my body.

At least I'm no longer worried that he's going to toss me into the sea. That's an improvement.

Lazlian was capable of many deceptions, but being the object of his lust was safer than his loathing. *Right?*

"You're still sad," Laz said, frustration roughening his voice.

"It's… strange being back here. Willingly, I mean." I gave a small laugh, trying to lighten the mood. My mood. "I spent my time in High Spire as a prisoner. You stole me."

Lazlian nuzzled my ear. "You wanted to be stolen." He pressed closer, his hard, bare body tight to mine. "It was just the wrong man."

Sighing, I bit back a hundred things I could say. There was no point in arguing with Lazlian.

"I've changed my mind about our schedule this afternoon," he declared in my ear. "I have plans for tonight and we both need to recover."

"What. Plans?" I grit out. I briefly registered that he might be redirecting me again and I could tell from his tone that I needed to brace.

"You're wearing traditional attire to the feast. And when dinner concludes, we'll return to my chambers," Lazlian announced, his breath making me shiver. "And I'm going to give you the whipping I've always vowed."

CHAPTER 18

AN OFFER
Kirwyn

He didn't need to say it, but he did.

"This is what awaits your Elowan princess when you lose," Jori warned, green-gray eyes shifting to the parade below to reinforce his meaning. "She'll be sold into slavery. The same fate will befall the Dorestes and they'll be sterilized to prevent future heirs. Your wife, however," he trailed off dramatically, then continued, "there will be a bidding war to make offspring with her."

A tinny sound rang in my ear. I forced my breathing to remain even, but I knew I wasn't fooling him.

"Your son," he tilted his head side to side and shrugged, "could go either way. He's a half-breed so maybe they'll want his seed."

"Keep your goddamn hands off my wife and my son," I gritted out, clutching the armrest.

"Or maybe they'll castrate him."

"I swear to god if you lay a hand on my son-"

"Does he have a nice singing voice?"

Red tinged the edges of my vision, consuming the world around me into flame as I leapt from my seat and shoved Jori to the wall. Before I knew how I'd gotten there, I'd pinned him with my forearm pressed against his throat.

"He's a baby," I growled. "You leave my son alone. What the fuck is wrong with you people? If you touch my family, I swear I will burn this city to the ground and everyone in it," I pushed harder against his larynx, making him choke. "I swear you will live the longest life possible and I will torture you for every day of it, in ways no man could ever imagine and no man has ever endured. I swear I will drive you so far into madness you will forget your own name and know only one thought -- the wish for death. Do you understand me?"

Gleeful roars erupted for the show below. I tried not to think about what they cheered and how easily it could be *her,* Zaria terrified and humiliated, paraded as a war prize. The idea momentarily turned my vision from red to black, and I had to blink to clear my sight. With the last vestiges of reason in my head, I relaxed my arm enough to allow Jori to reply.

"I understand you more than you know," he said, calm despite having to work to catch his breath. Jori took a moment to arrogantly straighten the collar of his shirt, then continued, "When I was taken, my mother and father were captured with me, and they were brought up onto that stage. I will spare you the details, but my father was able to break free long enough to swipe a gun from the nearest guard. In front of the crowd and in front of me, he killed my mother to save her. He shot at me, missed, and then quickly turned the gun on himself before the Spades could take it."

I searched Jori's face for the lie but found none.

"My father could guess what fates the High Twelve planned for them both. Can you guess what they want to do to you, hm?" Jori mused, smug with knowledge I did not possess. "Corine and Banya want to forget you; they want you to toil away in obscurity as a slave in the mines or the far fields. But your love story with the Queen of our Hearts is famous... whichever version is being parroted," Jori said with a shrug. "Larius would rather exploit it by making you a Beast of the Bowl. He thinks you might be good with a blade and that many would find it entertaining to watch you fight. You lose, you die. Any matches you'd win, you'd earn a night *with her.*"

Rage rose in my chest and Jori knew it.

"You can see the entertainment value as it echoes your real love story," Jori said, eyes hard. "If Larius has his way, you'll fight to the death once a fortnight for the privilege of spending a few hours with *your wife.* You won't last long, though. You may be fast, but you haven't the brute strength to win against the bigger men he'd eventually send."

Jori moved slowly as he reached for a glass of wine, not wanting to make any sudden moves and to show me he had no tricks up his sleeve. Head spinning, I watched as he leisurely sipped.

"I, however, think your talents lie elsewhere," he declared. "I think you can be persuaded with better choices. You've risen from nothing and I respect that."

I sneered at Jori, at the notion that I'd be interested in anything he offered. Yet I couldn't help but picture the alternative. Glancing down into the bowl, I saw myself there, torn from Zaria and having to kill another man just to see her again. Hearing crowds cheer when I did. Would they hide her from me? Let her watch? Force her to watch me die when I was finally paired with someone I couldn't beat?

"I don't resent my father for what he did, he couldn't have known how high I'd climb," Jori said, bringing my attention back to him. "But had he waited... I was able to assimilate and ascend to the highest of ranks. I would have been able to save my parents, eventually. At the time, I was too young to make the choices I'm now offering you. You, however, are not a child."

I scoffed at his condescension and didn't back away. "You should hate the High Twelve for what they did to you and seek your revenge, not lick their boots. You're a traitor and a coward."

"One day the world went dark," Jori said, sagely. "Lights everywhere flickered out and they did not return until the Spades re-lit them. Think of what that means to the people here. It's not as simple as you believe."

"I'll make it simple for you," I spat. "She is my *wife*. He is my *son*. You will not touch them."

"I will be doing very little directly, yet most of you will die in this war regardless," Jori said, smoothing the non-existent wrinkles in his shirt. Having made his point, he was happy to chatter now. "Any surviving Elowans and the highest in Rythas will be taken for unspeakable use. The only power you have is in choosing a few people to save, and even that is limited to your household and the High Twelve will require much in return. Your allegiance. Your service." Jori finished inspecting his shirt and met my eyes as he continued. "For your support, you will be given status here. Position and power. A luxurious estate and slaves at your attendance. Servants, if that bothers you," he quickly amended. "All I'm asking is for you and your wife to take the Spade citizenship I'm offering."

"All you're asking me to do is turn traitor and betray the entire kingdom and its people," I snarled, waving him away as I stepped back.

"Who is your allegiance really for? The kingdom? Or her? You can't save both," Jori warned. "You know it. I know it."

"You don't know shit about what I can do," I swore, and stormed out of the Bowl.

CHAPTER 19

DIVINE SLUMBER
Zaria

What did Lazlian mean, exactly? *Surely not an actual whipping.*

I could say no. *Couldn't I?*

I managed to dress myself and when Lazlian returned, he rewarded me with his hot stare. Laz was oddly fascinated by my back, and yet, I knew it wasn't the kind he preferred: soft, slim, and not shaped for the sea. It made me both self-conscious and, at the same time, annoyed that I felt that way. But the clenching of his jaw told me Lazlian fought an erection when I spun at his command.

The silken gown he provided bore no embroidery, but the style was unmistakably traditional. Black and flowing, like a dark river on a moonless night, it ran to the floor and beyond, blending into a long train. Held up by two thin straps, the backless dress dipped as low as possible without being totally obscene. It was as if the dressmaker worked a modern take on a traditional gown, retaining the cut but not the heavy fabric or embellishment. I wore no jewels but a simple gold diadem and one golden cuff, high up on my right arm. Servants had come earlier and prepared my hair in a style swept to the side and loosely arranged in twists, allowing for the unobstructed viewing of my exposed back.

The unobstructed access for whatever Lazlian planned to do to it later.

Whipping, I thought. *Say the word.*

I glanced at the keylord. "You don't mean it literally, right? As one would attempt to scar or to kill a man?"

Lazlian traced his thumb over my lips. "No blood will be drawn."

I gulped but nodded. I could always tell him to stop... although I wasn't entirely sure why I hadn't already. I'd raised protests and Lazlian said something about our odds of conception being higher if I stopped stressing and turned my mind off completely. I gave up arguing because every time I advanced, he'd parry in return, and it continued until I was exhausted... or he ended the disagreement by fisting my hair and guiding me down to his cock.

One of Lazlian's preferred methods to cease debates was to stuff me so that I couldn't speak, always claiming it was for my own good to stop my racing mind. In reality, I only found myself on my knees when my mouth was saying things Lazlian didn't want to hear.

Returning me to the moment, Laz stroked his fingers slowly down my back and I shivered.

"You're like the Queen of the Night flower," he said from behind me, sounding far away.

"What's that?" I asked, narrowing my eyes as I spun quickly to face him.

"One of the rare plants we have in the courtyard," Lazlian replied nodding his head to the inner garden. "Juls found it first. Figures. He told me of an unbelievable white flower he'd seen blossom one evening only, and I didn't believe him as it sounded too fantastical. A flower that blooms for only one night? It became like a myth between my brother and I," Lazlian said, leaving me to cross to his dresser. He shrugged into a flattering and finely cut black jacket with silver embroidery, then fixed a thin silver crown onto his head. I wondered if he wore one because it was a formal affair, or because I wore one, or to lay the groundwork for possibly taking the throne. Lazlian had rarely donned a crown in the past, I had thought, in order to quash the rumors he now wanted to cultivate about being the true first-born son.

Either way, I had to admit that he looked ridiculously striking in that ensemble.

"And then, one night before you arrived, I was in the courtyard alone," Laz continued. "It was just past midnight and I'd been out drinking. But I saw it. Delicate petals and a scent you can never forget. The entire courtyard smelled of it... like jasmine but better. By morning, the flower had died," Lazlian said with a shrug. "Gone with the sun's rise."

He leaned back on his dressing table and stared, lost in the memory.

"Seeing it with my own eyes drove me to research, and I eventually found out it's called Queen of the Night, or sometimes simply, Moonflower. It only blooms once a year, only at night, and only for a few hours."

In the heavy silence that followed, my heart ached, understanding that I was Lazlian's Queen of the Night flower, blooming for him this final evening and gone by morning. But there was nothing I could do. I felt bad about leaving and wretched at the thought of staying. I missed my family terribly. Guilt made it difficult to breathe. Shame was something I couldn't even begin to tackle yet.

And yet... I crossed to Lazlian and kissed him. He stiffened at first, then his hand wrapped around my waist to pull me tighter. I realized I'd never kissed Lazlian before -- at least, never had I initiated a kiss outside of sex.

I only felt more confused when it ended.

"We'll arrive together but leave after everyone else, so that they cannot know for sure what is happening," Lazlian said. "It will cause just enough suspicion to start rumors, but not enough to spread wildly. Though," Lazlian said, hand encircling but not squeezing my neck, "It's not a lie. You are my mistress now."

The possessive threat in Lazlian's voice made me wary.

"You're not yet king and it's only for one more day," I said.

Lazlian's eyes twinkled, and I was reminded that he lied about... something... the day we met at my table to discuss making the heir. Laz couldn't lock me up in his room, I assured myself. As king, Juls would never stand for it.

But what did Juls have to do with Lazlian's lies? Because the keylord hadn't told me the truth about why his brother had hit him.

As we walked, Lazlian's hand found the small of my back and I stiffened. This was Kirwyn's place; he always held me there to guide me into a room. The casual intimacy of the familiar act jarred me, made me recall all the times Lazlian had been my enemy and his hands, a threat.

How had we gotten here and... was it real?

∾

CANDLES high and low lined the castle hallways leading to the dining room, which had been expanded to accommodate more guests for Merie's frequent entertaining.

For the Divine Slumber, the room was transformed into a warm wonder of rich tapestries and multitiered candelabras, but the best feature was the potted plants and trees from northern, mainland forests. They filled the space to make it look as if we dined in a woodland, each tree aglow with soft fairy lights and pine scenting the air.

It was said that anything could happen during the Divine Slumber because the gods weren't watching. They were believed to be at rest, dreaming up new events for the coming year... though there was an ever-going debate about whether one mortal night was the same in divine time, or whether it lasted much longer... but that was a question for the theologians.

What *was* agreed upon was that it was a night fates were determined, and while anything might happen *to* you, mischievous children were advised not to seek trouble. It was said, "*though they sleep, you will reap,*" a caution that while the gods weren't paying close attention, what one sowed during the time, one could expect to reap in the coming year. Since it was a bit contradictory, I'd often wondered if the consequences were tacked on a later date to deter the rise of trouble-seekers, or if the holiday was supposed to be some sort of test. It made me think of parents stepping out and not watching their children but checking to see if the little ones had been well-behaved when they returned.

Juls sat at the head of the table and Merie, Laz, and I sat nearest the king. The rest of the table was filled with noble couples save Lida, who I was happy to see, and Navere, who I was not. Involuntarily, I gulped under the scrutiny of his calculating glare. There had never been proof that the Commander encouraged his soldiers to dispose of me, but I knew I dined with a man who'd murder me, given the chance. A third solo guest entered when Raoul, looking dashing in a deep indigo jacket with black trim, moved to the chair at the table's other head. Before sitting, he gallantly bent and kissed the hands of the women nearby.

The feast was as glorious as I'd imagined, and from the cooing delight of the nobles, I knew I wasn't the only one impressed. Tapers had been lit and they glowed in myriad colors -- not just the wax itself, but the fire as well. Flames of azure, violet, coral and emerald flickered at various heights throughout the lush spread of fragrant greenery. I'd never seen anything like it and could only assume the candles came from the Spades.

It was Merie, I was sure, who'd brought out the best flatware from High Spire's reserves. Each fork handle culminated in a crown design, every spoon bore a smaller, queen-like tiara, and the knives were decorated with a key at the end. Plates were painted with a rendering of the castle itself, and on that dinnerware the Dorestes served a feast to end all feasts. Tender beefsteak, roasted rabbit, and spicy goat aside pots of herbed, heavy sauces were scattered throughout the table. Fresh clams and oysters piled atop towers rising higher than our heads. I grimaced at the hearts of mourning doves in little trays with tiny skewers, Lazlian's favorite. Finally, more side dishes than I could sample in an evening were set before us.

Above, a music sphere played festive songs to add to the ambiance. In one corner of the room, a clever pyramid of wine bottles had been constructed.

"A gift from Mal-Yin's reserve," Lazlian whispered,

seeing my gaze on the fifty or so bottles. Surely, they couldn't all be consumed in one evening?

I drank to calm my nerves but didn't overeat, preoccupied with what would soon happen in Lazlian's room. Everyone waited with palpable anticipation when our plates were cleared, indicating it was time for dessert.

"Fortune en Flambé," Lazlian said, as if I didn't already know -- though I had to admit I'd never seen it prepared like this.

Fate on Fire was the traditional dessert served for the holiday. Whatever was revealed in the cake or the candy balloon, supposedly revealed the fate the gods had planned for the recipient in the coming year.

But the Dorestes didn't *just* serve cakes to each guest. Every plate contained a slice and an edible balloon, but between the dishes themselves servants constructed some sort of pathway whose purpose I couldn't glean.

Juls spread his hand, beckoning Merie to do the honors. Smiling, she stood and crossed to the other head of the table, by Raoul. Merie lit and dipped one candle into the path's origin and stepped back as, to our collective delight, an immediate trail of fire blazed across the dining table. Each time the fire reached a guests' cake the alcohol was set aflame, the heat burst the sugared balloon perched above, and the fortune-telling trinket was revealed as it fell. *Pop, pop, pop* echoed across the room, followed by giddy laughter. The flames raced down the table until they reached the four of us at the other end, Merie having scurried back.

Lazlian knit a brow somewhere between disgruntled and curious as he eyed the gold coin, indicating a boon of wealth. My heart sank to see I'd received the rock, the only mixed omen, foretelling a difficult path ahead. Whether it led to ill fate or to a brighter future was a toss-up, but it was never without strain.

I knew Lazlian was disappointed that neither of us received the little baby. From the shrieks and laughter, I could tell a noblewoman at the other end of the table had the divisive token. She threw the miniature baby and a small game of hot-potato began as the nobleman facing her didn't want it either.

Glancing over, I saw Juls received the tiny crown, indicating power. I couldn't help but wonder if Lazlian and I would be unsuccessful, leaving Juls to rule for as long as he could hold onto the throne. Merie examined a tiny book, the symbol of a path of learning or knowledge ahead. It was a favorite of apprentices, and a generally good omen overall.

With dessert and fortunes served, couples began to wind down their conversations over the next hour and depart. Lazlian and I remained, as planned, until we sat alone at the table.

"Lazlian, what are using to... you know. Like... not a real whip, right? Because you said you wouldn't scar me or draw blood."

"You can cry and beg but I don't want you to talk for the rest of the evening," Lazlian instructed, his thumb stroking my lips. "Give yourself to me and I'll give you a baby."

I huffed. There were many things wrong with what Lazlian just said. It was much too casual. It was insulting. And he had it backwards. But at this point, I was honestly so desperate to move past the unbearable pressure, I'd try anything.

"I promised that if you followed my lead, you'd get pregnant, didn't I?" Lazlian asked. "It's a vow, and I always keep my vows."

"You can't promise that, Lazlian."

He laid a finger on my lips. "What did I just say?"

I rolled my eyes and quieted, though I could feel my heart beat faster as Lazlian rose and took my hand.

Juls, not a particularly superstitious man, had left the crown beside his empty plate and I watched as Lazlian pocketed the trinket. The little toy baby, upside-down and forgotten, lay at the other end of the table. Passing by, Lazlian casually swiped that one as well.

You can't steal other people's fates, I wanted to say, but, forbidden from speaking, I said it all with a chiding look. Lazlian's raised eyebrows and half-smirk might as well have replied, *the gods favor those who dare.*

Maybe he was right. They weren't looking at us anyway tonight, were they? I hoped not. I didn't want anyone to see whatever Lazlian was about to do to me and certainly not an immortal who'd remember it eternally. My footsteps were heavy as Lazlian's determined hand firmly clasped mine, leading me back to his chambers.

Entering his room, I gulped and blushed. A sturdy-looking hook and rope contraption had been attached to the ceiling, and a table placed beneath it. *Servants must have set this up.* They knew. Maybe Lazlian didn't have as tight a hold on them as he thought and they'd gossip. Maybe he wanted them to. Either way, they'd certainly look at me with knowing, judging eyes.

Maybe Lazlian wanted that humiliation for me.

A jerk of his chin told me what to do, and I stepped out of my shoes, climbed hesitantly onto the table, and raised my arms. In heavy silence, Lazlian tied them tight above my head. True panic set in once I was secured. No arms, no speech, and nothing but the pleas in my eyes to stop the keylord if he went too far.

You can cry out at least. He promised.

Lazlian flourished a dagger but he didn't use it to toy with me. With two quick swipes he cut each strap of my beautiful gown and let it fall, pooling onto the table beneath my feet.

I stood in nothing but my tiara and one golden arm band.

Lazlian unrolled a length of fabric onto the dining table and I couldn't look away fast enough. Black, ominous tools of all sizes met my eyes. Flat, leather implements. Thin, whippy rods.

Sweat gathered at the back of my neck and anxious butterflies frenzied in my stomach. I couldn't remember why we were doing this. Distractions of some kind... they were working because I could focus on nothing but Lazlian's hand selecting a wicked-looking length of black leather and coming to stand before me.

His eyes darkened as he moved, circling to my back. I felt him raise his arm. And then he brought the leather down on my rear with enough force that I jerked my head back and gasped.

CHAPTER 20

HIS MARKED QUEEN
Lazlian

"Oh my god, look at you," I said, letting my eyes rake over every vulnerable inch. "I could do anything to you in this moment and you'd not only allow it, you'd moan for it. No matter how depraved, no matter how painful. I could clamp your nipples and you'd arch for me. I could whip your pussy and you'd soak yourself. I could do unspeakable things that would make you sob in the light of day and right now you'd only weep if I stopped."

Zaria's reply was a deep groan and the lolling of her head.

I'd shattered her like glass. Outside my chambers, she was obstinate. Strong, even. I could admit that. She persevered under the scrutiny of the people and she refused to be dissuaded from what she wanted, even when my family opposed her.

But here, I thought, rubbing my achingly hard cock. *My*

little whore is just as I'd always known. Ruled by her swollen sex. This was why she needed to be contained, to be kept behind closed doors.

I'd started slower, with medium force, but the more I struck her, the more she could take. Her body implored and I obliged. Lubrication dripped, soaking her thighs as if she'd wet herself. I wondered what might frighten her so much that she did, and the idea made my cock twitch. What would it take to scare her into the ultimate degradation, until she was a trembling mess of fear in my arms, sobbing and shaking for any soothing I'd provide?

Forgetting herself, Zaria's legs had slackened and closed, so I gave her one sharp smack between them and she immediately yelped and spread for me.

Pleasure shot down my spine and I felt pre-cum leak. I craved this. As often as possible. Seeing her brought to this state was like the first dose of some next generation drug that eternally hooked the user, ruined a man in an instant... the kind that sometimes emerged in Mid-Spire and we tried to contain, the kind my father had always ensured Juls and I never went near.

I'd succumbed to another addiction entirely. She bore the angry weals on her body, but I was the one who felt whipped. Her ruination was my ruination. She looked beautiful, this creature crafted for me, the first-born princess, born for the first-born prince.

She needed it, she just didn't know it. The harder you whipped a girl like her, the harder you fucked her, the harder she came.

Two opposing thoughts dominated my mind. The first was that I would stab her husband to death if he walked into the room at this moment. The second was that I would disgrace myself and beg, compromise, offer anything he wanted not to take her from me. Which made me want to stab him all over again.

Running my fingertips down Zaria's vulnerable sides elicited her pained whimper of wanting. Her eyelids fluttered, mind lost in some state of desperate desire. Her mouth parted in silent pleas for my attention. Her skin, golden in the candlelight, glistened with a light sheen of sweat.

My sovereignty, writ in welts upon her flesh. Mine for a day, said the lighter bruises. A week, proclaimed the darker marks. An angry line disappeared down between the crease of her ass and I wondered what it would be like to carry her out to the throne room and let them all see. To spread her wide and show them her sore, swollen sex and the lines of my leather crossing over even the other opening.

The Queen of our Hearts. What would they think of her like this?

Who cared what they thought? They were leagues beneath the both of us.

Piercing the silence with a grunt that surprised even myself, I kicked the table from beneath her, sending Zaria swinging in mid-air as she scrambled for support. Finding none, her wrists were forced to bear all her weight and I did not know how much it might hurt because she was too far gone to know herself. For a moment, I soaked her in; naked, bruised, and dangling helplessly. Then I charged forward, almost without thinking, drawing her up and wrapping her legs around my shoulders. Zaria's wrists supported her upper half, but I carried the weight of her lower body and, despite the odd angle -- half-slanted, half-sitting on my shoulders -- I dove into her cunt, lapping.

The cries of pleasure she made couldn't be called human.

Oh, how she wanted what only I could give her.

Whatever discomfort Zaria suffered, strung from her wrists and dangling in the air as I buried my face in her needy sex, didn't deter from her ecstasy. I could tell from the tightening of her thighs that I drove Zaria to an orgasm faster than ever before, and from her screams it was one of the most powerful.

She shattered, jerking against my mouth, and I continued to suck her clit as she rode what turned out to be the longest orgasm she'd ever had with me. A rush of dominance and a thrill of power shot through my head. As she came down, nonsense tumbled from Zaria's lips between gasps for air, and I licked her gently through her descent.

I'd broken my rule that she never come without my come inside her. I didn't regret it, but it had to be addressed -- immediately because I'd never been so painfully hard in my life.

Yet I helped Zaria down slowly, first pushing the table back beneath her feet. It didn't do any good, she could hardly stand. I untied her hands and when she collapsed into me, I swept her into a bridal carry and laid her carefully on the bed. Throughout the transfer, she seemed to have one foot in this world and the other in the dream land in her head.

I removed my clothing and meant to fuck her -- my cock was throbbing for it -- but instead I moved to her ankles, kissing. I worked my way up her bruised thighs, kissing the marks of the crop. Zaria made a sound like she'd winced, so I rolled her half-over, guessing the punishment she'd taken on her rear was too much and she'd rather sleep on her stomach.

I pressed my lips to those angry bruises on her soft bottom and up her sensitive back. I kissed the mark of

Rythas on her shoulder blade. It should have been me holding her down as she took it, but at least it had been my command. I kissed the unbruised skin on the hollow of her long, regal neck. When she began sighing and softly rocking her hips, I spread and bent her top leg, desperately needing to sink myself inside her. With Zaria half face-down, half on her side, I slid my fingers cautiously into her wet sex. She sucked in a breath, then groaned.

"Does it hurt?" I whispered.

She made an attempt at a nod, still rocking against my fingers.

"Does it feel good too?"

She gave a pleasured whimper and the almost imperceptible inching of her leg wider. Opening for me, inviting.

My beautiful whore of a queen, offering herself to the king who'd just whipped her.

From behind, I slid into her soft, hot cunt and a deep groan reverberated through my chest. I wrapped my right arm around her torso and Zaria tried to thread our fingers, I think, but she was too dazed and instead clutched my hand in hers and clasped it against her heart. The night's festivities, the alcohol, the whipping, her orgasm... it was all bearing down on her, forcing her beyond the fuzzy-minded state she occupied and into a true slumber.

We were pressed as tightly together as possible, my chest to her back and our bodies both dampened with sweat and the juices sliding down her thighs onto mine. I kissed her gently as I thrust, deep and slow. She was fading, too tired to orgasm again, but my seed would find its target inside her. The thought made something warm unfurl in my chest.

One final thrust, another hot kiss upon her neck, and an intense pleasure raced down my spine as my balls emptied, shooting deep within my pliable little queen. She accepted what I gave with a passive moan, succumbing further to the pull of sleep.

Even when my cock softened I kept it inside her, squeezing her limp body tight to me. I didn't know where the surprising words came from next, but I said them.

"I love you, Zaria," I breathed against her ear.

"I love you..." she murmured, and an instant, blinding starlight filled the room as my heart swelled against my ribcage.

"Kirwyn," she whispered sleepily.

Something like the crack of thunder boomed above -- or maybe it came from my goddamn chest -- silencing the world around me and plunging it all into darkness.

UTTER ANNIHILATION
Kirwyn

atrik, the artist in our group, arrived at my assigned manor late in the evening. I made no attempt to hide his visit as I showed him into the large, sunken gathering room, centrally constructed in the lavish house. Floating above, relaxing melodies played from the music sphere. Before us, candles flickered, adding a soft glow to the dimly lit room.

Back stiff, Patrik continually shifted on the couch, never seeming to find a comfortable position. When I attempted to meet his gaze, his eyes darted to the floor. He was clearly nervous, but that was good.

We chatted idly for a few minutes, sipping a cocktail I'd intentionally asked one of the servants to create. As the evening progressed, I subtly moved closer to Patrik. We spoke about our planned journey back to Rythas the following day, and we both expressed a bit of reluctance to return.

It helped that Patrik was somewhat good-looking. Still in his twenties, he was fit and had a full head of hair.

When we'd emptied our glasses, I suggested we pop into the adjoining kitchen to raid the cabinet for something stronger. Grabbing the nearest bottle of Spade spirits I could find, I poured two drinks and met Patrik's eyes meaningfully.

Okay you pricks, I thought, slamming back the liquor. I blew out a puff of air, skirting a cough from the repugnant flavor. *You want to watch and report? Watch this.*

When Patrik replaced his now-empty glass on the counter, I moved into his personal space and wedged my knee subtly between his legs. It was enough to look like I tried to hide my actions, but past the point where one man would press his leg against another's.

Fuck it.

I grabbed Patrik's hair as if I'd broken self-control, yanking and holding his head so that I could whisper in his ear. Pulling back, I cocked an eyebrow and nodded in the direction of my bedroom. Finally plucking up the courage to hold my gaze, he nodded in return.

I led Patrik across the sunken gathering room and made sure he'd collected his satchel before we conspicuously entered my bedroom together and closed the door behind us. Wasting no time, I turned on some music from another sphere. Then I stripped my shirt and sat on the bed, before thinking better of it.

"Would you prefer it if I laid down?" I asked Patrik.

"If you don't mind," he said. "It's going to take a while and it might hurt a little. You should get comfortable."

I laid on the bed while Patrik retrieved the necessary tools from his satchel.

While I waited to begin, I imagined the salacious whispers outside my bedroom. Not only would tongues wag with the story of the philandering prince, but giving them a man to gossip about was sure to distract those spying servants from what was really going on behind the door.

Patrik needed to temporarily cover my Rythasian tattoo and convincingly apply a Spade mark over it. Impersonating a Spade was an offense leading to a quick death for anyone caught, but it wasn't like I hadn't done it before. It was trickier this time, however, as I both needed to make the mark of Rythas disappear *and* craft a sign of the Spades that would pass closer inspection.

Patrik turned out to be as good at his job as I was at mine. He first applied a false layer of flesh on top of my mark, blending it with my own skin. The adhesive took an hour to cure, after which Patrik worked the Spade tattoo onto the blank canvas.

"Don't get it wet," he advised. "Bathe around it, if you must, or better yet don't bathe at all."

Once finished, Patrik slipped out of my room in the middle of the night, with tousled hair and an untucked shirt. Alone in my bed, I forced myself to sleep, knowing many things could go wrong and I needed to stay sharp.

But the next day, we had a stroke of luck as the skies opened and it *poured*. Instead of waiting for the rain to pass, our convoy departed at the height of the storm. I observed their departure from the shadows, making sure to keep myself dry. Very few people braved the storm to watch my duplicate leave the walled city, and his hood was pulled tight around his head to shield him from the rain.

The dark skies also helped me escape notice as I moved onto the next part of my plan. Darting into a bathroom in one of the drinking halls, I shaved my hair and my short beard. My reflection was considerably more severe without hair to soften it, but it was still recognizable as my face. Making a spur-of-the-moment decision, I shaved my eyebrows too. Changing my clothing, I slipped into something the impoverished of Spade City would wear -- though still above the attire of a slave -- and snuck out of the hall.

I'd previously identified a small room for let in a part of the city where people didn't tend to ask many questions for the right price. I paid enough, though not so much as to raise suspicion, and secured myself what amounted to little more than a closet. The space only allowed for a bed so small my feet hung off the end, and a row of shelves holding a few dusty books on the wall. My stomach turned as I sniffed the stale air. A chamber pot had been shoved into one corner, and, from the look of it, the porcelain had seen frequent use and less frequent cleaning. It was a stark contrast to the modern plumbing I'd been afforded in the sleek manor of this highly-stratified clan.

It's only for a few weeks, I thought, surveying the dismal space. Intending to spend as little time in the room as possible, I flipped my hood back over my head and slipped into the rainy streets.

OVER THE NEXT FEW DAYS, I mapped out the parts of the city I'd previously been denied accessing, sketching from memory when I returned to my room. Keeping my head down, I listened in drinking halls late at night, and was able to learn more about how people other than the Aureum viewed their clan. There didn't seem to be enough unrest for me to hope we could destroy the Spades from within, but I was encouraged to hear the dozen factions did not move as cohesively as the High Twelve purported. Perhaps, one or two pieces of the pie could be sliced and devoured?

In the evenings, the Spades kept darkness at bay by lighting the sky with continuously-glowing electric lights, especially atop their thick walls. An attack at night, where they could shine beams to illuminate soldiers below, provided no tactical advantage. In fact, it would be a disadvantage.

While I counted myself lucky to not have been caught and to glean what I did, I was frustrated to progress no closer to the odd silo at the city's center, nor did I happen upon anything extraordinarily useful.

Ten days after I'd taken the room, I heard the knock on my door, well past midnight.

I jumped from the bed and froze, listening to see if the visitor would move on. After a full minute, the knock came again. Tucking my gun into the waistband of my pants, my muscles coiled as I reluctantly opened the door.

Jori stood before me, a hood pulled over his head of gray hair. He wasn't wearing his gold medallion and his clothing was more subdued than usual.

How the hell did he know I was here? More importantly, did anyone else?

"I came to tell you you're wrong," he announced, by way of greeting. "I know a lot about what you can do. That's why I'm here, talking to you now."

I folded my arms and said nothing. If he sought an invitation inside, he wasn't going to get it. I wanted to ask him several questions but knew I wasn't going to get much from him either.

"Come. Indulge an old man," he prodded. "I want to show you something. It's safe. I've told no one you're here."

After a quick debate in my head, my curiosity was

piqued enough that I grabbed my own hooded coat and followed him through the empty, dimly lit side streets. I thought Jori would lead me along the outskirts of the city, but we moved inward. The further we walked, the quieter the city grew. As the central, municipal area contained no houses and few businesses, no one had reason to linger at this hour. We moved toward the heart of the walled city and in the direction of the strange, circular building at the city's core. My pulse picked up speed as we approached. Was he going to show me what it housed?

Jori and I descended a wide, darkened ramp leading to two heavily armed guards in front of an even heavier-looking door, set within an impenetrable gate. It was clear I had no hope of sneaking into this place on my own.

"You will touch nothing," the guard on the right said. It was not a question.

"You will tell no one," Jori replied, the command also leaving no room for uncertainty.

The left-side guard held out his hand and Jori dropped a heavy bag of what sounded like Spade tokens into his waiting palm. Then the first guard turned and entered a code I could not see onto a metal panel beside the door. I waited, feeling my heart beat faster but trying not to show too much interest on my face. The door swung open and Jori raised his hand, indicating I should walk first.

As I stepped into the room, lights flickered on all around me...

...illuminating the doom of kingdoms.

There was no hiding my open-mouthed shock. I spun, taking in the variety and volume of complex weapons I'd never seen before. Machinery *no one* had ever seen before, though its menacing construction left little room to question its purpose. Peering downward, I saw the circular room continued to several levels beneath the ground, and everywhere my eyes landed caused my stomach to further sink. I couldn't stop turning, taking in what looked like the stockpile of an advanced army before The Great Decline: guns attached to lean, nimble tanks, explosives in sleek casing, projectile weapons to rapidly nullify many soldiers from a distance. There were devices whose function I couldn't even fathom.

No clan could defend themselves against artillery such as this. So why was it hidden? Why hadn't the Spades used it before?

Scrambling for hope, I wondered if maybe everything I viewed was useless.

I was quickly disappointed.

"This is the defeat of everyone who isn't us," Jori said. "The council has been toying with the clans, giving them false hope, while our technology grows. Now you will be baited into a war you cannot win."

I stared at Jori's gently weathered face, looking for the lie, for some reason to disbelieve I stood amongst the means to destroy us. Again, he answered my thoughts.

"Once we unleash these weapons, all other clans will be wiped from the mainland and Rythas will fall as well."

Seeing such unarguable defeat, I swallowed a lump in my throat. But I pushed the thought from my mind because there was a more pressing matter to attend -- why I was here.

"Is this your persuasion?" I asked, sneering to cover my concern. "Showing me how we lose to sway me to your side?"

"I'm risking my neck to show this to you," Jori snapped. "If anyone knew, I'd be executed. If you tell anyone, we will both be killed."

"You're an opportunist or you wouldn't be doing it."

"I'm presenting you with a chance for an alliance where we both come out ahead," he advised. "Make no mistake, every clan will be destroyed. But if you defect and throw your support to the Spades, you'll dampen the fighting spirit in Rythas and we'll make quicker and cleaner work of it. Less deaths on both sides."

"What a deal," I mocked, spreading my hands wide. "You get to parade Zaria and I as your shiny new prizes, winning the esteem and envy of your peers. She and I get to live. Long enough to be paraded privately instead of publicly."

"To live a life of opulence," Jori corrected.

"We already do," I countered.

"Not like it would be here."

"We prefer it there."

Jori shook his head and said darkly, "*There* will soon cease to exist."

CHAPTER 22

THE LIAR'S LAIR
Zaria

My body was a bas relief, a map of dominance carved by the keylord, livid lines and wrathful welts. I sat up in Lazlian's bed with a growing pit of anxiety in my stomach as I gently traced my fingers over the bruises from my thighs to my breasts, thankfully only wincing at the worst. Apprehension and shame made me second-guess what I'd done, what I'd agreed to do. These were deeds for the darkness and the sun's light made them seem utterly scandalous. I tucked my knees under my chin, curling into myself, needing... assurance? Affection? I wasn't sure *what* exactly would assuage my nerves.

"On all fours," Lazlian said, making me snap to attention. I hadn't realized he'd awoken and I blinked at his curt order. He rose and stroked his cock, readying himself.

"Lazlian, I-"

"Head down, ass up. Show me what a whore you can be."

I closed my mouth, and, trying to ignore the rise of injured feelings -- trying not to let him see them -- did as I was told.

Not that it mattered. If, somewhere in the back of my mind the night before, I'd thought that submitting to Lazlian's commands bought some measure of affection, he disabused me of that notion as he pushed my legs wider and ran his hand up the back of my neck and beneath my hair, gripping a fistful to yank my head back as he pushed inside me.

I wished I could say it wasn't enjoyable, but the truth was, pleasure took over as he thrust. At least, physically. Two vital organs in my body had two separate ideas entirely, and while my heart was a little bruised, it wasn't enough to stop my climax. In fact, I think Lazlian liked it, stroking me with extra attention to make me come despite his condescending treatment.

After my moans died down, Lazlian removed himself from my body with rough fingers and a small shove.

"What are your exciting plans tonight?" he asked as we lay together, staring at the ceiling. "Sitting alone in your manor and having dinner by yourself at that rickety table in your sun parlor?"

"I like that table," I replied curtly. I'd curled my legs up, partly from habit and partly from some protective instinct. "Kirwyn and I built it together."

"You're shit at carpentry."

I laughed. "That's true. We try. You'd think Kirwyn would be better at domestic work, having to fend for himself his whole life. We can hunt, fish, and forage, but building, cooking... even gardening." I shrugged. "We get by but have no real talent."

"Not enough physical range," Lazlian said.

"What?"

"You're like children who can't sit still. When the task requires you remain in one place, you lose interest."

"That's not true," I said, scowling. "Besides, Kirwyn loves to read and to play senorok, even if I don't."

"Those activities engage his mind enough," Lazlian replied, waving his hand. "But if he's not challenged mentally, he needs to be moving."

I didn't like what Lazlian implied. I pushed myself up to face him. "And by that assessment, what does that make me, moving and mindless?"

Lazlian's smirk was cruel. "Do you need me to say it?"

"Stop it," I snapped. "Just because I don't read as much fiction as Kirwyn or as many technical manuals as you, doesn't make me any less clever. I have outwitted and escaped you both on occasion-"

A knock sounded on the door, interrupting me.

"Stay," Lazlian ordered, and he rose to answer what turned out to be servants arriving with breakfast. Lazlian took the trays himself and brought each to the dining table. The warm scent of fried bacon hit my nose first, followed by the fruit of guava tea. I realized I was ravenous and immediately leapt from the bed, grabbing the short, light robe to cover myself. I didn't care about Laz's rules and didn't want to be naked right now, but his stare made me pause as I reached for a morning bun stuffed with paw-paws.

"You should remain in High Spire," Lazlian declared, and I could see the wheels in his head turning. "When you're pregnant and in labor, here is the best place for you. You can't give birth unattended in the surf somewhere. Without proper doctors and modern medicine, there were complications the night my son was born."

"Complications? Wait, night?" I asked, perplexed. "You said your son was born during the day."

"Right," Lazlian agreed.

"Well, which was it, day or night?" I pressed. The piping hot food on the table was suddenly forgotten as the unsettling idea that Lazlian had skipped out on his son's birth caused coquina clams to climb up my spine. "And if you weren't there, why not? That's a big deal."

Lazlian didn't reply.

"Lazlian, the time of day matters to my people and being present at the birth of your child matters to every woman. I refuse to believe that you are so cruel as to not care, not when you clearly cared about his life. Tell me the truth and don't start lying," I ordered, voice raised. "Was it night or day or were you not present because you're so callous as to not even bother to be there? And don't try to make up excuses and say you were away in some battle when he was born."

Lazlian let out the longest sigh I'd ever heard.

"I don't know when he was born because I wasn't in their lives yet." His eyelids fluttered shut as he paused. "He's not my son."

"What do you mean, he's not your son?" I asked, uncomprehending. "Of course he's your son."

Lazlian's jaw twitched as he clenched it. "Not... biologically."

Biologically? Confused, I searched Laz's guilty face.

Biologically... what the...

No, no, no. The world tilted on its axis so abruptly, I stumbled.

"What are you saying, of course he is," I insisted, maybe to myself. "That's why you slept with Merie. Because you know you're capable of producing an heir because you've already had a child. You wouldn't lie to your brother, not with something like that."

"I didn't lie," Lazlian said. "I'm capable, I know it. I just didn't have the chance to prove it. Merie and I only tried twice before it became too awkward. Just because he wasn't mine doesn't mean anything about the future children I can make."

Denial, the first stage of grief, quickly departed and seemed to take the room's stability with it. The floor dipped again, dizzying me. I clutched my stomach, feeling as if someone had punched it with full force.

"You didn't have a natural child on the mainland," I whispered, staring at the large canopy bed where Lazlian had taken me several times. "You didn't impregnant Merie," I said, growing both hot and clammy all over. "And you've failed to produce an heir with me as well."

With a pounding heart, I gazed at Lazlian and declared, "You have no proof you're capable of fathering a child. And a string of evidence to indicate you're not."

As soon as I said it, a wretched cry escaped my lips. I brought my shaking hands to my head. "You've been making me fuck you and lying this whole time. You tricked me, you're not virile!"

"I am," Lazlian growled through clenched teeth, stalking toward me. "I just haven't proven it yet. You'll see."

"You can't make an heir, Lazlian, that's why it never worked!" I cried. "Think about it. All this time we've been unsuccessful because you *can't.*"

"No!" Lazlian shouted. He winced a little, averting his eyes and admitting, "The samples we used... I might have sabotaged some of them, decreasing their potency."

I was going to be sick.

"Which samples?" I asked, almost to myself.

"All but the first and the last one," he confessed. "I couldn't figure out how to do it the initial time, with Lida watching. And the most recent... when you were alone after the Fae Fête... I gave it one honest go and decided that if it wasn't successful, that was fate telling me to bed you."

"Oh, *you* decided?" I laughed as I cried. *"You* decided? Half the first sample dripped out of me and I didn't insert the last one!"

"Why not?" Lazlian asked, surprised.

"None of your landdamn business," I shouted. I was the only one entitled to ask questions and I didn't trust Lazlian to give me honest answers. My hands shook with fury and my blood ran hot through my veins. The shame and anger made me sweaty and feverish as I descended into near-hysterical rage. Blind by it, I had trouble making sense of what was happening as I attacked Lazlian.

"Liar! You fucking liar!" I cried. Lazlian tried to stop my fists by grabbing my hands and pulling me to him, but I kept swinging. Even when Lazlian swooped me up and carried me to his table, I punched him again and again.

Even when he lowered his pants, I writhed and kicked him.

Even when he kissed me, my tears sealed our lips.

Even when he drove his cock into me, I pulled his hair with blinding anger, whimpering and grinding back against his hardness. I dragged my nails down his arms as he thrust inside me. I wept as I clung to him. He rammed into me and I arched to meet him, moans morphing into pained groans and back again.

"You fooled me," I sobbed between kisses and punches.

"I'm virile, you'll see," Lazlian swore as he panted, locking me to him so that it was harder to get a full swing. I beat his back and he took it, grunting when I got a good hit but never breaking the rhythm of his hips.

My heart shattered into a million pieces and still I came, shaking and calling his name like a curse. I could feel him come too, but it didn't matter. Nothing he did mattered anymore.

Sweaty and done, I pushed Lazlian off my body. He'd come so hard he stumbled backward and didn't fight me.

I hated that I'd come hard too.

I stood on shaky legs, grabbed the dress I'd first arrived in, and threw it on as I ran to the door. I didn't make it.

"You might already be carrying my child," Lazlian said, racing to block my path.

I laughed so maniacally I swallowed all the hot tears streaming down my face and into my open mouth.

Fool. You deserve to swallow your own tears.

"If you don't let me out of here right now, Lazlian," I gritted between clenched teeth, "I think I'm mad enough to pitch myself out the window and onto the stone."

I might have meant it, but for my family.

"You used me. I will never again allow you to use my body. I will die before I let that happen. Do I make myself clear?"

Lazlian didn't move but I could see him debating what to do.

"You know, I used to envy your family, the way you all cared for each other. But maybe it never extended to those who don't share your blood." I used the moment to lunge past Lazlian. I made it to the door before he caught up, slamming his hand above my head in a move that angered me even as it made me jump.

"Then share it. Share my blood," he said, breathing heavily. "We've done it before, do it again."

"I didn't need to share blood in any ceremony to have Kirwyn treat me the way I want to be treated, to bind us. And I'm threatening that for what? A good fuck."

"This is more than just fucking!" Lazlian shouted, baring his teeth. "It could be, but you never let it."

"No, Lazlian, you never let it!"

Landdammit. I'd started crying again and I hated it.

Gasping, I covered my mouth as another realization came over me. I looked up at the keylord, who still hadn't moved from the door.

"Juls found out you lied to him, didn't he?" I wondered aloud. "That's why he punched you that day."

"Juls assumed he was my son, I didn't lie," Lazlian said. The muscles in his forearm tensed as he tightened his fist with insistence. "And even if I did, it was for everyone's benefit. When Juls started thinking about alternate plans, *he's* the one who suggested you first. Maybe I subtly nudged him in your direction," he admitted, and I laughed because I knew that's exactly what happened.

"But I didn't want to sleep with Merie, and Juls certainly didn't want me to. If my brother believed it to be a plan with even *less* chance of success -- if he didn't have the evidence of my fertility -- the decision would have weighed even more heavily on his head. Don't you see? I took that burden from him and bore it alone."

"Oh my fucking god. You will justify anything, won't you?" I said, snarling. "Did you take that burden from me too? Should I thank you? How would you like me to thank you, Lazlian? On my knees or on my back?"

I pushed Lazlian's hand from the door and he backed away reluctantly, with flared nostrils and wild eyes telling me he might change his mind at any moment.

The truth hurt so much I didn't think I could handle it. I

felt used and stupid and I couldn't handle the shame. I'd been so focused on what Lazlian might *do,* I'd failed to realize the worst might be what he'd already *done.*

"All your fascination with whipping my body is pointless," I said, voice cracking. "Your cruelty alone flays me to the bone."

I grabbed the door handle.

"You just can't see it," I said, flinging the door wide. "You never do."

PART II
COMMUNE WITH DESPAIR

DARK KEY, SHADOWED MOVES
Zaria

I turned away the messengers without accepting their messages. In my rageful moments, I was angrier at the keylord than myself. In my indulgent ones, I permitted bursts of self-pity. Guilt threatened to suffocate me. Frustration boiled inside my veins, making me want to scream.

But outside, I simply gazed at the ocean as I considered what actions to take. *We* were the ones who were supposed to make things better, and instead we'd made it all worse. Now, a reckoning was coming for Rythas *and* for me.

My world contracted to the borders of our estate. Teddy and I ran beneath the broad leaves of the Elephant Ear field or swam in the sea. Mazriah helped us prepare simple meals of roasted fluke or snapper, sugar apples and pawpaws and fresh bread. We milked the goats together and shared warm milk. I didn't need anyone else except Kirwyn, but he wouldn't return for some time and...

...in truth, I was frightened of how he might look at me now.

When a firm knock sounded at my door after many days -- or weeks, I wasn't quite sure -- I ignored it. But when the lock turned and the door swung wide, I jumped.

Jesi stepped into the house and I blinked at her sudden appearance.

"Lord, Zaria," she said, taking stock of my appearance, "you look terrible."

"Is there a reason you're here or did you just come to insult me?" I asked, frowning.

"Now, now," she tsked, closing the door behind her and stepping inside without invitation. It was far from the first time she'd done so. I should have never given her the key. "Don't get angry at me for trying to help."

"I don't need any help," I said, turning and walking back into the seating room.

"If you think attending the coronation looking like that is going to be acceptable, then you're beyond my help."

I froze. "What coronation?"

"Mine," she said sarcastically, half-rolling her eyes. "What coronation do you think? Lazlian's, of course."

Little minnows darted about my stomach. I shook my head and blinked several times. This couldn't be real.

"Lazlian is not king," I protested.

Jesi gave me a look I hadn't seen since I'd first come to Rythas. As if I were mad.

"Zaria, he's been named king for days now. Haven't you heard the news? There will be a coronation and fealty cere-mony tonight, followed by a ball. The Dorestes are working nonstop to pull it together."

Stunned, I collapsed into a chair. A bit breathlessly, I confessed, "I refused the messengers."

Jesi sucked in a long breath. "Well, High Spire is a little chaotic at the moment. Juls revealed that Lazlian was really the first-born son, and thus the rightful heir. It's been... divisive. I'm summing up a lot here, but Juls is relinquishing the crown and giving it to his brother. It's done."

"What is so easily done can be just as easily undone," I snapped, struggling to believe what was happening. "This isn't how we planned it."

"Tell that to Lazlian yourself," Jesi said, flicking her curls. "I think part of his haste was to force you to talk to him."

"Well that's a good reason to jeopardize the kingdom," I dead-panned.

Jesi gave a carefree shrug and smiled. "I'll be back before sunset to help you get ready." She rubbed a section of my hair between two fingers. More precisely, it was a clump. With knots. "Do me a favor and wash the sea from your golden tresses before I get back, okay? This looks and feels like a gull's nest."

I scowled. She gave me another smile and a patronizing pat on the head.

"You've been hanging around Lazlian too long," I said, pinning her with my eyes. "He's rubbing off on you."

"He's rubbing off *to* you," she remarked cheerfully. "Although he'd much rather prefer on."

"Ugh." I dropped my head into my hands, never quite having managed the level of comfort around sex that Rythasians had. Jesi, especially.

"I'll be back before dusk. Oh, and practice this," she said, rising from my sofa and handing me a scrap of parchment.

"What is it?" I asked.

"The fealty vow," she replied. "You need to publicly swear your loyalty to Lazlian."

My eyes fluttered closed. *Of course I did.*

~

L*AZLIAN IS KING*, *Lazlian is king,* I marveled at the fact as I washed the sea from my hair in a trance-like state.

Mal-Yin's words from long ago rang in my head.

Changing kings is easy. Changing minds is hard.

Having someone as ruthlessly determined as Lazlian on the throne might prove *disastrous.* Once, he'd implied an openness to advisement and to change. But given recent events, I didn't believe that Lazlian would truly listen to counsel when necessary.

As promised, Jesi arrived shortly before sunset. She was already dressed in a gown of scarlet and midnight-black with high slits. The silver bodice over her muscled frame leaned more toward fighting than frivolity, reminding everyone she was the First. I thought it was a clever move on her part, wearing both the previous king's and the new king's favorite colors. And while her gown wasn't sparkling or glittering, she'd pulled her hair half up in an intricate manner, with small braids interwoven in the top half and curls cascading in the lower. I didn't need to see anyone else to already know she had the best hairstyle.

Jesi called to people apparently standing just outside my door, and four men sprung into view, carrying an obscenely large box. It was as tall as me, three times as wide, and wrapped in a black bow, like a present.

"I come bearing gifts," Jesi announced. "Well, the new king does. Well, not so much gifts as-"

"Requirements," I interrupted dryly, narrowing my

eyes. "Whatever is inside that thing is obligating me... somehow." I leapt backwards. "Is there a guard in there? Is someone about to seize me?"

"Calm down," Jesi laughed. "It's just a dress." To prove it, Jesi untied the massive ribbon and the box folds sprung open, revealing Lazlian's *gift*.

I'd expected to be presented with something black and sleek, like the traditional gown Lazlian made me wear to the Divine Slumber, but what I received was the exact opposite.

It was a work of art. Clearly a Rythasian style, the soft white dress bore dazzling metallic thread and sparkling stones, like sultry moonbeams dancing in the night sky or tropical starlight or...

A moonflower coated in stardust, I thought, remembering Lazlian's description of the Queen of the Night flower.

The design wasn't at all like a heavy and embroidered traditional gown; this dress was meant for dancing. Similar to the one I'd worn years ago at my Presentation Party, the garment was light and layered, with sheer, airy panels, allowing for easy movement. Sashes hung from the back of the dress, near the top, to float as a lady danced. The corset-like mid-section held the gown firmly in place, but only came as high as the region beneath a woman's breasts. Like my presentation dress, this had a soft, silky layer to cover the breasts themselves. Unlike my previous dress of deep scarlet, however, I could already tell the shape of my nipples would more readily show through the white.

The glittering threads of gold and silver combined with small, shimmering stones made the garment look as if it had been made for some kind of celestial queen, casting starlight as she twirled, and the slightly distressed layers of the gown fell and floated, giving the wearer the look of a half-ravished princess who'd spent the night running beneath the moonlight.

I was almost afraid my mortal touch would sully this goddess gown. It was perhaps the most stunning garment I'd ever seen in my life. I wondered if it was the most beautiful dress ever created in the history of the world.

I hated it.

"I'm not wearing that," I said. Already I imagined whatever in my closet was most unlike this gift. Something blue, plain, and with a high neckline.

"He said you'd refuse," Jesi replied, grinning. "And to tell you that he can't be held responsible for what he does if you show up in something other than this gown."

I frowned. "What's that supposed to mean?"

Jesi shrugged. "With Lazlian, it could be anything. He said it's a fair deal. If you behave, he behaves."

"That's not what this is," I protested. "It's manipulation by the book. I submit or he'll make me sorry."

"He is the king," Jesi pointed out. "He could do worse than make you wear a pretty dress." With no shame, she added happily, "And it's not like you're not already fucking him."

I blinked at her easy declaration, but I supposed nothing escaped Jesi's attention -- if Lazlian hadn't told her outright already. And though I knew she loved Kirwyn, Jesi always possessed a more casual attitude about, well, everything.

"He's only the king because a baby with me would help him hold the throne," I gritted out between clenched teeth. "Or it was supposed to. This move? It wasn't our plan. It's hasty, it's sloppy, and there's going to be consequences."

Despite my protests, I sat, and Jesi put a highlighting cream on my cheekbones, browbone, and the cupid's bow between my lips -- nothing as glittering as one would wear at the Fae Fête, but a subtle shimmer that made me look like I glowed from within. She coated the waves of my hair with a light oil, making them shine too. Pinned at random intervals in my tresses, Jesi fixed tiny diamonds to catch the light. The only concession I would have been afforded was in my choice of crown, and I'd have selected the most subtle tiara I owned, as everything else about my look was already overwhelming.

But having committed to helping Tomé's friend with the jewelry shop, I was honor-bound to wear an intricate diadem that had been delivered to my doorstep several days ago -- the only package I accepted. It sat upon my head like a bold, regal proclamation that I'd arrived planning to be the girl to watch, though nothing was further from the truth. All I wanted was to disappear, to be alone, and to sort through my life. *Let the others celebrate,* I thought. *You can swim in the sea for hours and no one will find you.*

But failing to show up and swear my allegiance might be equated with treason, and I was sure Lazlian would find some excuse to hold me in the dungeons for it.

Despite my displeasure, I donned the dress. It fit perfectly, caressing my skin like a lover's fingertips. It *felt* like Lazlian's hands all over my body. A dress of this complexity, made to my specifications, had to have begun creation many moon cycles prior... meaning Lazlian had planned this for quite some time.

"Oh my god, Zaria," Jesi marveled, stepping back.

"I can't arrive like this," I protested, though my voice sounded breathless. "It's too much."

"*Everyone* will be pulling out the stops tonight," Jesi insisted. "You'll see. Especially the girls who want Lazlian's attention. But I have to concede that if Laz wanted all eyes on you, he's going to achieve his goal."

I can't upstage the queen, I thought, before I remembered, with no small shock, that Merie was no longer queen.

This isn't right. It's happening too quickly.

I walked, and the gown shimmered. If I had thought Lazlian would please me and send me a dress like the sea, I was certainly disabused of the idea. This gown floated so airily it reminded me of that element itself. The fanciful part of my mind took the idea and ran. If Lazlian was fire, being of air would be the most useful to him now, spreading the flames of his rule like the wind, carrying his popularity over the towers of High Spire and throughout the land.

Not to mention remaining quiet and unseen as I moved, like an obedient little consort.

The image pricked at my already-bruised heart. Was I simply useful to Lazlian? Was he playing a very long game? *He couldn't do that, could he? Pretend and plot for years and years?*

He desired me physically. I'd felt the evidence inside me, it was real. But inside himself... could he still despise me? To the point he planned to use and discard me once I'd served my purpose?

I straightened my spine, stepping through my door and facing the night sky.

It didn't even matter what was true. The fact that Lazlian was *capable,* the fact that I questioned it at all, was enough.

~

We rode under a bright, full moon to High Spire, and I continually looked up, wondering what it foretold. This hasty abdication and coronation made my stomach twist with writhing eels. It wasn't like Lazlian or Juls to maneuver so carelessly. On the other hand, Laz didn't shy away from risk. Could it be as Jesi said, and he'd pushed Juls... because of me?

Once inside the castle, the immediate hum in the air made my heart beat a little faster. Jesi entered the throne room first, and I glimpsed around the corner while she was announced. The decadent array of silken gowns, sparkling glassware, and fairy lights was almost too much to take in at once. I appreciated that real candles weren't used, which would have been both hazardous and hot in the crowded hall. I knew I'd be glad for the revealing style of my gown once the dancing further warmed the room. I almost felt bad for the men in their stiff jackets and pants.

Princess Zaria Holt, Raoul called as he gave me a cheeky wink and I stepped into the doorway.

Lazlian sat directly opposite me at the far end of the hall. Our eyes locked and I gulped involuntarily. All the nobles had stopped and stared when my name was announced, but Prince Lazlian was already watching the door, anticipating.

King Lazlian.

That would take some getting used to... time I didn't have. I sucked in a deep breath, held my head high, and walked.

Juls sat the throne as if he'd been born to it; his posture comfortably firm and his face alert and receptive. Lazlian sat the throne as if he'd conquered it. His arms rested on either side of the chair and his legs spread, commanding space with languid insolence. I had to admit his arrogance was an asset right now -- that aggressive energy might have bought him loyalty and it certainly bought him time. Even the few who knew of and supported the change in rule never thought it'd come about so suddenly. However unconventional the traditions of Rythas, they *were* traditional. But the current unpredictability made the nobles look more nervous than rebellious. For now.

Unlike Juls, with a palette of red, gray, and white, Lazlian wore all black. No surprise there. Black boots, black pants, and stiff, black jacket. The only color was the glinting of his silver cuff, ring, and crown.

He looked really fucking sexy and it only made me angrier. It made the dagger he'd plunged into my heart twist with post-stab menace.

Lazlian never possessed Juls's beauty, the kind that made a girl gasp when he looked her way. Laz's lips were thinner and slightly crooked... but now I liked their character. I liked how they seemed more masculine than the pouty mouth I'd once found so kissable on Juls. Lazlian's eyes were cruel, but now I felt drawn to how cunning they were, intrigued by how much that keen gaze captured. What Lida once said was true -- Lazlian was hot in an unconventional way. A way I might not have appreciated when I was younger.

Not that he'd appreciated any of my assets when we'd first met. Not that he ever looked at me then, the way he stared darkly at me now. He reeled me in with his gaze like a fish on a line, fit to be smacked onto the table and skewered upon arrival.

Flayed open. I could practically feel him sharpening the blade as I walked.

Oh god, I wished the conversation had continued as I crossed the floor. *Fucking Lazlian and his landdamn dress.* He knew everyone would stare. Candlelight caught the gown's shimmers, sending sparkles dancing on the floor as I moved, like faeries chasing my steps. At least the musicians were professionals, never ceasing the enchanting float of their bows. But that music only seemed to heighten the tension of my walk, adding melody to the moment.

Something awaited me at the end of this journey and everyone was playing an unwitting part in it, as if Lazlian spun a spider's web and caught us all in our places, immobilized.

Except for me, spiraling powerlessly toward my own ruination.

Fuck you, Lazlian. Wipe that look off your face.

I reached the keylord-turned-king, ready to prostrate at his feet. Other than my rage, I didn't have reservations about the actual act. It was no big deal compared to what I'd already done in this hall, at his feet, mere weeks prior. It was no different from what every other noble -- even Juls -- had presumably just done.

I would have rather kissed Lazlian's feet than endure what happened next.

Before I could lower to the ground, Lazlian sprang to the edge of his seat and grabbed my elbow, stopping me.

It took all my control not to smack his hand away.

"Princess, you shouldn't trouble yourself with kneeling," Lazlian said, with saccharine sympathy. "Not in your condition."

My eyes flew wide, my lips parted with ill-concealed shock, and my throat made a tight, strangled sound.

In your condition.

Who heard that? What did they think it meant?

Lazlian's eyes gleamed. I wanted to claw them out of his head. He knew exactly what he'd done and knew I was spinning, looking for a way out and not finding it. If I protested, I'd only call more attention to any argument he'd ultimately overrule.

In your condition. He might as well have announced to the hall that I was pregnant, and with a husband who may or may not have been in the kingdom to contribute to the event.

Offering me his hand with false, exaggerated grace, Lazlian said, "You may pledge fealty by kissing my ring instead."

While my heart pounded in my ears, his eyes danced with triumph. If anyone had missed his comments, they'd certainly notice my lack of kneeling. The best course of action was to get it over with quickly.

"I - I pledge my loyalty to King Lazlian," I said. "I vow to serve your will. My lands are your lands, my sword is your sword, my life is your life. I vow to do... whatever my king asks of me. From now until my death."

Why did the words of a fealty vow mirror that of a wedding ceremony, but with a thousand times more subservience? Why did it feel like I was pledging away my soul?

Bending just my torso, I kissed Lazlian's onyx ring.

"I accept your service and devotion," Lazlian answered, just as he must have replied to a hundred other men and women already. But it felt different when he said the words to me. "I vow to lead and protect you. I will not demand your land, your sword, or your life without just cause. I vow not to ask of you anything beyond that which you are capable of giving. From now until my death."

Ha. You and I have very different ideas of what I'm capable of giving.

I fought the urge to snarl or storm off, knowing it would

only draw more attention. Or worse, give Lazlian another excuse to tell me not to exert myself.

Bowing and seething, I spied Juls and Merie seated at a table for royals, I presumed. I made my way to it and I braced for anything to happen as the night unfolded.

CHAPTER 24

TO CATCH A KING
Zaria

Jesi was right -- due to Lazlian's eligibility everyone in the hall was dressed for competition. I watched the girls watching him, scrutinizing every flick of his wrist, every dish that caught his eye, every bit of gossip that captured his attention. On this spellbinding night, one lucky noblewoman might catch a king, and the air hummed with hope.

Lazlian's sudden ascension and availability must have seemed like a gift from the gods. Locked from becoming queen when Juls had been betrothed to me, all the noble families were unexpectedly bequeathed a second opportunity with his brother.

I realized some would hate me if they found out Laz planned to make the heir with me, and I also understood why I was the Dorestes' best choice. I had known before, but now I *saw* it. It didn't matter who Laz favored, whatever noble families *hadn't* been selected would use his hasty and unusual coronation as cause to conspire. But with the people on my side, they could only go so far. The popularity I'd strived so hard to achieve to protect me *from* the Dorestes, I now used to protect *them* from usurpers.

Possibly. Unless we'd miscalculated the whole land-damn thing. *And did I even want to get pregnant, did I want to be a part of the Doreste scheming after what Laz did?*

I fought the urge to collapse my head into my hands. We were floundering in the darkness, making decisions that would affect generations, kingdoms, and possibly the world. *How did you know if you were making the right moves when there was never anyone around to guide you?*

I eyed Juls, kissing the hands of noblewomen and clapping noblemen on the back, confident and composed. I hoped he was doling out promises and promotions to any who could be persuaded.

As we dined, the nobles cautiously shared his celebratory tone; the prevailing mood, opportunistic.

What the hell are the Dorestes doing? The glances in many seemed to ask. *And more importantly, how can I benefit?*

"Lucky Raoul came forward with that evidence he'd found about our birth order," Lazlian remarked, sipping his wine beside me. He spoke as if I had no reason to be furious with him.

So that's how this transfer of power happened, I thought. *Makes sense. Everyone trusts Raoul, maybe even more than Juls.*

"It's good for the people to have a wartime king right now," Lazlian mused, stroking the rim of his wineglass in a subtly sexual manner, "since the Spades are getting uppity."

"The people don't generally like you, Laz," I reminded.

"Which only proves their small-mindedness," he joked. At least, I hoped he was joking.

"Perhaps the contempt with which you treat everyone isn't so easily brushed aside by them, the way it is by the nobles, because they don't readily seek anything from you," I pointed out, lowering my voice as a young, beautiful couple danced close by our table, accidentally-on-purpose. The lady had a bright smile she made sure to maintain until it could be firmly angled into Lazlian's view. I bit the inside of my cheek to keep from rolling my eyes. To spark jealousy and confer desirability, the noblewoman feigned adoration of her partner almost well enough to believe, never once tearing her loving gaze from his face.

Clever, that one.

A sort of... unwelcome satisfaction flared in me when Lazlian failed to notice all of it.

Once the couple danced out of ear's reach, I added, "Or perhaps it's because the people remember the time you made them empty their pockets to fund my supposed rescue mission, instead of opening your own heavy, royal purse."

"You're responsible for that one," Lazlian countered, drumming his fingers on the table to purposefully annoy me. "If I hadn't known how much it would pain your tender heart, I wouldn't have thought it up in the first place."

My mouth dropped. "What in the blame-shifting is that? Do you study some kind of ass manuals in your spare time so that you can apply the manipulative tactics and warped logic?"

"What," Lazlian barked a laugh, "is an ass manual? You've been here for years and you still don't get it right. I think the word you might be looking for is asshole." He chuckled. "Though if you find any ass manuals in the royal library, then by all means, please share."

I felt my cheeks heat as I fidgeted in my chair. People tended to speak politely in my company so maybe that *particular* nuance escaped me.

"And the answer is no," Lazlian replied with a satisfied grin. "Such tactics must come to me naturally."

"Ugh. I hate this version of you," I said, frustrated with the persona Lazlian retreated into whenever he felt attacked or at a disadvantage.

"Whatever the nobles feel, they *know* I'm a better choice to lead us into what's coming," Laz insisted. "The Spades fight dirty and Juls doesn't like to dirty his hands."

I said nothing. The idea of a *clean fight* was pretty oxymoronic but the notion that there be no fighting at all was childishness I'd left behind in Elowa.

As most of the guests had finished dining, more couples swirled onto the floor, but no one at our table had yet joined them. When he rose to his feet, it occurred to me they were waiting for Lazlian.

The mere act of the new king standing commanded everyone's attention.

My heart skipped a beat when Laz turned to me and extended his hand, and inwardly, I groaned. The gesture actually made sense. Lazlian couldn't give his first dance to Merie when Juls sat right beside her. Any other hopeful noblewoman would set off immediate suspicions, if not rivalries. And the act itself seemed chivalrous -- cheering the sad princess who sat alone, amusing the wife whose husband was busy on the mainland. To most, I was a neutral choice.

But I didn't believe for a second that Lazlian did it for

logic's sake. He did it to piss me off and to make a point. I had no choice but to take his hand.

Lazlian led me out amongst the couples who respectfully stepped aside, clearing the floor for us. When Lazlian began dancing, I was shocked to realize he was skilled at the High Twine. Not as much as when he danced the Sea of Flames, but still talented and better than me by far. It served to remind me how much he'd failed to properly move with me the first time we danced in this hall six years ago, instead holding me at a distance, as if I'd contaminate him. In a reversal, I was now the one touching as little as possible.

"Pull away and I'll pull you tighter," he threatened. "Then everyone will know."

"They very well may after your little stunt with the fealty vow."

"You kneel to me in my bedchambers. Not here."

Lazlian said it as if he'd just presented me with jewels. I rolled my eyes.

"If you're looking for a lady to swoon from such a generous token of affection, you've picked the wrong girl."

"Right girl, wrongly reared," he said. "We're working on that."

I strained to keep my wrath from showing, smiling tightly instead. "The fact that I can never tell how much of this you truly believe versus the extent to which you say sexist and sadistic things to rile me, is alarming."

"You haven't even thanked me for your gift, which far exceeds whatever gown you'd planned on wearing," Lazlian remarked. "I'd say that's poor manners."

"I hadn't planned on any gown at all because this night wasn't supposed to happen," I whispered, seething. "Not like this."

When the song ended, I rushed back to my chair. It didn't take long for Lazlian to sprawl lazily in the one beside me. I ignored him and focused on people-watching.

At the far side of the room I spied Tomé and Marcin, bedecked in Rythasian attire of cream and white, dancing amongst the crowd. Jesi chatted with Erisio, completely in her element. Courtiers preened and flirted in Lazlian's direction, but, interestingly, a few struck up conversations with the king more reluctantly. It was clear to me they would rather *not* catch his eye and were being prodded, likely at the behest of pushy families. *Allies at court,* I thought with relief. I imagined some women already had suitors and dreaded being the object of the king's fancy, an experience I knew first-hand.

Or they were simply terrified of the cruel new king.

Wise, I thought. *And if you knew how he likes to wield a whip behind closed doors, you'd see your fear is warranted.*

Or perhaps Lazlian's reputation in the brothels was already known to these nobles? I remembered how Juls once intervened in Laz's hobby of taking women to his bedroom and wrapping his hands around their necks. Perhaps the more skilled players in this game would use that information to their advantage, with hints and innuendos about what they'd like him to do to *them* behind a closed door.

I was largely ignored as any competition. While my dress may have stirred envy when I arrived, it did not progress beyond fashion. Happily married, I was a threat to absolutely no one.

Until Lazlian's lingering gaze made me so.

"Lazlian, you're being obvious. Go flirt with someone else. Preferably many others."

"There's a tight, jealous press to your lips I don't think

I've ever seen before. It doesn't flatter you at all, yet I can't say I dislike it."

"The tall girl with pretty waves of chestnut hair," I suggested, undeterred. She wore a gorgeous gown the color of a blood orange, which was clever because no one else wore a similar shade. As she walked, it glistened like the inside of the fruit. "Kelody, I think is her name? Her family is wealthy and powerful, so she'd make a good match."

"Kels? I've had her before," Lazlian remarked off-hand-edly, possibly using callousness to get a rise out of me or possibly because those thoughts came naturally to him. It could go either way with Laz.

"You're right though, she's very well-bred. You could learn from her," Lazlian noted, and when I didn't respond as desired, he coaxed, "Do you know what she offered me tonight?"

"Enlighten me," I said, replacing my wine glass on the table and keeping my gaze on the colorful array of dancers.

"I think it would make you blush," Laz taunted. Despite not deigning to give him the attention he sought, I could hear his grin and feel my cheeks heat with anticipation.

Overtly, I rolled my eyes and huffed. But I was pleased at having been right. Hearing the new king had his dark proclivities sent the cleverer girls to learn as much as they could about what fantasies they might fulfill.

"Perhaps I shouldn't," Lazlian teased, spinning his onyx ring with feigned consideration.

"Stop playing games," I snapped, hardly hiding my curiosity as well as I'd have liked.

"I think she's heard whispers that you're my mistress," Lazlian began, drawing it out. "It's hard to say. She has a competitive spirit." As he spoke, Lazlian leaned closer, his tone more seductive. "Apparently a friend of hers is a tattoo artist and piercer. Do you know what she offered to let me pierce? Can you guess?"

"I can guess," I lied, tossing my hair back. What was the big deal? Lots of girls had piercings in Rythas.

I bristled at Lazlian's low, mocking laughter as he drew nearer.

"Her nipples, little queen," he said by my ear, and my eyes flew wide. *Why would someone... wouldn't that hurt?*

Beneath the table, Lazlian snaked his hand between my legs and it took all my restraint not to jump and give away what he was doing. The gown had parted to allow access where he sought. Lazlian traced one finger above my clit -- or as best he could with my thighs pressed together.

"And here," he whispered.

Where?

At my furrowed brow, Lazlian said, "That's right. She said she'd like me to pierce her clit. With a little tag hanging down on it, bearing my name."

A strange mixture of revulsion and arousal made my breath quick, shallow. Or maybe it was Lazlian's husky voice; his lips at the shell of my ear, saying dirty things in a room full of nobles, at a historical ceremony of the utmost decorum. Part of me pictured what he said, another part of me turned away from the horror.

"I must admit her suggestion had appeal," Lazlian rasped near my ear. Beneath the table, his finger stroked my now-erect clit. I wasn't sure when he'd gained access. "But it was you I pictured, tagged with my name."

"You've never struck me as a particularly imaginative person, but you must be," I replied in a throaty voice I barely recognized. "Because that will never happen in reality."

Lazlian sat back abruptly, a small frown twitching at his lips, like a little boy who'd been denied his pudding.

"You know I could command it if I wanted."

"There are few women who are untouchable to you, Lazlian," I countered, "but I am one of them."

Lazlian waved his hand. "Once it comes out that you're my mistress, who would stop me? Who would speak out against what happens between two consenting adults in the privacy of their own bedroom?"

"That's just the point," I said, eyes narrowing. "It wouldn't be consenting."

"A mistress's word against the king's," he dismissed with a one-shouldered shrug. "Of course, your word might bear more weight if you were queen."

Lazlian might as well have been twirling a ring between his extended fingers as he'd said it. The threat was clear. *I can painfully force you do things as my mistress or I can respectfully request them of you, as my queen.*

I turned to face him fully. "Lazlian, if you haven't figured it out by now, threats and deals and manipulations don't get you very far with me."

"They got you into this dress. They got you into my bed." He cocked his head with mock consideration. "Actually, they work exceedingly well with you."

I let out an exasperated huff, one hand fisted on the table. "You know what I mean," I said, voice rough with repressed rage. "They won't make me love you, Lazlian. After what you did, I'm trying my hardest not to hate you all over again."

Instead of getting through to him, the annoyance on his face told me the walls he liked to build around himself rose higher and grew thicker at my words. What right did he have to act defensive when *he* was the one who'd wronged *me?*

"Stop making baseless threats," I told him. "You need me. The people don't like you and do you think Kirwyn would allow you to harm one hair on my head?"

I'd raised my voice too loudly and clamped my lips shut as Kelody shot a look in our direction. I didn't think she could discern what I'd said, but she'd clearly made out that Lazlian and I had been arguing.

"Lazlian," I said softly, worry cracking my voice. "The girl who offered to let you pierce her... Kels... her family is *very* powerful and I know she's related to your mother's side somehow."

"You've been brushing up on our ancestry," Lazlian remarked, sipping wine with no concern.

"If she marries Navere that would be a troubling alliance."

My eyes rounded as beneath the table, Lazlian put his hand on my belly. I stiffened, worried someone would see.

"Anything Navere does would be too late," he said, voice low. "You're already pregnant, I know it. When the Savior of the Bloody Shoals, the Queen of our Hearts... and the newly crowned king, the true, first-born son of Grahar... when we stand together and proclaim the new heir, who will oppose it? The people will rejoice in the streets."

I knew this to be partially true -- some would celebrate. Most, I hoped. But certainly not Navere or Kels or anyone vying to marry into the Doreste family.

"They like Merie, everyone likes Merie, but they *love* you," Lazlian said. "You saved them all when you swam out to destroy the Oxholde ships and I designed the weapons you carried. Not Navere, not Kels. It's *us.*"

My stomach sank as that feeling hit me again. Like

Lazlian was just using me. Like he didn't want the throne to claim me, he only wanted me to claim the throne. Was it all just a long game?

"Navere led Rythas to victory at the Battle of the Glass Gardens," I snapped. "And Kels isn't a nobody."

"Even if he takes her as a bride, they're just two." Laz's fingers tightened on my belly. "We're three. And royal."

"With a bastard, not a legitimate heir born in wedlock," I whispered through clenched teeth.

"You know the solution to that," Lazlian returned.

I shot to my feet, refusing to entertain this discussion again and not trusting myself not to strike Lazlian -- an offense leading to scandal, at best, or an excuse to throw me in the dungeons, at worst. There was absolutely nothing in the world that could make me divorce Kirwyn and if I paused and thought too much about Lazlian's never-ending lies, I was going to scream.

Abruptly leaving the newly-crowned king at his table, I made polite conversation with nobles for the rest of the evening. Lida and Raoul, twins in diplomacy, tirelessly worked the room to smooth the transition. Juls and Merie retired early, but the lively celebration continued as if it would never end.

Every so often I glanced at Lazlian and found him in his element, drinking one goblet of wine after another, with one noble and the next. When I couldn't force myself to smile and dance any longer, I snuck out the royal doors behind the throne, hoping to make a discreet exit.

I was only halfway down the hall when I heard Lazlian's footsteps behind me. I thanked Keroe and all the Rythasian gods that this hallway was off-limits to anyone outside the royal family because the king wasn't subtle in his stalking.

"Lazlian-" I began, whirling to face him. I was cut off by

him pushing me against a wall. I winced as he cupped my pussy with one hand, easily accessible by shoving aside the thin layers of my skirts.

"Come back to my chambers," Laz whispered, nuzzling my face with his scratchy beard. "I can't retire yet, but I'll meet you up there as soon as I can leave."

Was he drunk? Did he really believe I'd say yes?

"I don't want to. I'm going home."

"This is your home," Lazlian said, sliding his fingers beneath my undergarments.

"It never was and it never will be."

He frowned, stopping his exploration abruptly. "Why aren't you wet?"

I laughed at the same time tears pooled. *Was he serious?* "Do you really think that after everything you did to me I could simply grow wet at your touch?" I pushed him from my body.

"I'm going home, Lazlian. I wish you a long and prosperous reign."

I took two steps forward before turning back around and pointing.

"You know, most of the people in that hall want something from you. And that kind of commodified relationship is a transaction you understand. So why don't you go back out there and find it? I'm sure you'll gain satisfaction, though maybe not happiness. But don't look to me to fill that missing hole in you."

As soon as I said the words, I realized how true they were. Lazlian was utterly alone. And I might have felt badly if he hadn't caused it all on his own; if he hadn't used and made a fool of me. Juls would soon leave High Spire and Laz had irrevocably damaged their relationship. As king, Lazlian could never know if the friendship anyone offered was real, let alone the truth in any love professed to him by the female courtiers who wanted to be queen.

He'd accomplished what he wanted, climbed to the highest of heights and bedded me many times over in the process. Yet I never pitied Lazlian more.

For a moment, we stared at each other.

Then I turned and left the new king standing by himself in the dark and dusty hallway, looking very lonely.

SAVE HER, DAMN YOURSELF
Kirwyn

"I'm giving you the chance I never had," Jori said. "If I'd been older and could have assimilated sooner, saved my family somehow, I would have. With what's coming you will be *lucky* to die quickly in battle. I'm offering you a better alternative than hope of a quick death."

I ran my hand down my face and cursed, running plays in my mind as I desperately searched for a path to victory. The cold, hard truth was that we couldn't win against these weapons. No clan could, not even all the clans united.

Dammit.

If I took his offer, I'd be betraying everyone I knew and trusted, everyone she knew and trusted. Abandoning them, condemning them.

But she'd be safe. Zaria and Theo would be protected.

Or...

Or we'd all die together. If we were lucky enough not to meet a fate worse than death.

I clenched and unclenched my fists. My arms tingled, the tinny buzz rang in my ears again, and my stomach roiled with queasiness.

There was no choice. I had to get Zaria out of Rythas.

It was going to be ugly. She'd never willingly abandon the kingdom and she knew I'd never hurt her, so threats were useless. The only way to do it was through force. Rapidly, I worked through scenarios in my head. As much as I wanted to slip something into her drink, I couldn't knock her out. She'd never forgive me if I didn't let her say goodbye to our home, if she woke up on a ship somewhere. God, she was going to scream and fight me every step of the way. I'd have to bind her and carry her onto a boat. Gag her so she couldn't alert anyone.

Teddy couldn't witness this; I needed someone to take him while I kidnapped his mother.

Fuck, that sounded bad.

I only had to keep her contained until she calmed down. Which would be a few weeks. Months.

Stay with the nanny just a little while longer son, daddy needs to keep mommy tied up in our room until she comes around to seeing things my way.

I let my head collapse into my hands. Funny, I was on the floor and didn't even remember sitting.

It's the only way. Or... a life in hiding? No, especially not while being hunted *and* likely pregnant or with a newborn.

At the thought of Lazlian, violent rage rose within me. It was all his fault for endangering her.

I could bring Mazriah to help me with Teddy and two house guards to help me with Zaria. Everyone else... everyone she loved was going to die or live to endure a worse fate. Jesi, Lida, Saos, Alette, Tomé, Marcin, and the Dorestes. She would never forgive me for taking her away from everyone.

But at least she'd be alive to hate me. Maybe after several years...

Or maybe I could save some of our friends if I charmed the High Twelve. If I told clever jokes and chummed up to the Aureum, cheering beside them at the Bowl, leering at those Rythasians who didn't die in the war. I'd be forced to watch our friends taken as slaves...

As a scholar, Lida might be spared such a fate to find a more academic path forward in Spade City. She reminded me of that adage about a clever cat who always lands on its feet. But Jesi, Tomé, and Marcin were fighters. I didn't want to think about it, but they'd likely perish in battle. Saos and Alette might be granted permission to live out the remainder of their lives in whatever became of Rythas under Spade control.

I was surprised at how the image of a smoking, half-destroyed Rythas made my gut twist.

The Dorestes would be publicly humiliated, as Jori said, stripped and paraded through the city. Royals would never be killed, it was too kind a fate and only created martyrs. Trying to play out the probabilities, I realized it was entirely possible that Juls and Merie might do something stupid and honorable toward the end of fighting and lose their lives for it.

Lazlian was the most likely to survive, darting into a hole to hide like the snake he was. And when he was captured...

In my mind a twisted picture flashed -- Zaria, Teddy and I, living in an opulent Spade manor with Lazlian enslaved to the Spades.

Degraded. Brought to his knees and sold.

God, a scenario I'd never imagined was entirely possible.

Zaria would make me take in any surviving Dorestes. She'd insist I save Lazlian, especially if she carried his child. And how could I deny her when I'd helped destroy everything she loved? If -- *when* -- Rythas lost, Lazlian could very likely survive, and Zaria would make us spend whatever gold and tokens we had to buy him. Like a fool, I'd agree to make it up to her for what I'd done.

I'd never be rid of the asshole. Goddammit, I'd be sleeping with one eye open for the rest of my life because there was no way he wouldn't try to slit my throat in the night.

From keylord to king to slave. As much as I wanted the prick brought low, the mere word made me sick. This was an entire city of horrors. I could shut down my feelings, look away and survive, but dragging Zaria into this world would destroy her. It was almost the anthesis of Elowa or Rythas, it was everything she feared and hated.

We should have run away when we had the chance, all those years ago.

The thought was a punch to my gut. I'd supported her decision to stay in Rythas, even encouraged it, and now it was too late to convince her to leave. She was happy there. Teddy thrived. Even I felt a sense of peace and purpose, for the first time in my life. But Spade City was far from the sea and even farther from all Zaria held dear in her Elowan heart.

"If you capture the royals and high-ranking nobles," I said slowly, thinking aloud, "they'll be sold as slaves."

"An example must be set," Jori agreed, with regret of indeterminate sincerity. Tricky, that one.

"It's repugnant," I gritted out.

"Many share the view," Jori replied, moving his fingers and watching the artificial light glint off his golden ring. "Maybe the best way to change it is from within."

I stifled a snort at his manipulative persuasion, then looked up with hard eyes. "If they live, I want rights to buy the Dorestes, especially the keylord, Lazlian Doreste."

His pause told me I'd stunned and confused him. Quickly recovering he scoffed, "There's talk he might be crowned king. That's quite the prize."

"So are Zaria and I. Do you want us to defect or not?"

As Jori thought it over, I surveyed the stockpile of weaponry no clan could beat. Peering down into the cylindrical levels filled with metal tanks, guns, and gadgets, I didn't even know how half of them functioned. And what I *was* familiar with would easily decimate Rythas and her people. I ran the odds through my head and came out estimating very little survivors. The Spades would win no matter what any of us did, but perhaps I could spare some lives...

...if I helped end the war faster.

I'd already sold a piece of my soul to save Zaria, why not carve out a few more chunks for a few more lives?

Fuck, who was I kidding? There would be nothing left of my soul with my next words.

Chin up, I told myself. *Maybe souls don't even exist and none of this matters.*

"I know the keylord well, I know how he thinks. The king, the commander, all of them," I waved a hand. "I can help you win the war with less bloodshed. When I return with my wife and my son, I'll counsel you and prove it. But I want a guarantee that no one *ever* touches Zaria or Theo, no matter what they say or do."

I made the stipulation because I could not foresee a scenario in which Zaria didn't get herself into serious trouble by speaking out against the Spades. Or worse, by doing something rash.

"I will handle my wife, not you. And if the keylord survives, he belongs to *us,* the Holts. He becomes our personal slave."

Jori considered me with a gaze I was sure made many men flinch under its keenness. "I'd worry it wouldn't be a fitting punishment for the keylord... but the gleam in your eyes tells me this is a *personal* vendetta."

The curiosity in Jori's voice told me the little conniver was probing for details, and the gleam in *his* eye confused me. Jori wasn't bloodthirsty, but my vengeance seemed to intrigue him.

"It is and it's none of your business." I paused to let him think that was all he was getting from me, then added with thinly veiled relish, "But if you need to sell it to Larius, I can tell you there could be no greater punishment you could ever devise than to have the keylord beneath my boot. Given the choice, he'd rather be publicly whipped to his death than face anything I've planned for him."

Jori was, above all, an opportunist. Believing us to be of the same ilk would gain me his trust.

"I can't make that second promise, but I can promise to support it," he concluded.

"I think you have a way of getting your way," I remarked.

"My slice of the pie is a rather generous one, despite its rank," Jori agreed, referring to the command over his division.

Closing my eyes and sighing, I gave Jori one small nod.

"Excellent," he said. When I opened my eyes, I thought

Jori would appear to gloat, but I was surprised to find him more... pensive? He stared at me for a few moments and said, "Often in life there isn't a good option, only a less-bad one. I know where you are right now and trust me, you chose the path that saves not only the most lives but those you most love."

I shrugged one shoulder. I didn't want his empty attempts at comfort.

"I'll begin the arrangements for your estate," Jori announced and, with a wink, added, "And I'll help you sneak out the gates."

I was surprised by his offer until I realized that Jori likely didn't want to brag to the High Twelve that he'd claimed my allegiance. Not yet. Too much could go wrong between now and me returning with my family. I could change my mind. We could be killed in some skirmish. Unrest could grow in Rythas.

With some resentment, I accepted his help and was able to make it through the city gates without incident when I departed, ten days later. I met up with the Rythasian party who'd been waiting several weeks for my return, and we quickly journeyed back to the coast. As we sailed, I played out potential outcomes.

Maybe I'd get lucky and Lazlian had been successfully assassinated before my return. *Slim chance. But possible.* The likelihood that Lazlian lived through the coming war was not insignificant, and Zaria wasn't going to like the deal I'd struck.

She'd be livid, disbelieving I'd saved the keylord as an act of mercy.

She'd be right.

I froze as a horrible vision popped into my head. It could be far worse than I'd imagined.

What if she hates me forever, and buying Lazlian to be with us is the only way to help her find some happiness? What if I have to watch the two of them find love in each other's arms, while she can't stand to look at me for what I've done?

What hellish irony.

I'd be the bad guy she despised. But at least she'd be alive.

I closed my eyes as the gut-twisting truth sank in.

It didn't matter if Lazlian lived or died or became a slave or to whom. Not when it came to me keeping Zaria's heart.

No matter how it played out, one thing was certain.

What I had to do to save her life would cost her love.

WRONG TARGET
Zaria

Gazing at endless sparkles the sinking sun cast over the ocean, I ran soft grains of sand through my fingers. Back in the house, Mazriah had taken Teddy for night's feast. He and I had played together since he woke at dawn, and I appreciated the much-needed break. The only other moment I'd had to myself was briefly in the afternoon, when Theo spontaneously napped beneath the many arches of Golden Chalice vines, which thankfully provided some shade. After chasing him through the Elephant Ears for hours, I was a little tired too. The tall plants dwarfed his small body and he was tricky to find beneath their leaves.

I decided against using any energy to wade into the surf, but watched what I thought might be a good sunset, even if I was alone to enjoy it. Long ago, I'd watched many sunsets alone in High Spire, thinking of Kirwyn somewhere across the ocean and wondering what he was doing. It was unsettling being here again, with the God Sea between us and him on the wrong side of it. Whatever he was up to, I hoped he stayed safe.

The sun sank further and a slight breeze from the east picked up. It carried the scent of frangipani from our garden to where I sat, making me wrinkle my nose at the cloying sweetness.

Mid sand-dig, I froze. Then I inhaled deeply, nearly gagged in disgust, and knew.

I'm pregnant. Oh my god, I'm pregnant.

It was just like it had been with Theo. The scent of sweet flora seemed to carry right down to my stomach, making me sick. And how had I missed that I was feeling more tired than usual?

Oh my god, I'm actually pregnant with Lazlian's child. We'd done it. I brought my hand to my belly, marveling that a sweet little baby was growing inside me.

Who was I kidding? However he or she turned out, sweet wouldn't likely be the first word people would use to describe a child of Lazlian's, raised to rule. *Feisty. Tricky. Proud.*

Mine.

Ours.

Tears welled in my eyes and I gasped from relief as the wretched weight of the past few months, the weight of a kingdom, lifted from my shoulders. We'd be safer now, more stabilized. At least, Rythas would be, and that was more important than my personal life, which was about to grow more chaotic.

I dreaded telling Lazlian. I was annoyed that he'd been right, livid at his deception, and wary for more. How would Lazlian, hot-tempered and unpredictable, react?

I didn't know. And there was only one way to find out.

I stood up, wiping grains of sand from my hands and feeling a little superstitious. As much as I enjoyed sunsets, learning I was pregnant while viewing one at the same time seemed a little ominous. I licked my lips, nervous. Now that I thought about it, the moon was in a waning cycle as well.

Too many signs symbolizing endings instead of beginnings.

It's the end of uncertainty, I lied to myself as I lifted my chin and walked back to the house. *The end of our distress.*

I waited a few days to be sure, but I didn't want to wait much longer. Kirwyn could return at any moment and I wanted to deal with Lazlian alone.

When Mazriah brought out the little guava cakes for Theo and I fought the urge to vomit, there could be no doubt. I donned a loose, white dress, strapped on a pair of leather boots, and saddled Nixie for a ride to High Spire. Though it was still light, it was getting late. Before I left, I read to Theo his favorite dolphin book and tucked him into bed. He'd be safe with Mazriah in the room beside his, and it was entirely possible that Kirwyn could return in the night.

A short while later, I climbed the long stairwell of High Spire's royal tower, and, feeling like I returned to the scene of a crime, grew angrier with each step. Lazlian opened his door and considered me with guarded hope. It was an expression I'd received from him countless times since we met, though I didn't know it until now. I brushed past him and closed the door behind me. I ignored the bed where we'd lain, the table where we coupled, and the ceiling where he'd tied me up.

Strung me up *and* along.

Although, I thought with resentment, *he'd been right, ultimately.* Lazlian was virile and he'd proved it in the most inarguable and permanent way possible.

There was no point in stalling.

"I'm pregnant," I told him.

My own words rang in my ears, as if they weren't true until I'd spoken them aloud.

Lazlian's face lit up like the Fae Fête at its height. For several seconds he said nothing, though his lips attempted to form words before breaking into a grin.

"You're sure?" he asked, dropping to his knees.

"Yes, I'm sure," I snapped, while Lazlian laid reverent kisses on my midsection. "And before you insult me by asking, yes I'm sure it's yours."

"I wouldn't," he breathed between kisses, "question you."

I didn't know whether to believe him but said nothing as he stroked my still-flat belly. "My son," he murmured. "My daughter." He laid another kiss. "My heir."

Back on his feet, Lazlian kissed me. I did not kiss him back. In his exuberance, I didn't know if he noticed. Too many conflicting emotions swirled in my head, tossing me from one to the next. I'd never been seasick, but I imagined this is what it felt like to other people.

"It's as it always should have been." Lazlian spoke almost to himself. He wasn't hurried, yet there was a tinge of mania to his tone, raising the hair on my neck. He turned his head, looking around the room but not really seeing.

"You'll move into my quarters immediately," he declared.

My stomach lurched.

"Lazlian, no. I must be with my son, with Teddy."

"We'll bring him here."

Panic swelled in my chest. "Lazlian, *no.* He needs his father."

Laz gave an irritated, twitchy movement of his neck and shoulders. "We'll discuss it later."

"Listen to me." I backed away from him, coquina clams racing up my spine. "Kirwyn is my husband and Theo's father. We need to be together."

"He shouldn't be your husband," Lazlian said, brow knit. "It endangers our child. I'm the king, I can decree the union dissolved and we can marry before anyone knows you're pregnant. The heir will be born in wedlock, unquestioned."

I backed up several steps and tried not to shout. "You're not thinking clearly, you're being emotional and not logical."

"It is logical," Lazlian yelled. "It's the *most* logical thing to do to keep the dynasty safe."

I closed my eyes, dread creeping over me. *I knew it.* Give Lazlian the smallest space to move and he'd claim the board. I was speaking to a madman.

"Kels won't like it, but she's a smart girl. I'll arrange a good match for her."

"Kels?" I asked.

"Mm," Lazlian replied absentmindedly, quickly crossing to his dressing table and grabbing an embroidered jacket. "Kelody knows we're more than we appear and she's been sniffing around High Spire, angling to be my wife or mistress. But once she finds out you're pregnant, she'll realize neither is going to happen. It's better this way. Saves her from her mother's fate."

"Mother?" I asked, struggling to keep up with Lazlian's rambling. Why was he getting dressed?

"We discussed this. My father spurned her mother. She was the mistress he used to encourage *my* mother to marry."

The one the king kicked out of her position once your mother came around, I remembered, stomach twisting a little. *No, you never said her name.*

This was eerily close to history repeating itself and I was sure Kels wouldn't like it.

"Wipe that look off your face, Zaria," Laz chided. "Kels has no real desire for me, she just wants to climb the royal ladder."

"And with you unavailable, that sends her straight into Navere's arms," I reminded.

Lazlian snorted. "I trust her to do the right thing for the monarchy more than I trust *you,*" he said, irritated. "Kels is ambitious, not evil."

"But Navere is," I cried.

"It doesn't matter because *we have the heir,*" Lazlian insisted. "Why are we talking about this anyway? There are more important matters at hand. You don't understand, we *have* to marry now, quickly, before the heir is born, or else-"

"Or else the baby won't be born in wedlock, I know," I spat. "We've gone over this-"

"*No.* You don't understand-" Lazlian growled, but he was cut off by an insistent knock on his door.

"I do not wish to be disturbed," he shouted, remaining still until he heard retreating footsteps. "We have to move quickly," he said, crossing to his chest of drawers to retrieve something.

My eyes widened as Lazlian spun his hand upward, revealing a ring clasped between his thumb and forefinger. One singular diamond had been masterfully cut into the shape of a star. There were no accompanying stones, but it didn't need any, nor was there room. I'd never seen anything like it.

It was far too beautiful for such an ugly moment.

Lazlian grabbed my left hand and tried to slide my sea-ring from it, but, sweaty and swollen, it wouldn't budge.

"Stop, you're hurting me," I cried.

Relenting, Lazlian grabbed my other hand and lifted his diamond ring. The gem's many facets sparkled, casting twinkles about as Lazlian forcefully pushed the star-stone onto the ring finger of my right hand. I didn't try to remove it as it fit so tightly that I doubted I could, nor was there time when Lazlian next flourished a dagger I hadn't previously noticed.

Had he gone crazy? What was he doing?

I fell to my knees, shouting protests while Laz held my hand aloft.

Binding our blood to marry us right now?

Everything was happening too hastily and all wrong, just like when he'd claimed the crown. Laz squeezed my flesh, perhaps to mitigate the pain, then raised his dagger.

"Lazlian, stop!" I cried. "Please..."

I trailed off, woozy as I swayed. The impending threat of a gash combined with whatever was going on in my stomach made me nearly faint.

The dagger clattered to the ground and Lazlian fell to his knees beside it.

"I'm sorry," he said, clutching my biceps. It was the first time I'd ever heard him apologize. He'd never even done so when he tried to take my life. "I can wait a bit..." Laz added, not sounding much like he could or wanted to. "You need rest. Lay down. I have some things to do and I'll return as soon as I can."

"Lazlian," I pled. Tears spilled over my lashes and slid down my cheeks.

"I can't let you leave," he declared, with the nerve to look at me almost pleadingly for a moment, as if *I* was the irrational one who needed to understand. "Not with my child inside you."

Lazlian glanced around his chambers and said, "I need to make arrangements, but I'll return shortly. Don't make me chain you to the bed. I trust that you won't hurt your-self. That you'd never do anything to hurt a baby."

"What is wrong with you?" I cried. "You've lost your mind. Of course I wouldn't, but you are. Can't you see that? Let me go."

Lazlian gave me one firm shake of his head. This was the version of Laz that I hated, cruel and unbending. I knew the further I pushed, the further he'd retreat into it, but I couldn't stop myself.

"I'm a person, Lazlian, not a prize. I have the right to pursue my own choices in life."

"Zaria, I am your king," he said, frustratingly soft, but firm. "You have only the rights I allow."

"If this is the kind of king you are, then it would have been far better to keep Juls on the throne!" I shouted. "Let the dynasty die with him, let the whole kingdom die with him."

Lazlian's eyes flashed. "You're hormonal, you don't know what you're saying."

"Yes, I do," I swore. "Will you throw me in the dungeons? Whip me for treason? Go ahead. You think I care whether you lock me in your room or a cell? It makes no difference. You are locking me out of my life."

"This is your life!" Lazlian shouted, pointing angrily at his floor.

I knew he couldn't be trusted. He'd shown me that again and again. I just never thought with something this big...

Though I shouldn't have been surprised. Lazlian wasn't himself lately, his hasty move to take the throne before we'd laid the groundwork proved that.

The king opened the door and called for his men.

"Don't let her leave for any reason," he instructed the guards. "She's slippery, she'll try to persuade you. Know that I will send you to the Isle of Walking Corpses if she's not here when I return. Do I make myself clear?"

Ignoring me, Lazlian closed his thick door and the guards somehow managed to lock or barricade it from the other side, because it wouldn't budge when I tried the handle.

"Lazlian!" I cried, banging the door so hard my fists would likely bruise and my bones felt as if they'd break. "Let me out!"

When it became clear he wouldn't return or relent, I broke off in a pitiful wail and sank to the floor, closing my eyes.

Lazlian knew how much I hated being powerless to Juls's orders and yet he'd always threatened worse. So why was I surprised that he'd stolen my choices and locked me in a bedroom?

He hadn't changed.

I opened my eyes.

But I had.

I'm not a helpless girl anymore, I thought. *Cowering under your commands.*

I had to move fast. Whatever Lazlian was doing, it was bound to be damaging. Maybe he was making announcements or calling a Rythasian Priest. He probably thought I'd rage around, trashing his room and, admittedly, I wanted to. But I had better ideas. Ones he wouldn't expect.

I raced to the balcony overlooking the courtyard. Lazlian may have locked the door, but he didn't bar the windows.

It was a steep drop, but I was good at escape. Determined, I scanned the room. There was nothing I could use to lower myself, the ropes Lazlian once employed to string me to the ceiling had been cleared. I would have to jump.

Figuring that it would help to disguise myself, I hurried to Lazlian's wardrobe. It wouldn't be the first time I'd dressed as a man to escape the castle.

Laz's trousers were too big, but I belted them and rolled up the cuffs. I tucked the smallest shirt I could find into the pants and twisted my hair into a low bun. Scrounging around his drawers, I fished out a hooded cape. I'd never seen Lazlian wear the ceremonial garment, but I figured regal robes could only help my concealment. I wouldn't fool anyone who spared time to consider me, but from a distance or a quick glance, I might pass for the king. Or, at least, not myself.

Assessing the balcony I again wished there were a tree tall enough to climb, as there had been outside my bedroom in Elowa. The best I could do would be to shimmy over the other side of the railing, hang off the edge, and fall into the relative padding of the flowering bushes below.

Peering down, I cringed. It was further than I liked.

That was the thing about land; too many sharp edges, steep falls, and gravity, with its invisible fingers, always threatening to pull a person to their death -- or at least, to serious injury. To me, the sea was always softer, safer.

Without allowing myself time to second-guess, I shimmied onto the other side of the rail and crouched down on a tiny ledge. Resolute, I took a breath and slid downward until I was held up only by my hands with my legs dangling in the air.

There was no turning back as I didn't have the strength or the room to haul myself up if I wanted to.

With another breath, I let go, and as soon as my feet smacked the ground I fell onto my rear. My hands instinctively flew to my stomach, where my baby would grow, but the brunt of the impact had been taken by my knee and my tailbone. I ignored the pain as I wiped the dirt from my hands and dusted off Lazlian's cape. With a quick check for any leaves in my hair, I pulled the hood over my head and darted across the courtyard. Maintaining a sprint, I bounded straight to the construction areas on the opposite side of Lazlian's chambers. The darkened arches, towers of building materials, and half walls without clear pathways or guarded posts made it the easiest route to avoid discovery.

I crept through the shadowed labyrinth until, rounding a corner, I practically slammed into a party of darkly dressed men. I didn't immediately recognize any, though it was difficult to make out faces in the dim light.

Not guards at least, I thought, relieved.

But the next moment, one of the men withdrew a dagger and I jerked backward from the threat. The hood of my cape slid from my head with the act, and, at the same time, I saw the gleaming blade plunge toward my unprotected neck.

My own shock was reflected in my attacker's eyes.

"Who are you?" he growled, hand frozen mid-air.

I formed words with my mouth but no sound came out.

"That's the princess," came someone's stunned whisper.

"Shit," I heard another voice curse.

Realizing I wasn't about to be stabbed, I screamed, "Help! Somebody help me!"

"Kill her!" a woman's voice cried.

"No, not *her,*" the man with the dagger argued.

"Shut her up!" I heard a different man shout.

The assassins rushed forward in a blur, readying blades but not striking. Instead, they postured, bursting into arguments about what to do with me. Someone plucked up the courage to muffle my next scream before I got it out, holding his hand over my mouth while I thrashed to free myself.

"No gun!" I heard one man growl to the woman. "Too noisy."

Jerking, I turned to glimpse a gun raised at my head, so I didn't immediately see what was coming on my other side. Amidst the chaos, someone pushed forward and brought a wet cloth to my mouth, forcing me to breathe noxious chemicals.

The world faded away.

WORST-CASE SCENARIO
Kirwyn

I stood on the bow, watching our boat part waves, but I couldn't look at the sea without wanting to drown Lazlian in it. I hated him even more for the nagging idea that his survival of the coming war was probably the best outcome for Zaria, once I moved her to safety and she hated me forever.

My trip back to Rythas seemed to take twice as long as my journey leaving it. The sun beat upon my unprotected scalp and neck, and it would be months before my hair regrew to its old length.

When our small boat finally neared my manor, I saw the keylord -- regrettably still alive -- and Raoul, standing at the end of my dock.

What the hell are they doing here?

A dread like heavy rocks grew in the pit of my stomach. Something in the keylord's posture alarmed me. Was it shame? Caution? Contrition? Whatever to call it, I'd never seen Lazlian affect the look and it wasn't an encouraging one. Tension formed at the base of my spine and ran right up my neck.

After transferring to the dinghy, I gave the men a brief but friendly goodbye, waving my transporters on to their next port. Striding across the dock, I continually glanced behind the keylord, looking for Zaria and already knowing something was wrong and I wouldn't see her.

"Where is Zaria?" I demanded, coming face-to-face with Lazlian. "Where is *my wife?*"

"She's been taken," Lazlian said, keeping his voice low to not attract attention from the departing boat. My stomach lurched as if someone knocked the wind out of me. "Someone kidnapped her and-"

I tackled Lazlian to the ground before he finished and unleashed a relentless onslaught of blows to his face.

For my wife.

For my son.

For me.

You son of a bitch. Inserting yourself into our life and fucking it up.

Hands grabbed me, yanking me up and off the bloodied man.

"This solves nothing," Raoul counseled, struggling to hold me back and stealing glances at the departing dinghy. As if I cared that we made a scene.

"Where is my wife you son of a bitch?" I shouted, letting Raoul restrain me from finishing Lazlian's beating only because I needed answers.

"You cannot hit him, it's a crime punishable by death, and the behavior is unfitting of your new station," Raoul scolded, still holding me from behind. "He has been crowned *king*. You have been named *keylord*."

"I don't give a shit what anyone is," I yelled. *"Where is my wife?* Where is my son?"

"I don't know where she is," Lazlian said, panting. He struggled to his feet, bloodied, his hand spread gingerly across his stomach. Head bent, he looked up at me miserably and mumbled, "I believe she's been taken somewhere on the mainland."

"You let someone kidnap her!" I cried. My head spun in all directions and I forced it to stop because none of it was helpful at the moment.

"I couldn't prevent it," Lazlian said, still fighting to catch his breath. "I... wasn't there. It happened last night, here, at your house. Perhaps you need better guards. Your son is safe, my men are with him in the kindery and they've swept your manor for clues. Nothing has been taken; it doesn't look like they want a ransom. I've sent a party of trackers to the mainland-"

Ignoring Lazlian, I stormed in the direction of the house.

"Where are you going?" he demanded.

"To get her back," I replied, not turning my head as I continued walking.

"Wait," Lazlian said. "I'm coming with you."

Now I halted, if only to sneer to his face.

"You'll just slow me down," I spat.

"I've spent more time in the backlands than you have these past few years and I've ingratiated myself into several clans in a way you never have," Lazlian argued.

I paused. That was likely true. My uncle and I hadn't spent any time with other clans and Lazlian had been doing *something* on the mainland the past few years.

Laz quickly added, "More importantly, I'm the best bargaining chip you've got, if it comes to that."

I folded my arms, waiting for him to elaborate. Fast. We were wasting time.

"As king, I'm a better prize than she is. If they've taken her as a hostage, perhaps we can negotiate an exchange. Me for her."

I searched Lazlian's face for a lie, hating that I needed him to be telling the truth. Would he give his life for her? And was he really a better prize if they were looking for Elowans or for Zaria specifically?

"There's something else you need to know," Lazlian said, wiping blood from his mouth with the back of his hand. "Zaria's pregnant."

For months, I'd dreaded those words; thought my world would collapse upon hearing them. But now, all I could feel was fear turning the rocks in my stomach to chunks of ice.

Dear god, no. How could this be any worse?

Zaria was alone, terrified, and pregnant. Lazlian was suddenly king and however it had happened, this wasn't the meticulous, stable transfer of power we discussed.

"Does anyone know?" I asked, forcing myself to focus on facts over feelings.

"I'd told a few people, but largely, no. It's safer for the baby if whoever's taken her doesn't know it's mine."

Kicking sand, I cursed. If Rythas wasn't a mess already, it was about to be.

"You can't announce the heir or it might endanger the baby," I said, staring at the beach and thinking out loud. *And that will kill her.* "But securing an heir was the move solidifying support for your reign. The people don't like you and half the nobles don't back you either, regardless of whatever fealty they swore. Why did you have to go and crown yourself? It'll be chaos whether you're here or gone."

"I've thought of that," Lazlian said. "And there's something I need from you."

I flicked my eyes to the insolent king, and, without moving a muscle, waited.

"In the event that I don't make it back alive, in case..." he trailed off, not wanting to say it. *In case something unspeakable happens to my wife and the child she's carrying inside her you piece of shit.*

"I'm naming your son Theo in line for the throne," Lazlian said. "After my own children and any Juls may have."

Thrown by the ridiculous declaration, I scoffed, "What does that have to do with anything? And you can't. No one will accept him, he doesn't have a drop of Rythasian blood."

"No," Lazlian agreed. His tongue tapped his lips. "But his wife will. I'm going to announce his betrothal at the same time."

It took a second longer than it should have for his words to sink in.

"He's three years old!" I shouted.

"And he's a prince," Lazlian countered, with more arrogance than he should possess for someone who'd just been pummeled. "You seem to want to be a part of our family. This is how we do things."

I was seconds away from losing my mind and beating the shit out of Lazlian again.

"You want to do to my son what you did to my wife?" I growled between clenched teeth. "Do you think I'll allow it? Do you think Zaria would?"

Lazlian paused, the severity of his face momentarily relaxing. He ran his hand roughly over his stubble, forgetting that I'd just battered his jaw and wincing at the soreness.

"Fine. I'll leave it open and taunt the prospect to all, the same as I've done with myself," Laz conceded. "When Theo comes of age, he can choose any girl from a noble family. Except in this case, it will be a decree that *must* come to fruition. It doesn't matter if he's never near enough the throne, he will always be a prince and that will always be appealing. But I can't fail to deliver on this declaration, especially not when they realize their hopes for me to marry one of their own will never come to pass."

"Or you could remain here and marry one of them and stay the fuck out of my life!" I roared.

"It's too late for that. Any child I'd ever have would be a threat to the one she's now carrying. Do you want that for her?"

I closed my eyes and dragged long pulls of air through my nose and into my lungs. It did nothing to calm me.

"Further, Saos and Alette need to bring Theo to High Spire twice weekly," Lazlian announced. "We'll arrange playful gatherings with the other noble children. He needs friends."

"Theo has plenty of friends at our camp," I said.

"Commoners," Lazlian dismissed.

I snorted. "And you wonder why they don't love you? Why the people don't want you as king without *her*?"

Raoul stepped forward, straightening his already-perfect tunic. "At High Spire the nobles will clamor for a chance to befriend Theo," he explained. "It will serve as a distraction and no one will want to make any unnecessarily violent moves when the prospect of peacefully securing a better position next to the young prince, either as his wife or his companion, hangs in the air."

"Call it like it is," I grit out. "You'd make a prize of my son."

"Yes, I would, and to keep her safe you would too," Laz said. "What kind of future do you envision for the baby she's carrying? That too must be a marriage according to station."

I ran a hand down my face and shook my head, unable to consider anything beyond getting Zaria back.

"There are plenty of girls to choose from within the elite ranks," Lazlian said quickly. "If the nobles think there's a chance, it will distract them from a bloody fight for powerful roles they can instead seamlessly marry into."

"He's three years old!" I repeated, shouting. "You are throwing my son like a sheep for the wolves to fight over. To buy our success with their distracted scheming."

"Have you a better idea?" Laz asked.

I did not. Yet. I had to admit that Lazlian was better at the intricacies of Rythasian politics.

We should have left when we had the chance.

"This was all her choice," Lazlian said, breaking the prolonged silence. "You came here forcing us to make changes, to weaken my family's power within Rythas and her power in the world beyond. Zaria chose to help rectify that as best she could."

He was right, we did contribute to this instability. Were we forever doomed to pay for it, until there was nothing left for Zaria or me to give?

"I need something more," Lazlian added.

I let out a low laugh. He didn't need to finish.

"My gold," I said, already having worked it out. "You want to bribe the army to maintain peace and loyalty in your absence."

"If the kingdom is in chaos upon her rescue she'll have nothing to return to," Lazlian said, nodding once.

As if I care. I had half a mind to take the gold and buy my family a new life in Spade City. If only I could get Zaria out of wherever she was, which wasn't a purchasable feat if they hadn't done it for a ransom. There might come a time when I'd need soldiers to save her, and for that reason alone I agreed.

Her fate is tied to the heir, and the heir to the kingdom, and the kingdom to this insolent king.

And her heart? Was it still to me?

The question brought me to my knees. The irreversible fact was that mine belonged to her. I scooped up a handful of sand and spread my fingers, letting it fall through my grasp and back onto the beach, feeling as if my life was equally slipping away.

"Take it," I whispered, defeated. "Take all the gold. Leave enough to run our household and pay the staff, if you're able. Make sure Mazriah is cared for. Our dog, Finley, goes with Teddy."

From the corner of my eye, I saw Raoul nod. "Saos and Alette will take good care of Mazriah, as well as Teddy," he said. "Juls and Merie will treat your son as their own. With so much love and all the abundance of High Spire, he'll want for nothing."

Nothing but his parents.

Lazlian slid an onyx ring from his finger and handed it to Raoul. Dimly, I heard him instruct his advisor on transporting our fortune and preparing excuses for the king's prolonged absence. Raoul's trustworthy presence was the only thing that gave me any assurance in this situation.

"All you do is take," I grit out, rising to my feet and staring hard at the imposter king. "My wife, my son, my gold. You'd better be prepared to give your life for hers, if it comes to that."

Back inside our house, I tried explaining to Teddy that

mommy and daddy were going away for a while, and that we'd return as soon as we could. He was too young to understand anything beyond the exciting prospect of spending time at Aunt Alette and Uncle Saos's house. I left Theo in Raoul's capable hands and quickly grabbed a few items from the house. Lazlian watched, observing quietly. I didn't know what was going on in his head and I didn't care. He wasn't a king; he wasn't even a man as far as I was concerned. He could travel with me only as a bargaining chip, and if he slowed me down, I'd cut him loose.

In our back parlor, I paused with my hand on the doorframe, wondering if it would be the last time I set foot in our house. If something happened to Zaria, I'd either lock myself inside these rooms and go quietly mad or take Teddy and never return. My hesitation made Lazlian speak, though he misinterpreted my pause.

"She's stronger than you think," he had the audacity to say. "You shelter her so much you never get the chance to see it."

"You think I don't know that after all we survived together?" I snapped. Inwardly, however, I was a little irritated to acknowledge a kernel of truth to the prick's words. I hated seeing Zaria hurt and the more time passed, the more I shielded her as much as possible.

"She's more vulnerable than *you* think," I threw back. "You torment her so much you never see anything other than her defenses."

The new king flinched and tried to cover it up. Good.

Attempting to wrest control, Lazlian began instructing, "We'll head to the weaponry and arm ourselves-"

"No need to waste time." I cut him off with a wave of my hand as I strode out of the manor. Lazlian trailed at my heels as I led him to the stockpile of guns and explosives we concealed in a hidden cavern beneath a folly in our garden. The dim chamber wasn't large, but it contained enough to heavily arm more than a dozen men.

Stooping to enter the low-ceilinged room, Lazlian's eyes widened as he scanned the contents. "This goes against the treaty," he spat, as if his army didn't have their own illegal stockpile he'd just referenced. "You could start a war. Possessing these weapons is strictly prohibited."

"We both know war is coming either way," I countered. Then, with a sneer, I threw his own words back at him.

"You seem to want to be a part of our family." I tossed Lazlian an unloaded gun, which, to his credit, he was quick to catch. "This is how we do things."

CHAPTER 28

PATIENCE
Zaria

Not only was I fuming at the audacity of these men, I was annoyed that the growling in my stomach would soon announce that I'd awoken. So much for eavesdropping.

Deposited in the cabin of a boat, I'd been listening to my group of abductors argue about what to do with me for what I estimated to be twenty or thirty minutes. They debated about the boat's route too, and if I didn't speak up and convince them to turn west, they'd get us all killed.

At least, if we sailed where I thought we sailed. It was hard to guess, having been knocked unconscious for an indeterminate amount of time.

I laid a nervous hand on my stomach, again praying that it hadn't affected my baby and hoping Teddy remained safe, back in the manor.

Relieved to at least have been left unrestrained, I emerged from the cabin without trying to hide myself. My sudden presence startled the group of what turned out to be four men and one woman. The woman shot to her feet and aimed a gun at me.

"There are five of you, I'm unarmed, and we're at sea," I said, exasperated and blinking in the bright sunlight. "What exactly do you intend to accomplish by pointing that at my head?"

A man sitting central on the boat's bench seat laughed. He had brown hair and sharp, green-gray eyes, as well as a curved scar running along his forehead and around his eye, toward the ear.

"Put the gun down, Breyline," he ordered, sounding annoyed as well. "She's no threat."

The woman named Breyline shifted her weight and didn't meet the man's eyes as she argued, "She snuck up on us without hearing. She could have taken one of us out."

"And then?" I asked, folding my arms. "What would be my brilliant plan? How would that help me escape this boat?"

The man laughed again. His laughter came easily but it wasn't particularly friendly. As soon as he stopped, his aura settled back into what appeared a natural state of emitting so much danger it made my skin tingle all over.

"She's got you there." The man turned to me. "My name's Hektir. Sit."

It wasn't a request. Sighing, I sat.

"I don't suppose asking nicely for you to return me to Rythas will do any good," I tried.

"We can't do that," Hektir replied, smiling coldly.

"Would it make any difference if I told you I'm pregnant?"

Hektir cocked his head and took a few seconds to reply.

"No. But I'd send my congratulations to your husband if I could."

Something in the tone of his voice caught my attention. Surprised, I asked, "Do you know my husband?"

"I met him not long ago," Hektir replied, vaguely.

I rubbed my temples, frustrated. Kirwyn's visit to Spade City was a fairly large-scale event. He probably met many people.

Stroking his chin, Hektir remarked, "You're quite calm for a captive."

"This isn't the first time I've been kidnapped and you're not even the best at it." Considering, I shrugged. "You're not even third."

Chuckles from the men followed my statement. Breyline's gaze darted between me and Hektir. The maniacal smile plastered on her face did not meet her eyes.

"Glad I amuse you." I re-crossed my arms. "Seeing you all gutted will amuse me."

Hektir slapped his knee as everyone again laughed.

"You're feisty," he proclaimed, grinning the compliment.

Letting out a long breath, I leaned back casually against the seat and announced, "There are only two ways this ends. Either I kill you or my husband does. There is nothing anyone can do to change this certainty, so why fret?"

My declaration earned more appreciative smiles but Hektir raised his hand in a cautionary manner.

"Make no mistake, if you don't do what we say, you'll meet The Daggering. It's my way. But we like you. We like Prince Kirwyn. We'll do the best we can to accommodate you for now."

I rubbed my temples again. I needed water and something to settle my stomach. "You mean until you figure out what to do with me."

"No one wants to harm you or your baby," Hektir assured me. "You're just a princess and not a Doreste. But you're Elowan and we can't let you go."

Way to show your hand, I thought. *My god, you're incompetent kidnappers, and I've met my share to know.* The blunder was so severe I had to wonder if it was actually a clever trap, but Hektir's arrogance told me he didn't think the information was worth concealing from a captive in an ostensibly helpless position.

I considered the ragtag band before me, lounging around the small boat. *So you want the royal family dead or overthrown,* I reasoned. *And perhaps you want the Elowans captured, exempting me only for my status or to use as a pawn in this game.*

I fought the urge to bring my hand to my belly as coquina clams raced up my spine, but I visibly swallowed. What would become of my baby if they knew it was Lazlian's?

I won't let them hurt us, I vowed, fingers tensing against my thighs.

"Seeing as how you have a desire for me to continue living," I began, "you're going to need to accommodate that condition, which will be in increasing peril as my pregnancy progresses. I require special care. Are you capable of providing it?"

"We can't let you go," Hektir repeated.

"Maybe she-" a man began.

"Maybe *you,*" Hektir bit out, voice snapping like the crack of a whip, "can shut your mouth."

It chilled me how quickly he jumped from friendly to frightening.

"I require water and will likely need it intravenously in the near future," I explained gently.

Hektir stroked his chin. "I'll take that into consideration when choosing our location."

Scanning in all directions, I saw only clear, sunny skies and open water. Thankfully, the ocean breeze kept me cool.

"How far are we from Rythas?" I asked.

"Why do you want to know?" a portly man returned.

"Because you're headed north and if we pass near Oxholde we're as good as dead. I need to know how far we are. I'd advise sailing west if you want to avoid a battle we're sure to lose. I'd also advise heeding my counsel and releasing me if you want to live in general, but I will only waste time attempting to convey such reason."

Hektir ignored my wisdom and scoffed, "Oxholde is deserted."

"No, it's recently infested with pirates. Sail through those waters and we'll all find swords in our bellies. If not other parts of our bodies first, if you can understand my meaning."

I wasn't sure if the latter rumors were true, but I certainly didn't want to find out, and the additional motivation to make the foolish crew do as I said could only be helpful.

Hektir tilted his head, considering me.

"I'm a princess of Rythas," I reminded, sternly. "I would know about threats to our people, wouldn't I? And I have nothing to possibly gain from redirecting your course, other than saving all our lives."

Hektir held my gaze for a long time. The scar around his eye was hook-shaped, almost like a question mark. It made me wonder what it would take to push him too far, beyond that genial laughter and into whatever a Daggering was.

Finally, he announced to a man named Jemmy to chart a course due west. In a business-like manner, Hektir proceeded to make introductions. Jemmy was portly and a little gruff. Ollier, a slight man with a kinder face, was the one who'd interrupted Hektir earlier, and the last man, Murlow, had a severe face just as dangerous as Hektir's.

But it was the woman, Breyline, who unnerved me most. A malicious energy radiated from her fake, foolish smile. Her eyes were glassy and vapid, yet a threat lurked behind them. It was strange... I'd become so used to seeing a keen intelligence underneath cruel maneuvers in adversaries such as Lazlian, that I'd forgotten most evil lurked behind a wall of willful ignorance. I got the feeling this woman was malevolent *and* foolish and that made her even more dangerous. An intelligent person could be reasoned with, they had some sense of consequence to their actions. An ignorant bully simply followed their hate where it led, dismissive of the damage it caused to others or even themselves.

"You almost got us all killed," I remarked to Ollier as our boat took off in the direction I'd instructed, putting comforting distance between us and Oxholde. "You're shit as kidnappers go."

"You're pretty good as captives go," Ollier said, giving me a small smile.

"I've had a lot of practice." I gave him a smile in return and announced, "I'd like some water, please."

"You heard the prisoner," Hektir said to Breyline, whose wide, creepy stare and idiotic grin seemed plastered on her face and pointed in my direction. It made me feel like insects were crawling up my skin. "Get her water."

"I can get my it myself," I announced to Hektir, rising.

"Sit," Hektir ordered. A jerk of his head in Breyline's

direction was all the command needed to tell her to fetch the water for me. Her nostrils flared just a hint in my direction before she ambled down into the cabin.

Ugh, not her. There was nothing I could do to make Breyline hate me less, but being commanded to serve me would certainly make her hate me more, and for my baby I did not want that.

I couldn't be sure Breyline wouldn't spit in the water and it seemed like the men were oblivious. I could almost understand. With a cursory glance at Breyline, I wanted to say her gaze was vapid, her eyes empty... but there was a nastiness behind them too.

On an equal playing field, she'd be an opponent I could crush or preferably, ignore. I think Breyline knew this and it stoked her hatred of me. She seemed like the type who, given power, would wield it with gleeful cruelty. Something in her covetous face made me sure of it.

Nervously, I stroked my belly.

Mean *and* stupid was a dangerous combination.

Thinking of my baby, I wondered if Lazlian would also leave Rythas to find me. He'd done so before, but now that he was king, I didn't see how he could abandon the throne. Did he care for me that much?

I remembered a conversation I'd had with Jesi, the day of Tomé's party.

"Out of all the men I've met," I said, trying to explain why I'd agreed to make the heir. "Kirwyn and Lazlian are the only two of whose feelings I can be sure. Well, not always with Lazlian. But in some ways."

"What do you mean?" Jesi asked.

"So much in this world is fake, just a trick of the light. But I met them both when I was young, before I knew how superficial it can all be," I said, stroking my cheek, self-consciously. "Had I

met Kirwyn under other circumstances, later in life, I might have thought he wanted me for more superficial reasons and I'd have been hesitant. But now I know it's more than that, that he's more than that. Kirwyn has never taken advantage of the power I've given him to do... certain things, intimately. He's never abused the privilege. So many men would."

I took another sip of the cocktail before continuing because Lazlian was harder to explain.

"And Laz wasn't even attracted to me at first. Not enough to stop him from trying to kill me. So I know it's not a surface level desire with him either."

"Let me get this straight," Jesi said, dropping her empty drink into the sand and using her hands to emphasize her words. "You know Kirwyn really loves you because he's never taken advantage of or mistreated you when you're vulnerable... Depressing, but I suppose not unwarranted, considering most men. And you know Lazlian really cares for you because he's more than taken advantage of or mistreated you, he's tried to kill you. Which, while I sort of understand your reasoning, is really messed up."

Of course Jesi hadn't hesitated to wield her blunt tongue. I could only shrug. It did sound messed up when she said it that way.

No matter what happens, it's best to focus on keeping myself safe, I thought.

Imagining the spit in my drink again, I jumped from my seat and announced, "I'll join Breyline. I need to get out of the sun."

Finding Breyline sitting on a cushioned bench below deck and not making any haste in retrieving water, didn't surprise me. Ignoring her, I shuffled through the cabinets until I found a glass, and I poured myself a generous cup from a container resting on the small counter.

Breyline snorted. "You've got some nerve, little Elowan whore." Her voice was strangely melodic; it didn't match her eyes, glittering with malice. "Making threats that your husband will kill us all. How many husbands have you had now? I don't know why Hektir put up with that."

"It wasn't a threat, it was a generous warning you've chosen not to heed," I said, taking a drink. The water felt like a dream as it went down my throat. I hoped I could keep it there. That had been the problem the last time I was pregnant.

"I'm going to be quite ill for a while. I need to focus on keeping myself alive," I told Breyline, shrugging. "I don't have time to worry about you too."

Which is true, but the more helpless you believe me to be, the less you'll worry about my scheming, I thought.

"You have so much faith that your husband will come and rescue you?" Breyline harrumphed. "You haven't seen our fortifications."

"You haven't seen my husband."

I savored another long, refreshing sip of water. *You haven't seen me.* But again, I bit my tongue, because the more they thought I was simply waiting, the less they'd suspect I'd plot anything.

I'd already found the weak link to pressure -- Ollier. I just had to work out how I'd use him to my advantage.

CHAPTER 29

HIS FAULT
Lazlian

Anxious as I was about both Zaria and the open ocean, it delighted me that Kirwyn had fumed as we'd sailed. That I knew better where to start our search when he considered himself the expert on all things mainland, knocked the smug upstart down a peg or two. And he couldn't even truly resent it. Not when he wanted to get her back as desperately as I.

We benefitted from a quick and easy crossing to the mainland -- no storms and no adversarial ships on the horizon. *It was about time our luck turned for the better.* As we journeyed, Kirwyn and I discussed the best places to begin our search, but only one of us had spent recent years with other clans. So what did he know?

I knew to bring us to The Exchange. He wasn't even aware of its existence.

The Exchange, or the Ex as most called it, was a hodge-podge establishment about four hours inland and buried deep within the woods. Its three primary functions were to serve as a drinking hall, a safe roof under which to catch some sleep, and a *mostly* war-free zone for emissaries of various clans to meet and forge deals and alliances against the Spades. Information being a prized commodity there, the Ex was the first place we should start.

Though, admittedly, I had to begrudge Kirwyn *some* respect for getting along so well in his mainland endeavors without the benefit of knowing this place.

"Keep my identity a secret," I ordered before we entered the Ex. "Both of ours."

"You don't say?" His voice dripped with insolent sarcasm and he rolled his eyes.

"It's not just that," I replied, pausing at the threshold and rubbing my finger as I searched for my phantom ring. I hoped Raoul had delivered it to my brother and that, in my absence, Juls had successfully stepped in to rule again. "Part of what I was doing here the past five years was fostering friendships and potential alliances. But you know the clans. To make a friend in one place is to make an enemy in another. It's possible I might be recognized by an acquaintance or... something else."

"Some hate you as Rythasian anyway," Kirwyn remarked with a shrug.

"I know. I was working to smooth that over," I replied, annoyed.

Mainlanders had, at times, requested aid from my father... and his father before him and so on. Rythas instead chose to shroud itself in greater obscurity and to strengthen her ties with the Spades. I didn't blame my ancestors, but the choice no longer served. Those clans that knew of our kingdom, however, did not forget what losses they suffered when Rythas ignored their call for aid.

"I couldn't patch up ages of resentment in a few short years," I admitted. "And fighting *with* one clan means fighting *against* another."

There were no passwords to speak or any examination of our marks to enter the Ex. While it was a seedy, secret establishment, it was intended as a safe-zone. If a person knew of its existence, that was good enough.

We're all friends here, united in our hatred of the Spades.

The largest section of the establishment was its meeting area and drinking hall, but even that wasn't very spacious. While fights broke out, it was generally discouraged to carry a weapon inside the peaceful walls. The guideline was rarely enforceable, however, since some clans were distrustful and a body contained so many clever hiding places. Sleeping compartments were little more than underground burrows only large enough to fit one bed.

Were we to be delayed, Kirwyn and I would take the forest floor instead.

Without revealing our identity, we entered the main building, ordered something foul passing as ale, and questioned the patrons and servers. I used my familiarity with the various clans to ease my way into conversation, and Kirwyn used his charm. I tried not to roll my eyes with how well it worked on the few ladies present, who looked up through lashes they batted hopefully.

But I *did* spit out my tepid ale when he made a show of propping a foot upon on a bench and resting a cocky arm on his leg as he leaned over to question two starry-eyed girls. I imagine, had his hair been the length he was used to, he would have tossed it back with the act.

Did this shit work on Zaria?

But for all our efforts, we learned nothing of value and the hour grew late. The Ex wasn't an actual, bustling drinking hall with many patrons hanging about. People tended to come for a purpose -- a message to be delivered, an exchange of goods to be acquired -- and, having achieved the goal, departed.

Kirwyn and I sat despondent on a bench, each of us quietly running through ideas for our next course of action. The longer we lingered, the further away Zaria might be spirited.

When the door swung open once more and a man entered, I hadn't much expectation. But I did a double-take when I saw that beneath a rather half-assed disguise, it was Brekett, the Spade Emissary. He was unmistakable with that weak chin and those watery blue eyes.

Kirwyn noticed him too, at the same time Brekett caught sight of us. The emissary's mouth dropped and he froze. While we were unusual for the establishment, *his* presence was cause for action.

As a Spade, if anyone knew he'd sauntered inside, they'd tear him to pieces.

But there was more than that in Brekett's eyes. There was a fear in seeing *us*, in particular.

He knows something about Zaria.

Brekett turned on his heel and fled into the woods.

The prick.

Kirwyn and I grabbed our packs, knocking over our benches as we jumped to chase him. We'd been disadvantaged from our position across the room and the emissary was surprisingly fast. He was also better acquainted with the terrain, so it took longer than I'd have liked to catch him through the dark trees.

Finally, Kirwyn tackled Brekett to the ground, while I withdrew my gun and held it to his head.

I blinked.

The act felt like a declaration of war. This wasn't something I'd have ever dared to do to a man of his station or to any Spade, back in Rythas. And while I was sure they suspected we had firearms, flaunting them wasn't something I ever imagined either.

Let alone pointing one at an emissary's head.

"You're going to answer some questions," Kirwyn gritted out, fishing rope from his pack and roughly tying Brekett's hands behind his back. For extra measure, he secured the man to the nearest tree. I watched, stunned at the feeling of having crossed a bridge and burned it behind me.

Could we even let him live, after this? He'd report our actions back to the Spades and then... how would they retaliate?

"I'll tell you anything you want," Brekett said quickly. I frowned, disgusted by how easily he offered it all without a single threat or even a question on our part. I'd caused plenty of men to break down in my father's dungeons, but most at least tried to hold up under the beginnings of torture.

"Where's Zaria?" Kirwyn demanded. "What do you know?"

"They're taking her to a satellite compound," Brekett confessed, referring to the outposts ringing Spade City at various distances. He rattled off an approximation of how to locate the one holding Zaria. "She's in good care. There's medical equipment at the southernmost, I directed them there myself. They'll take good care of your baby."

Kirwyn flinched.

"What do the Spades want with my wife?" he gritted out, grabbing Brekett by the collar of his shirt and pressing his face close to the frightened emissary.

"N - nothing," Brekett insisted. "They didn't have a choice but to take her."

Shit.

I yanked Kirwyn off Brekett. The sudden act startled him enough that, reluctantly, he let me pull him a few steps back. The rage on his face morphed into confusion as he stared at me with a furrowed brow.

"There's something I neglected to tell you," I admitted. "Well, I may have misled you."

Kirwyn scowled, self-righteous hands on his hips. God, this was going to be awful.

"It's my fault Zaria was captured," I confessed. "It didn't happen in your manor. I had tried to... contain her. She was running away from me and ran right into her abductor's arms. They weren't even looking for her."

Nostrils flaring and eyes wide, Kirwyn shouted, "You know, I always thought I'd have to do something to get you out of the picture, but I don't need to lift a finger. You fuck things up to bring about your own demise. Now what the hell really happened?"

"I tried to lock her in my chambers and she escaped by crossing the inner courtyard to the fourth side of the royal tower, the one under construction," I said, hating that he was right. "She'd been disguised as me, it was really me they were looking for. She was just in the wrong place at the wrong time." Trying to smooth things over, I insisted, "That is how I know they'll make an exchange and take me in her place."

Kirwyn, having frozen as I spoke, now paled.

"What did you say?" he whispered.

I growled, "You heard me perfectly well, don't make me repeat it."

"She was taken... from the rooms under construction... they were looking for you?"

"Yes," I snapped. "Whoever's done this came with the intent to kidnap me and she was unfortunately taken in my place."

Kirwyn swayed on his feet, the color now completely drained from his face. "They didn't come to kidnap you. They came to kill you." He looked like he was going to be sick as he said, "And I sent them."

I'd only cocked my head before it was my turn to freeze.

Kirwyn, still dazed, murmured, "I was eavesdropping in a drinking hall one night, back in Spade City. But a man saw through my disguise. Caught, there was little I could do but listen to him talk. We shared a drink and a mutual hate for you. I happily secured his silence by telling him the best way to sneak into the castle to assassinate you. I described what Merie showed me... how the wing under construction was dark and lightly guarded. A part of me hoped you'd be dead before I returned, though realistically, I never thought he'd attempt it or even be successful."

I'll admit that I was so stunned by his words that it took me a second longer than usual to react. Then I was on top of Kirwyn before he could move.

"You tried to have me killed, you fucking rat!" I shouted. Besides being with Zaria, nothing in my life had ever felt as glorious as my fist connecting with his face. "You tried to end my life?" I cried, hitting him again on the side of his head. "It's *your* fault she was taken!" I yelled, unleashing another barrage of punches.

Kirwyn took the beating he deserved up to the point when self-preservation instincts took over and he was forced to defend himself or be destroyed. For nearly a full, foolish minute, we thrashed in the dirt, kicking and shouting and causing a regrettable ruckus.

Several shots rang out across the forest, instantly sobering us. Kirwyn rolled away, and, keeping low to the ground, withdrew his gun as he searched for the source.

Having taken a similar position, I noticed the gunshots hit Brekett in his chest and he'd slumped, dead against the tree. We'd nearly forgotten him as we brawled, but there wasn't time to react as more shots rang overhead.

Kirwyn fired back and I heard a man squeal, but the bullet seemed to hit rock instead of the intended target.

The next instant, someone at our backs growled impatiently, "Put down your weapons. You're outnumbered." Striding into our view, he declared, "Shoot any of us and you're dead."

At the same time, five other men, all with guns raised, emerged from the dark wood. Kirwyn and I exchanged a look of furious defeat. With a sigh, he stood slowly and dropped his weapon to the ground. I did the same.

"He shot at my head!" one of the men cried, examining the rockface. "If I hadn't already been slipping, he woulda killed me."

"Next time, try not to shoot first and warn them all we're here," the leader scolded a large man with slightly long, curly brown hair. He eyed Kirwyn appreciatively, then toed Brekett's corpse. "Maybe we coulda used this one for something too." Turning back to the large man he ordered, "Check their marks."

Kirwyn and I were gruffly stripped from the waist up to reveal our tattoos.

Noting the black crown and key, the leader asked with ill-concealed disgust, "What in the world are men of Rythas doing on the mainland?"

"We're scouts," Kirwyn lied, and I had to stifle a snort at his old cover.

"I don't know what you know of Rythas, but some of their royals have gone missing," I added. "We've been sent on a mission to find them, and to gather any information we can. Some believe war is coming."

"War is already here, it's *been* here," the leader said, scowling at me. He was a short man with short, spiky hair and a misshapen nose, likely the result of repeated breaking. "Rythas has been sittin' pretty avoiding it all these years. Hell, until recently not many even knew 'bout you." He spat and proclaimed, "Spade whores."

I licked my lips and replied, "Yes, we don't agree with the decisions their kings have made over the years, but we're only soldiers, bound to do as we're told."

"What's your name?" the leader asked.

Before I could speak, Kirwyn replied, "This is Callum and I'm... Finley."

I frowned. Wasn't that his dog's name?

"May we have the pleasure of knowing what clan you belong to?" Kirwyn asked.

I listened, curious, as I'd spent plenty of time on the mainland and couldn't place the men either.

With a smirk verging on a snarl, the leader turned around and slid the top of his jacket from his shoulder. Wearing no shirt underneath, I immediately saw the grotesque scar of flesh having been flayed from his body.

The clanless.

My eyes unintentionally rounded. Unlike freeborns, these men had once belonged to a clan, maybe various ones. They'd either left or been kicked out -- for reasons that were never good. Likely for crimes so atrocious, they'd been exiled from clans who didn't put monsters to the sword. Circumstances varied but the men either had their marks forcibly burned or flayed from their skin... or they'd done it later by their own volition, to prove themselves worthy in some twisted way.

I couldn't be sure if being burned or flayed would be our fate. Especially if they hated Rythas and knew who we were.

"Tie 'em up and put 'em in the cart," the leader ordered the men. "Search the dead one and leave his body."

Fuck.

Kirwyn and I were restrained and marched into the cart, which wasn't much more than a jacked-up wheelbarrow hitched behind a horse. Rough sacks were found and tied tightly around our heads, so that we didn't know where we'd journeyed as we were bounced and tossed about. The only thing useful we learned were the men's names. Gerod was the leader, Squeo the one who was lucky to escape Kirwyn's bullet, and Craigory was a mountain of muscle with curly brown hair. The other three, Pelor, Mige, and Nico, were quieter but no less dangerous.

An hour or two later, we were removed from the wagon and marched into a dwelling of some kind. It smelled musty, a scent that only increased when we were led down a set of stairs.

The bags were lifted from our heads to reveal a small, dark basement with two cells built into the walls. They were only about seven feet in both directions. Pressed together, one side of each cell shared a wall.

Kirwyn was shoved into the right, and I, the left. We were roughly searched, Gerod claiming all our weapons, gold, and tokens. When they finished, Gerod removed my silver cuff, the one with Zaria's hair. I wanted to cut off his hands for even daring to touch it and for forcing me to stand submissively while he did so. My only consolation was that he didn't play around with it, instead pocketing the bangle and curiously eying my torso.

"What's this?" Gerod asked, fisting my key necklace. When it didn't budge as he painfully tried to yank it from my neck, he slipped it off instead.

He doesn't know. Let's hope he never does.

"One of the keys to my family's shed," I lied, badly. "Where we store our grain."

"Fancy key for a grain shed," he remarked, turning the symbol of power over in his hands.

I looked down and lied better, "We store guns and ammo in there too." Angrily, I added, "The rulers of Rythas don't allow us to protect ourselves the way we want to."

"The world would be a better place if they were all dead," Gerod agreed.

I didn't need to share a look with Kirwyn to know he was thinking the same thing I was. It was bad enough coming from Rythas. If these men knew who'd they'd really captured, we had no chance of survival.

Gerod locked us in our cages and tossed the key to Squeo.

"I'm off for part two of tonight's plan. Keep 'em here until I return. If I'm held up, it could be awhile. Keep 'em alive. I've always thought Rythasians needed a taste of what it's like for the rest of us. Let's give it to 'em when I return."

The men thumped up the stairs and I tensed, not intending to stay locked up for long.

My wrist and chest felt naked without my cuff and my key. I shot Kirwyn a look he read too well. Boldly, without even waiting for the men to fully disappear, he opened his mouth and let the ring fall onto his waiting hand. The tricky bastard must have hidden it under his tongue before we'd been tied. I hadn't thought to hide my silver, hadn't been quick enough. And now they were gone.

I fumed at the smug cock of Kirwyn's brow as he quietly slid the ring into his pocket. I knew the object well. Neither Zaria nor Kirwyn had opted for another wedding band, choosing instead to wear a single ring -- hers with the blue-green stone he'd given her, his with a dark green gem I knew she'd gifted him as a symbol of the earth.

"Aren't you a nimble little rat to purpose your mouth so quickly?" I mocked.

"Agility with my tongue isn't the only reason she chose me over you," he shot back, "but her screams prove it didn't hurt."

I gritted my teeth but could do nothing more until the men ascended the stairs. The moment the cellar door slammed shut, I leapt to the lock. To his credit, Kirwyn did the same.

Unbuckling my belt, I broke the prong off the buckle and inserted it into the lock, playing around until I heard the most satisfying *click*.

Amateurs.

Free, I swung my cage door wide and stepped out. Behind me, Kirwyn angrily shook the bars of his cell.

"How did you do it?" he demanded, panic edging his voice.

"I'm the keylord," I declared, barely glancing over my shoulder as I scavenged the sparse room for something I could use. I found a metal pipe in a corner. It would have to do. "I know very well how to pick a lock."

Leaving the prick to the fate he deserved, I walked toward the stairs.

"Let me out!" he whispered between clenched teeth, truly panicked now.

As I walked, I tilted my head toward the ceiling, savoring his desperation. *Glorious.*

"If you don't let me out," Kirwyn threatened, "I'll scream and they'll come rushing through that door. You can't beat them all and they'll throw you right back in that cell."

I paused. He had a point.

But if I found Zaria and delivered her news of Kirwyn's death... told her the tale of how I tried so hard to save him, risking my own life and failing...

Let the prick scream, I decided, after debating for a bit. It was worth the risk of a fight to come. Who knew what awaited on the other side of that door anyway?

But by the time I reached the stairs, Kirwyn hadn't screamed. In fact, he'd gone mysteriously quiet.

I paused. Suspicious of a trick, I asked, "Why aren't you screaming?"

After a pause of his own, he replied with defeat, "If I scream, she'll lose us both."

Rage like wildfire coursed through my blood. I snarled as I turned to hiss, "You think you're better than me? You're not the better man!"

"I don't give a shit what you think," Kirwyn said, looking around his cell in a fruitless effort to find something useful. "Just go. I'll figure this out myself."

"So that you can die here and become her martyr? The man she'll never forget, the hero no one else will match?" Crossing to his cell door, I worked my prong at the lock and declared, "I don't think so. You can face her and tell her of your broken promise. Tell her that's the real reason she was captured in the first place." Through gritted teeth I insisted, "See what she thinks of you then."

Having struck a nerve, Kirwyn glared.

With a satisfying *click*, the lock sprung open. Fine. He'd be useful for whatever we met up those stairs anyway.

My hands were on the door when I heard another scrape.

Fuck, I thought, stomach lurching at the sound of footsteps atop the stairs.

"They're out of their cages!" someone shouted. "Hurry!"

Two seconds later, the clanless men charged down the steps and we were instantly overwhelmed, our escape embarrassingly futile. With multiple guns trained at our heads, we didn't even put up a fight, though they beat us like we did before tossing us back in our cells.

I groaned, both in pain and defeat as multiple chains were locked around our doors. I couldn't pick that many.

"Gerod just left, but you'll be sorry when he returns," Squeo taunted.

The men clomped back up the stairs, closing the door and leaving us in complete darkness.

"You fucking asshole," I grit out in Kirwyn's direction. "If I hadn't have come back to let you out, I would have escaped."

"If you had let me out right away without stopping to debate over it, we *both* would have escaped," he shot back, before breaking off in a pained moan.

Alone, Kirwyn and I quietly nursed our wounds. The clanless did not return for hours. Maybe a day. Maybe two. Exhausted and needing to heal, I fell in and out of sleep, making it difficult to tell. When I was awake, there was nothing. No light, no food, no sound.

The only thing to exist would have been our voices in the darkness, had Kirwyn or I deigned to speak to one another.

We did not.

DARKNESS BEGINS
Kirwyn

We didn't speak until the shit made us. Literally.

It was inevitable, caged for days. Squeo occasionally descended to give us some water in a small cup or a few Spade bricks, with no consistency to help us track the hours and snickering maliciously throughout. Our cage contained no blankets, pillows, or anything other than a handleless, metal bucket.

Lazlian and I quickly ascertained its intended use, and I supposed I should have been grateful for even that comfort.

The crux of the issue was the only means to do anything with our waste existed in the form of a shoddy pipe built into the floor outside my cell. The drain wasn't quite what I'd seen developed as a toilet in some dwellings after The Great Decline, but it wasn't just a hole either. A misshapen lid covered most of the opening and a chemical pit resided in the bottom.

The problem lay in the fact that only I could reach it by dumping my waste through the bars of my cell, to the far side of Lazlian's.

Occasionally, Squeo placed the stub of a candle on the basement floor, and I thought the concession was half-torture. Lazlian and I were granted but a few minutes or hours of dim light, before being quickly plunged back into darkness. I used that time to take care of bodily needs and turned to see Lazlian looking at me with arrogant expectation.

"I'm not emptying your fucking shit bucket," I spat, disgusted.

Lazlian shrugged. I cursed and kicked my own bucket.

It didn't take long before I broke down, gritted my teeth, and emptied the chamber pot like his goddamn servant. The process was made worse by the fact that the bucket didn't fit through the bars and he had to tip it over to transfer the... contents. I repeated the process on the other side of my cell, disposing of the waste in the drain.

I needed to maintain health to escape, and unsanitary conditions weren't conducive to that goal. My only consolation was that Lazlian seemed even more horrified than me at the whole situation. He tried to hide it by affecting nonchalance, but I could tell through his twitching lips that the insolent king was humiliated and enraged to be degraded thus. Our cage was a far cry from the comforts of his castle, and I wouldn't have been surprised if his ancestors had servants to wipe their royal asses.

When Lazlian did not thank me for the assistance, I gritted out, "Of course you expect me to do your dirty work, that's all your family does -- endlessly take."

"We take? You've got that backwards," Lazlian hissed, clearly pushed to the brink as well. "We endlessly give. My brother and I gave you protection in Rythas, made you a prince, and permitted you to marry the woman who was meant to belong to *our* dynasty. You, a selfish fucking prick from nowhere. And after all that, you try to assassinate me."

"I plan to do more than that," I gloated, making a conscious decision to attack, even if it was a risk. I wanted him to know, wanted to rub it in. *We might never make it out of this hell anyway,* came the intrusive thought. "I've worked out a deal and I'm taking Zaria to Spade City. She'll be safe there, with me. And can you guess where you'll likely wind up after the war?" Knowing Lazlian suspected as much, I rolled back on my heels and considered him. Allowing my estimation to come up short, I shrugged, "Perhaps I'll buy you if you're cheap enough."

The diminishing candlelight allowed me to make out some of the rage crossing Lazlian's face and better yet, I could *feel* it rolling off him. It was worth the disclosure to see his fury.

"After all we've done, you wanted to steal her away to bring her to our enemies? To work *against* us?" Lazlian slammed his hands against the bars between our cells and shook them. I couldn't see any spit fly out of his mouth in the dim light, but I amused myself with imagining it did. "You fucking traitor. I will see you sent to the Isle of Walking Corpses! And I will swim there myself before I allow you any authority over any aspect of my life."

"You have done nothing but endanger *her* life," I said, snarling. "Whether it's the Spades or whoever has her now. Maybe I sent him, but it was *you* he wanted. Do you want to tell me why the man who took her wants to kill you so badly?"

"How the fuck should I know?" Lazlian scoffed, waving

an arrogant hand in the air. "I'm king. Assassins wanting to kill me comes with the position."

"No," I growled. "This man had a vendetta before you were king. I don't know his name. I didn't bother asking to receive a lie. He had... brown hair and sharp eyes. Kinda mean-looking but mostly forgettable but for a curved scar around his right eye."

Shock registered on Lazlian's face. Slowly, with wide eyes and an open mouth, he gripped the bars of the cell again, as if for support. After a long pause, he mumbled, "I hoped he was dead. His name is Hektir and doesn't just want me. He wants my heir too."

"Start talking," I ordered coldly. "Why?"

"None of your fucking business, traitor," Lazlian spat.

"Fuck!" I swore, realizing the danger Zaria was in. "You went around starting rumors that the baby is yours. How many people are aware? Does the kingdom know? Does Hektir?"

Lazlian shook his head and shrugged.

I ran a frantic hand down my face. *Maybe he thinks the baby is mine,* I consoled myself, closing my eyes and wishing it to be true. *We hit it off, in a weird way. Hektir has no reason to harm a child of hers and mine.*

I opened my eyes just in time for the candle to flicker out, plunging the cellar into darkness, and I wondered if the ominous timing was a good or a bad sign. On one hand, it reminded me of candles blown out for a birthday wish upon a cake, a custom still employed in some places. On the other, the sudden envelopment of total darkness at that moment felt undeniably foreboding.

I wondered why I was thinking of these superstitions at all and considered that I might be losing my mind in such confinement.

It was too soon to go insane, so to pass the time and keep nimble, I did push-ups and crunches. I didn't want to expend too much energy without knowing when I'd next receive food or water, but losing my sanity to the abyss didn't appeal either. I ran through all the exercises I could before tiring and laying down to find sleep.

Lazlian, who'd been quiet the entire time, suddenly broke the silence by accusing, "You are not a prince of Rythas, you are nothing. You gained the title only by marriage. Everything you are you owe to her. You use her."

I threw my head back, laughing deeply. It felt good to piss Lazlian off by doing so. "You are no king, you can't even hold a throne without tying yourself to her through an heir. I wouldn't sling about insults of *use* if I were you. Then again, honesty was never your family's best policy so lying to yourself must come naturally."

"If she didn't meet you first, she would have been happy with me," Lazlian seethed. "None of this would have happened."

"I just warned you against deluding yourself," I scolded haughtily, knowing it would get under his skin. "We *were* happy. You endanger and objectify her."

"You overprotect and infantilize her."

"Me?" I scoffed, adrenaline rose as my body prepared for a physical fight that couldn't happen with bars between us. "You're the one who locked her in your room!"

"What do you expect me to do?" Lazlian shouted into the darkness. "I had to stand by and watch her marry someone else. Twice."

"So did I!"

Seething, he replied, "Well, she carries your name now."

"And your fucking heir!" I roared.

Long moments of silence passed. I fisted and unfisted

my hands until they'd be sore in the morning. I counted the minutes until I grew bored. Sleep eluded me.

Breaking the quiet, Lazlian asked with relish, "Do you know how I was finally able to get her pregnant?"

I scoffed. "Yeah, actually. I do."

I didn't need him to tell me what I already knew transpired in my absence.

"She comes at my command, you know. I've trained her like a dog." Lazlian made a musing sound and added, "Well, I can't take total credit for the masterful instruction, part of it was innate. She hears my voice and my wishes and submits to them naturally."

I indulged in the fantasy of digging my fingers into the flesh of his face and tearing it off, but I tuned him out, refusing to give him the anger he desperately wanted to goad. I craved cutting out Lazlian's tongue for all but calling Zaria a dog. Instead, I bit my own. Lazlian was predictable. He enjoyed setting little traps for people to stumble blindly into.

If the prick could only amuse himself in the darkness by trying to instigate something with me, I'd simply cut off his supply.

I turned over and finally found sleep.

DAYS AND NIGHTS were indistinguishable in the pitch-black cellar, but I felt like many passed before Gerod returned. I was instantly alert, pulse racing and bracing for anything. When the leader and his men clomped down the stairs, Lazlian and I had the benefit of both the small candle and the light from above coming through the doorway.

Gerod considered us with his hands on his hips. Lazlian

and I were on our feet, facing the cell doors and waiting. I didn't want to say anything to attempt persuading Gerod. I wouldn't until he spoke first, and Lazlian was smart enough to do the same. We needed somewhere to begin, an angle to work with.

"Which one of 'em picked the lock?" Gerod asked.

"That one," Craigory said, lifting his chin at Lazlian. "Tried to escape and armed himself with that pipe." The large man tilted his head in the direction of the discarded metal pipe, forgotten in a corner of the basement.

"This one?" Gerod asked, crossing over and stooping to retrieve it.

My muscles coiled. Something was happening and it wasn't good.

Gerod bid his men to unlock Lazlian's cell door.

My adrenaline spiked, pulse skyrocketing. *What was Gerod doing?*

"Hold him down," he ordered, and his men jumped to obey, pinning Lazlian to the floor.

Oh fuck. No, no, no.

I watched in horror as Gerod swung the pipe downward and with a sickening crack, unmistakably broke both of Lazlian's legs. It was the first time I'd ever heard the king scream and I winced, choking back my own.

Lazlian moaned feebly on the floor. To his credit, he didn't cry or faint, though I wouldn't have blamed him if he did.

"We should kill this one," Craigory said.

Good. Kill him and I'll finally be rid of him, I couldn't help but think. *He was prepared to let me die.*

"He's more useful alive," Squeo argued, rubbing his nose. "Keep that one in line on raids."

"Seeing as how we can take his life at any time will keep him in line enough," Craigory returned.

But if Lazlian dies, I can't use him to free Zaria.

Gerod, ignoring the chatter, raised his arm and poised for another strike. Stomach dropping, I watched in helpless horror.

"Not if you want to let him off leash," Squeo said.

Off leash? What were they talking about?

"He needs range if he's going to be a good shot," Squeo argued. "That means he needs incentive to behave."

My heart pounded. Lazlian groaned, sweat matting his hair to his face.

I need him alive to save her.

"I'm not convinced his friend's life matters all that much to him," Gerod said, tightening his grip on the pipe. "They were fighting when we found 'em and who wants the responsibility of the broken man?"

My mind raced, putting the pieces together. Frantically, I shouted, "He's more valuable than I am!"

Craigory looked at me and snorted. "He's not as valuable as he was two minutes ago."

"He can still use his hands and his mind if you don't break them," I argued, speaking as fast as I could because Gerod had lowered his arm.

"Better than any of your men, I bet, when it comes to repurposing Spade technology, or anything else you scavenge." Gripping the bars, I cried, "He's doubly useful to you. His captivity will keep me in line like you want, and he'll earn his keep while he's here. Just... he needs a splint and something for the pain!"

The men stared at me, unmoving.

"You want my gun? You want me to be your sure shot on raids, right? Is that it?" I cried. "I'll do what you want, but you have to keep him alive. And for god's sake, help him!"

Gerod grinned widely. He tossed the metal pipe to Craigory and away from Lazlian. I exhaled, letting my shoulders slump with relief.

"And that, men," he gloated, "is how you tame a pistol pet."

CHAPTER 31

PILLARS OF PERSUASION
Zaria

Knowing Kirwyn was coming didn't stop me from missing him, or Teddy. *Or Laz,* I had to admit. Even when I hated him for what he'd done, I couldn't shake him.

I snorted. *Well, I'd willingly accepted a part of him to take root inside me, after all.*

Captive in the Spade compound, I had no hope of fighting my way out of the sophisticated building or beyond my five captors, even if I were well. But with a bit of persuasion, I might flip the allegiance of Ollier as one flipped a magnet, attracting him to my aid instead of opposing it.

Unfortunately, this required my being conscious and I slept an appalling amount. Having my grand plans of escape foiled by needing a nap was a rather humbling experience, but to be awake was to be violently ill. Days and weeks passed in a blur of slipping in and out of sweaty

294

awareness. I flinched but did not fight the needles pricking my tender flesh, infusing my body with the hydration I couldn't ingest orally. It was the same as my last pregnancy.

The part I most hated to admit was that with the Spade's technology, I was receiving the best possible care.

Kirwyn had theorized the severity of my wasting might partially be due to my keen sense of smell. What was an advantage in many circumstances worked against me when pregnant, and every scent turned my stomach. I actually preferred the antiseptic odor in the sterile medical room where I was kept most of the time. If I couldn't be near the clean scent of the sea, it was the next best thing.

I missed Teddy so terribly the agony stole my breath and tears pooled at least a dozen times a day. Endlessly tossing on the stiff hospital bed with little to do, I played the *what if* game. Infinite scenarios unspooled before me, had I made different decisions, behind me.

It did no good, and I had to force myself to stop, or a good vomiting session took me out of it. Wiping my mouth clean, I'd try to take a realistic look at the effect my past had on me, and what that meant for the future.

I was different, and denying it only wasted time.

I wasn't made for the mainland. If I were honest, I wasn't made for many things others were, and it wasn't just geography. My time in Elowa had shaped me and it wasn't easy to parse out what was for the better or the worse. It had happened and, like an animal long caged, I could no longer survive quite the same in some environments. Or rather, I could survive but not thrive.

Despite Lazlian believing me to be a wild, savage princess.

The thought brought a sad smile to my sweat-soaked face.

Rythas was my sanctuary. It had been, for many.

Kirwyn would balk if I told him, horrified at a seemingly defeatist notion. But on some deeper level, I thought maybe he knew, and it was one of the reasons why he didn't push for us to leave the kingdom. I wasn't at all saddened to come to this realization, and I wasn't alone. Many had crafted a new way of living when they fled to Rythas, long ago. We were not defeated. *We are the descendants of those who dreamed and those who dared.*

It had happened gradually, the spreading of my roots in the island-kingdom. I hadn't looked upon High Spire and instantly fallen in love. I hadn't known in my bones from the moment I set foot upon her sand. But it didn't diminish the truth in the least.

Rythas was where I belonged.

I wasn't incapable of surviving, if forced to remain on the mainland. It simply wasn't best for my spirit or my soul. I'd be like a tree planted in the wrong soil, the wrong sun. Determined to live, she'd rise from the ground, but she'd never flower, never flourish. If war came to Rythas and annihilated the kingdom and me with it, I'd still prefer that course. I'd rather blossom and suffer the woodsman's axe, then never bloom at all.

A dull pain spread through my stomach and I shifted uncomfortably. *I'd gone beyond blooming,* I thought wryly. *I'd been fruitful.* And now there was more to consider than axes swinging for my head or the Spades claiming us as war slaves.

I had Theo and this little baby to protect.

With effort, I pushed myself into a sitting position on the bed. My disadvantages were many and unhelpful to dwell upon, so I ignored them and listed my assets instead.

I held both royal power and the love of the people. I still might be able to leverage them to bribe Ollier, though I was cut off from each at the moment. The best tools I had at my disposal were those I could use now -- my wits and my charm.

On que, bile rose in my throat and past my lips, making me dribble a nasty bit of sick onto my lap.

Scratch charm, I told myself, groaning as I wiped my face clean with the back of my hand.

Wits, then.

I didn't see much of Breyline and for that I was thankful. She'd been assigned the lowly job of gathering news from some Spade outpost. The glassy-eyed woman resented the duty, but I was pleased that it kept her away for days at time whenever she traveled back and forth.

Ollier was the weak link; I simply needed to find where to apply pressure. What did he want?

Another wave of nausea hit me so fiercely that I pitched myself onto the cool floor to help mitigate my dizziness. Arms and legs sprawled, I stared at the ceiling feeling utterly pathetic. My only consolation was that I could sink no lower.

Yet what is a floor if not a foundation, I thought suddenly, an idea forming in my mind. *The groundwork upon which to build.*

Until the worst of the wasting passed and I entered the second trimester, I couldn't hope to escape anyway.

Instead, I vowed I would stay as still as I must and build a trap around me. It would be like constructing a house, I told myself. One where I could invite Ollier inside and ensnare him. So what if I was, quite literally, writhing on the floor? The foundation always comes first. If I looked like a helpless captive in need of aid, so be it. I'd swoon on cue if I must.

It was a start.

Whenever Ollier entered, I perked up enough to converse with him, but not so much that I didn't allow myself to look as sick and vulnerable as I was, hopefully pulling his heartstrings.

Ollier wouldn't be persuaded to assist in my escape -- yet -- but as I engaged him, he brought me news from Spade City and the nearby clans. I listened, glad for diversion but never finding anything useful in his tidings. After a few weeks, I decided it was time to build upon the foundation with flattery and encouragement -- the twin pillars of persuasion.

"You really have a good heart, Ollier," I whispered, clasping his hand when he next came to bring me water. The skinny man averted his eyes and reddened at my praise. It wasn't a lie. While, admittedly, he'd enmeshed himself in an assassination and kidnapping plot, I got the feeling Ollier could have led a much different life, had he better opportunities. When he came again and checked my vitals on the complicated equipment, I studied him as if in awe of his abilities. When he entered sullen, head bent, I guessed Hektir had berated him once more and mused, "With all the work you do, it's a wonder you're not leading your own gang."

My praise lit Ollier up from the inside. He was a full head shorter than the other men and rather bony. I wondered if he'd been taken advantage of, if not outright abused for most of his life. Perhaps that was what had kept him from breaking away from Hektir's unkind treatment. I would forgive him if he helped me successfully escape. He'd have a much better life in Rythas. Maybe not one he deserved, at the moment, but could have the opportunity to earn.

One afternoon, Ollier snuck me some berries Hektir had

rationed for his crew only. One look at the slick, red skin made my stomach lurch, but I forced myself to eat them slowly, gratefully. I could vomit when he left.

As if debating something in his mind, Ollier watched me carefully while I chewed.

"A few weeks ago, Breyline collected some news from the outpost. The king of Rythas has been missing since around the time we took you," Ollier admitted suddenly.

I nearly choked on my berry but said nothing, hoping to encourage him to elaborate.

"Hektir thought he might use you to coax King Lazlian into a trap, but with him gone, there's nothing Hektir can do to get at him. Your husband is missing too," Ollier added in a whisper, unable to meet my eyes.

I sucked in a deep breath.

Any number of infinite possibilities could be the cause of their disappearances. But knowing how Kirwyn and Lazlian had worked together in the past to assassinate Navere's men, I was almost positive they were working together to look for me now. The only thing I couldn't puzzle out was why no one had seen them.

If something happened...

No. I wouldn't allow myself to think on it.

"Without a formal declaration of war, the High Twelve would demand Hektir return you to Rythas," Ollier informed me, playing with the collar of his ill-fitting shirt. He was too scrawny and it swam on him. "He's hoping either King Lazlian makes an appearance or war breaks out. He doesn't know what to do with you in the meantime and he's been stalling."

I moaned. So there was no plan but to wait and see. *Effectively proving that idiots are just as dangerous as clever men. Perhaps more so.*

"Why does Hektir hate King Lazlian so much?" I asked, thumbing the star ring on my right hand. Thankfully, no one had stolen either ring from me. With my fingers swelling, I didn't think they'd come off anyway.

"When he was playing at being a commoner, the king killed Hektir's younger brother in one of the clan skirmishes. It effectively put an end to Hektir's bloodline as he has no children of his own and no other kinsmen to make them. Now he wants to end Lazlian's life, or his line."

"Then why not go for his brother, Juls?" I asked, puzzled.

"Hektir would take a shot at Juls if he had one, but his hatred is for Lazlian first and most," Ollier said, shrugging. "Plus the rumor back in Spade City is that Jullik is infertile, else he would have made an heir by now. His line will die out and he might lose his crown before that happens. But after the skirmish, Hektir found out that Lazlian had a son with some woman in the camp, so he's capable of making another."

I bit my lip hard to keep the fear from my face. *What horrid irony. That child wasn't his. But the one in my belly, is.*

I needed to speed up my plan. One, in case something had happened to Kirwyn and Lazlian, and two, because the best time to move would be when the wasting subsided in my second trimester, which was quickly approaching.

Returning again to my image of a trap house within which I'd lure Ollier, I pictured windows and doors. I thought of each as the favors I might do for Ollier, and for those I might ask for in return.

My resources and my skills were admittedly limited. I couldn't trim his uneven hair into something more fashionable. I couldn't cook him anything special -- not that I was much of a cook anyway. But Ollier's clothing was patchy and frayed and no one made efforts to find him something better.

I still had Lazlian's royal cloak... somewhere.

When Ollier next arrived for what was becoming our daily chats, I requested he bring me a needle and thread, as well as the cloak I'd been wearing when they'd taken me from High Spire. My sewing skills weren't much better than my cooking; the only experience I had was in stitching fish nets back in Elowa, or the minor mending of Teddy's soft toys. But it was easy enough to cut the embroidered trim from Lazlian's ceremonial garment and sew it onto Ollier's shirt. The stitches weren't close to even, but no one would notice with the black thread and cloth, and anything was an improvement upon the original garment.

Not to mention, being given a piece of a royal cloak was quite a boon.

"T - thank you," Ollier stammered when he donned the shirt.

"I would be indebted to you if you could find me some ginger or mint," I told Ollier the following day. "It would help with my nausea."

Lies. No mere herb would mitigate the wasting. But the request would encourage Ollier to feel a sense of pride and perhaps an obligation to help me.

Doors and windows.

And finally, to complete my trap house and seal the structure, I'd lay a roof over it all with the oldest trick in the book.

I'd make Ollier think helping me escape was his own idea.

"You'd look good in Rythasian attire," I mused to him one evening, when he brought some mint tea. Then I lightly teased, "Maybe one day you'll get to travel there for a real visit and not a murderous plot."

"I tried to kill the king and captured you," he mumbled, head bent. "I'd never be granted the permission."

Ollier was only a year or two younger than me, but he seemed almost childlike at times, with his uneven head of thin brown hair and sunken eyes. Stilted in growth, perhaps, from a lack of love in his life.

"You've shown me such kindness in my time here, Ollier," I told him, a bit manipulatively, though sincerely. "I won't forget it. When I'm back in Rythas, perhaps I can implore the king to pardon your involvement in this plot and to grant you a permit to visit... or to stay."

I kept my eyes focused on my swelling belly, letting him come to his own conclusions.

It only took a fortnight before Ollier approached me with an idea on how to sneak me out of the compound.

At his words, I bit back a smile. But I blinked and tears of relief leaked from my eyes.

I'm getting you somewhere safe, sweet baby, I thought, laying a hand on my stomach. *Teddy. Kirwyn. Lazlian. I'm coming.*

It was perfect timing -- my second trimester had just begun and I'd been able to keep food and water down on my own.

Over the next few evenings, Ollier sneaked into my room and we whispered together as he explained the layout of the satellite compound to me, detailed everyone's schedule, and discussed the best possible routes to flee to safety. We'd bribe our way back to Rythas together, never revealing our true identities.

"You're a good person, Ollier," I said, shortly before our

escape. I laid a hand on his cheek, "You just got caught up with some bad people."

That was what the mainland did -- distorted and denied our true identities. Elowa had been safer, but not better.

"In Rythas," I said, "You'll get the chance to be who you truly are."

That was one of the many gifts of my home.

And my loved ones...

War would come to our shores, I knew. And when it did, I would fight beside them.

CHAPTER 32

REGRET
Kirwyn

True panic set in, but I didn't allow the space for despair. That would never help Zaria. Yet the reality of the situation was that it would take months for Lazlian's legs to heal, and he'd need weeks, if not months, to build up his strength after that.

The bitterness of knowing where Zaria was and not being able to get to her ate away at me.

With his hatred of Rythas, I couldn't reveal Lazlian's identity to Gerod without risking the clanless man killing him. And I couldn't escape without Lazlian because he was my best chance at getting Zaria back.

The black cellar was worse for the broken king, who couldn't move much. For the first few days, I tried to encourage him to use his arms to exercise, but he was too weak or too disinterested. I didn't know what went through his head or how often he was awake. The pain medication

Squeo brought seemed to vary, and I suspected some of it lulled Lazlian into sleep.

At least they'd set each leg in a splint.

I hated myself in the darkness, tracing everything that happened back to my decision to send Hektir after Lazlian. I hated Laz too, tracing our horror back to his choice to lock Zaria in his room.

When the stumpy candles burned out, no one came to replace them for hours or days. Not even when they brought a pittance of water and Spade bricks. I quickly learned to keep my cup in the same place, or risk knocking it over in the dark and losing any hope of a drink. My constant companion was the cold -- not to the bone but enough to never be comfortable unless I was exercising. The smell in the air alternated only between the musty cellar walls and the foul, chemical pit, depending on where I stood.

For whatever reason, the men had taken a break from their raids and turned to torturing us instead. It began with beatings and smaller horrors, like ripping a fingernail or two, until bored, they took it to a new level.

Craigory couldn't have known when he hooked up the hose. That goddamn fucking hose. I wanted to grab it and beat them with it. I wanted to tie it around their necks and choke off *their* air.

They couldn't have known Lazlian was afraid of the sea, and, I suspected, drowning. The king was already half-immobile from his broken legs, so it didn't take any effort at all to hold him down and waterboard him with freezing cold water until his lungs nearly gave out. His injury didn't spare him in the least. As the clanless supposedly needed me for an eventual raid, Lazlian suffered the brunt of Craigory's cruelty. Once they saw the fear in Laz's eyes, they delighted in nearly drowning him as often as possible.

The clanless loved that icy water and I knew first-hand how horrific it was on the occasions they chose me. When I was held down and gasping for air, I thought of Zaria. In case I didn't live through it, I pictured meeting her again, on the other side.

In my weakest moments, I begged them to stop. I knew it wouldn't do any good, yet it seemed an instinct I couldn't prevent.

Sometimes it was worse being chosen, and sometimes it was worse listening to Lazlian's tortured gasps.

I missed my wife and my son so badly. That pain was the worst torture of all.

Whenever they weren't tormenting him, Laz didn't speak and barely moved. He simply lay, mostly sleeping, barely existing. As weeks passed, Lazlian descended into his private, inner hell.

I lived in hell too, and it was a surprisingly cold and dark one.

Keeping despair at bay grew difficult. I began fantasizing aloud to Laz, telling him what we'd do when we escaped and turned the tables.

"We'll wake *them* with waterboarding each morning," I said. "They'll never sleep for fear of it."

Lazlian didn't reply.

"Hey. You awake?"

I heard him grunt as he turned, giving me his back, I assumed.

The king was too weak to talk after they waterboarded him. He could only lay, wheezing and moaning. I hated those pained sounds, yet I prayed for them. When Laz slept it was too dark to tell if he still breathed, and I never knew if

I stood watch over a corpse, if his lungs or heart finally gave out. I wondered if they'd leave him there to rot. I wondered if anyone would ever know that the Rythasian king met a gruesome end in a dark cellar of the backlands.

Over the weeks, I sustained myself more on revenge fantasies than on the meager crumbs of Spade bricks. These men didn't know what I knew, they hadn't read what I'd read. Some of them couldn't even read at all. I knew ways to make them scream, ways in which they could never hope to conceive. So did Lazlian. Hell, he knew more than I did in that department. I tried to encourage him to talk about it, but he retreated further into silence.

We were alone in that darkness, our boredom broken up only by the beatings.

The clanless tended to confine my pain to injuries that would heal in a few days, so I suspected they'd soon need me. Fighting back earned me more blows, so I tried to grit my teeth and take it, making sure to protect my head as much as possible. Headaches I hoped weren't concussions commonly pained me in the days of endless dark.

Don't knock out my teeth, I'd think. Zaria loved when I grinned and revealed my canines. She liked me to bite her with them.

I wanted my teeth for her. Even if I never smiled again.

THE REAL ROYALS
Merie

My heart sank, seeing Juls on the bed with his head in his hands. When I entered the room, he looked up with dark-rimmed eyes that told me he hadn't found sleep the night before. I suspected he'd been strategizing with Raoul until dawn.

"He's not dead," Juls insisted. "I'm livid at his deception, but he's still my brother, my twin. I would know, I would *feel* it if he were dead."

"I believe you," I said firmly, crossing to sit beside my husband and draping my arm around his shoulders. "He and Kirwyn are alive and still searching for Zaria."

Juls rubbed his temples, frustrated. On his left hand, he wore the onyx ring Lazlian had given Raoul to deliver. It was fairly similar to the one Juls wore on his right hand.

Outside, the sun shone brightly, but Juls had pulled the curtains. I hoped he intended to nap. No one could keep going like this, not even him.

"So why haven't they found her yet? Or if they've been captured as well, why hasn't a ransom note arrived?" he mumbled. "Lazlian left a mess for us to clean up." Juls finally looked up, but only to wave an angry hand in the air. "To chase her, he's jeopardized our reign and his own life."

"He's chasing his heir, too," I said, *"the* heir."

When Raoul had delivered the ring to us, he also carried the surprising news that Zaria was finally pregnant. I couldn't figure out how these events were connected, but I knew somehow, they were. It was too coincidental.

"The gold for the army has bought us time," I reminded. "And caring for Teddy when he comes to High Spire has brought some comfort, has it not? He's such a delight. He won't have any trouble when it comes to his betrothal, which has intrigued many of the nobles. I've heard the ladies talk, you know."

Juls only let out a *humph*. I chewed my lip.

Juls and I hadn't even had the chance to relocate to Low Spire, as we'd planned to do when Lazlian was crowned. We'd only begun packing when Zaria was suddenly taken and Laz and Kirwyn sailed to the mainland to find her.

To say it was a thorny problem was an understatement. Having publicly claimed in the past that Zaria was kidnapped when she'd actually run away, telling the people now that she'd been abducted for what would seem a *second* time, smacked of egregious incompetence in our security. Instead, we announced her pregnancy and told the white lie that she'd traveled to the mainland for special treatment, along with her husband. Juls made an emergency declaration that the king had also journeyed to the mainland to continue his work with the various clans in preparation for any forthcoming conflicts.

I grew weary of these constant deceptions and I wasn't

sure how much the people believed about Laz's sudden departure, right after being crowned. But everyone knew war with the Spades was a looming threat, so that helped.

My heart ached for Juls, left to bear the weight of it all and having to clean up everyone else's messes. Did he think I would someday let him down too?

In Lazlian's absence, Juls and I stepped in to rule once more, but it felt as if our reign was held together by string. One firm pull and it would all fall apart.

Or worse, I thought, standing by the balustrade above the Garden Gate a few weeks later. *One matrimonial kiss and it would all collapse.*

Below, I watched servants scurry in and out the gate as Rythas prepared for the wedding of the year. For weeks, special shipments had been delivered to our shores. Flaky pastries, candied flowers, shimmering ribbons, and one hundred caged doves to release. All had been ostentatiously ferried into the castle beneath our watchful eyes.

As my brother and Commander of the army, Navere would be married in High Spire.

With each new sack of fruit or towering box of specially-designed flatware, I felt the divide between my brother and I grow into a chasm that could never be crossed. With temperaments so dissimilar, we hadn't been especially close in our youth, but we'd played together and I had fond memories of the little boy I once knew.

I couldn't see him any longer in the ruthlessly ambitious man he'd grown into.

I'd known for a while that he'd take my crown if he could, but sometimes, I wondered if he'd take my life too. Once, I'd assumed my brother would exile Juls and I if it came to that, but now I questioned everything.

Kelody's family footed the bill for the forthcoming

extravagance and she didn't hesitate to let anyone know. Giddy and preening with her upcoming nuptials, Kels strode through vendors in the marketplace or surveyed the gardens, issuing commands and orchestrating one aspect of the party or another.

I didn't begrudge her happiness, but her popularity worried me. The wedding was all anyone talked about. With her money and beauty, and Navere's power and influence, I didn't know that Juls and I could thwart a coup.

Watching the sea for his brother's return each morning, Juls worried as well. I always stood beside my husband and took his hand in my own, wanting to say so many things, but failing.

NOT A CLOUD CLUTTERED the sky on my brother's wedding day and the sun was gentle. A soft breeze carried the scent of High Spire's many flowering verandas throughout the castle halls as if Kels commanded the wind to freshen the fortress for her special day.

I'd granted her my private rooms to ready for the ceremony but kept a respectful distance. That I was not invited to join her bridal party set off alarms that neither Juls nor I needed to discuss to understand.

Kelody and my brother were an immediate threat to our rule.

Lingering by the doorway to help direct the proceedings, I glimpsed the bride every so often. Nobody could deny that Kels was stunning. Tall, slender, and with long, shining brown hair, she'd had her pick of noblemen. Much like her mother, I knew she wanted the best, and for a long time I'd wondered if that would be Lazlian. He *was* the best choice if her aim was to join the royal family.

If her aim was to overthrow it, however... I thought, nervously eying her intricate gold wedding dress.

Kels twirled, showing off her gown, and I caught a look on her face as she smiled for the twelve bridesmaids. Her grin didn't touch her eyes.

Curious, I crept closer.

Was it my imagination, or were the whites of her eyes a tad... pink? Bringing attention to the beading on her hem, Kelody spoke in a voice a bit too loud as she gushed to her friends that she couldn't contain her excitement. There was something contrived in it.

Quietly, I backed away from the door. Retreating to my bedchambers where Juls currently dressed for the ceremony, I grew increasingly sure of an idea with each step. By the time I'd entered our bedroom, I hadn't worked out all the implications, but I knew one thing with certainty.

"Kels doesn't want to marry my brother," I announced, causing Juls to turn. He furrowed his brow and I continued, "I don't know what this means for us, but I don't think she's scheming with him, at least."

"Did she tell you this?" Juls asked, face lit with surprise.

"No," I admitted. "I just... know."

Something like pity crossed Juls's face. It was almost the look an indulgent parent might give a child.

Out of nowhere, all the tension of the past year and recent events seemed to become too much to handle. To my surprise as much as Juls's, I snapped.

"You all dismiss me because I can't play court games as well as others," I cried, words tumbling from my mouth without knowing where they originated. "You secretly mock me because I like pretty things and my education wasn't as robust. But I know one thing and maybe I know it better than anyone else in this court," I said, shaking with indignance. "And that's love. I know how a bride's eyes light from within when she's marrying the man who holds her heart in his hands. I know what love looks like. And that's not it."

Never having spoken to Juls this way before, I had his full attention. He looked at me like he'd never even seen me before. It made butterflies frenzy in my stomach and I couldn't decide if I liked it or not, but I pressed on.

"I know what Zaria looked like the day she married you and I know what I looked like that day too," I confessed, jutting my chin and aching to remember. Juls and I never talked about it. I was always too afraid. I pressed my hand to my heart. "And I know what I looked like the day we finally wed."

Having paused in his dressing, Juls stared at me, rapt. I took a minute to catch my breath, smoothing my hair and, for some reason, fighting tears. I *needed* Juls to believe me. I thought I'd go mad if he didn't; thought it would solidify that wall that had been building between us to a degree where it could never be torn down.

"That bride down there doesn't resemble any of those things," I insisted, still shaking with the need to be understood. "I can't tell you for sure what's going on behind her guarded eyes, but it looks something like... like... stoicism covering pain. Either she never wanted to marry Navere or something happened and she regrets it. Don't dismiss me, don't tell me I'm wrong, Juls."

"I'm wrong," Juls said, unblinking.

"What?"

"I'm wrong and I've been wrong awhile."

"I - " I stammered. "I don't understand what you're saying."

"You're right, and even if I don't see it, I believe you. I see *you*," Juls said, coming to stand before me, "and I see *me*."

We weren't discussing Kels any longer but I didn't know what we were talking about. Even more confused, I asked, "What are you saying?"

Juls took my hands in his. "My divorce from Zaria made me into something I don't like, made me forget who I am," Juls said softly, leaning down to kiss my hand. "My marriage to you, my love for you, reminded me."

I whimpered as a tension banding my heart unexpectedly released. It was a weight I'd barely acknowledged but had carried for six long years. In the wake of everything that happened, Juls had changed. He'd become like some prickly fruit whose sweetness was shielded with a bitter skin. In time, that skin had thickened, toughened, and I'd feared I'd never see the happy Juls I knew from our youth again. It wasn't just Zaria, I knew, it was all the losses he'd suffered, shaping him into this new, short-tempered and distant creature.

Absolutely stunning me, Juls asked, "Can you forgive me for not being the man I should have been, the man you deserved these past few years?"

"Yes, of course," I immediately replied, laughing. The tears streaming down my face had surely ruined my makeup but I didn't care. I knew I'd remember this moment forever. I kissed my husband's hands as he'd kissed mine. "Cynicism never suited you, my love. Courage has always been your color."

Juls wiped my cheeks with his fingers and kissed away the remaining tears. I hadn't felt this happy in *years*. And with a war coming! But if Juls was by my side, we could face anything together.

"And I, I lost myself too," I confessed. "I think I... fell into a role of pleasing you as a way to reach you, to soften you."

It was regrettably true. The more Juls withdrew, the more it had chipped away at my confidence, turning me into someone who'd reshaped herself -- reshaped her whole environment, in an effort to bring him back to his old self.

Juls shook his head and declared, "No more."

"No more," I agreed.

"I believe you," Juls said. "And while I'm sorry for Kels, I'm happy for us. It makes our job easier."

"What job is that?" I asked, though I suspected I knew. I just wanted to hear him say it.

"Holding down the fort until my brother returns," he said with ease.

My eyes fluttered closed as I smiled. That was the Juls I loved. *Assured. Confident.*

"Playing defense," I noted, smiling and teasing him a little.

"Do I look like I was born to play or to rule?" Juls asked, with a gleam in his deep brown eyes that melted me. He stroked my cheek with the backs of his knuckles and my heart raced in response. "Although I think tonight, in private, I might have some playful activities in mind."

I was sure I blushed from the crown of my head down to my toes. He took my chin in his hands, forcing me to look at him, which only made me flush *more.*

Cocking that dashing smile that could leave no room for doubt, Juls clasped my hand and said, "Now let's get down there and remind them all who the real royals are."

CHAPTER 34

OMNI LUCI EST UMBRA
Kirwyn

Instinctively, I screamed as I woke to the freezing blast of water pummeling me. Craigory stood above, wielding his torture, and I tried to shield my face from the aim of the dreaded hose. It didn't do any good. He pounded me with a stream of ice until I gasped, forced onto my hands and knees, head bent.

"Wake up, pistol pet. Gerod wants your gun today."

It took every ounce of willpower not to grab Craigory's legs and pull him to the ground, not to take that hose and twist it around his neck until he choked to death, or to shove it down his throat and turn it on, spraying water until he drowned.

Instead, I suffered his muddy boot as he pressed it to my head and gave me a shove, forcing me to fully collapse on the floor before him. After he'd smushed his dirt-encrusted heel against my face long enough to satisfy his sadism, I was led up the stairs and through the black door, still soaked. As my eyes adjusted to the blinding sunlight, I saw Gerod considering me.

"Squeo is staying with your friend," Gerod informed me. "Underperform and he's dead. Turn your gun on any of us, and he's dead. If we fail to return by tonight, he's dead."

"And what if something happens to prevent us?" I asked. "Something that's not my fault?"

Gerod shrugged. "Hope it doesn't." He nodded in Craigory's direction and the brute brought me a horse. It was an old, slow steed in need of serious grooming, but as we traveled he followed the other horses well enough, and not so well that I'd be able to outride anyone. I'd been given a dagger too, and the familiarity of weaponry strapped to my waist was some comfort. Yet I was torn between soaking up the sights and scents of the forest while I could and fighting the growing dread in my stomach. When we reached Gerod's chosen destination to continue the ambush on foot, we dismounted beneath the foliage.

"They got any women?" Craigory asked, grabbing his dick. "I've got something for 'em."

If they had, I hoped one of them managed to cut off everything he palmed.

"Few, but choice," Gerod answered, stroking his chin. He withdrew a spare gun from his waistband and considered me again.

Fighting my own sneer, I said, "I can more than imagine what you will do to me or *my friend* if try anything funny." Beating him to his repeated threat was the only satisfaction I could have in this situation. "I fully understand that I have no hope of killing all of you and freeing him. You might think me many things, but to save time let's both agree that I'm not stupid."

Gerod didn't fight his sneer. "If this raid goes wrong, I rebreak his legs. If it goes right, he gets more pain meds."

I held out my hand. "Have the medicine ready when we return."

He snorted but gave me the gun.

"You first," Gerod said, lifting his chin in the direction of the small settlement we were about to ambush.

With no better choice, I did what I had to. I led the attack.

The first scream was quickly followed by the second, spreading and alerting people to our raid. The villagers' defense was immediate and, I knew, futile. To live in this warfaring area was to know battle, but they couldn't have been at it very long as their resistance was poor. I shot those who shot at me, and I didn't miss. Pushing forward, I led, with the others winging out behind me until we reached the village itself, or whatever the few, scattered dwellings could be called.

Men would die and we'd claim the spoils. It was nothing new for the backlands, but it was new for me. Theo and I never stole, never attacked, and never fought without provocation.

I blocked out the screams and cries of the fallen. I hoped there were no children. I hoped those who could escape, did.

As we pursued those with firearms, I lost the other men. Choosing the first house I came upon, I burst through the door.

The small home consisted of one room to serve all purposes. A roughly constructed fireplace for cooking stood opposite the door and on the right side of the dwelling, cozy blankets with a cheerful floral pattern covered a floor mat used for sleeping.

Nothing that happened in the bed would be cozy or cheerful, because in the center of the room, a slight girl shook before me as she brandished the only weapon she had -- a kitchen knife. Hair as voluminous as Zaria's fell wildly across her face, almost obscuring her wide, fearful eyes. As if it would do any good to save her, she stood behind a table centrally placed in the all-function room.

I heard men yelling outside the house and estimated I had less than ten seconds to hide her -- not enough time. I could shoot her as a mercy. Lazlian wouldn't hesitate and he'd pat himself on the back for it. Or worse, he'd let her get captured and never give her another thought.

There's one more way.

Without wasting any more time, I rounded the table and swatted the knife from her hand, cringing when it landed with a clatter louder than I'd have liked. In the same move, I shoved her to the table and pushed the girl's face until it was pressed against its surface. She fought me like her life depended on it, which, to her, seemed the case. She even managed to pop up once before I could effectively pin her.

"Stay *down!*" I ordered through gritted teeth, but she continued to fight me. Struggling was good, would make it look real, but she was going to hurt one of us if she kept it up this wildly, as well as ruin her chances of survival.

Better some bruises than the brutality they'd render, I thought, shoving her back against the table's edge and slamming her wrists on top.

I wanted to assure her the tears weren't necessary but there was no time to explain. Her cries made it believable, but they morphed into shrieks as I pushed down my pants and lifted her dress, all while keeping one hand on her wrists. I'd meant to leave her underwear on, but what she wore was so threadbare it wasn't much help, exposing half her ass. I immediately reached up and covered her mouth in case she said something stupid.

I don't want this either, I thought.

In the last seconds before Craigory kicked the door wide, I slammed my hips into the sobbing girl.

"Find your own," I growled, sparing Craigory a glance. "This one's taken."

The fucker laughed and if I could have gotten away with it, I would have stopped what I was doing and stabbed him in the mouth. Craigory paused a beat, during which I was forced to keep fake-fucking the hysterical girl beneath me.

I'm probably scarring her for life. But at least she'll have a life.

I'd never been more flaccid, but I kept ramming into her as if it wasn't. Not understanding what was happening and expecting to feel me inside her at any moment, she kept screaming against my hand and flailing on the table.

Catch on, I thought angrily. I knew it wasn't a reasonable thought, but she endangered us both if she escaped my hold.

"Don't want this one anyway," Craigory said, sneering. "They found better options on the other side of the settlement."

Liar. The poor girl beneath me was beautiful and even if she wasn't, it wouldn't save her from Craigory or any of the others. He'd only said it because he was pissed I'd gotten to her first.

Finally, he left, and I pantomimed sex for another few seconds before releasing the girl's wrists and backing away. I yanked my pants back to my waist as the girl bolted upright, panting. She eyed the room and it was painfully obvious she was looking for a weapon.

Oh fuck, she still doesn't get it. She probably thinks I tried to rape her and couldn't get it up.

I spread my hands wide and said as calmly as possible, "I just saved your life but if you don't listen to me, it won't be for very long."

To my relief, she paused, head cocked.

"I'm on your side. If you hurry, you can escape. Use the window and head east down the dirt path."

She didn't move.

"This isn't a trap!" I shouted, exasperated. "If you don't want to save yourself, I'll have to kill you now rather than risk your exposing me. I don't think either of us want that. So *go.*"

I could see the moment she came to her senses as her face lit with gratitude.

"Thank you," she breathed, and bolted toward the window.

"Wait!" I called, racing to where she'd halted. I shoved the dagger I hadn't previously bothered unsheathing into her hand. "Take this. But cut me first." I sliced my hand across my side, showing her where I wanted the wound. "Here. On my waist. Not too deep."

Lifting my shirt, I winced as I braced.

She didn't hesitate to follow instructions with a slice deeper than I expected. I hissed and let a string of curses fly from my lips.

"Sorry!" she cried, hands waving so wildly she nearly dropped the blade. "I'm sorry."

Hunched in pain, I gritted out, "Just go!"

Fuck. I fell to the floor, trying to staunch the blood. *At least it's believable.*

When the girl reached the window, she hesitated. "In

the cabinet, there's herbs you can use to make a poultice. It prevents infections."

I nodded my thanks, still gritting my teeth and unwilling to divert energy into speaking. Before she opened the window and fled, the girl paused once more.

"My name's Grethen. Thank you."

I nodded again, not watching her leave. She wasn't my problem now; it was up to her whether she escaped or not. I was already on my way to rummaging through her cabinet to see what I could use. I spied dried herbs in a small, porous bag and grabbed them. I took a sniff but couldn't identify what the bag contained. I poured water from my bottle over it anyway, wincing as I pressed the poultice against my gaping wound. When I departed the hovel, I didn't look back.

Outside, I paused, sensing quiet to the east. None of Gerod's men lingered; their combined hoots of glory came from the west. Even injured, I might escape. My muscles instinctively tensed.

Zaria. I'm coming.

I gritted my teeth.

I'm not.

I needed Lazlian. If I left him, they might kill him. If I couldn't trade him, I might never get her out.

I had no way forward in that direction, no choice but to keep things as they were until a path presented itself.

As I'd waited for Zaria at Volmar's manor for so long.

Hating every step, I headed toward the men's voices. They were gathered by one of the dwellings, thankfully alone. I didn't think I could handle seeing prisoners. Only Nico was missing, guarding those who remained alive, I presumed.

Craigory was the first to spot me.

"Didn't know you had it in you," he taunted, casually wiping someone else's blood from his dirty chin. "Think we're rubbing off on you."

"Keep a man in a cage long enough and what do you expect will happen when you let him out?" I replied, lifting one shoulder. Craigory sounded casual but I knew he was angry that I'd gotten to the girl first.

"I see she's escaped. Did you get a chance to pull up your pants before she carved out a piece of you?" he mocked, pointing his gun in the direction of my wound.

"I got a chance to gift her with a piece of me before she took out this one," I volleyed, morphing my grin into a sneer of disgust as I ignored my roiling stomach. "What she took will heal, but what I gave her might grow."

They cackled like animals, but shame clung to me, covered me. It was like molasses coating my limbs, making it hard to suck in air, to walk. Like I'd never wash it off. Despite having saved Grethen, what I'd done to do it, what I'd said... even just walking next to these men felt like a I'd grown a skin of shame I'd never shed.

She might be scarred, I told myself, *but at least she has hope.*

The others... I closed my eyes like it could stop the picture forming in my mind. *The others who cross my path over the next few weeks...*

I couldn't give them the same chance.

THEIR FACES, like their screams and pleas for mercy, blended together. They morphed to create new faces that never existed, multiplied until a sea of victims wailed in my head, drowning out everything else.

In reality, I hadn't killed many. Small raids, small villages not even proper clans. Large stains on my soul, although I wasn't even sure I believed in souls. They were all armed men, and that was a consolation. After the first raid, any meager villages we attacked were ready to fight back and had already gotten the women and children to safety. Gerod raided to steal and to kill. Squeo sold whatever they got their hands on, sometimes travelling back to the Ex.

Lazlian's curiosity got the better of him, and he began speaking a little. From his few, snide comments, I knew he resented the privileges being a pistol pet afforded me -- namely, getting time out of the basement. Yet I would rather have suffered the isolation of the dark cell than be forced to shoot innocent people.

"I know you would have killed the girl," I accused Lazlian when I returned from the first raid.

"It would be the most efficient and effective course of action," he replied, unrepentant. "Surely you killed many during your years scurrying around as a mainland rat. And what about your schemes with Mal-Yin?"

"Only those who attacked us first," I said, staring into the darkness and unmoving. "We never raided. And with Mal it's not like this -- unprovoked. There's a line. I don't know where it is exactly, but I know I've crossed it."

I had no intention of declaring my thoughts to *him,* but I couldn't stop from muttering, "How can I live with myself for the rest of my life? How can I look at her?"

Lazlian was quiet for a while. I didn't think he meant to reply to a question I'd never meant to announce. But he spoke.

"I've done more than that in the name of Rythas and

while you were still a snot-nosed kid running around and playing make-believe games in your library."

I didn't respond, didn't even shrug. I just stared at a ceiling I couldn't really see. The privileged prick had no idea what it was like to grow up in the backlands, to be under constant threat of death before you were even born. Yet Theo and I had managed not to engage in whatever horrors Lazlian undertook in his cushy castle.

What I was doing now was different than what I'd planned to do in taking Zaria to Spade City, or even in providing information to help quicken the end of war. At least, that's what I told myself. It was hard to sort out much in the endless darkness.

Lazlian's dark morality didn't help.

"You're speaking half-truths," he declared when I failed to reply. "That's your problem. You didn't kill innocents, you killed innocents to save Zaria. Never neglect the end of that sentence. Repeat it over and over until it's inseparable in your brain."

I stayed quiet, sure even refuting his unsolicited advice would only encourage it.

"After a while you can shift your focus to the last part, that critical part, and start to ignore the first. Concentrate long enough and one day you'll no longer even require telling yourself the first half," he said, his words echoing off the walls of the empty cellar. "You saved Zaria. That is all."

I snorted. "That's how you become a sociopath."

"That's how you become a survivor."

"Maybe they're the same damn thing," I said angrily.

"Maybe," he agreed.

~

THANKFULLY, as opportunities died down, many of Gerod's next missions simply had me on lookout, paired with Squeo or another man to act as potential sharpshooters. Occasionally, materials were brought to Lazlian, testing his ability to repair electrical equipment. He was always thoroughly searched and the items accounted for, making stealing a spare bit of metal impossible.

But mostly, Laz remained in the dark with nothing to do. Speaking and moving less and less.

On a whim after a raid one day, I stooped and tore a fistful of grass from the earth, pocketing it before I could be seen. When I returned to the cellar and the door swung closed with its ominous thud, some light remained from the lone burning candle.

I stretched my hand between the bars and held the springy clump of grass, earth clinging to its base, for Lazlian to take.

"What's this?" he asked, frowning.

"Grass." I shrugged, stating the obvious. It suddenly felt like a stupid gesture. This was the kind of gift Zaria would appreciate, something to help her hang on. Lazlian wasn't the type who sought out nature. Save riding, he seemed to distance himself from physical activities outside the castle walls.

"You bring... dirt?" Lazlian mocked. "You couldn't smuggle a piece of metal we might fashion into a key or at the very least something to eat other than crumbs of bricks?"

"You know I would if I could."

"The most abundant resource in the world, and therefore, the lowest. That is what you bring. If you courted Zaria with such presents, it's no wonder she sought the benefit of my good breeding."

It was painfully obvious that Lazlian only said such words to wound, and I was secure in the knowledge that he was wrong -- I could and had outspent him. I also understood why he lashed out and wisely bit my tongue from putting him in his place.

But I tossed the grass across the floor of his cell with a sneer. Which, admittedly, might have been childish, but in my estimation still made me the bigger man.

"Get fucked," I said, and turned away.

"Your wife isn't here for the enjoyment," he retorted.

I didn't turn back. "Mention fucking my wife again and I'll cut off the parts of your body you need for the act."

I might not be able to, but I could probably coax Gerod into something horrific and Laz knew it.

That night, the candle burned out and I laid in the darkness, unable to sleep. I knew from Lazlian's breathing he'd drifted off into a slumber so deep that he did not stir when the black door atop the stairs opened. I shot up, bracing, readying for anything.

Thump, thump, thump... footsteps echoed to reveal Squeo. I sighed as he wordlessly shoved a cup of water into my cage. Quickly, he turned and departed back up the steps.

But before the door closed, reducing the coveted square of light until it was no more, I caught a glimpse of Lazlian's sleeping form.

He lay on his side, fingers curled around the grass splayed beneath his nose and against his lips.

CHAPTER 35

MONSTER
Zaria

Tomorrow night, I escape. Ollier and me. We run.

Excitement coursed through my body like some modern, electrical current. I hadn't been this energized in months. It had taken that long to earn Ollier's trust and to sway his loyalty.

The wasting calmed in the second trimester, so I ate my fill of whatever Ollier brought me. This night it included boiled potatoes, hunks of roast pork, and all the bread and bricks I could stomach. Unsure what we'd meet on the road ahead, I wanted as many calories as I could consume. After dinner, Ollier even snuck me a piece of berry pie that was reserved for Hektir and whomever he favored that week. This time, I kept the berries down.

Ollier and I said nothing when Jemmy or Murlow entered the room, but we snuck knowing, anticipatory glances at one another.

Tomorrow night, they seemed to say.

I rubbed my belly and thought, *I told you we'd escape.*

Having stuffed myself more than ever, I was laying on my birthing bed to rest when Breyline sashayed into the room. Immediately, I sat up. Being in a vulnerable position around her always discomforted me.

"You think you're clever, don't you?" she snapped.

Here we go again. Unprovoked, Breyline often said biting things to me whenever she deigned to enter my room.

Annoyed with her nastiness more than usual, I shrugged and quipped, "Well, lying to myself is something I've learned not to do, so..."

The look she gave me could wither entire forests. I bit back a grin.

"Hektir making *me* fetch messages was terribly rude," Breyline glided around my bed, centrally placed in the room. I didn't like how it gave her the effect of a picture I'd once seen in a book, of sharks circling to attack. It made the hair on my neck rise. "But everything has a reason and God's purpose in that was to deliver me unto greatness."

"What are you talking about?" I said impatiently.

"I received news from Rythas," Breyline drawled. Her brown eyes shone with something new, something fresh. No, it was rotten. Like a decaying corpse rising from the bottom of a swamp to the surface. "Do you know what the rumor in Rythas is?"

Breyline's eyes flicked pointedly to my belly and I felt the color drain from my face before I could stop it.

"Multiple marriages weren't enough for you, were they? They say you've taken a position as His Royal Mistress and that the baby inside your womb isn't your husband's," Breyline gloated. Giddiness barely contained, it bubbled to the swamp's surface like rancid pockets of air. "That baby is

King Lazlian's. An heir Hektir would love to get his hands on."

My stomach lurched. *To torture. To kill,* came the dizzying thought. I did my best to keep a straight face but my weakened state didn't improve any ability to lie.

Please god, no.

Breyline cackled, delighted. "I wish you could see your face! Once a whore, always a whore."

"What do you want?" I whispered, knowing whatever it was, I'd give it to her. She knew it too. *Money, position, power... who cared?* I only needed to promise enough until the next evening, when I'd escape.

"First, you will not take that tone with me," she snapped. "Then we are going to Hektir together. You're going to confess that you've been conspiring with me. You and I have been working on a plan this entire time. Doing my bidding, you set up Ollier, rooting out a traitor in our midst."

I was sure my heart stopped beating.

"Oh yes," Breyline cooed in that strangely melodic voice. It did not at all match her hateful eyes. "I know all about that too. You think I haven't been listening to your late-night talks? Ollier's planning to help you escape tomorrow. Don't insult my intelligence by denying it."

"Why would Hektir believe for one moment that my allegiance has changed to *you?*" I asked, stalling, desperate. My heart and blood pressure climbed while my entire body trembled. I tried to control it because I worried what such stress would do to the baby inside me.

"Because you'll *make* him believe it," Breyline said, snarling. "Why would you be so different from your disloyal and traitorous husband anyway? Men are easily persuaded by things they don't understand. Tell him us girls stick together or you were impressed by my brilliance. I don't care how you do it."

Convince Hektir I think Breyline is brilliant? He wasn't stupid and knew I wasn't either.

"Hektir would kill Ollier for betraying him," I whispered.

"Yes," Breyline said, though it came out almost like a question, as if it didn't bear discussing at all. "And you will watch The Daggering with satisfaction. If you cry one tear, I will tell him about your baby and then you'll be crying a lot more."

"Don't do this, please," I begged, shaking my head and clutching the edges of my bed. Tears leaked; I couldn't stop them. Even if I'd felt energized by my plan, I'd spent months losing physical strength. While my belly swelled, everywhere else I shrank, losing weight from my inability to keep food down. Malnourished, weakened, and frequently in pain, I wasn't a worthy adversary to anyone in my current state.

Ignoring me, Breyline continued, "Secondly, you will write a letter to your sister, requesting the deliverance of three Elowan specimens -- two females and a male -- and you will not tell Hektir about that part. Not yet."

Elowans? What did she want with my people? Wasn't impressing Hektir with manipulating me enough? Or did Breyline's ambition carry her on to bigger and better things?

"Why do you want Elowans?" I asked, not really expecting an honest answer, nor did I get one.

"It's not your concern," Breyline snapped, annoyed. "The Aureum will take your island anyway, once war is declared. I will be the one to get the pretty little Elowans in hand, *now.*"

I often struggled to imagine what the Spades would do with my people, but I'd heard stories. Their scientists acted as if we possessed genetic keys to unlock their clan's own grandiose potential, instead of acknowledging my people for what we really were -- the descendants of some cosmetic engineering ages ago, concentrated by mating with one another due to the limited number of partners on our island.

Well... maybe the genetic selection *had* gone beyond a surface-level beauty to include some other talents and abilities, but I didn't think we were as extraordinary as the Spades wanted to believe. Sure, we possessed better odds of conceiving, but it wasn't like they needed more people, considering how many they stole and enslaved.

But they can experiment on us anyway, I reminded myself. *Breed with us. Who knows? I'd be consigning three people to that fate with any letter I wrote to Aewna.*

"You're wasting my time," Breyline said, annoyed at my prolonged silence. "Stop crying. We both know you'll do anything to save the king's baby and hold onto his power."

My stomach rioted, seconds away from emptying all that food I'd overeaten. "Please don't make me betray Ollier."

"He dies or your baby dies. You decide."

Oh god, what kind of choice was that?

Unable to swallow back the bile, I raced to the nearby sink and vomited a continuous stream of everything I'd just consumed. By the time I'd finished, I was gasping for air. Still I stalled, cleaning my mouth slowly and longer than necessary with water running through their metal pipe.

I wasn't stupid enough to hope that Breyline wouldn't tell Hektir about my baby as soon as I'd done as she commanded. I'd lose both. Ollier, and next, my child.

But if I didn't do as she ordered, I'd lose my baby *now*. The only thing I could buy was time...

...and buy it with Ollier's death.

This can't be happening.

My legs wobbled as if all the strength had been sucked from my muscles and my bones had turned to jelly. I didn't trust myself not to collapse. Slowly, I hobbled back to my bed and hauled myself onto it. By the time I'd managed it, tears soaked my face and I'd let out embarrassing little whimpers for Breyline's enjoyment. I wiped my nose with the back of my hand so that mucus wouldn't drip into my mouth as I spoke.

Curling into myself, my voice cracked as I said, "I'll do it. Just please don't hurt my baby."

I thought she'd cackle and gloat, but Breyline didn't even acknowledge that she'd won. I guessed she already knew. Instead, she drew back her hand and violently slapped me across the face. My own hand flew to my check, and the other to my belly, on instinct.

"I said stop weeping!" Breyline ordered.

Before I could even decide how to react, she grinned with triumph and said, "Apologize for making me do that."

"What is wrong with you?" I cried, sore and admittedly scared for what she might do next.

"You're an untrustworthy little whore with no sense of honor. I need proof that you're cowed enough and won't try your deceptions on me. Apologize."

"I apologize." I couldn't keep the bite from my tone and instantly regretted it. Frightened, I dipped my head lower in submission and begged, "But please, don't make me do this."

Breyline looked at me with glee in her glazed eyes.

"Dry your tears, they don't work on me. First, we'll

report to Hektir together, and you better perform. Give the performance of your life, because your baby's depends on it. Then we'll sit down and write to your sister requesting the Elowans." Breyline narrowed her eyes and added, "And don't get your hopes up, I'm not sending them you."

I hated Breyline more than I ever hated anyone. I wanted to cut out her tongue so that she couldn't speak her evil any longer. I wanted to cut off her hands so that she couldn't even write to tell Hektir about my baby. But I could only cower and cry as she lorded above me and laid out my orders. Breyline would collect me in the morning and I was to confess our supposed scheme to Hektir. I'd tell him of how *we* collaborated, instead of Ollier and me. I'd tell him I tested Ollier at Breyline's behest, as she suspected he was a traitor.

And I'd prove it all by betraying Ollier. When he came to collect me for our planned escape, Hektir would be waiting in the shadows for the trap to spring.

Ollier would be seized and executed. Throughout the Daggering, Breyline insisted, I would show no emotion except satisfaction for having our plans fulfilled.

When she concluded, Breyline studied me, her mouth set into an angry frown. She was too young for the creases beside her lips to have set, but I knew she'd formed them from repeatedly making that face of disgust.

"You know, you must have some cunning in you to have convinced Ollier to do your bidding. You almost escaped. I'll give you that. You're good," Breyline said, bringing her face so close to mine I could smell her powdery perfume. She smiled and concluded, "I'm better."

THAT NIGHT, I resolved myself to my fate.

I would do what I had to so that I could return to those I loved. I would do it for Teddy and for this little baby. What other choice was there?

Breyline was not the clever schemer she believed herself to be. She was rash, short-sighted, and vain. But it didn't matter. Given power, a foolish person can cause just as much damage as a clever one -- likely more.

I had no better choice, but I knew I'd never be the same after I did this to Ollier.

This was different than all the other deaths I'd been responsible for. This was not an enemy in battle.

He wasn't the bad guy. I was.

HEKTIR REMAINED HIGHLY suspicious of my supposed *Breyline is so brilliant* motivation to team up with her. He was even less convinced by my trying a *girl's stick together* tactic.

But when the trap was sprung and Hektir caught Ollier in the act of betraying his little gang, the frightening leader was convinced.

The look on Ollier's face when he realized I'd betrayed him would haunt me until I died. I added it to the little girl in the wagon when Kirwyn and I were in the backlands. But this was much worse. Now, I was wholly responsible for everything horrifying about to happen to the terrified and whimpering man.

Hektir dragged Ollier to the communications room. I was seldom permitted within, but either my trickery gained me access or this was a warning Hektir wanted me to witness.

Ollier was tied with rope while he screamed his protests

and innocence. When that didn't work he cursed me. I hadn't known the extent of mainland curses but I was sure he'd given me every one and even surer I deserved them.

Hektir, Murlow, Jemmy and Breyline withdrew their daggers. Ollier's blood-curdling screams began before they did.

Oh god, oh god, oh god. Sweat dripped down my back and my hands shook.

Don't react, I screamed at myself. *For the love of your baby, your kingdom, Teddy and Kirwyn and Laz... don't cry.*

Hektir drew first blood, cutting Ollier with his dagger, and a dance of death began around the skinny man. Everyone took a turn, circling him and striking at random.

I bit the inside of my cheek to keep from sobbing. If my performance was less than perfect, any flaws went unnoticed as Ollier, wretched in his pain, kept everyone's focus. It didn't take more than a few slices for his horrified gaze of betrayal to leave me. Lost to the agony of a slow death, he looked everywhere as he cried. Each shriek was excruciating enough to pierce the fabric of my soul and carve a scar I'd carry forever.

It was a deserved wound to bear.

None took pity and ended Ollier's life quickly with a deep, penetrating stab. They danced in a circle of bloodlust, drawing sharp blades across tender flesh and letting him bleed out, one cut at a time. My betrayal reduced Ollier to a howling, wretched boy on the ground. There had never been and would never be a desire greater than I had at that moment to grab a gun and end his agony.

With all the effort in my body, I made my hands stay at my side.

Murlow skipped toward the bloodied man and sliced again, causing Ollier to scream.

"A princess's ears shouldn't be subjected to such horribly offensive cries," I snapped, before I could stop myself. "Either end them or I'm leaving."

Hektir raised his brows at me appreciatively, as if he hadn't remembered my royal status until now. He gave me a slight, playful bow, then turned to Ollier.

"Please don't kill me," Ollier begged, huddled helplessly on the floor.

Hektir tossed his dagger in the air and caught it by the handle. In one quick move, he knelt and plunged the blade into Ollier's heart.

Ollier's body lurched, curling inward before falling back, lifeless.

It was over.

I pushed myself to the silence under the sea. I was there, not here. Floating in a quiet ocean. I'd be just as silent and serene.

Breyline escorted me back to my room. The more I yearned to hang my head in shame and misery, the higher I lifted my chin. Stoicism was the only defense I had against something like a Daggering happening to my baby. There'd be dark, endless days and nights to sob alone. Not now.

"Sit, whore," Breyline commanded in my room. "It's time to write to your sister. And don't try anything funny, don't try to send her any secret messages. You will write *exactly* what I say."

I sat. I wrote.

I made sure my hand did not shake so much that my unsteady penmanship marred the strokes.

I made sure my tears fell onto my lap and not the letter.

And just as I was told, I made sure *Breyline's voice* came through, unfiltered in my words.

CHAPTER 36

MADNESS
Lazlian

I wished that Kirwyn would shut the fuck up.

In the early days of our imprisonment, he chattered as if his words were keys to free us.

Gerod had added better locks, so that wasn't likely.

I didn't need her prince's talk, I needed my legs to heal. I needed something to occupy my mind in this hellscape -- something other than his attempts at conversation.

Kirwyn returned from his raids so morose I could feel his self-pity infecting the air and expanding to encompass the entire cellar.

It was offensive, too. *Poor baby.* I would rather have been conscripted to killing missions than to waste away in the endless, tomb-like darkness. Sometimes I thought that if had to endure another hour, I'd go mad. Sometimes I thought I already had. It mattered not -- another hour came and there was nothing I could do to stop it.

Zaria's emotions tended to take up space too, but I

enjoyed that. Her arousal revealed her when it permeated the air, wrapping me in that needy cocoon of desire she begged me to sate.

For years I had three distinct fantasies of the little queen -- which worked out rather nicely as she had three distinct holes. I liked to shuffle them in the evening, before falling asleep. In the first, I'd imagine my father had selected her for me and this time, she'd arrive *untouched* for the despoiling. My second fantasy was under similar circumstances, only in this version, when Zaria was naked and pinned, she'd laugh. The little queen would have the gall to tell me -- just as she had when we'd once negotiated in the war tower -- that she'd taken the birth control shot and would give me no heirs.

Calmly, I'd nod and flip her over, ass in the air. It would be my turn to laugh as I told her that if she couldn't give me an heir, I would amuse myself with other areas of her body until she could.

My third fantasy had entertained me often, as, for a long time, it was the only one plausible. The others had been stolen from me.

Laying on my bed in High Spire, I used to picture returning to my room after some business with the Assembly of Elites. Zaria would be waiting on her knees with her mouth open and wearing the bejeweled body chain. Nothing but the adoration in her eyes would fill the space between us. I'd lower my pants and she'd take me in her eager mouth, sucking away my stresses of the day. If I felt generous, I'd use my fingers to make her come, rule her head by my hand.

It was as much of a surprise that the little queen got off so lewdly on my fingers, as it was that I enjoyed it. There was something degrading about it, using a simple, everyday part of my body to stimulate the most private, sensitive part of hers. In those moments, it was as if I held her entirely in the palm of my hand.

Everything changed when she yielded to make our heir; everything I wanted was possible.

I never imagined that, not only would it all be snatched away again, *she'd* be snatched away and I'd be caged in a cellar with *him*.

Mentally I snorted, remembering there was a time when I believed the three of us could work together in some fashion. Maybe I'd been desperate, but I said it to Zaria at her manor and actually meant it, for a moment.

Look at the three of us now. We aren't fit to lead anything. Thank the gods for my brother.

Juls would keep the kingdom together in my absence. He was the steady one who could be relied upon. I was the fuck-up and I'd fucked it all up.

Wait, no. None of that Kirwyn-style self-pity for me.

My water was within reach, so that was good. Sometimes Squeo placed it near the cell's door and I had to degrade myself and crawl like a broken thing to retrieve it.

Once I sat upon a throne and she crawled to me.

Not that Zaria was broken as she took me in her mouth that night. She'd been exquisite. Although, to get us there I'd had to break some rules, break some of her ties...

I rolled my neck and concentrated on the future, on how long it might take for my bones to heal. At least the pain in my legs was manageable. I supposed I had to thank Kirwyn for that. Not verbally, of course.

I'd have taken a thousand broken bones over the waterboarding. I despised the hose and how I embarrassed myself with obvious fear before the water even began to flow. They knew. Craigory saw it in my eyes and relished it.

That particular torture haunted my nightmares so frequently that there was little difference between sleep and wakefulness.

Squeo found it funny to tear off our fingernails, a torment that only stopped when they decided I would soon need use of my hands, though the promise of equipment hadn't materialized.

Perhaps I deserved some of the torture for how many years I'd inflicted it upon others, and I'd been far more creative than these men. But that was the thing about pain -- you didn't need to be intelligent, didn't need to find cunning ways to cause it. The end result was the same.

Agony. I was sentenced to float in the endless abyss, broken up only by the agony.

Weeks of alternating pain and blackness had passed when I heard Kirwyn sniffle one day... or night. It was all the same so there was no way of knowing.

Was he crying?

I glanced at the mainland rat to find him with his knees drawn to his face and his head bent between them.

"Kill many today?" I drawled.

"No," he said after a pause. "I missed the shot and he got away."

"Did you miss on purpose?" I asked, not really believing there to be another option.

"No," he said, surprising me. "And that's what makes it worse."

Ooh, that had to tear him up.

After a few seconds, Kirwyn wiped his nose and shrugged. "I'm sure they'll exact revenge for it."

I sucked in a long breath and exhaled slowly, wondering what fresh hell they'd soon visit upon us.

There was nothing we could do but wait, and as

expected, the clanless came that night. Morning. Whatever it was. They made Kirwyn whimper, while I was made to listen.

When Kirwyn was curled up in a ball and nursing his wounds, he seemed so pathetic... and no different than how I looked every time. It pissed me off. He was a prince of Rythas. How dare the clanless bring him so low? Who the fuck were they?

I didn't know why I said something; I just needed Kirwyn's moans to stop. I couldn't sleep with that racket. And anyway, he'd been cajoling me long enough that I thought it might buy me some time and shut him up for a bit.

"Zaria will forgive you for breaking your promise and trying to have me assassinated," I said. Hoping it would be a little encouraging, I admitted, "She hates me. Not just because I tried to lock her up and it's partially my fault that she was taken..." I paused and my lips twitched before I could get out the next part. "But because I lied to her about my son."

Had telling him proved my madness? It wasn't just the endless dark, it was his tortured cries. They were irritating and needed to stop.

Kirwyn's moans had dulled a bit, so I continued. "He wasn't my biological son, it was just easier to let everyone think he was. I met his mother shortly after he was born and we fell into a... companionship for a while. But too soon, there was a spate of clans clashing."

I swallowed, then admitted, "I couldn't protect them when it happened, when they were... killed."

I'd never said the words out loud and certainly never imagined doing so under these circumstances and to *him* of all people.

"Hektir is a Spade in name only," I said, hurrying to move onto the pertinent part. "Half the time he's AWOL, stirring up trouble on unsanctioned raids. It's more common in satellite compounds and villages. The Spades are not as unified as they'd have you believe."

"I know," Kirwyn said. His voice was weak but laced with some encouraging impatience. "I was there. But they're still united enough to defeat us."

I ignored his pessimism and continued, "Hektir liked to join the warring clans. For him it was an amusing way to pass the time when there wasn't an official Spade sweep. People were always happy to have his gun, hoping it would bring favor in the future and not understanding that the High Twelve didn't know of his diversions and if they had, they wouldn't have approved."

Kirwyn's moans had dulled to heavy breathing.

"Hektir led the attack that killed my son and his mother," I said, trying and failing not to picture it. "In return, I killed two of his men... and one turned out to be his younger brother. During the fight, I gave Hektir that scar and I thought I'd killed him too. He lay on his back as I stood above him, and he recognized me. He cursed me and screamed that he'd see me dead, see my entire family dead, see my dynasty brought to an end. The usual nonsense."

I didn't want to return to that day in my mind's eye, but I saw it. The battle was so thick it had drawn the attention of other Spades, and we didn't even have time to bury the dead before we were forced to flee. I hated Hektir for that too.

It seemed like another lifetime, one with sunlight. I'd been half wild then, fueled on fury for everything that had happened in Rythas and perhaps taking risks with my life because of it. But it wasn't just to forget. I'd forged ties, as well.

We were going to need them.

"I suppose Hektir didn't want to involve the High Twelve, because he'd have to confess to what he was up to. Or maybe he just didn't want to admit he'd been beaten."

Or maybe Hektir just likes to take matters into his own hands.

"I haven't even told Zaria the full story," I admitted. "I didn't see the point, as I thought he was dead. But the baby is safe," I quickly added. "As long as Hektir believes it's yours."

"No one is safe," Kirwyn whispered, so softly I wasn't sure I heard him at first. "No one but the Spades."

And then, voice heavy with defeat, Kirwyn told me of an unbelievable stockpile of weapons the Spades held, one that no clan could go up against. Not even all the clans united.

I didn't believe him. I didn't. But the sinking in my stomach did.

HELLFIRE WILL RAIN
Aewna

Bright beams of sunlight shone through the windows of the palace and onto my desk where I'd spread out my correspondence. A vase containing colorful Dahlias decorated one corner. Mal took every opportunity to slip new buds inside. In return I'd slip a particular stem into a book of his, or beneath the door to his room when he was in Elowa and staying at the palace.

It was a secret way we communicated when we could not outwardly show affection.

I sighed at the stacks of correspondence before me. Mal was not going to be pleased with the show of affection contained within.

Affection for my sister, more accurately, and what he would say was a lack of affection for him... but was really just defiance of his wishes.

In all fairness, Mal had been rather sneaky with his

weapons deal for the Spades. He had no right to get angry that I too handled some matters on my own.

I picked up the thin, white paper, examining it for the hundredth time.

I knew my sister's handwriting well enough to be sure the contents of the letter were real.

I knew my sister's heart well enough to be sure the sentiments conveyed within, were not.

Zaria was being held captive at an undisclosed location and someone had forced her to write this letter, imploring me to send three Elowans to a secret Spade compound for unknown reasons. The wording made it seem like Zaria was in agreement with this plan, that she herself desired it.

My sister would never.

My eyes fell upon another letter, one written in pretty penmanship with a crown and key emblem atop the parchment. Zaria's plea meant Merie's other letter must be true. Not that I'd doubted her integrity -- but Merie herself had left some room for uncertainty when she'd written, because she hadn't confirmed the fact with her own eyes.

Though my sister mentioned nothing of a baby, I knew Zaria was pregnant. The *only* thing in the world that would force her to write a letter requesting three of our own people was if someone had made a threat to her baby.

Beyond my bedroom wall, I heard Mal-Yin drop his weapon into the basket before entering through the secret passage. He wore a crisp, white shirt, clinging beautifully to his slim torso. The heat had caused him to unbutton the first two buttons, exposing the top of his chest, and to roll up his sleeves, revealing his forearms. This was as close as I could persuade him to dress for our weather. Mal had never worn a tunic and even trying to imagine him in one was almost comical in my mind.

Mal-Yin took the seat on the opposite side of my desk and over the next few minutes, I explained what had transpired and my decision for the demand I'd received. I'd never kept a secret from Mal before. But if he knew, he'd only have tried to stop me, and the fact that he still quietly did business with the Spades hadn't pleased me either.

"I have offered myself in place of the three requested Elowans," I told him. "It is done, I've already written my intent."

Mal stilled. Nothing gave him away, he might as well have been carved from marble as he carefully asked, "And they've agreed?"

"Perhaps they think me arrogant, or foolish, believing I can sway them by negotiating in person. Perhaps they're blinded by seeing a Braeni, or the queen regent, and cannot resist the opportunity to capture the bigger fish."

Whoever was behind this, they weren't as smart as they thought they were. Mal's shoulders subtly relaxed, but a muscle in his beautiful cheek feathered, betraying that he'd clenched his teeth. "Do you think I'm going to allow you to simply walk into a Spade stronghold and surrender yourself as some kind of hostage?"

"No, I do not," I answered the question I'd been anticipating. Folding my hands and placing them on the desk, I declared firmly, "But I think you respect my decisions too much to physically stop me."

Mal studied me with dark, dangerous eyes. "Are you punishing me for selling the Spades the FLO weapons? I *told* you, I added another letter to their design," he reminded. "Or are you forcing me to commit to a side now?"

"They believe me to be a fool?" I asked rhetorically, gesturing to the letter demanding hostages. "A soft-hearted, Elowan princess who knows little of how to navigate the world beyond? Let them. They know nothing of who I truly am and nothing of our relationship beyond your political aspirations." I lifted my chin and explained, "I will walk into their compound like the martyred queen they believe me, sacrificing herself for her people. But I will wear that tracker bracelet like you've long desired. You can follow at a safe distance with your men. Once I've been taken to whatever satellite or village they intend, you'll ambush it, saving both me and Zaria."

It was a good plan, and though I still didn't like the idea of being tagged like an animal, there was no better solution. It was a fair compromise, too. I wanted Mal and I united both in our aims *and* how to achieve them.

Mal-Yin smiled and there was something odd to the curve of his lips. I cocked my head, trying to work it out. *What about this situation could possibly cause him any satisfaction?* I'd briefly imagined he might shout, furious with me for offering myself up to the enemy... or at the very least, subject me to a lengthy lecture. Neither was his style, but I knew this played upon his greatest fear -- my endangerment at the hands of an enemy. Instead, Mal stood and walked around the table with a quiet, predatory gait; that feline saunter that meant he was up to something.

"They will check," he announced. "The Spades will search you for devices like that and remove them."

"Oh," I breathed, deflating. *Is that why he'd smiled? To crush my plan so easily? No, Mal was many things, but cruel wasn't one of them. Not to me.*

I tried not to panic, yet my entire scheme rested on him being able to find me with that bracelet.

"There's only one way I can track you and have it concealed from any sensors the Spades would use to detect such a device."

I instantly perked up. *Of course he has a solution.* "Yes?"

Mal half-sat on the desk, looking down at me as he declared, "The device will need to be implanted inside you, surgically. The Spades will search but won't find a locater beneath the surface of your skin. Not that deep, anyway."

I stared, waiting for Mal to tell me he was joking.

"You want to walk into a snake pit, that's my offer."

"You're lying," I said.

He raised his eyebrows. "You of all people know that I'm not."

"So I'll be permanently tagged somewhere *inside* my body, with no way to remove this tracking device unless I undergo another surgery?"

Mal dipped his head in a nod.

"Where, *exactly?*"

"May I?" Mal asked, scooting down to lift the hem of my dress. I nodded and he slid his hand underneath the material, raising gullbumps all over my skin. Mal's fingertips reached somewhere around my abdomen or my appendix or... I didn't even know where. It was terribly difficult to pay attention when Mal was caressing my bare skin, staring at me with his mysterious eyes, and hovering so close to my lips he could kiss them if he moved just a hair closer. Mal's fingers tensed and his breath caressed my face as he said, *"Here."* After the briefest moment, those same fingers moved downward, softly stroking the sensitive skin above my undergarments.

"I..." What were we talking about again? Mal's fingers dipped lower on each gentle pass. My cheeks heated, knowing he'd reach beneath the trim of my underwear if he kept going. "I..."

Tracking devices. I blinked and shook my head rapidly to

clear it. Leaning back, I guided Mal's hand away from my waist and chided, "You can't seduce me into being tagged."

The declaration came out rather breathy, but Mal let me push him away, resuming his half-lean on the desk. "I don't need to," he said. "I don't need to do anything at all except listen."

"Listen?" I repeated, perplexed and suspicious.

"Yes, I'll listen. Tell me your plan," he ordered, a bit smug. "What is your idea to accomplish this mission if it doesn't include tracking you? I'm listening."

Pointedly mirroring my earlier position, Mal folded his hands in his lap.

I let my mind scramble for several frustrating, fruitless seconds before giving up. Narrowing my eyes and crossing my arms, I said, "How is it that you always get your way? Everyone thinks you're the devil and I'm starting to believe it. Even when it seems like you have a temporary setback, something else just comes along that's better than what you originally wanted anyway. It's uncanny."

I knew that I pouted and resented the loss of composure. Mal seemed to bring out a side of me no one else could.

He gave me a satisfied shrug. "Make no mistake, I'm one-hundred percent against this entire plan. But since you're determined, this is the way it must be done. We'll travel to my compound where we have the staff. Only then can you surrender yourself to the Spades, and I will stay back and track you." Mal gently took my chin in his hands. "Do we have a deal, my darling?"

"I suppose," I sighed. "I'll write to Juls and Merie to let them know our intentions-"

Mal squirmed and dropped his hand. "I'd rather you didn't."

"Why?" I asked, suspicious. "So that you can rescue Zaria and come out the hero?"

"Well, yes, but also because they'll want to handle her release more... diplomatically. The delay will unnecessarily stall matters, and it may occur while you're inside the compound as well. I'm not willing to take that risk," Mal concluded.

I knew that while what he said was true, Mal also relished having information others did not.

"Whatever Juls intends will only interfere with my plan," he insisted.

I sighed. Juls never trusted Mal and was likely to oppose whatever he planned just to spite him. But in this case, I understood what else was happening.

"You're going to storm the location of wherever I'm held and kill everyone inside, aren't you?"

"Yes."

I closed my eyes. "Is this going to start a war?"

"I could say you started it the moment you inked that letter. When you promised to deliver yourself, knowing I'd follow." Mal stroked his chin and continued, "I could say they started it when they captured Zaria and wrote the demand in the first place. Or that it began when the Aureum turned hostile toward Rythas. Or when their scientists started pressuring the High Twelve to experiment on Elowans. Any number of events could be counted as contributing to this cold and escalating tension that's been going on for years."

Mal leaned back, resting his hands on the desk behind him. "But the first shot being fired? Yes, it will be the fury I'm going to unleash."

I took a steadying breath. I'd long known war was coming, but I never expected it to begin this way. The likeliest catalyst, I'd imagined, was the Spades invading Rythas and their army taking out the kingdom before moving onto Elowa.

I wondered why the Spades hadn't done so already. *Why bait us with messages written in the blood of rabbits and random estates set ablaze in Low Spire? What was the point?*

Now Mal would make a bloodbath of some satellite or secret military base and it could not go unanswered. This wouldn't just be the spark that lit the fuse, this would be an explosion in itself.

"You'll tarnish the image you've worked so hard to create," I protested.

Mal tilted his head and cocked a half-grin. "Or I'll polish it. Time will tell."

"Time?" I asked rhetorically. "Whoever wins this war will be the only one telling anything. I think the word you're looking for is victor."

Mal licked his lips and smirked. "I prefer the term liberator."

THE FIRST LETTER I wrote was to my mother, Enith, requesting her presence in Elowa. From our recent correspondence I knew that she'd had enough of Pama and Volmar's shenanigans and was ready to leave them to it. As Jona, Gereth, and Naseroson were all too young, Enith, protected by Mal's guards, would have to step in to oversee matters until I returned.

With Elowa settled, I exchanged letters over the next few moon cycles with Zaria's captors, confirming a location on the mainland where I'd arrive alone. The delivery address was a fortified outpost the Spades used for mail and trade, unhelpful in determining Zaria's actual location and dangerous to invade as Zaria's life might be at risk should we do so.

Several weeks later, Mal and I sailed across the God Sea in an unmarked ship, and, under the cover of night, traveled to Mal's heavily-guarded compound. It hadn't changed much in the years since I'd last walked his halls, but I had. Never would I have imagined returning to Mal-Yin's underground lair so willingly or holding the devil's hand and allowing him to place a locator inside me.

"Try not to look so smug," I told Mal when the doctors explained how he'd possess a corresponding device to keep tabs on my location at all times. Then I donned a flimsy robe, laid upon a table, and was promptly put to sleep.

When I awoke it was as if no time had passed. Mal and I were alone in a brightly-lit room. It took me a minute to clear my head as he told me there had been no complications. I didn't even feel the tracker inside me.

I did, however, see the mark.

"You'll remove this device once we've rescued Zaria, won't you?"

Mal didn't reply.

"*Won't you?*" I insisted, scowling.

"You always counsel patience," Mal said sagely. "So let's just take it one day at a time and see how things go."

I huffed, throwing Mal a look of displeasure.

"You forget that I can tell when someone's lying," I snapped. "You don't intend on ever removing this."

"Is it so bad, having me able to locate you at all times?" Mal tucked my hair behind my ear and pledged, "I will do whatever you ask, of course. But I ask that you wait until the war is over to decide. Or when we return here, I can have the surgeon put one in me as well. You can keep tabs on my location in return. Fair?"

"Yes," I said. "I'm holding you to that."

~

THE NEXT MORNING, Mal took my hand in his, leading me out of his compound. The day was bright, but brisk. Too chilly for the Elowan tunic I wore.

"My best guess is you're going to a satellite and once we storm it, chaos will ensue. The most important thing you need to do is use that time to get yourself away from the fighting and hide. I'll be able to locate you anywhere in the building, but if the Spades figure out what's going on, they'll use you as a hostage. If you're able, find Zaria and take her with you."

I nodded and my heart picked up speed just a little. I wasn't sure what to expect inside a satellite complex, but I was quick on my feet and good at hiding.

I didn't try to talk Mal out of a massacre, not when his worst fear had come to pass. I could tell he was reluctant to let me go as he continued stroking my hair. He wore camouflage clothing and was armed with more weapons than I could count or even find on his body. Not that I expected Mal to lead the charge, but he was always somewhere with his men.

"It's not luck," Mal said. "Well, not just luck."

"What is?" I asked.

"How things work out for me so well," he explained. "It's a two-part formula. When I think back on everything I've accomplished in life, nothing of value ever came without *both* components, they're inseparable. *Great risk and great effort.* Everything that means anything to me required both a huge risk and a monumental amount of work."

I smiled at his rather sensible confession. Inhaling, I caught the whiff of Verdnal smoke on his camo jacket. I knew that he'd smoked because he was nervous and tried not to show it.

"That's my secret to power. Boring, I know."

"It's not boring, it's admirable. And it's not the only factor in your favor," I insisted. I tucked that errant hair behind his ear, though I knew it would soon fall forward again. "I swear, diabolical forces work behind the scenes to bring you fortunate outcomes. Maybe you're not the devil, but perhaps you've sold him your soul."

"Well then, you've fooled us all," he replied, eyes twinkling with mischief. "Although many say the devil comes disguised as an angel."

"Me?" I asked, confused at the change in subject.

"You're the one in possession of my soul, so if you're the devil I've sold it to, your disguise is astounding."

I laughed and lightly smacked his chest, unsure whether to be flattered or insulted. He was stalling, and so was I.

"You look like an angel in your Elowan tunic," Mal mused, stroking my cheek. "Don't be afraid. I'll be tracking you every step of the way."

"I'm not," I replied truthfully. Well, I was a bit nervous. But not frightened. Not with Mal behind me.

I heard the rustle of his soldiers from the trees and knew it was time to go. Aric, Mal-Yin's closest guard, stepped forward and knelt before me.

Head low, he said with his whole heart, "I swear that I will accomplish my mission." Layered in mottled greens with a bulletproof vest beneath, the short, dark-haired man was also dressed for camouflage and for combat.

"Aric will lead the charge. This plan is in capable hands." Mal's eyes hardened and his jaw clenched as he swore, "If it's an army of demons I've got, know that I'm about to rain hellfire on the Spades for this."

"I know," I said gravely. I pitied them, but I would not cry tears for those who warfared, for those captured and enslaved, and for those who would experiment on my people.

The events that were about to unfold were inevitable. I would do anything to get my sister back, and Mal would stop at nothing to punish those who would harm me. Nothing could change that. This was who we were at our core.

Somewhere hidden in the forest, these Spades awaited my arrival at a village outpost or some secret satellite. But I was walking toward a compound of corpses.

They were all as good as dead, they just didn't know it yet.

CHAPTER 38

TETHER
Kirwyn

For a long time, I'd hoped to rouse Lazlian with promises of revenge, to entertain him with detailed stories of how we'd inflict pain on the clanless in return.

It hadn't worked.

I feared that if we ever escaped, his mind would be so broken he'd hardly be useful. But there was a glimmer -- he'd engaged me, once. He'd even gone so far as to confess a secret. Perhaps, regretting it, he'd retreated further into himself.

In the endless days and nights, my thoughts continually turned to Teddy and to Zaria. I wondered how she fared, scared and alone. Zaria had a goodness, an innocence. It made you want to protect it, posses it, play with it. *Corrupt it.*

That's what Lazlian wanted, I was sure.

If… *when* we found her, would she still be the same? Or would whatever she'd endured have permanently changed her? Would she look at me the same, or had I morphed into a man she didn't recognize?

Surely, I had on the outside. Gerod didn't allow Lazlian and I to shave or to bathe. We hardly ate. I passed my reflection once and quickly looked away. I didn't need to see it; I saw it in Lazlian. We were twins in filth, with threadbare clothing, matted hair, and beards covering our sunken cheeks.

Maintaining muscle through daily exercises was the only control I had. Although it was all for naught if we were to rot in the darkness, disappearing into the black hole that felt as if it would swallow us up and forget about us…

"You know she saved me," I said suddenly. "Zaria found me washed ashore one day, and she dragged me from the beach to her secret cave. I only found that out later when I regained consciousness."

Lazlian didn't say anything.

"When I awoke in a strange place, I assumed another clan had taken me. She entered the cave and I ambushed her. Pinned her to the ground and demanded to know who she fought for." I nearly smiled, thinking back. "She didn't know what I was talking about, of course."

Rubbing my hands over my scratchy beard, I continued, "I made her lower her dress so that I could see her mark. She wasn't too happy about that. I had to threaten her a little."

Lazlian remained quiet. I kept talking. For him. For me.

"When I saw her bare shoulder, I thought she was a freeborn. She used my confusion to grab a jar and attack me. Smacked it hard into my head."

I heard a small sound from Lazlian, a breathy laugh through his nose. "That sounds like her."

"Fucking hurt," I said. I gave a small laugh back, relieved that he'd spoken. "She fled the cave and I had to chase her. But she stumbled on a rock, cut herself, and cowered on the ground, visibly afraid."

Lazlian snorted. "That definitely sounds like her. She'll fight until she fails. Then she'll flee. And when she's caught, she'll fawn. Look up at you with those big eyes and expect you to forgive her for any damage she's done."

I didn't want to admit that he'd nailed her pattern. "Yeah, she can be a bit of a-"

"Brat," Lazlian snapped.

"I was going to say challenge," I hedged. After a pause, I added, "But you have to admit, even when she's running or when she's quiet, she never truly stops fighting. She's just biding her time. It's one of the things I love about her."

"I find it infuriating," Lazlian said dryly.

There was a long moment of silence during which I thought the conversation was over. But Lazlian spoke, stirring hope in my chest.

"So what happened next?" he asked, not bothering to hide his curiosity.

DARKNESS MAKES a man do funny things. Under the cover of night, when the moon or the stars still provide some glow, he might only go so far as to cheat or to steal. But in the endless black of that cellar, it was as if we existed in an abyss without time or consequence.

So I talked. I shared our past, Zaria's and mine,

revealing more as the darkness dragged on. What was the point in keeping secrets when we might not keep alive another day?

I told him how I liked her blushes. What caused them. What it sounded like when I kissed her neck and she whimpered, melting into me.

Some things are sacred, I swore, saving the most private matters to myself. How it felt when Teddy was born. How it filled me with love and pride just to look upon him. Times Zaria awoke from nightmares about the world and I caressed her until she calmed. How she looked when she smiled at me in the morning as sunlight haloed her golden hair. How hard she came when I held her down.

But when the clanless entered with the hose or brass knuckles, when Lazlian or I were curled on the floor and barely breathing from the pain, it was as if the darkness all around us seeped into my soul and the only way I could cast it out was to speak the secrets I hid in my heart.

Over the months, I shared every soft, beautiful moment, laying on that bloody, shit-stained floor.

Part of me did it for Zaria. Because I wanted Lazlian to take my words with him, should I die and he make it out alive. I wanted him to carry them back to her, for her to know that in my final moments I thought of her, loved her.

Part of me did it for him. Lazlian fared far worse than I did, and when vows of vengeance no longer tethered him to reality, only glimpses into her life and her mind had the power.

But part of me did it just for me. What began as a lifeline for Lazlian became my own way of holding on. We floated without end in that abyss, with nothing to anchor us in reality, in sanity. Nothing but our voices.

I listened as Lazlian confessed that he began tinkering

with equipment as a way to calm himself after what his father forced him to do, as well as to secretly defy Grahar with the forbidden act. I learned that he so deeply resented his father having died before he could confront him, that Laz sometimes wished he could find the late king's corpse at the bottom of the sea, raise it, and kill him all over again.

I even listened as Lazlian told me everything that happened after Zaria came to his bedchambers one day and he closed the door, fully intending to seduce her.

It was strange that I learned Lazlian so well, he could not so much as pause half a second too long without my discerning his hesitation. He could not say one word and mean another, without my gleaning his true aim. I knew Zaria didn't even know the king so well, and at times I doubted his brother did.

And then I realized that Juls could not. Whoever Lazlian was when he entered the darkness, he'd emerge a different man, if he emerged at all.

Like me.

I hated the clanless for that, how they irrevocably changed me, hurt me, and I hated my helplessness to the endless pain, the molding. I hated that they kept me from my wife, my son. My *son,* who should have been laughing on the beach with me. I hated them so much it consumed nearly all my thoughts in the quiet. I could create fantasies that lasted for hours, about how I'd torture them in return if I ever gained freedom.

It was my nourishment, and Lazlian's. We fed on love for her and hate for them, fantasies of coupling and killing. I dreamed of candles on a guava cake for Teddy's birthday, and then flames licking Craigory's face until it melted. I dreamed of stroking Zaria's hair and kissing her lips, and then breaking their noses with my forehead and tearing their flesh with my teeth.

I would have judged a man for such thoughts before I'd entered that cellar. But the darkness doesn't judge; the darkness knows.

And so did he.

THINGS IMPROVED when Gerod finally brought Lazlian some equipment to work on and more importantly, when Lazlian's bones healed and I could motivate him to regain muscle. The rods passing for his legs were inhumanly thin when the splints were first removed, and he couldn't put weight on either foot for very long. It took several weeks of pacing his cell before he was functioning normally. Eventually, we were able to compete on the floors of our respective cages -- push-ups, crunches, and anything else I could think of.

Not knowing when the torture was coming and what it entailed was a torment equal to whatever they ultimately decided.

Craigory waltzed into my cell one day and strapped me to a small, rickety chair. Needing to restrain me was already a dire sign. My heart hammered when I saw the container of oil -- this was new.

From his cage, Lazlian unleashed a string of curses. I guessed all the workouts had brought his testosterone levels *and* his arrogant temper back to their old heights.

I only half-heard him, needing to concentrate on surviving as Craigory poured a circle of a strange chemical around me. I smelled oil and... something else... and it was all too near. *He can't kill me or damage me too much,* I tried to reason. I'd become too effective a pistol pet... although missions had been scarce lately.

"Hey!" Craigory yelled at Lazlian gruffly, spitting as he spoke. "Shut up or I'll rip out your teeth. One at a time. You don't need your teeth to work."

Stop, Lazlian.

Instead, he added slamming fists onto the bars as he shouted.

Turning, Craigory threatened, "One more word outta you, just one, and I'll take a tooth. A tooth for every word."

I could see in Lazlian's eyes he read it as a challenge.

"Shut your fucking mouth, Callum!" I yelled, praying the son of a bitch listened for once in his life and thankful that I remembered to use his fake name. "Do you hear me?"

When the circle was complete, Craigory moved with cruel, exaggerated slowness as he fished a lighter from his pocket and flicked it. My pulse skyrocketed as I prepared for anything. Something had been added to that noxious oil. I had a feeling it was a bolstering agent of some kind, coaxing flames to intensify. Out of the corner of my eye, I saw Lazlian banging on the metal bars, growling and flashing his teeth like a wild animal. But he did as I said and kept from uttering actual words.

You won't die. You won't burn. You'll just sweat a lot, I repeated in my mind.

When Craigory dropped the lighter onto the oil, I took and held a deep breath.

A circle of hellfire erupted around me, accompanied by the brute's laugh. Torturous seconds dragged on. It was so intense I wondered if I suffered third degree burns, and my lungs screamed for air.

Air.

I need air.

A shot of frigid water from the hose quenched the fire as Craigory blasted it directly at me. It beat my flesh and slammed my chair onto the floor and back against the wall. He made sure to keep it near my face so that I still struggled to breathe.

Finally, all torments disappeared and I gasped, inhaling stale and smoky air that had never been sweeter.

Craigory cut my bonds to remove the rope and the chair, lest I find use for them in the future. I was too exhausted to stand, even after I was freed. Bored now, Craigory tromped up the stairs and I managed to curl into myself for warmth.

Lazlian did not offer words of encouragement.

"I am your king," he growled. "Don't tell me what to do."

"Then act smart and I won't have to."

The retort was hard to get out. My teeth chattered from the icy water, loud enough to be heard in the quiet cellar.

Lazlian pulled his threadbare shirt from his back and tossed it through the bars.

"Get out of your wet clothes and put this on," he said. "If you catch pneumonia, we'll never get out of here."

I grunted, but he was right. It seemed a monumental effort to make my limbs move, but I peeled the wet clothes from my body and pulled Lazlian's shirt over my head. I didn't have a chance to feel awkward about it because I was so exhausted, I passed out.

~

UNBEARABLE MONTHS PASSED.

"Zaria will have the baby soon," I said, staring up at the black ceiling after the lone candle had burned out. I wasn't sure exactly how long we'd been caged, but Zaria had to be in or nearing her third trimester. The idea that Hektir might deduce the baby as Lazlian's from his or her appearance, gnawed at me. Would he immediately kill it?

"Is it true that we can't beat the Spades?" Lazlian whispered to the darkness. To me. "Even with all the clans uniting and Mal's firepower?"

My voice seemed to merge with the dark and together we replied, "I have gone over every possibility in my mind and there is no way we win this war."

Somehow, the truth made the room even darker. Lazlian was quiet for long seconds. I shifted on the concrete floor, imagining soft bedding I might one day have again.

"If we escape and save Zaria, I want you to take her," Laz said. "But not to Spade City. Take Zaria, take my son or daughter, and run. Sail back to Rythas and collect Teddy, but then flee somewhere safe. Everyone probably thinks we're dead already and they might still believe the baby is yours, so no one will come looking for you."

"You want me to take your baby for you?" I asked slowly, with disbelief. "Somewhere in the backlands or the Southern Continent or..."

"Who is more invested in protecting her and her child? Who is more capable? I don't have a choice," Lazlian said gravely. "I must fight with Rythas, even if it's futile. It is you who must flee. Raise my child with her, somewhere far away from all this." Lazlian allowed a tinge of hope in his voice as he said, "Perhaps someday when he or she is grown, help lead my heir back to reclaim the throne we'll lose."

I was stunned speechless.

"Raise the babe like you... but not too much," Laz said with a snort. "That fucking arrogance is annoying."

"As if I could raise it *out* of a child from your blood," I snapped. "Your family is insufferable and you're the worst of them."

Lazlian said nothing and I imagined my words only pleased him. I pictured him smiling in the darkness.

"But you don't understand," I said, stroking the coarse beard I couldn't wait to someday shave. "She's not going to forgive me for what I've done here to the innocent..." I trailed off before my voice cracked.

"Oh, she will," Lazlian replied. "You'll have tarnished your blindingly shiny armor a bit, but she'll understand. She's forgiven me for worse."

"Maybe. But she won't forgive me for trying to assassinate you when I swore I wouldn't."

It was almost as if I could feel Lazlian roll the statement around in his head, considering it.

"She will be angry and you'll have to suffer her wrath. But she'll eventually come around. Deep down, she'll secretly be flattered, though she won't even admit that to herself."

I considered his words. It was possible. But then I admitted the last betrayal, the worst. "She won't forgive me for plotting to kidnap her out of Rythas. For betraying the kingdom. She won't understand."

I heard Lazlian inhale deeply through his nose, then slowly exhale. "That will require a grovel of immense proportions. I suggest you kneel as you beg, and often. Prepare for your knees to bruise, as it will take years for her to soften. Trust me, I know from experience," he quipped. "But you have one thing going for you that I didn't. She feels guilty too."

"You can't possibly be suggesting I exploit that," I said. *But of course he would.*

"I'm just saying," he protested, "you'd be justified to express your feelings about what she did in your absence."

I groaned, aching to ride, run, or even swim. I just needed to *move*. It helped me think.

"Alright," I said running my hand down my face. "If we live, I'll do what I can to fix this mess. The mess all *three* of us made."

CHAPTER 39

RISKY OPERATION
Aewna

I was resolute in performing my two jobs to the best of my ability. Unfortunately, the first was impossible to execute.

Focusing all of my attention on the second, I asked many questions about the Spade compound as three guards marched me discreetly through the metal and concrete halls. The dour-faced soldiers didn't always answer, but I could glean the truth when they did.

Mal-Yin didn't possess the details of every Spade satellite, but I was comforted by the fact that he must know *something* of this location where I'd been brought, as the complex was too large to be hidden. Half of the fortified buildings were above ground, and half, under. I was perplexed at having been brought into a military base over a lab of some kind. As I was quickly escorted through what appeared to be intentionally-emptied halls, it also became clear that pains were taken to ensure my presence remain secret from the Spades within.

It was wasted effort as Mal wasn't going to take any prisoners.

Our attack would come swiftly, and my second job was to get myself somewhere safe as soon as I heard gunfire. Carrying no weapons and surrendering as meekly as possible, I gave the Spades no reason to restrain me or to find me any threat. I hoped.

I'D BE a liar if I said my heart didn't race when the first sounds of our takeover reverberated through the echo-y compound. In the chaos, it was no trouble at all to bolt, shrink myself into ball, and hide in an air vent until the sounds of combat died down. But I didn't feel comforted by the ease with which I knew we'd succeed, as my heart already sank for how we'd failed.

It only took a few minutes before I emerged from the vent with my hands raised. Mal's men knew better than to shoot now, but guns made me nervous regardless.

When I spied Mal amongst his soldiers, the world around him faded. It blended into the gray of the corridors, and he was the only thing remaining in color. My leg twitched, wanting to race to him as Zaria would to Kirwyn, but I was conscious of so many eyes on us. Instead, Mal and I waited until we were in a room alone, but his arms were around me the second the door closed.

"You're safe," Mal sighed to himself, cradling my head against his chest.

"I am, but I couldn't save Zaria," I breathed, pulling back to look up at him. "She's not here."

I caught the flare of surprise in Mal's dark eyes -- an expression he rarely showed. A crease formed between his brow, another unusual occurrence.

"Not only am I now concerned with where she may be, but why?" he asked. "If the aim was to gather Elowans here as leverage or for experimentation, why is she being held separate?"

He didn't pose the question because there was no single answer, but rather, because there could be any number of reasons.

My sister might have pretended she'd betrayed us and had been granted special privileges elsewhere for it. We might have been kept separate for the simple sake of risk mitigation. *Don't put all your Elowan eggs in one basket,* I thought, wryly. Or... there could be more than one faction in this game. Players playing one another.

From his frown, I knew Mal came to the same conclusion. Someone would pay for making him a piece on the board, instead of the director moving everyone else around.

"They wanted to keep my presence hidden," I told Mal. "So I don't believe the Spades know I'm here. But whoever is behind the letters couldn't have originally guessed that I'd offer myself instead. Whatever their intent with this move, I don't believe it was to start a war."

Mal surveyed the carnage around us and fished a Verdnal cigarette from an interior jacket pocket. He lit it and took a drag before speaking.

"Well it did," he said simply.

IN REALITY, it wasn't that simple and it wasn't truly Mal's

doing -- or mine. The Spades had long been planning *something.*

But of the handful of clan members Mal kept alive, they knew nothing of the whereabouts of Kirwyn, Lazlian, or Zaria, and little of value about the High Twelve's intentions. Whoever it was that had coordinated with the person writing to me, they must have been killed in the fight. After Mal questioned each and I confirmed they were telling the truth, he executed them. I didn't feel overly remorseful for the deaths of these militant slavers who would bring me harm... but I still I flinched when Mal fired.

The hour grew late by the time Mal and I walked down an artificially-lit corridor to what would be our chambers. He told me he'd claimed the best rooms for us, and I didn't fight him on it. I insisted I stay with him at the newly-captured base, and he didn't fight me on that either.

Safe places for anyone to exist were quickly evaporating. Unless I traveled beyond the Cold Mountains or to the southern continent, I'd be endangered anywhere now. I suspected, in Mal's mind, keeping me close was the best alternative to sending me far away.

My feet ached as we walked to our new bedchambers, and I yearned for a bath. The compound didn't contain many private suites, most of it consisted of barrack-like accommodations where men and women slept by the dozens on cots in one large room. Five spoke-like hallways led to ten individual rooms for the higher-ranking officials. They seemed serviceable enough, if a little sterile.

Mal and I reached ours to find the light switch wasn't working, so we moved around in the darkness, looking for a table lamp. I heard Mal's knees hit a nightstand and then he fumbled with his hands until he found what he wanted. A click sounded, followed by light flooding the room.

I gasped as three things happened in rapid succession. First, I noticed a man in a wheelchair who sat near a wall aiming a gun at my head, yet he did not pull the trigger. Secondly, almost at the same time, Mal-Yin fluidly drew his own weapon and pointed it at the man.

Thirdly, my heart leapt into my throat and I squeaked.

I'd never stared down the barrel of a gun and it was every bit as frightening as I'd imagined, especially in the hands of a nervously-sweating enemy.

"Over here," Mal said, and I was sure to anyone else's ears he sounded calm. He wasn't. Standing seven or eight feet to my right, Mal might as well have been a thousand miles away. He couldn't make a move toward me and risk the man pulling the trigger. "Point your weapon at me. It's obviously me you want."

The man in the wheelchair let out a breath bordering on a pained hiss. He had floppy brown hair, a pointed chin, and looked to be in his thirties.

Through clenched teeth, the man protested, "You'll shoot me before I aim."

My stomach dropped the same way it did when a boat hit large waves and tossed me about, giving me a momentary sense of weightlessness, groundlessness. Maybe I wasn't the target, but I was now the leverage.

From the corner of my eye, I saw Mal's left hand twitch, aching to join his right to ensure a steadier shot if needed, but not wanting to make any sudden moves. Instead, Mal rose his hand in the air gradually. It was a cautionary, peaceful gesture.

"What is the alternative?" Mal asked. On the surface he sounded as cool and smooth as an undisturbed lake, but I could see beneath the level façade. Currents rushed, waters churned the lakebed, and a maelstrom brewed beneath his exterior. "You shoot her and then I shoot you?"

"I'm dead anyway!" the man cried. Sweat glistened off his face, so I could only imagine how much greased his nervous trigger finger. "I kill her, you kill me. I put the gun down, you kill me anyway. I know who you are."

I swallowed but did not move another muscle. Shock gave way to absolute terror and a cold sweat broke out all over my body.

"Care to keep things fair and tell me who you are?" Mal-Yin asked.

The man deliberated for a moment, then confessed, "Sergei."

"Sergei," Mal repeated, almost like a question, an invitation.

"My name is Peri, but everyone calls me Sergei, after the composer," he said in a nervous rush. "I compose. Play."

"I enjoy the music before the Great Decline and possess an extensive collection in my stronghold," Mal-Yin said. The dulcet tone of his voice swept gently across the room like music itself. "Rachmaninoff or Prokofiev?"

Sergei's lips curled into what might have been a smile, though it was full of mockery. "As if you care." He laughed a little manically, which increased my panic.

"Sergei," Mal pointedly used the man's name again. "Can you guess what I care about? I'm going to begin by admitting that I will do anything to keep Aewna alive. You have power over me. Very few in this world can claim such an achievement," Mal confessed. "There are moments where our choices have the ability to affect the rest of our lives. This is one such moment for us both. I'm going to offer you a proposition in which we both come out *having* a life. What do you want from me? Name it, and I will give it to you if you put the gun down."

Sergei flashed his clenched teeth. It was from indecision, I was sure, and not any lack of strength at holding his weapon. With arms more muscled than Mal's, were it a contest of pure stamina, we'd lose. Though more likely, guards would find us before that happened and we'd perish in a shootout. It was odd that no one had come by already.

"Do you want me to rain down gold and tokens upon your head?" Mal asked. "Give you a position of power and authority over others? Tell me what you want in exchange for her life."

"I don't want anything and I don't believe you," the man cried. Tears of frustration welled in his eyes and he had to blink to clear them.

I whimpered a little again and cursed myself. In desperation, Mal was actually telling the truth, but there was no way I could convince Sergei of it. Or rather, Mal believed his own words, for the moment. I couldn't swear he wouldn't take revenge on Sergei once his mind cleared the bargaining stage.

"A guard of mine, a man named Aric, was to have swept these chambers," Mal prompted. "It's unlikely he missed you. Either he's grossly incompetent or he betrayed me. Why don't you tell me the truth about what happened before Aewna and I entered this room?"

I blinked, startled at what I should have easily reasoned myself but had been too distracted by my life hanging in the balance.

Sergei's deliberation crept by for agonizing seconds. "He gave me the gun and said if I killed you, he'd spare my life. I don't believe him either, but if I didn't take it, he was going to kill me on the spot. Or you'd just shoot me like you shot up everyone else so I was dead either way. I would have shot you already, but I mistook her for you," Sergei said, minutely jutting his chin at me.

Aric is a traitor. How did I miss that?

It would explain why the guards hadn't stumbled upon us by now -- Aric was likely keeping them away. I blinked my confirmation to Mal. Sergei was telling the truth. Unfortunately, there still was no way to have the man trust that *we* were.

Unless... Sergei didn't *want* to shoot me.

"Sergei," I whispered, speaking for the first time. "I know you don't believe that Mal-Yin won't kill you as soon as you lower your weapon, and if I'm honest with you, you'd usually be correct. But I'm hoping you will believe me. I can be your guarantee. I will swear to you that if you drop your gun, we will take no harmful action against you in retaliation."

"Tell me, what do you do here when you're not composing?" Mal-Yin asked.

"I work in the backrooms. Tech," Sergei replied almost automatically. A bead of sweat dripped from his forehead onto his chest.

"You value logic, do you not?" Mal-Yin argued. "Think it through. The only path where you have any hope to continue living is by trusting us."

Sergei whimpered and cursed. Finally, he said, "I want my life." His eyes remained on me. "And my piano. It's been modified for me."

"Done," Mal promised.

With another curse, Sergei finally lowered his gun and Mal swiped it from his lap.

Are you okay? Mal asked me with his eyes and I nodded. I wasn't -- but I would be. As soon as this awful day was done and my reward was that I'd sleep in bed next to Mal, feel his arms around me.

Ignoring Sergei for the moment, Mal-Yin stepped into the hallway and called for Aric and several of his guards. A moment later, he re-appeared, entering the room with four others -- two men and two women.

Mal raised his gun at Sergei, whose eyes widened at the betrayal. Aric's were guarded, but alert.

Traitor.

"A man tried to kill me today and he'll die for it," Mal announced.

After a pointed pause, Mal swiveled, aimed his gun at Aric, and shot a bullet directly into the guard's head. Aric dropped dead to the floor. The other four guards gasped, and one jumped. I knew it was coming, but still started a little when it happened.

"He tried to assassinate me and takeover *my* clan using this man," Mal-Yin calmly told his guards. "He nearly killed Aewna in the process. Dispose of him outside the building and make sure his body is seen as you drag him through the hall." Dismissing them, he added, "Spread the story of what happened here."

With his hands on his hips, Mal turned back to Sergei.

"You're going to kill me now too, aren't you?" Sergei said, slumping in his chair.

"No. Now I'm more interested in you than I was when I walked in this room," Mal told Sergei, tucking his gun into the waistband of his pants. He pulled a chair opposite Sergei and sat, leaning toward the wary man. "Your skills are a welcome boon. I've got another proposition for you."

Sergei's eyebrows rose and he regarded Mal cautiously, as if he suspected Mal might pull a secret, secondary gun from thin air at any moment.

"We'll see that you're reunited with your piano. Compose an opera about today's events if you'd like, in your free time," Mal said, spreading his hand in offering. "But on the clock, I'd like to see what those fingers can achieve with the Spade comms. Show me your loyalty and you'll be rewarded with as many instruments as you desire. Attempt any trickery and you'll die slowly."

After a moment's hesitation, Sergei nodded. He was escorted from our room and promptly put to work. However, guards quickly took his place, combing every inch of the chambers for possible weapons of attack. An hour passed before every nook was sufficiently explored.

Once Mal and I were left alone, I fell into a chair and slipped my shoes from my aching feet.

"We still don't have Zaria and the Spades will retaliate," I said. "But the day is won, we're both alive, and one asset remains whose skills might prove useful. Are you pleased?"

"It's as I said," Mal replied, cocking a half-grin, "Great risk and great effort."

"It's as *I* said," I argued, "Every time you seem to have a setback, something else just comes along that works out in your favor even better. It's positively devilish."

"Will you come and kiss the devil?" Mal-Yin asked, tossing his gun onto the table and away from me.

"I thought I was the devil," I teased, suddenly re-energized. Barefoot, I crossed to where he stood. "The one you sold your soul to."

"Take pity on your wretched servant then," Mal said, tilting my chin up. "And grant him the mercy of your soft lips."

I melted into the wet familiarity of his mouth, but we'd only kissed for a moment before we were interrupted by a knock on our door. I bit back a tired sigh.

A female guard of Mal's apologetically entered the room and handed him a piece of paper. "It's from Sergei," she said. "Without anyone left to obstruct him, he's been able to access more of the Spade systems. Unfortunately, this was all he could glean before this complex seems to have been permanently cut off from Spade City."

Looking down at the paper, Mal's eyes widened slightly.

"Is it about Zaria?" I asked, hopeful. "Or where Kirwyn and Laz are being held?"

"This doesn't contain any information on the missing royals." Mal shook his head, brow knit. I could tell that beneath that look, his mind raced with plans. "But we've got a much bigger problem to deal with."

CHAPTER 40

COLLABORATION
Kirwyn

I hadn't been let out of my cage in a while, but the cellar was still warm, so I knew that fall hadn't fully arrived. As much as I ached to feel the sun on my skin, a part of me was secretly relieved. If given a chance, I didn't think I could deny myself the opportunity to break away, to run and find Zaria. But I knew the unspeakable horrors my escape would condemn Lazlian to, and I couldn't do that either.

Imagining the abundance of the summer beyond my cell, I dreamed of the ripened mangoes and paw-paws from our garden. Warm goat's milk and soft cheese right on the rickety table in our back parlor. Potatoes, oversalted to my pleasure and roasted chicken, dripping in juices for night's feast. I wondered if Spade bricks prevented scurvy and what nutritional deficiencies I might have, forced to subside on them. I knew Zaria wasn't eating much better if her pregnancy was like the last one.

We were afforded some diversion in Lazlian's repairs. Once, we thought we might be able to construct an explosive and blow our way out of our cages, but Gerod never provided the right materials and we were both physically checked, ensuring nothing had been stolen before the items were re-collected. We could perhaps hide something smaller, like a bolt or a screw, the same way I'd hidden my ring in a dirty corner of my cell. But with the newer locks Gerod had installed, even Laz couldn't pick his way out without something better to manipulate, so it wasn't worth the risk of getting caught.

The tortures continued. Now that Lazlian's legs had healed, Craigory only toyed with him more.

One day when the weather turned colder, the brute entered Laz's cell and before Craigory even finished removing the equipment out of it, he started swinging his fists. Having stuffed his pockets with the last of the metal plates, screws, and wires, the giant of a man turned his yellow-toothed grin to Laz, and I knew he wanted to rough him up for the fun of it.

I was forced to helplessly watch as Craigory punched Lazlian to the ground, then gleefully kicked him. But as he continued kicking, a wire sprung free of Craigory's pants pocket and uncoiled onto the filthy floor.

My eyes snapped to the metal, as did Lazlian's. Like a game of senorok, moves unfolded in my mind and hope trumpeted in my chest. There was no time to consider the consequences of failure, of getting caught. We only had a moment to act on the chance or lose it forever.

Before the brute could see the object, I called out, "Hey! Don't you think he's had enough?"

Of course I knew the answer, but I needed to buy time for Laz. Craigory turned to me, provoked by my audacity.

Move, I willed with my thoughts, heart thumping wildly. *Hurry.*

I kept my gaze on Craigory, but out of the corner of my eye I saw Lazlian crawl, stretching out his arm to grab the fallen wire.

"No," Craigory replied with a snarl. "Not yet."

I cursed that he was a man of few words as he turned back to his target, but to my immense relief, Laz had secreted the wire somewhere amongst his clothing. I watched, grimacing, as Craigory dragged Lazlian to his feet, only to punch him in the stomach several times, causing him to collapse onto the ground again.

As the brute stood above the king, Lazlian made an unusual sound -- a plaintive whimper. Its incorrect pitch was the most pleasing false note my ears had ever heard.

Some battles begin with a war cry, the beat of a drum, or the shot of gunfire.

This attack was signaled by Lazlian's lie of a lament.

Craigory threw his head back, roaring with laughter, and the fallen king's eyes met mine. Sweat dripped from his brow to the floor, but his gaze was cold and calculating. I could see what Laz planned; I'd worked out the same idea. In a fraction of a second, I knew the moves I needed to make and what Laz determined to do in return. We didn't need verbal cues any longer, all the words and sentences we'd used to dispel the darkness those long months had filled our cages to the brim, and we swam in each until we'd swallowed the other's; his thoughts became declarations that mingled with my own and we absorbed them in equal measure.

It now took only a glance for one of us to know the mind of the other.

"He's got no fight left in him," I called to Craigory, voice low and menacing, enticing with my insolence. "Try *me.*"

Craigory flashed a hungry smile in my direction, kicked Lazlian once more, and left him locked in his cage. Too much adrenaline raced through my veins for me to give in to the fear of Craigory's enormous size and his thickly corded muscles as he entered my cell, locking the door behind him.

My pulse raced at an alarming speed and sweat dripped down my back. I wasn't big enough to beat the brute, but I didn't need to.

Now. Now's the time we do it.

As soon as Craigory positioned himself, I lowered my head and charged like a wild bull, roaring as I pushed him against the cell wall and held him in place. I could only hope Lazlian didn't take long to work the wire through and around Craigory's neck. Painful seconds passed as I struggled against the force of Craigory's overdeveloped muscles. Finally, a grunt from Lazlian and the corresponding jerk in Craigory's body told me he'd done it.

"Hold him!" Lazlian shouted.

I grunted as I pushed, my muscles straining with exertion and screaming in pain. It would have been impossible to take Craigory down on my own, but fighting both my lock around his waist and Lazlian's wire at his throat was a dual attack giving us some hope of success. Craigory was torn between trying to yank the wire for air to breathe and raining stunningly painful blows upon my back for release. I prayed to all the Rythasian gods that he was too frantic to concentrate a hit to my spine. The slick sweat ringing his waist mingled with my own and threatened my grasp.

"Keep holding!" Lazlian grit out the encouragement. I felt Craigory's body twitch as Lazlian, I assumed, tightened the wire. I could see nothing, but I savored the brute's hideous noises.

With a final jerk, the fight in Craigory went out abruptly and I found myself supporting dead weight. I let go, and his body slumped to the floor.

We'd done it. We'd actually done it.

Triumph swelled in my chest. Through the bars, I met Lazlian's gaze and knew the same bloodlust in his eyes was mirrored in my own. We panted in unison, grime running over filthy, sweat-soaked skin.

Neither of us spoke. Checking to ensure Craigory was dead, I knelt and found the keys in his pants pocket. My heart beat a curiously steady pace as I unlocked my cell door and then Lazlian's. As many times as I played out our escape in my head, I'd pictured us gleefully rushing to freedom, with Lazlian spitting snappy insults at the corpses littering the floor. Yet we moved methodically, quietly.

Perhaps it was because we'd only just begun our escape and too much was still at stake, but it felt like something weightier. It was as if the moment held too much reverence for us to profane it with noise.

Before we departed, I took two things from my cell -- one, the ring I'd hidden in a dirty corner all this time, and two, Craigory's gun. Lazlian grabbed the metal pipe that had been used to break his legs all those months ago. Finally, we ascended the stairs and opened the door to freedom.

I almost wished we met more of a fight in the clanless. With the men asleep -- or awake but unprepared -- it was easy to pluck them one by one, restraining, gagging, and marching each man into the darkness.

We didn't kill them. Lazlian and I dragged our abductors to the cellar, shooting kneecaps if necessary. We tied them in the cages they'd built, most along the bars, but the ones with fresh bullet wounds we simply laid out on the floor.

Lazlian and I did the things we always talked about. The things we couldn't tell her, not in great detail.

It lasted for hours. If Lazlian's feigned wail was the best false note I'd ever heard, their pleas were perfectly pitched. When Lazlian took the lead, I closed my eyes and listened to their music. I knew no one on the outside would condone, let alone comprehend our actions in that moment, no matter how we explained the suffering we experienced. It could only be endured to be understood. Laz and I delivered those demons back to hell, we dragged them to death's door and kicked them onto the mat, bloody and begging to be taken that extra step.

We denied that that mercy and left, locking them tightly in their cages and leaving them for the unbearable pain and darkness to swallow.

Before departing, Lazlian scrounged around the small house to find his keylord necklace and silver cuff in an upstairs cabinet drawer -- such powerful symbols, utterly forgotten. Laz turned the key around in his hand a few times, then tossed it to me. I caught it with one hand.

"It's yours. I should have given it to you when I named you."

After a pause, I slid the necklace over my head. "You didn't really mean it then."

He wiped the blood that had splattered onto his forehead with the back of his hand and nodded. "I do now."

"Do you need a break or can you travel?" I asked, impatient to leave. "We can take food and supplies but I want to move quickly." *She kept us alive all this time,* I thought. *We have to move now to ensure we do the same for her.*

"I'm ready. Remember what you swore," Lazlian said, holding my gaze. "You have to take her and the baby far away. Look after them, protect them. It's for your own good -- all of you, and the kingdom too."

I shook my head. "It's a tempting offer, but I'd need her compliance. Even if she forgives me, she's not going to abandon Rythas and certainly not you. She would never tear you away from your child."

"She will under the right circumstances," Lazlian said ominously. I narrowed my eyes, not liking where this conversation was headed, nor the fact that I didn't entirely know how far he'd take it.

"And what circumstances are those?"

"If she hates me."

I half rolled my eyes. "She doesn't hate you."

"Oh trust," he replied with stoic assurance, "that I can make her hate me."

CHAPTER 41

PANDEMONIUM
Zaria

I wallowed. I wept. I *wailed.* I'd thought determination was my special gift, my power. Short of losing someone I loved, I didn't think I could despair this deeply.

Or maybe I did lose someone I loved -- the girl I'd been before I made the decision I'd made.

So many deaths in my wake, and each worse than the last.

It was hard to breathe when I thought about what could have been. Hektir learning the truth *might* not have meant an immediate death sentence for my baby. Maybe he would have instantly killed us both... maybe not. Hektir seemed to care for the continuation of my physical life, however little value he placed on my heart, on the devastation he'd render should he harm my child.

It was *possible* that even if Hektir knew Lazlian had fathered my child, he might have waited until the baby was born to murder it. And in that time I could have escaped, or been rescued. I could have risked it. I could have refused Breyline and stood by Ollier. I could have called her a liar to try to save Ollier's life. Breyline would tell Hektir the truth about my child, but by then he might have been so distracted with the power to enact vengeance on Lazlian's heir, that he dismissed any concerns about Ollier's loyalty.

If, maybe, possible, perhaps...

The chance, however slim, made me sob. It wasn't only that I'd betrayed Ollier, it was that I did it while there existed *some* possibility, however miniscule, that we all could have made it out alive. It was that I weighed my baby's life against that risk and decided not to take it.

Kirwyn would say it was logical, and it was. Lazlian would scoff that I'd care at all for a man who'd been part of the assassination plot, and he was right too.

Maybe someday those truths would soothe my conscience, but right now they felt cowardly.

Normally, I'd have regained strength as the wasting temporarily receded, but I lost it, having no will to eat. Breyline forced puréed food down my throat. I had no will to swallow it, but even less to fight her. I felt like a pig, fattened for the slaughter. Not my own, but my baby's.

The absolute, most horrendous fear that reverberated in my head was that I'd done it all for nothing. When my little one was born, Breyline was most likely going to rip him or her from my arms and present my baby to Hektir like a prize, having strung me along with false promises to gain my cooperation. In her eyes I had to live, so that Lazlian's offspring lived, so that his or her death could be used to gain favor.

My third trimester began and the end barreled down on me. I clutched my belly as if I could hold my baby in, keep it safe. He or she kicked back, as if to encourage me, and I wept harder because I was failing him or her.

I always know what to do. Eventually. But now all my plans and schemes had disappeared. Nightmares of my child's fate were unspeakable, although I found some words when I awoke because I was screaming.

Hektir investigated a few times and Breyline blamed my despondent behavior on my pregnancy. I probed her for news on the three Elowans and she refused to reply, although something about the question irritated her.

It was late one evening when I curled onto my side, protecting my heavy belly and wishing I could touch the sea.

That was my last thought before a sudden *boom* reverberated from outside the compound.

Or in? In between? An explosion?

Before I could ruminate, gunfire followed. I heard a lot of it, and this time, the sound was unmistakable.

I threw myself off the birthing bed where I spent nearly all of my time and scuttled barefoot down the hall to the communicator room. Generally, I wasn't allowed, but Hektir was too busy watching the screen to prevent me.

My heart leapt out of my chest, but it must have found its way back because it thumped wildly against my ribcage. Even with the distant footage and distorted images, I knew those men anywhere.

Kirwyn and Lazlian had found me.

I couldn't see their faces, covered in overgrown hair, but I knew the movements of their bodies like I knew my own.

My stomach lurched when I heard more gunfire and realized Jemmy was outside the compound, shooting at them.

"No!" I cried, alerting Hektir to my presence.

"Get her back in her room!" Hektir ordered, strapping a gun to his side and tucking another into the waistband of his pants. "Back us up once she's secured."

This is it, this is my chance.

But I hadn't the physical strength to take it -- to do *anything* about it other than scream my protests as Murlow seized me and half-dragged, half-carried me out.

Before I was pulled from the surveillance screen, I caught one final glimpse at the monitor and I watched something terrifying unfold, something not to be believed. A bullet from Jemmy's gun whizzed in the air and Kirwyn went down.

No.

No, no.

I didn't see that.

It was just like when Kirwyn went under the water the night he was ripped from me in Elowa. It was fine. He'd be fine.

Except... oh god. I didn't see him get back up again.

Murlow dragged me down the hall and shoved me into my room. I was forced to brace my stomach against his roughness rather than waste energy on a fruitless attempt to fight back when he locked me inside.

I went as still and silent as death, palms and neck sweating. There were no monitors to see outside, so my imagination ran wild.

Kirwyn fell into the sea one stormy night off the shores of Elowa. Twice, really. Once before I met him and once the night I was ripped from him. But he'd popped back up again each time, even if I wasn't there to witness it. So he must have this time too.

Except this wasn't the sea. This was the land, where no Elowan god reigned and anything could happen.

Only the sound of my heavy breathing filled the air.

Then I jumped when the distant blast of gunfire boomed again. Had I more time, I might have thought to scavenge the room and arm myself, but seconds later, Breyline entered. Dreadful. Smug.

"Your husband is dead."

I didn't believe the declaration, not for one second. I didn't even hear her words. Yet, somewhere deep in my body they must have resonated because an unbearable pain came from my womb. I doubled over and wetness spilled between my legs.

Oh god, not now.

Too soon. No, the baby shouldn't come this soon.

I had difficulty knowing what happened next; it was as if the world around me existed on another plane. Breyline's voice babbled nonsense, buried under layers of an impenetrable fog. Beyond that, all I knew was pain.

Kirwyn is not gone. My husband lives. You are wrong, wrong, wrong.

I was on the birthing bed, writhing in agony. It felt as if my entire body shrieked and convulsed to announce my baby was coming. This wasn't like when I had Theo, when the cramping began gently and escalated to a significant, but bearable, crescendo.

My love, my love, where are you? Not dead. You are not dead.

Something boomed in the air far away and I wondered if it was gunshots. Lazlian? Oh god, would he die too?

Agony ripped me back to the material world, to the birthing bed where I writhed. Breyline busied herself with hooking me up to a needle I knew was designed to bring medicine into my veins. *Why did Breyline even care to help ease my pain?* I felt like I was dying. Why not let me die?

Breyline moved around the bed with the maniacal

gleam in her eyes shining brighter than ever. As she hooked me up to more wires and machines, I knew the cause of her efforts and it made my heart scream. My worst fear was true.

Once my baby was born, it would be her prize to Hektir.

Once my baby was born, he or she was as good as dead.

Everything I'd done with Ollier had only bought me time, it didn't save my child's life.

No. I couldn't let it be in vain. I had to do something. *Use the time I'd been given. The time I'd stolen.*

Breyline's mouth was as glazed as her eyes from the repeated, anticipatory licking of her lips.

"Don't hurt my baby," I wheezed, tears slipping down my cheeks. I knew it would do no good, but I couldn't stop myself from begging.

Breyline's eyes darted to me. Her mouth cracked into that horrific, plastic smile.

Pitifully, I sobbed, knowing as soon as my little one came out of me, Breyline would snatch my newborn away. I might not even get a chance to hold him or her before she brought it to Hektir, along with the truth.

Please, god, no. Not my baby too.

I had to do *something* and might only have minutes to do it. Pain nearly consumed my thoughts entirely; if it escalated to another level, I wouldn't be able to act. Between cries and groans, I eyed the sharp, metal tools on the rolling bedside table. My hands, like the rest of my body, were slippery with sweat. If I attacked Breyline, I'd risk pulling the needle from my body -- the one flowing medicine into my veins. It was the only thing going to make the pain manageable. But if I didn't seize an opportunity to stop Breyline now, I might not get another.

I desperately wanted the pain to end. Second only to

needing Breyline dead. She was inhuman; pure evil embodied. The monster hovered over me, delirious excitement behind those big, dumb eyes. I needed to close them forever.

Don't think about the consequences.

When Breyline's back turned to check something on her electronic screen, I stretched out my arm and grabbed the nearest, sharpest scalpel.

For my baby. I won't let you hurt my baby.

Breyline turned back around and moved close to my head.

With a primal cry of rage, I pushed myself off the bed --

-- and plunged the scalpel right into her big, glassy eye.

Again.

And again.

I had the advantage of surprise and of injuring her severely on my first strike, but Breyline had the advantage of strength. Adrenaline muted my pain, but the wasting had weakened me. With the force of her weight, Breyline pushed me onto the ground and I was further disadvantaged by trying to protect my swollen belly.

Please no.

I couldn't throw her off me and I couldn't roll away. With the spare second I had, I used it to stab Breyline's other eye. Her hands immediately flew to her face and I scuttled out from under her while she collapsed onto the floor, screaming in pain.

Breyline tried to grab me and to push me away, but I rose onto my knees above her and stabbed wildly all over her face. Breyline howled and flailed. I couldn't get deep enough. I didn't care where I hit, I just kept coming at her, screaming and stabbing. I wanted to penetrate right into her brain, to end the horror of her existence forever. I didn't stop when she stopped moving. I needed to make sure she never moved again to threaten my child.

It was only a sharp pain in my abdomen that forced me to halt, gasping for air as I finally noticed that Breyline lay dead in a puddle of blood, her face utterly mutilated.

It was the most horrific sight I'd ever seen, and I'd caused it.

I began screaming and crying hysterically. Not for Breyline, but for myself. Which made me scream and cry more, guilty and confused. I wept for what she made me do. I sobbed because my baby couldn't be born near this... this mutilated corpse.

Groaning, I crawled away from the dead body, my hands and knees aching against the cold floor. The room tilted and spun. I coughed through an attempted retching, splatting bile and what I hoped wasn't blood onto my chest. It was impossible to tell if the blood and sweat covering me was mine... or hers.

Kirwyn, I love you. Please don't be dead.

I couldn't regret what I'd done. It was Breyline or my baby. But what omen was this? What curse would befall my child, whose mother murdered while she was in the womb? Bringing life with death? Being born beside it?

The only thing I could do was crawl as far away from the corpse as my arms would allow. When I couldn't make it another inch, I collapsed, sobbing on the floor.

Kirwyn. Lazlian. Where are you, my love?

My sweaty hair clung to my face and neck. Agony shrieked through my abdomen. I could mitigate the pain with the IV drip, but I didn't have the strength to pull myself back onto the bed and reinsert the needle. I was too weak to even move another inch.

But I protected you. I saved you. The secret of your father died with Breyline.

I thought I heard more gunshots but I was distracted by pain lancing me like a sword and making me howl again. I'd foolishly thought that since the babe was coming early, it would come fast. Or I'd vainly believed that because it was easy the first time, I'd had something to do with it and I could do it again.

But it wasn't up to me. The baby wasn't coming anytime soon or maybe even at all. It was just endless pain, a river of fire coursing us both toward death.

To Kirwyn? And Lazlian too?

Covered in blood, I lay alone on the cold floor and screamed.

BLESSED BY THE MOON
Zaria

"*She's in here!*"

"*Zaria, Zaria!*"

How strange. I'd done what the Mystics said was possible -- meditated so deeply, I was hallucinating. And oh, I was good at it. I'd always thought the Mystics were full of goatshit, but I was wrong. I heard Kirwyn and Lazlian's voices so clearly, it was like they were in the room with me.

"*Zaria, hold on. We've got you.*"

And then I was floating, lifted from the floor and up, up, I supposed, to the mainlander's afterlife above...

...But no... then I was sinking back down, and none of my unbearable pain had stopped anyway.

Ah, hell.

That was probably fitting, given what I'd done to Ollier and Breyline, given how many deaths I was responsible for in my lifetime. I'd been a catalyst for chaos in my time on

Earth, causing a wave of destruction and leaving death in my wake.

Did my baby survive? Please let my baby survive my death.

The voices of Kirwyn and Lazlian had been sent to this hell to torture me. Fingers pushed and prodded to hurt me. I was too weak to swat them away. I wished I could have held my new baby just once and been permitted to hug Teddy one final time. I ached to tell him how much mommy loves him.

If I could not hold my sweet son, I would cling to his image instead. I pictured my favorite thing in the world -- a beach with cool waves lapping my feet. Perhaps if I waded into those waves it would keep the hellfire around me at bay. In my mind, Kirwyn stood on the sand beside me and Teddy held my hand and my new baby was in my arms and...

Lazlian. He was there too. I could hear his voice.

"It's this switch," he said. *"This is the way it works."*

Why would my beach have switches? I didn't want them there. I didn't want anything metal and modern, clicking and clacking. Why were such noises on my beautiful beach?

The fire consuming my body began to recede, moving outward like an expanding ring. With every inch the flames retreated, a sterile room advanced, taking its place. The birthing room in the Spade compound. Irritatingly bright, fake light all around me. Sharp edges and cold metal and...

...two faces peering down at me.

Male.

Mine.

I gasped, eyes focusing.

Was this real?

Kirwyn and Lazlian laid desperate kisses on my head,

hovering anxiously over me. But they were so different from how they always looked, I didn't fully understand what I was seeing. Tangled hair grew well past their ears and bushy beards nearly touched their chests. Sunken, dark-rimmed eyes brimmed with alarm. Taut, sinewy muscles stretched over concerningly lean bodies.

But I knew those eyes. One set a deep, serene green like forest, and the other, an otherworldly hazel, brown and olive flecks as conflicting as the man who possessed them.

"You're alive." Words I meant to speak I wept wildly, my bliss spilling forth as blubbering, as endless, happy hysteria.

"I love you. I knew you'd come," I cried. *I always knew. I just worried it wouldn't be in time.*

Both Kirwyn and Lazlian were rushing around me, sweeping my hair from my face, arranging my legs, jostling back and forth to figure out the complicated workings of the Spade mechanism, but it wasn't enough. I wanted them in my arms, holding me, and both were curiously restrained.

Why?

They must have done something correctly because relief flooded back into my veins, dulling the pain with wonderous Spade drugs.

I brought my hands to Kirwyn's gaunt, grizzly face, poking and prodding to ensure he was real.

"Careful, we don't want to infect you," he cautioned. His hand shook and flexed, seemingly fighting with the urge to push me away or pull me toward him. "We're unsterile."

Oh. I understood his logic, but I had to *feel* him. Tears spilled over my lips. I didn't think I could cry any longer, but it was as if I'd never run dry. Shaking as I reached up, I prodded Lazlian the same. His dark eyes watched me nervously through a filthy tangle of overgrown hair ringing his face and clinging to his cheeks.

You're both too far away.

"How are you here? Where have you been? Are you hurt? Where's Hektir? Are you hurt?" My questions came out as pleas; appeals to know that they were not *physically* harmed beyond any recovery. Because one look and I knew they'd suffered deeply, with inner wounds I could not yet imagine.

"We were detained," Kirwyn replied. He was firm but dismissive, as if he'd simply come home late one evening after having chatted with a friend he ran into on the way.

Liar. Always trying to make me feel better.

"Ask questions later," Lazlian said, although it was somewhat of an order.

Bossy. Always trying to tell me what to do.

"Hektir's dead," Laz related, at least. "It was a standoff, and that's why it took us a while to reach you. But they're all dead now."

My mind struggled to catch up, and it felt extra difficult amidst laboring. Ollier and Breyline were gone. That had left Hektir, Murlow, and Jemmy guarding the compound. The gunshots I'd heard.

Three against two, but in any battle, I'd bet on Kirwyn and Laz.

You're alive, you're here, and I love you.

"Is Teddy okay?" I pled the question to Kirwyn.

"He's safe with your aunt and uncle," he assured me.

"The baby's coming," I cried, which was rather obvious, but the words tumbled forth regardless. "It just," I broke off in a sob, feeling horribly guilty that I'd caused this premature birth. "I thought you were dead and then it happened."

"I know," Kirwyn said, clasping my hand. "We've got you connected to the correct medications, I think. We came to rescue you, but we'll remain here until you have the baby. Then we'll flee."

"No, Kirwyn," I wailed. "Something feels different. It's not like before. The baby is coming but it isn't. Not fast anyway."

There was a pause, during which Kirwyn and Lazlian exchanged a look. Then Laz said in a low voice, "She could be in labor for hours. Days. We can't move her, and the Spades might send someone to investigate the attack."

Kirwyn nodded, once. "We stay. Take shifts. One to watch over Zaria, one to guard the compound."

"Sleep," Lazlian added. "We need to sleep in shifts too. You look like you're going to pass out any second and we need to dress your wound."

My eyes snapped to Kirwyn, but before I could ask, he said, "A bullet grazed me, I'll be fine."

Scanning the room, Lazlian's eyes fell on Breyline's corpse. "We need to get rid of the body and sterilize everything. Clean ourselves up and her, as well."

"We should also lay whatever traps we can," Kirwyn offered.

Kirwyn and Laz rapidly made plans above me. I meant to hang onto their words, to them. But with my pain finally dulled, I dozed. The medications allowed the rest my body demanded. I could no more stop sleep from taking me than I could stop the baby from coming.

WHEN I AWOKE, it was with a jolt. My head had cleared and my body wasn't in too much pain, thanks to the medicine.

Immediately, I spied Lazlian -- this new, strange Lazlian covered in hair.

"Where is Kirwyn?" I cried.

"He's sleeping over there," Laz tilted his head toward a cot against the wall where Kirwyn laid, bruised but no longer bloodied.

I knew you'd come. My heart swelled but my eyes widened with fear. He too had a Spade device strapped to him.

"I haven't figured it all out, but look," Lazlian said, pointing to a monitor near Kirwyn's cot. "See the screen? It scans the body and it shows his vitals are good. I think he collapsed from exhaustion and blood loss. I've cleaned and bandaged him. His heartbeat is strong; he just requires rest. His body is forcing him to take it at the risk of his life if he doesn't."

Kirwyn pushing himself to the brink of death didn't shock me nearly as much as the knowledge that Lazlian had dressed his wound or the idea that Laz had cared for him when he could have killed him. Perhaps Laz didn't even need to expend any effort, perhaps he could have done nothing and just let Kirwyn die.

Maybe I really was hallucinating all of this.

Fresh pain in my womb and a beeping of the Spade machinery brought me back to reality.

"How long have I been asleep?" I asked, but as soon as I spoke the question, I realized this was far from the first time I'd awoken. Were the Spade drugs messing with my mind? Fuzzy memories came back to me of passing in and out of consciousness. Kirwyn and Lazlian had cleaned themselves and then sponge-bathed me as best they could, wiping all traces of Breyline's blood from my body. "How many hours has it been since you came?" I asked.

"You've been in labor almost a day," Lazlian said, anxiously glancing from me to the electric monitor. "But I think the baby is coming now."

His words sent me into a panic. In a reversal of my labor with Teddy, I was in much less physical pain now, but my spirit agonized at the location and circumstances of this birth.

Struggling to focus on Laz's face, I was hit with a wave of contractions and cried, "We're too far from the ocean! The baby can't be born here. Where is the sea? What time is it?"

"It's night," Lazlian said, smoothing my hair from my brow. "But this is the heir to Rythas, we don't have the same superst-" he cut himself off and concluded, "beliefs."

"This baby is half Elowan," I protested. "A Braeni. My baby needs to be born with the sun, by the sea."

Lazlian furrowed his brow in helpless frustration. I knew I wasn't being completely logical and rushed to qualify, "I'm not saying it's *bad* to be born in the evening, it's just an extra blessing during the day. One he or she should have, as the heir."

"The sun is a star, remember?" Lazlian said, taking my hand and squeezing. "Think about it. This baby has not one but millions of suns blessing his or her birth."

I wanted to believe that. "You sound like Kirwyn," I marveled, searching his scraggily, bearded face, twin to my husband's. Though they'd both scrubbed themselves as clean as possible, neither had taken unnecessary time to cut their hair or shave their beards.

Lazlian's nostrils twitched with irritation. "I've been around him too long."

I wanted to ask so many questions at that remark but couldn't. I let my head fall back, groaning and giving myself over to the contractions. Thankfully, they were dulled with the medicine.

"Should we-" I began.

"He can barely stand," Lazlian replied, though he seemed to be debating whether he could handle delivering a baby on his own. I doubted he'd ever planned for that possibility in his princely -- kingly -- repertoire. "Let him sleep, I'll wake him if there's trouble."

I was again taken aback. Not because I thought Lazlian said it to exclude Kirwyn from the birth of his heir, but because Lazlian gave the order to me with something different in his voice -- a desire not to disturb Kirwyn's healing.

The idea was too bizarre for me to wrap my head around and I hadn't the time to focus on it anyway.

It was time to push.

And I pushed, as I'd done before, as billions of women for hundreds of thousands of years had done. But it also was not as I'd done before. Like each life on the planet, each birth was unique, with as much difference between them as one snowflake to another, as one star to the next.

And as treacherous as any battle ever fought, coming out the other side covered in sweat and blood, and hopefully, all souls making it through together.

I counted myself lucky that my baby and I lived through it.

"It's a girl," Lazlian breathed as he beheld her, as her cries filled the room, joining my own. I was elated and exhausted all at once. I wanted to memorize every monumental second while Lazlian cleaned us both.

I was speechless as Lazlian, the king, held a new young queen in his arms.

But right now, she's just my baby, I thought, when he

placed her on my chest. Our teeny baby girl. Heart-breakingly beautiful and seemingly healthy, despite her preterm birth.

I could not say the rest of us fared well, but we were alive. My joy at holding my baby in my arms and at having Laz and Kirwyn with me was immeasurable.

And then, somewhere in a dark, nervous corner of my mind, I worried... because Lazlian said a male bastard was easier than a female to slide onto the throne, and he wasn't wrong.

But looking into Laz's eyes, I sighed, seeing only pride and protectiveness reflected there.

MAYBE HE WAS RIGHT, I thought, gazing at our little one as Lazlian held her. Maybe the Elowan superstitions of birthtimes and birthplaces weren't predictors of any luck at all. Teddy had been an easy birth right into the afternoon surf, yet he'd been torn from his parents for more than half a year of his young life. This child's delivery began as horribly painful -- at least until the drugs took over -- and she'd been born into my captivity amidst death and darkness. Perhaps, in a reversal, she'd be fated a kinder fortune in the coming years.

"What do you want to name the future queen of Rythas?" Lazlian asked, gazing back and forth between me and our daughter. His skeletal frame seemed to emphasize his height. Yet he was still in possession of some muscles, abnormally taut and lean. Our baby looked so small and safe in his arms. It was doing funny things to my heart, but I knew them. I felt the same way when Kirwyn held Teddy in his strong arms.

"Fersanda," I answered. "After your mother."

Lazlian was quiet and thoughtful for a moment, as if considering how to react. "You don't want to use an Elowan name? One from your family?"

I was secretly pleased that he seemed willing to defer, but I shook my head. "No. Nor is it sensible. Linking her to your dynasty will help her claim. Only, we'll call her Sanda."

"Sanda," Lazlian said, lost in the awe of new fatherhood. He ran his long fingers down her tiny face, lightly enough not to wake her.

I glanced at Kirwyn, still deep asleep on his makeshift bed. The past day was extremely fuzzy in my mind and I didn't think I'd ever clearly regain the memories. Whatever had transpired, Lazlian must have been the one to do most of the work.

Taking care of us both, I thought, still shocked at the idea that he didn't leave Kirwyn to bleed out on the floor.

"I suppose you were right," I conceded. "About how we'd make the heir."

Laz flashed his crooked, smug grin and my heart thumped at the gleam in his eye.

"Will you take her outside?" I asked. "If we cannot wash her in the sea, we can bathe her in moonlight. My little moon babe. As you said, she's blessed by the stars." Hoping he wouldn't mock my Elowan ways, I asked, "Will you present her to them?"

Lazlian nodded, and I was flooded with relief. I should have known he wouldn't be cruel at this moment, but years of antagonism were hard to shake.

"As befitting for the offspring of the Queen of the Night," he said, referring to the flower he'd once compared me to. "Our little moon child."

I nearly snorted at the thought. *Of course a babe of Lazlian's had come into the world near the stroke of midnight. Should I have been surprised?*

~

FOR A LONG TIME I SLEPT, waking only when Lazlian placed Sanda at my breast to encourage her to nurse. My milk hadn't come yet, but Laz found the medicine-milk in the Spade stores to supplement. The ease with which it was all readily supplied -- medicine, milk, or machinery, gave rise to mixed feelings inside me.

Two days passed during which Kirwyn slept too, leaving Laz alone to tend to all three of us. He also tried to operate the Spade communicator in one of the adjacent rooms. Intermittently, I'd wake to find Lazlian had collapsed from exhaustion, curling onto a pile of blankets with Sanda tucked safely in his arms. With me on the birthing bed and Kirwyn in the cot-bed along the wall, Lazlian, the king, was left to the floor.

Was it an improvement upon what he'd endured? I worried.

On the third day, Kirwyn fully awoke, and I threw myself at him, pressing against the surety of his body and crying all over again.

You're here, you saved me, and I love you.

"Don't ever doubt that I'll find you," he rasped, stroking my hair.

"I didn't. I never," I swore, wiping my nose. "I just worried it might not be in time."

Stronger on my legs, I rushed to Lazlian as well, throwing myself into his embrace and nuzzling my head against his chest.

I let my questions come. Slowly at first and receiving

distant answers in return. I tried not to push either Kirwyn or Lazlian to tell me more than they were ready, and I did my best not to weep and make it worse when they did speak of their captivity. I relayed my story in much the same manner, but it felt inadequate -- like I didn't have the words because I couldn't yet process how much I changed from what I'd done. It was a stalled, stilted unraveling.

Laz and Kirwyn worked with the Spade communicator down the hall, trying to figure out how it operated. I guided them each to the bathing room to help trim their hair and shave their beards. Both were clearly malnourished, but at least they looked more like the men I remembered when we'd finished.

And how they gorged to make up for it. I'd never seen anyone eat as much food as they did over the next few days, voraciously attacking whatever they scavenged from the kitchens.

We simultaneously prepared to depart and braced for an attack that curiously, never came. With the three of us in less than stellar shape and a premature newborn, a journey through the backlands was treacherous. Laz made a plan to find one of the nearest clans he knew and to purchase our way back to Rythas with tokens we found. In the meantime, he tinkered with the communicator mechanism. Kirwyn buried his nose in all the manuals he could find, shouting instructions to Laz every so often.

Finally, five days after giving birth and with our health restored enough to travel, a soft, electric glow suddenly filled the communicator room.

Kirwyn and Lazlian had activated the Spade monitor.

Wide-eyed, I took in what it showed me -- the location of Spade City, as well as all the satellite compounds. For the first time, I could see where we resided on the mainland, clearly mapped onto a screen. I was impressed, but Kirwyn and Laz stilled.

"Fuck," Kirwyn said. "I think... it's been blank," he worried, running his hand through his hair. "Turned off, essentially. This isn't a large compound, maybe no one's been monitoring it. By turning this on, we've potentially provided a window in here, alerting others to our presence."

The three of us shared a nervous look.

"Give me a few minutes to check out the other satellites and then we'll prepare to leave," Lazlian ordered, hands moving over the many dials on the console. "We'll draw a map and note pertinent information. It could be useful in the future."

Twelve satellites in total ringed Spade city at various distances. Some were quite large, some, like ours, were rather small. Beginning with the one closest to our right, Lazlian electronically poked inside the buildings. In the meantime, Kirwyn and I raced through the halls, gathering supplies for our journey. We didn't expect the Spades to attack in the next few minutes, but we didn't want to linger either.

As we hurried around the small corridors to collect what we needed, Kirwyn and I intermittently popped back into the communicator room to watch Laz's progress.

Finally, he scanned the last satellite, the one to the left of ours.

I was passing by on my way to check on Sanda, but I stopped when Lazlian shouted, "Kirwyn, Zaria, get in here, now." With singular focus, Lazlian began moving around the device, fingers flying over the metal console as he tried to figure something out.

"I can't access the eleventh compound, it's gone dark

inside," he announced. "But it wasn't until recently. I was able to watch the feed before the communicator cut out and the data confirms it. Look," he said, running his hands over dials again until a picture appeared on the screen.

Never in a million years would I have guessed what the image would show.

It was my sister and a few armed men, walking into the compound next to ours.

Had I... was that from my letter? Did it somehow send her there, instead of three Elowans? And had Breyline known or was she cut off from receiving this news?

I covered my mouth, shocked, while Lazlian worked more Spade magic to show another image. This one was Mal-Yin's army attacking the other satellite.

"Oh my god, he's right here," Kirwyn whispered. He and Laz shared a look. Unlike them, apparently, I had more questions than answers. Mainly, what the hell happened in the time we'd all been in captivity?

"Your sister is in the compound next to ours," Lazlian said, running his thumb over his lower lip and tugging it gently. "Mal-Yin has captured it. And the Spades are aware, see," he said, indicating a screen of information I assumed to be confirming it.

"I - what does this mean?" I asked. Although I worried that I already knew.

"It means this compound is his now, and perhaps ours. All of ours." Kirwyn said, fingertips circling the image of the satellite, almost in wonder. The stronghold was a large one, and partially underground.

Turning around, Kirwyn's eyes were wide as he looked at us.

"I think it means this is where the war begins."

PART III
CARVE THE DESTINY

CHAPTER 43

SCAR HER, SAVE HER
Lazlian

War would break out any day, if it hadn't already been declared, and I, the king of Rythas, was missing. Presumed dead, most likely. My keylord fared no better, nor Zaria. And no one even knew of Sanda's birth.

It was time to move, swiftly and with finality.

Remember what you promised, Kirwyn.

I'd watched them reunite when she strengthened. Zaria clung to Kirwyn, as he clung to her.

A seed of envy planted in my heart and sprouted like some genetically-enhanced species, tendrils unfurling and seeking every inch of my body to infect with jealousy. Resentment. Not directed at Kirwyn, exactly -- for him I was grateful. Mostly. But for the fact that I knew she'd come to me next, and though I'd hold and kiss her just the same on the outside, inside it would be drastically different.

Their embrace was a connection, and ours, a departure.

When I'd laid Sanda in her bedding, Zaria leapt to me. She pressed her head into the place beneath my shoulder where it fit so perfectly, and I inhaled the scent of her hair.

My Queen of the Night flower. My chosen braenese.

The mother of my child, I thought, astounded.

Two days had passed since then.

Having discovered that Mal had seized the other satellite, Kirwyn and Zaria proposed we leave in the morning and travel to Mal's location. Instead, I planned to continue alone to Mal-Yin, and Kirwyn would take Zaria and Sanda to safety, as he'd promised.

I wished I had my onyx ring to gift Sanda, but I'd already given it to Juls. For the thousandth time, I wondered what was happening back in Rythas and hoped my brother fared better than we had. The only item of value I possessed was my silver cuff containing Zaria's hair, and I'd die wearing it into battle.

I was a king and yet I could give Sanda nothing -- not even a mere trinket, let alone a kingdom. All she'd have of me were the stories Zaria and Kirwyn would carry. If we lost the war -- and we likely would -- no one else would live to tell her of my existence.

Maybe... someday... if anyone can reclaim the throne we'll lose, Zaria and Kirwyn would be the ones to do it.

It had been a foolish risk the day I allowed Jesi to eavesdrop in the war tower, hoping she'd tell Zaria what she overheard about Kirwyn's gold. I could admit that now. Jesi might have just as easily told Navere, and Navere could have blackmailed Kirwyn for the coin. When I took the throne in haste, without having laid more groundwork, it created instability and drove the wedge deeper between my brother and me. The move had been woefully careless. I could admit that now.

And I'd set us all on this spiral of horror when I'd tried to lock Zaria in my bedroom. Now, I'd end this course of bad choices and worse consequences by letting her go. Making her.

Never let it be said I don't learn from my mistakes.

Zaria cooed quietly over Sanda, sleeping in her makeshift bundle. She was blissfully happy, for the moment. Blissfully unaware that I was about to destroy her.

Hearing me move closer, Zaria looked up with her soft, blue eyes shining.

Oh, fuck. It took years to get her to look at me like that -- with trust.

I cleared my throat.

It's for her own good.

"I've been mulling it over and I don't think it's wise for you go to Mal-Yin or even back to Rythas. At least, not permanently," I told her. "You know I love Sanda," I said, but my words didn't sound like love. I could make them do that. I could make the qualifying tone cause the hair on Zaria's neck to stand on end. I wasn't close enough to tell, but I was sure it had.

Zaria knew me too well. She rose to her feet, slowly, eyes narrowing.

"But if we're honest with each other, it's unfortunate that she's female," I said, matter-of-factly. "It's a problem. Claims could get messy down the line if we try again and a male child comes next. I think you should disappear for a while. Lay low. Elsewhere."

"Are you telling me that because she's a girl you want me to hide her away?" Zaria asked, jutting her chin. "Deny her birthright?"

"Would you rather I lie to you? We both know it would have been better for her to be born a boy."

I knew exactly what I was doing. More than anything, being born female had dictated the course of Zaria's life. Her fate had been sealed from the moment she was conceived. And to her, not for the better. Zaria carried a wound that hadn't fully healed and I was picking at it. No, I was driving the point of a knife to re-open the tender center and bring forth fresh blood.

"The more I think about it, the more I realize this is an issue," I told her coolly. "If you won't leave of your own accord or keep silent about her lineage, I will simply deny that she's mine."

Zaria's face was supposed to crumple, and she *did* look momentarily distraught. But instead of shrinking, she swelled. Zaria straightened and again lifted her stubborn chin, making my stomach sink so horribly it gave me the sensation of falling.

"You're lying," she spat. "You wouldn't dare, and even if you tried, who will the people believe? You or me?"

She had me there. It could go either way.

"I didn't want it to come to this," I sighed with just enough regret to make it believable. "You know I enjoy you. But if you insist on being a problem for me," I shrugged one careless shoulder and decreed, "then I'll be forced to banish you."

Zaria flinched and her mouth fell in temporary shock. She worked to form words and I pressed my advantage before that could happen.

"Kirwyn," I called. "His Royal Mistress and her child are creating a problem for me and are hereby banished. As keylord, you are responsible for escorting them elsewhere. I don't care where," I dismissed, waving my hand.

Kirwyn had been lingering in the doorway, but at my command, he'd stepped into the room. I couldn't see his face to know what he was thinking, but I hoped he soon speak up and make this easier for all of us. Zaria's eyes searched my face, then darted behind me, to Kirwyn, finally starting to believe me. Her breathing deepened as she fought tears.

You must leave with Sanda. It's for your own good.

"No," Zaria insisted. Her hands balled into fists, but her lip quivered. "I will not go. I don't... This isn't what you really want..."

Oh, the bloody irony, I thought, as she escalated her arguing. For the first time ever, Zaria was fighting for me, for us. The one time I needed her *not* to. Whatever it was -- love or stubbornness or something else entirely -- it was going to get her killed. She didn't know what Kirwyn had seen in the Spade silo. She wasn't scared enough. She should be scared.

I needed to scare her.

Zaria spoke rapidly, refusing me, fighting me. Her eyes blazed, her cheeks pinked with passion. I stared without speaking, wanting to remember how she looked at me this way, before I did what I had to.

The one thing that would sufficiently scare her. The one thing I could never come back from.

Even if she wasn't aware, I caught Zaria's barely-perceptible flinching at times, when my arm moved too fast. I knew what she was afraid of.

Long ago, when she'd been a prisoner in High Spire, my father had struck her and shortly thereafter, I'd threatened to backhand her just the same. It had seared into a deep, primal part of her brain, solidifying as a worst-fear. The unexpected, casual cruelty of a smack terrified her more than the stab of a sword.

There'd be no coming back from this. But she wouldn't come back either. She'd go where I needed her to go.

I didn't allow myself to hear what Zaria was saying and I shut down seeing her too, choosing to imprint the memory of her impassioned face in my mind, instead of the horrified one I was about to induce.

I flexed the muscles in my hand, readying to make good on what I'd threatened when we were younger. There could be no room for doubt in her mind, no room to continue arguing like this. She had to take Sanda and flee, *now,* and never return.

There was no time for me to wallow in self-pity and with any luck, I'd be dead on the battlefield soon anyway.

Looking down at Zaria, I sneered in disgust. She didn't yet notice, but she soon would.

The harder the blow, the safer she'd be.

Inhaling deeply, I tensed my arm, muscles coiling --

-- and in a rush that made me start, Kirwyn suddenly angled in front of me. He blocked my path, staring hard, like he knew. I blinked, positive from the accusing look in his eyes, that he *did* know.

I'd only managed to move my hand a centimeter, how the hell did he know what I intended?

What are you doing? I screamed with my eyes.

Kirwyn shook his head with reproach, fire in his gaze. Something like shame whirled with my anger at his interference.

How dare you? How dare I? The questions were in the same voice.

I balled my hand into a fist, ready to swing at him.

"We're not leaving and you're not taking the fall." Kirwyn declared, betraying everything we'd discussed. His hands were balled into fists as well, ready to fight me on it.

"You *swore*," I accused him.

"Yeah, well, I'm shit at keeping promises," he said. "Not when they no longer serve. I'd tell you to hang me for treason, but you've already tried that."

For the first time in longer than I could remember, I struggled for words. I wanted to shout at him that he was playing with her life, the life of our heir and the fate of the entire kingdom. But he'd messed with all of that in the past and he was right -- I'd tried hanging him for it and the prick didn't die.

Still, I was his king and he had no right; couldn't get away with the audacity.

"We can't keep doing this," Kirwyn grit out. "It's not working and you know it. We continue doing the same things and we're all paying for it. I don't want her to suffer. And I don't," he trailed off, then shrugged, "want you to suffer either."

Miffed that he had the nerve to interfere and even more pissed that he'd betrayed what we agreed upon, I cocked a brow and asked, "Are you saying you're stepping aside?"

"Fuck you," he returned. "You wish." Kirwyn ran his hand through his hair and sighed. "I'm saying, I guess it would be stepping up. Or... whatever. I'm saying look what happened when we lied and worked against each other. Where did that get us? I'm saying we do this together."

Zaria had been watching us with wide, keen eyes, trying to piece together what was happening. Having enough, she exploded.

"What the hell is going on?" she shouted. "How *dare* you both lie to me when you know I've been lied to for most of my life, and for my supposed protection. You'd break my trust in the same manner? After all we've been through?"

Kirwyn closed his eyes as he winced, pained. I gritted my teeth and groaned.

"I want the both of you to tell me the whole truth, right now," Zaria demanded. "*I* will decide what is for my own good."

Folding her arms, she plopped into a chair. It was a padded, gray thing, but she sat it as if it were the oaken throne, and looked at us expectantly, as if we were courtiers come to petition a queen. She was radiant in her wrath. Rather than stand above and talk down to her, Kirwyn fell to his knees. He tried to take her hands in his, but she drew them back with a scalding look.

Any hope I had of ushering Zaria and Sanda to safety slipped away as the confessions tumbled from Kirwyn's lips. He told her the full story of what he saw in Spade City and how he'd planned to betray us to them, stealing her away in the process. He admitted he'd sent Hektir to assassinate me. Still kneeling, Kirwyn told Zaria of the torture we endured by the clanless and the innocents he was forced to kill. He even told her an... overview... of how we escaped and tortured the clanless in return.

I watched Zaria's eyes widen and by the end, her lip wouldn't stop quivering and tears streaked her cheeks. She listened as Kirwyn confessed to everything possible under the sun.

Without consulting me.

"You'd align yourself with slavers and warmongers?" Zaria asked accusingly, though she quickly covered her mouth as if she wished she could take it back. Perhaps she realized a bit of the hypocrisy in her words, considering that Rythas had, for ages, depended upon a relationship with the Spades.

"I'd align myself with the devil to protect you," Kirwyn replied. "I've done it before."

My lips twitched, unsure if he meant me or Mal-Yin.

Kirwyn reached for Zaria's hands again and finally, she allowed it. To my surprise, he confessed to her what he considered a betrayal of their intimacies.

"You shared your body with Lazlian when you thought there was no other way forward," Kirwyn said softly. "And I shared with him all of our private, intimate moments when I thought I wouldn't survive. I betrayed you in the darkness just as I felt you betrayed me in the light. It's not the same thing, but I ask that you forgive me as I've already forgiven you."

I hadn't seen our talks that way and shifted uncomfortably at the idea. In the desperate dark of our captivity, I'd told Kirwyn secret intimacies too. They were mine to tell. By half, at least.

"You put me in an impossible position with the decision to make the heir," Kirwyn insisted, voice rough with frustration. "You'd resent me for not fighting for you and you'd resent me just as much for not respecting your wishes. I did the best I could."

Weeping, Zaria whispered, "I know you did, Kirwyn." She reached down to cup Kirwyn's face. "I'm so sorry, please believe me, and I forgive everything too. All I feel is everlasting gratitude that you're both alive."

Facing death did that to a person, I supposed. Burned away all the immaterial. After what she'd been through, the rest of it didn't matter any longer. Only he did.

Only I did?

Zaria looked up at me with her tear-streaked face, her eyes a mixture of hurt that I'd betrayed her, happiness that I'd found her...

...and pleading for me to stop. Stop lying, manipulating, disappointing.

The vulnerability in her eyes undid me. The raw hope. That look shamed me, shattered me. She saw through me and the memories of everything I'd done since before I even met her came barreling down on me, all at once.

It had been months in coming, but this was the moment I broke.

My Elowan princess. My little queen.

Falling to my knees before her, I was no different than Kirwyn as I confessed my wrongdoings and begged for forgiveness.

Truth be told -- which it never would to anyone outside of that room -- my pleading was even more pitiful. Refusing tears caused the lump in my throat to grow, which only made me hoarser as I begged.

The only upside was... she knew. And I could tell by the satisfied gleam in her eye that, whether she admitted it or not, my pain pleased her. Some part of her, anyway.

Was it entirely fucked up that something about that twinge of wickedness made me love her all the more?

CHAPTER 44

TRINITY

Zaria

I'd meant what I said -- *I* would decide what was for my own good.

If only it were that simple. It almost never was. I couldn't be everywhere at once.

Lazlian tried one last time to somehow make the Spade communicator contact Mal and Aewna, but it did no good as theirs seemed disabled.

"They're not coming," Kirwyn breathed, a far-away look in his eyes as he rubbed his thumb against his forefinger.

"Who?" I asked.

"Anyone to save us. Anyone other than us. It's us."

Kirwyn's words reminded me of something Lazlian had once said at his fealty ceremony. He took a deep breath, then continued, "Assuming the Spades haven't attacked yet, we have to leave for Mal-Yin, together, and join the war there." With a pointed look at Lazlian, he said, "Lead it."

Once again, they silently communicated between themselves.

"So you have a plan," Laz replied, astonishment tinging his voice.

"Not... yet," Kirwyn admitted.

"But you have faith in us," I said. "Faith that we can win."

Kirwyn wouldn't fight a losing battle. He was too logical for that.

To my disbelief he exhaled a long sigh and said, "I wouldn't bet on it."

My shoulders fell. "Then why?" I probed.

Kirwyn dismissed me with a shake of his head and a shrug. Either he didn't know himself or he wasn't ready to talk about it.

I wasn't sure how to feel about it. His allegiance had swayed and I'd missed a step somewhere along the way to getting him there. If Lazlian, of all people, was somehow related to Kirwyn changing his mind... that was hard for me to wrap my head around.

Much had changed throughout the long moon cycles we'd been separated and in the intensity of the past few days during which we'd relied upon one another. I had no name for this new thing we'd become. Parts were soft, malleable to the touch as they continued to form. Other parts had been forged in fire and were as strong as steel. If I moved in one direction, I met with more questions than answers, feeling as if I stumbled down a dark hallway whilst it was simultaneously being constructed. Yet angling toward another direction, I knew in my bones that there was nothing in this world of which I was surer than the strength of our bond.

The best word I could use for now was allies. United in

our defense of Rythas. Even Kirwyn, though he seemed unable to articulate why he'd joined what he deemed a lost cause. Personally, I didn't believe that. With the three of us on the same side, I knew it wasn't *hopeless.*

I swallowed thickly, glancing at Sanda. I had made a choice, and it was the exact opposite of what my heart wanted. Half my heart, at least.

Home. I'd been away from Teddy for so long, now that I was finally able to return to him... I couldn't. It was seemingly paradoxical, but no less true. The best thing to do for Rythas was to ride in the opposite direction of our kingdom. The best thing to do for my family was to keep it separated, for now.

Lest there be no kingdom to return to, no family left.

Determined, we made our final preparations to depart the following morning, needing the light. Nighttime in these woods, especially in the cold and with a premature newborn, could be deadly. I checked on Sanda and Kirwyn readied the horses Hektir kept in the stables. I'd ridden one of those same mounts into the compound when I'd arrived as a pregnant hostage many months ago.

I'd warned Hektir and his crew from the beginning -- there were only two ways this would end. Either I'd kill them, or my husband would.

Well, I'd been slightly incorrect. It turned out *both* had happened, with a bonus of the Rythasian king swooping in for at least one kill of his own.

We awoke at dawn the next morning, and the three of us bundled in Spade clothing we scavenged from the satellite. It chaffed my skin; made it crawl to wear the attire of my enemies. Yet I swallowed my disgust and put it from my mind.

Just before we departed, Lazlian lightly rubbed my

biceps and said, "Once we reach Mal, he'll provide an escort. You and Sanda can travel back to Rythas."

I cut him off with a laugh which made his nostrils flare, but I didn't care. "Did you learn nothing last night? The decision has been made and you're outnumbered. We stick together through the war."

"Is that how this is going to go?" Laz asked, brow knit in anger. "Two against one?"

"I don't know how it's going to go, but I'm telling you this and you *know* it. Working apart isn't working. We stay together."

"You can't bring a baby into a war camp," Lazlian insisted.

"It's a stronghold and I'm not leaving you." I pushed my shoulders back and gave him my most regal, commanding voice. "If we're truly going to war against the Spades, we need every asset we can get. I may not be skilled in battle, but my mind is sharper than any blade I might wield. I will give it to Rythas, just as I've given her the next queen."

Kirwyn, arms crossed, stood beside me. Lazlian's eyes flicked back and forth between the two of us. He grunted, groaned, then scrubbed a defeated hand down his face.

Partially relenting, he said, "We'll discuss the matter once we safely arrive."

I turned to Kirwyn. "Teddy is safe with Saos and Alette. I know he needs us, but the war needs us more right now," I insisted softly, half to console him, half to console myself. In Rythas, it wasn't uncommon for fathers or mothers to battle, but skirmishes tended to happen close to home. What I intended to do meant I'd be farther away than usual and possibly for a long time as well, when I'd *already* been gone for months.

In Rythas, everyone fights, I reminded the pain -- and guilt -- consuming my heart.

Kirwyn's eyes rounded and he abruptly gripped my biceps. "Oh no, there's two more things I forgot to tell you. I gave Lazlian all our gold to keep the army loyal and betrothed Teddy at his behest," he admitted in a rush.

My mouth fell and my eyes darted back and forth between the two men, unsure with whom to be angrier. *Betrothed? To whom?* I pulled away from Kirwyn's grip.

"Any noblewoman will do," Lazlian quickly amended. "I simply ordered it announced that as a prince of Rythas, Theo will choose a bride from amongst the elite families when he comes of age."

A volcanic rage inside me boiled beneath the surface. I tried not to let it explode. Sanda slept in the next room and I didn't want to wake her. Yet my breath huffed in and out of my nose in a heavy, bullish manner. Not at all regal.

"You *both* know what it did to me to be betrothed and you've gone and done the same to my son?" I cried.

They started talking at once, trying to tell me that it wasn't as bad as it seemed since Teddy would have his choice of many brides. He simply couldn't look *outside* the noble houses. Lazlian insisted some marriages are political only, to beget an heir. He argued that wouldn't be too unusual if Theo didn't marry for love but kept a common woman behind the scenes for a more romantic affair. Allowing for any outcome, Kirwyn and Laz assured me that if he loved a man, that could be arranged as well, albeit more discretely.

They were talking too much, pleading for my understanding, but the only thing I needed to know at the moment was that there was absolutely nothing left I did *not* know.

"Sit *down*," I interrupted, pointing to two chairs in the communicator room. "Both of you. Now."

They sat.

I reached back in my mind to Elowa, to the meditative exercises the Mystics used. Breathing deeply with my eyes closed, I pictured a calm ocean.

"What is she doing?" Lazlian asked.

"I don't know," Kirwyn replied cautiously.

I snapped my eyes open and said, "I want to know, right now, if there are any other lies. Omissions. Whatever. Anything else you've hidden from me?"

Kirwyn gave a firm, "No."

Lazlian paused. Finally, he said, "Well, there's one more thing."

A great expanse of a serene sea, I thought to myself, bracing.

"What is it?" I grit out.

"Do you remember when you first came to High Spire and fell ill?" Lazlian asked, shifting in his seat.

I frowned at the unexpected mention of a long-ago event, having imagined he was going to confess to something more recent.

"Of course I remember. I almost died."

Lazlian nodded encouragingly. "Exactly. You couldn't keep any medicine down and the doctor had to give you IVs to hydrate. No one knew if you were going to make it."

I remembered being on the brink of death and almost wanting to die at the worst of it.

"To keep Juls safe, my father didn't want him near you. No one was sure if what you had was contagious. But you couldn't keep medicine down," Lazlian repeated.

I'd been so sick I was in and out of consciousness, but I

thought I'd seen Juls standing in my doorway once. What was Lazlian getting at?

"Someone had to give you medicine and my father didn't want anyone else to touch you or to see you -- not in that way. You were the young queen and the future bride for his son..." Lazlian trailed off. I frowned, wishing he'd get to the point.

"Someone had to give you the medicine you couldn't take... orally," Lazlian concluded.

Kirwyn slapped a hand over his eyes and shook his head. I stared. What was I missing?

"I came into your room, flipped you over, and gave it to you through the only orifice you could retain it," Lazlian said.

Oh my god.

When his words clicked in my brain, it sent me into instantaneous hyperventilation. *Was Lazlian saying he put medication in my... No, no, no.* Was it possible to die of mortification from an event that happened years ago? *It might.* In fact, the distance between the occurrence and the admittance seemed to magnify my horror, giving it time to grow in the darkness.

"Y - you... in my..." I stammered, unable to even complete the sentence.

"And I may have saved your life." Lazlian folded his arms, unrepentant.

"I was unconscious!" I cried. It came out breathy as I fought not to picture what had happened.

"What would you have preferred?" Lazlian asked, waving a careless hand. "My father ordered it be done. Should I have let you die?"

I was laughing but it wasn't joyful. What came out of

me was more of a hysterical, unnatural giggle between gasps for air.

"He didn't order the next part, however..." Lazlian trailed off again.

My eyes widened with simmering rage and I pinned Laz with my stare. He leaned back in his chair, far too casually for this conversation.

"I knew you'd already slept with him," Laz said, tilting his head toward Kirwyn, "and I couldn't have you carrying a disease to my brother." He paused, scratching his stubble and having the decency to look a tad sheepish. "Since I already had your undergarments off anyway, I flipped you onto your back and checked."

I was going to die from some combination of shame and anger, I was sure of it.

"Are you saying you examined me?" I cried.

"I'm saying I saw every part of you that day, inside and out." He shrugged, fighting a grin. "Pretty thoroughly."

While I was unconscious.

My hands flew to cover my flaming face and the scream I'd been holding back finally came out.

All this time... All those months battling with Lazlian in High Spire and I didn't know he'd seen all of me.

"Do you want me to punch him for you?" Kirwyn asked in a deep, serious voice, but it wasn't helpful because I could hear him struggling to suppress a chuckle.

Lazlian snorted, indignant. "I likely saved her life."

"And insulted the both of us with your little examination."

"Oh, like you never thought the same about me?" Lazlian retorted.

Kirwyn scrunched his lips in thought and conceded, "Fair point."

"Well, I'm so glad you've both come to terms with all this," I cried, gesticulating with my arms spread wide, like some ridiculous bird trying to take flight. "I'm sorry if I might need a moment here to process it, seeing as I'm the one it happened to."

I tried taking deep breaths again as I held my head in my hands. *They'd both watched me give birth and we'd had plenty of sex. It wasn't like he hadn't seen all of me now,* I consoled myself.

But *then.* Without my knowing.

I folded my arms and shot daggers at Lazlian with my eyes. "All those times we fought in High Spire, did you just sit there and picture me whenever you wanted to? When I'd thought I'd gotten the better of you in some argument, did you just conjure up images of me, splayed and exposed and unaware?"

Lazlian didn't reply with words, but I'd never before seen him make the kinds of faces he made as he tried not to laugh, lips curling and uncurling. When Kirwyn started chuckling, Lazlian lost his battle of restraint.

When we were younger, I'd once tried to kick Lazlian's chair out from under him and he was quick to spring to his feet instead. This time, he was too busy laughing to stop me. Even though he wasn't leaning back and it took more effort, I knocked the chair legs from beneath him and pushed his chest to assist in my effort. With some satisfaction, I watched Laz fall onto his back.

Not that he cared.

To my infinite irritation, both Kirwyn and Lazlian only found my fury even more amusing, so I rushed Kirwyn and pushed him down too. It wasn't mature, but my rage needed a target and they were asking for it.

Unfortunately, they both found this even funnier.

Neither man made a move to pick himself off the floor, chortling as if they'd never stop.

With another cry, I spun on my heel and left them together on the ground, laughing like boyish idiots.

Well, I consoled myself, wrapping my clothing tighter as I braced for the cold I'd soon meet outside. *Let them. With what's coming, who knows when we'll have the chance to laugh again?*

CHAPTER 45

A BAD WAY TO GO
Zaria

Icy, bitter air blasted my cheeks as soon as I stepped outside, but my eyes met the most wonderous sight.

Snowflakes.

My god, they were beautiful, sparkling as they fell and crystalizing the wood in a dazzling array of shimmers. The forest floor shone as if it had been coated in fairy dust and trees glistened like they'd been set alight with a magical spell. My nose filled with this new scent of freshy-fallen snow. I hadn't the words to describe it, so crisp and other-worldly. I gaped in awe of such beauty, then frowned as a cold gust blew hard against my face once more.

Why did this enchantment require air so frosty that it felt as if I were being stabbed with a thousand frozen needles?

Wide-eyed at the snowy spell enveloping us, Sanda shared my wonder. She cooed and smiled as snowflakes fell upon her lips and lashes.

You're my little moon princess, I thought, worried about her warmth. *Not a snow queen.* Hugging her closer to my chest, I tucked my head into my shoulders and hurried to the stables with Kirwyn and Lazlian beside me. Every so often I shot them an angry look and they side-eyed one another, stifling chuckles they thought I couldn't see or hear.

Weakened from the wasting and labor, I hadn't the strength to hold myself in place for the entirety of the journey. We decided to double-up on the horses, with me alternating my weight between Lazlian's mount and Kirwyn's. Whoever didn't have me would ride with Sanda strapped to his chest.

In this manner we made sluggish, gradual progress through the icy wood. The distance to the other Spade compound wasn't too great, but we were slowed by what little pathway existed disappearing beneath by the ever-growing coating of slippery snow. Not to mention, every few hours we had to stop to feed Sanda. It was an ordeal where Kirwyn and Lazlian tried to shield me from the chill by huddling around Sanda and I and spreading their coats wide, while I exposed my breast for her to nurse.

I'd been through too much to worry long about what an odd scene we made.

The frosty wind didn't bother Kirwyn as much as it did me; he enjoyed the snow. Lazlian said it wasn't nearly as bad as it could be. He claimed that despite the snowfall, the air was on the warmer side for this type of weather.

If that was true, then I had no desire to ever know how cold the world could get.

Back at the satellite, I'd taken boots I was sure weren't Breyline's and stuffed the oversized shoes with extra padding. Yet my toes still froze within. I held onto either

Kirwyn or Lazlian's waist while they kept their hands ready to grab a gun if we met any *unfriendlies* along the way. Fortunately, there didn't seem to be any settlements on our path and the snow likely kept travelers at bay.

My anxiety mounted the further we traveled, the nearer we reached what might be the point of no return. Excluding Jesi, I felt safer with Kirwyn and Lazlian than I would with any other person in the world. Only, I didn't quite know how to act. In the compound I'd thrown myself at Lazlian with wild abandon, but I did not kiss him open-mouthed or murmur words of passionate desire. With Kirwyn standing beside me, I didn't know what was too much, too far. Physicality between us was the soft, pliable area that hadn't fully formed enough for me to feel the boundaries.

As was love.

The idea gave rise to more questions than answers, so I focused on the clearer problem ahead.

War.

I snorted at the irony, my breath coming out in a white puff of air as it met the cold. In war one either lived or died. The finite options were easier to grasp than myriad ways our alliance might unfold.

Watching Kirwyn and Laz move together, the way they spoke without speaking, reminded me of how Juls and Laz used to interact before Lazlian drove a wedge into their relationship, or how Kirwyn and Mal-Yin used to sync before Mal departed Rythas to spend more time in Elowa.

Several hours into our journey, Kirwyn pointed out a fox darting through the trees and following our trail. I wished I had something to feed it, but our food was packed away in the saddle bags. When we stopped a bit later so that I could nurse a heavily-bundled Sanda, I did not see the fox, but I left a Spade brick and half an apple in the snow just in case.

Laz was fairly certain we rode in the correct direction, but our progress was unclear. Hidden beneath a blanket of wet, gray clouds, the sun sank lower in the sky and the forest began to dim. Much like when I'd plunged off *The King's Light* to swim to freedom, we'd taken a leap and passed a point of no return. We hadn't the time to make it back where we started before nightfall; we could only go forward and hope we found shelter.

Please let us find Mal, or at least, somewhere warm, I prayed.

Coquina clams climbed up my spine because I didn't know what would happen if we were plunged into darkness in the middle of the icy wood with no shelter. The ride was a risk, especially at this time of year when we had shorter daylight to begin with. I didn't want to be outside when the temperature dropped at night.

The idea that Sanda could freeze to death in this dark, mainland forest, was too horrifying for me to think about and I mentally turned away from the dreadful image.

It returned with a vengeance.

Horrid scenes played out before me. Sanda, her tiny body frozen and lifeless. Madness following. Me, running into the cold wood to die or using the gun strapped to my waist. Or all of us expiring one at a time, watching the others die first.

I squeezed Lazlian's waist tighter. They were all bad ways to go.

"The last time I shared a saddle with you it was facing backwards in your lap," I said to Lazlian, trying to distract myself. "When you swept me onto your mount, trying to capture me before we made it to Mal-Yin's. What would you have done to me if I hadn't escaped?"

"You don't want to know," Lazlian replied ominously. "Perhaps if we survive, I'll show you."

I worked my hand beneath Laz's many layers of clothing, found the flesh of his abdomen, and gave it a hard squeeze. Lazlian grabbed my hand, stilling it.

For a while, he didn't let go.

Just before the light threatened to disappear entirely, I spied something moving in the gloaming. Blinking several times to be sure, I caught a glimpse of color other than the brown, green, and white of the snowy forest...

Flashes black, olive, and cream moved through the trees.

It was clothing. People.

Ours... or others?

I tensed, pulse racing as I readied to jump from Laz's horse and grab Sanda if we couldn't run. I had no idea what I planned on doing next, but my instinct was to shelter her, protect her. Dozens of men and women quickly dotted the forest before us, funneling from places I couldn't see and fanning out around us and --

-- I gasped. My entire body sagged with relief. One, because I recognized the people as Mal's men, along with a handful of Elowan soldiers. And two, because the sneaky way we'd been enveloped meant they had efficient lookouts in place.

My eyes fluttered shut and I thanked Keroe, finally feeling safe after being endangered for so many long moon cycles. I wanted nothing more than to rest my aching muscles after a full day's ride and to warm up somewhere away from the endless, biting cold.

Gasps broke out, followed by a ripple of chatter starting with the men and women closest to us and leading back into what I guessed to be the compound's entrance.

"It's the king!" the astonished whispers echoed from person to person. "The king of Rythas! And Prince Kirwyn and Princess Zaria!"

People rushed closer, shocked to see the missing king -- a man suspected dead -- riding out of the snowy trees along with Kirwyn, myself... and a newborn.

I remembered when my mother had planned to bring Volmar back to Elowa and present him as some sort of god having returned from the dead. We were treated in much the same manner, and these were only Mal's men. What would the people of Rythas make of the fact that we lived?

On one hand, we were disadvantaged; ignorant of critical events that had transpired while we were gone. On the other, our appearance on three steeds emerging from a snowy, enchanted wood after missing for several months, made us seem almost divine.

One figure, wearing black from head to toe, coolly emerged before all others. White snowflakes dusted his dark, shiny hair.

"I learned my lesson not to underestimate you a long time ago," Mal-Yin said, speaking to me. He reached up to help me slide off Laz's horse. My boots made a crunching sound as they smacked the snow. "I shouldn't be at all surprised that you managed to escape *and* to rescue the king and his keylord from wherever they've been all this time."

I think he was teasing just a bit with such an unlikely scenario. Although, had it not been for the stroke of bad luck in Breyline finding out about Sanda, it was possible that I would have both escaped *and* found Kirwyn and Laz, somehow.

"Hey," Kirwyn called out. "We rescued her."

"Only because it is the fault of you *both* that I was captured in the first place," I said, waspishly.

Mal-Yin and Kirwyn embraced with an affectionate clap on each other's backs, mindful of Sanda still strapped to Kirwyn's chest. Mal did not ask questions about our newborn, though his eyes gleamed with knowing. Lazlian and Mal dipped their heads at one another in respectful acknowledgement.

For me, Mal smiled warmly. At least, it was as warm a smile as I could say he was capable.

"Come inside. The compound is ours, your sister eagerly awaits, and we have *much* to catch up on."

WHILE YOU WERE DEAD
Zaria

I gaped as we were escorted into a cavernous Spade satellite. It was much larger and more well-equipped than the one where I'd been kept. About half the stronghold was underground, half above. Heavily fortified and guarded by Mal's men, it made a good base.

If this was indeed our war base, as Kirwyn speculated.

Aewna rushed toward us with the unexpected affection of an enthusiastic hug, and the expected sensibility of shoving a hot mug of tea in our hands. Like Mal, she too was dressed for combat in all-black, attire I knew she hadn't worn in years. She looked pale but healthy, and her appearance made my heart leap. Aewna's duties primarily kept her in Elowa and I, admittedly, was not disciplined in my correspondence. It took me longer to tear away from the sea, sit a desk, and to diligently write letters as often as Aewna did.

"And who is this?" Aewna cooed, taking Sanda from Kirwyn.

"Her name is Fersanda," I said, carefully omitting her last name, for now. Although with her tan skin and carrying the name of Lazlian's late mother, Aewna would have to be a fool not to know she was his. "We call her Sanda and she's your niece."

Half-niece. Or... second cousin? I still didn't know if Aewna and I were half-sisters or cousins. Though our height and frames differed, the creepy way all Elowan faces resembled one another made it hard to tell by looks alone.

As Mal-Yin led us deeper into the stronghold, there was a rush to speak. Aewna explained how she'd negotiated herself over the three hostages and Mal detailed how they'd come to recuse me and take possession of this Spade satellite instead. Kirwyn and Laz gave a brief overview of their captivity and I relayed my own ordeal, culminating in Sanda's birth.

After hearing Aewna's story, I snorted. "I could have told Breyline that you would have a plan and that Mal would follow you anywhere -- not that I would have. She's an idiot for thinking you are. I have no idea who she knew here, nor what she intended. But thankfully, whatever her plan, it wasn't a good one."

"Is Rythas at war?" Lazlian interjected, patience worn thin. "Are you with us? And what the hell has been going on since we've been gone?"

"It's easier if I show you," Mal-Yin said, leading us down another sleek, metal hallway. "We've been cut off from access, but we figured out there's twelve satellite compounds in total and the eleventh was dark, with no indication of its location. I've sent several parties to look for it over the past few weeks, but I never assumed you were this close," Mal said, permitting himself a light laugh. "They must have overshot you by miles."

We finally entered a room occupied by several soldiers flitting about. Spade technology lined the walls. A table with a map showing both the mainland and our islands had been centrally placed.

Mal-Yin didn't need to say it, we could see it. We stood in his headquarters.

Removing any doubt, he announced, "It hasn't been formally declared, but it has begun."

Kirwyn, Laz, and I drew a collective breath.

"Is this what I think it is?" Kirwyn drawled, pointing to a cluster of ships in the God Sea, never taking his wide, worried eyes off the screen on a wall before us. "Is this current?"

"Yes and no," Mal-Yin quickly replied, then instructed, "Please, sit down."

Sanda chose that moment to awaken and cry out her hunger.

"Do you have a room she can-" Lazlian began, but I laughed, cutting him off and earning his frown.

As if I'd relinquish a seat at the war table.

Lifting Sanda from Aewna's arms, I sat, arranging my hair and shirt so that I could feed Sanda while maintaining some privacy. I focused on what I needed to do as if nothing unusual was happening, because it wasn't.

"Continue," I commanded, perhaps with extra primness.

Maybe I was feeling a little defensive.

After exchanging looks and shrugging, everyone sat at the table displaying various clans upon a map. It looked a little like when Kirwyn and I had planned to attack High

Spire and had made a little model back in Volmar's estate using shells and rocks -- only this one was a hundred times more complex. The room itself reminded me of the war tower in High Spire, but here the table stood in an underground lair, moving our scheming from the sky to beneath the dirt.

"When we claimed this satellite, the Spades cut off our access," Mal said. "We're working on regaining entry. In the meantime, we maintain a tangible model here," he said, pointing to the table. "Primitive, but effective."

Mal turned to Lazlian when he spoke next.

"What you're looking at isn't yet an attack on Rythas, but it is a blockade. From what we learned, it is the Spades' aim to starve her, weaken her. Then they'll go in for the kill, bearing less casualties on their side."

Lazlian was as still as stone, save his eyes widening in horror and his nostrils flaring.

"We think their plan is to burn their way through Low and Mid-Spire, invading High Spire when she's near the point of surrender anyway. They want her intact, they don't want to destroy her beauty."

"Just her people," I breathed, images flashing through my mind, each more terrible than the next. Families fleeing, children screaming, soldiers bleeding, and everyone crying.

"A blockade?" Kirwyn asked, hand in his hair. "If they're successful then we'll never get our army out. We don't have *any* hope without the numbers Rythas can bring. We'll have already lost."

"It will weaken us, but I need to send a letter to my brother, instructing him to send our soldiers here," Lazlian said. His face was crumpled in pain. One hand half-covered his mouth, as if he couldn't believe he spoke the words. "It will leave Rythas exposed but some soldiers can remain to guard her, rather than risk *all* being locked in. It's a chance we'll have to take."

"It's already been done," Mal replied, holding up his hands. "As I said, what you're looking at behind me isn't current."

"What?" Kirwyn and Laz asked in unison.

"The bulk of your army has already sailed and is currently headed here, at our request," Mal-Yin informed us, pointing to the table. "See the crown and key?"

The change in Lazlian's body language was instant.

"Request? My brother hates you, and for good reason. You must have blackmailed him." Lazlian shot to his feet and stormed to where Mal-Yin sat. His sneer was full of disgust and I didn't blame him -- Laz took threats to his brother's safety very seriously.

I didn't blame Juls, either. Not only had Mal invaded High Spire at my behest, he continually chipped away at the monarchy's power by trying to spread new, more *modern* ideas that conveniently favored himself.

Lazlian's muscles tensed as if he readied to grab Mal by the shirt collar and yank him to his feet. Before I could blink, Kirwyn had wedged himself between the two men and spread his arms wide.

"You must have pressured him into this," Lazlian spat, speaking around Kirwyn but at least not pushing him out of the way. "Otherwise, he would have never submitted to your demand."

"He didn't," Mal-Yin's lip quirked, utterly unfazed. "Like any good man, he submitted to his *wife's* demand."

At Aewna's soft laugher, we all snapped our heads in her direction.

"I've long corresponded with Queen Merie," Aewna explained. "I wrote, telling her of the imminent blockade and urging her to send your army to the mainland before it was too late. Merie knows I have our best interest at heart. She trusts me, and Juls trusts her. Heeding her counsel, he sent three fourths of your soldiers here. A quarter remain to defend High Spire itself."

Kirwyn, Laz, and I were momentarily speechless. Clearly, they'd underestimated the power of female friendship and I, admittedly, underestimated the importance of keeping up with letters.

Mal-Yin rose and brushed past Lazlian, eyes on Aewna. He gently traced her shoulders as he spoke.

"My darling is ever so skilled with a pen. Only, sometimes she uses it to get us all into trouble," Mal said, giving her a teasing, chiding look, "and sometimes, out."

Aewna bit back a smile and bat her lashes at him, flirtingly. The way they were looking at each other made me feel like I'd invaded a private moment.

"We were lucky," Aewna explained. "The Spades were already planning this. If we hadn't come here when we did, we wouldn't have known."

My god, the irony. Everything Breyline had done to hurt us... had helped.

"What of Elowa?" I implored. "Is she safe?"

Aewna nodded. "A blockade there isn't very effective as she can survive on her own for a long time. And fighting the ships who guard her isn't yet necessary. When Rythas falls, Elowa falls. The Spades need only wait until there's no one left to protect her."

My stomach twisted and I groaned. Everyone re-sat, dejectedly.

"Once the Spades attack, Juls will shelter as many of your people as he's able within the city limits of High Spire. He will protect it for as long as he can," Mal-Yin announced.

Elbow bent against the table, Lazlian held his head up with one hand pressed to his weary forehead. "Then what of the rest of the kingdom? Juls simply plans to fall back, sacrificing Low and Mid-Spire to Spade forces once they start randomly burning buildings as they so love to do?"

"There's no better option," Mal insisted. "He cannot protect your island against the full Spade fleet no matter how many men he retains. There is no hope there, only here."

The room was so quiet I could hear everyone's forlorn, heavy breathing. It felt like I was witnessing the end of the world as we knew it.

Maybe I was.

Lazlian shot to his feet. "If our army is marching here, the Spades will pick off our soldiers on the way," he said, arms spread wide in a gesture that reminded me of Kirwyn. "We need to gather the clans to join them. That has always been my plan. At the very least, we need to send your men to help escort our army-"

Abruptly, Lazlian stopped. He blinked, brow furrowed. "Why haven't the Spades attacked you here yet? They know you've taken the satellite. What are they waiting for?"

Mal folded his hands and placed them on the table. "For us to do exactly what you said," he replied. "We think that is what they want -- for the clans to gather and attack at once, and thus, to defeat us at once. If we stay separated, they face what they've been facing for years. Prolonged and costly guerrilla battles up and down the coast. If we band together and attack as a force, they demolish us in one swoop," he explained.

Once again we quieted, letting the weight of Mal's words sink in.

"I don't think they're going to pick off your soldiers as

they march," Mal-Yin continued, shaking his head. "I think they're likelier to clear the trees and ease their path. In fact, I predict they'll only attack those clans who stay behind, prodding them to join us here and making it easier for the mass slaughtering."

"So they're doing the same here as they are in Rythas," Lazlian said, rage burning in his eyes. "Herding us. Using intimidation to funnel people into one place."

Mal-Yin nodded, his gaze assured.

Collapsing into a chair, Lazlian asked, "How do you think it will happen?"

"My guess is that they are setting a trap, an ambush. We march as one and deliver ourselves right into it. Perhaps in the hill pass, where we're narrowed, or the fields where we're exposed," Mal said, sliding his slender hand over the tabletop map. He clenched his jaw and stared with a rare, frustrated brow. "What I can't predict," Mal said, "is how far they want us to go."

"All the way," Kirwyn declared, resigned. "They're baiting us right through the city gates."

Mal cocked his head.

Kirwyn let out a defeated sigh, leaning onto the table as he explained. "They want us to attack Spade City because they've got a massive stockpile of weapons we've never seen before." He then described for everyone the multi-leveled silo Jori had shown him and we listened, rapt, though I'd heard it before.

"Why were they purchasing weapons from me when they're in possession of all that?" Mal pondered, irritated. "Misdirection? Or perhaps they find it amusing to use our own guns against us."

He sat back and his lip curled, almost like a smile but

not quite. Which would have been out of place because we certainly had nothing to smile about at the moment.

"This way, they don't have to move a single troop," Kirwyn explained. "We fight our way right into Spade City, cause chaos, and they, like heroes, unleash their mother-load of advanced weapons to destroy us in one fell swoop, probably with very little damage to their city."

It was one thing to have Kirwyn tell me about the Spade weaponry, it was another to see how it unfolded according to their plan. It stole my breath.

Staring at the tabletop rendering, I thought I'd much rather have preferred a battle at sea. Elowans and Rythasians were made from the sea, our bones as tough as bedrock, our maneuvers as swift and unpredictable as the currents. But the Spades claimed the advantage of their own territory. Here I was again in the mainland, with forests so thick they blotted the sky, and beasts so terrible my own nightmares couldn't conjure their horror.

Kirwyn ran his fingers over his lips and explained, "They've been holding back the big guns, literally. Once we invade the city and are trapped, they'll pick us off like flies, all while their people witness the triumph."

Kirwyn swore. Lazlian pushed himself up from the table with a furious grunt. I rocked Sanda, not wanting her to sense my unease and to emulate it, wanting to calm myself too, and failing.

"It's like a game of senorok, when you know you've won but your opponent doesn't yet see it." Kirwyn said between clenched teeth. "They'll study the board and you'll patiently wait as there's no move they can make which doesn't lead to their defeat." He looked up at all of us. "That's how they're playing. The Spades don't have to do anything because they know they've already won and we're just too stupid to see it."

I broke out in a cold sweat and breathing became increasingly difficult. I wondered if the rising terror inside me was akin to a panic attack.

How could we win a war if the only way to fight the Spades gave them exactly what they wanted?

CHAPTER 47

UNEXPECTED ALLIES
Kirwyn

Zaria and I were shown to a private room possessing a small, adjacent space we could use for Sanda. It was little more than an antechamber, but it was a larger area than most would receive once our army arrived.

Lazlian was escorted down the hall and into the next room.

Part of me was relieved that Mal-Yin's men had made the decision for us, but an unease crept up my spine. Forcing Lazlian to separate from his child was a shitty thing to do, and it hit me that this was the first time we'd not shared a room in many months. For so long, sleeping nearby enabled us to watch each other's backs. Losing that sense of security for me, for Zaria, and for Sanda, created an unwelcome discomfort and unnecessary vulnerability.

Neither Lazlian nor I voiced a protest, but I knew everything Laz was thinking as he turned and let himself be led to the next chamber.

I knew that Laz would sleep with a light on and pretend he'd simply forgotten to turn it off. Should he manage to get any rest, I knew there was a good chance he'd awaken from a night terror, covered in sweat. I knew what the dream would entail, and that the last thing he'd ever want was water to cool himself down.

LAZLIAN KNOCKED with the respectability of dawn, or close enough to it anyway, and the pretense of bringing milk for Sanda. I'd been awake, waiting.

He and I whispered at the small, round table in our room. Laz rocked Sanda to keep her quiet, allowing Zaria to sleep on the bed behind us. She'd awoken in the night, thrashing from a bad dream about stabbing Breyline. It was violent, yet I knew from experience that if we survived, the worst would come later. Zaria tended to cocoon herself in a protective shell when something bad was happening, but months or years down the road, it would hit her when she was ready to process it.

Once Zaria had relaxed, she'd taken the middle-of-the-night opportunity to nurse Sanda, and by the time she got back to bed, I knew she'd need to sleep in.

"I will send messengers to every clan this side of the Green Mountains," Lazlian whispered, holding his daughter on his lap. "They won't come for Mal-Yin, but they'll come for me. You know what I'm going to ask of you."

"I do, and I don't see how it can be done. I was able to leave, but no one can sneak *into* Spade City."

"Mal might know a way," Lazlian offered.

I shrugged. *Unlikely.*

"And with the blockade," I said, keeping my voice low, "no one can get to High Spire, either."

It was my way of telling Lazlian that I knew what frustrated him. He couldn't even send a messenger to let his brother know he was alive, let alone that he'd lead the army. Juls was entirely cut off from any news until we won... or were defeated.

We both turned our heads at the sound of Zaria stirring as she sat up, blinking at us. Zaria said nothing when she climbed out of bed and took Sanda in her arms, but I noticed the minute relaxing of her shoulders the moment she awakened and took in our presence.

It was obvious that, after what she'd endured, having Lazlian and I nearby soothed her. Being alone and pregnant, she'd suffered a different kind of hell than Laz and I had. Like me, I knew that she wanted us working together.

But I wasn't entirely sure what else any of us wanted beyond that.

AN HOUR LATER, we were called into a meeting with Mal and Aewna, happily finding steaming cups of strong black tea waiting.

"We have some hope with this," Mal-Yin said, opening his hand to reveal the golden data cube he'd claimed years ago, as the spoils of war with Rythas. Mal had taken it directly from the library's room of Forbidden Texts. Back when Zaria and I sought his help to capture High Spire, she'd offered the cube to sweeten the deal.

"We might be able to glean critical information about the Spades," Mal announced, "if we can read this."

"Wait," Zaria said, huffing and dropping her cup onto the table. "Are you saying that all this time you haven't been able to read the data cube? That you lied about having the technology?"

"I didn't lie," Mal-Yin corrected, placing his hands in his pockets. "You never asked."

"I assumed it when the device was a part of our negotiations," Zaria gritted out.

"I thank you for your confidence in me."

"I rescind it."

"But it's soon to be justified," Mal quipped, with that unbothered ghost of a smile.

I was surprised as well, but if Mal-Yin was anything, he was patient. To our shock once more, he introduced us to a man named Sergei -- apparently the only Spade he hadn't executed -- and explained his plan to hack the Spade systems. From Aewna's watchful gaze and folded arms, I got the feeling that Mal didn't want to reveal his asset and had only done so at her prodding.

Fantastic. I hoped this was all I didn't know. If we were keeping secrets from each other, we were doomed to fail. Lazlian frowned, but his concern took another direction.

"I think we need to develop an organizational plan," he announced, "with me named the leader commanding this war."

I looked between Mal and Laz. Rythas had the numbers, but Mal had the weaponry. In theory, they were both suitable candidates.

Too easily, Mal-Yin replied, "I agree. You will be named as our leader."

Why, I wondered, leaning forward and narrowing my eyes, *was Mal so accepting of playing second fiddle?*

"We have an idea," I said, both needing the meeting to progress and, admittedly, wanting to establish my own position. "I have a contact in Spade City and he's one of the High Twelve -- a man named Jori who tried to flip my allegiance. If there was a way to send him a message, I could meet with him and perhaps persuade *him* to flip to our side instead. The problem is that no one can sneak into the walled city, especially now."

Silence fell upon the table, then Zaria spoke up.

"No, that's not true," she said, stroking her lips as she thought out loud. She looked at me and said, "Remember, Farip Fabroni had a way? He implied as much when we first met. Maybe we could bribe him to help us. He's easily swayed by gold."

I sat up straighter, surprised I'd forgotten.

"True, but he's half-mad now, and even if we could rely upon him, we certainly can't find him," I pointed out. "He's a traveler, he could be anywhere."

Aewna replaced her teacup on the table and said, "I believe I know where he is."

We all whipped our heads in her direction and my heart leapt with hope. Aewna laughed softly and continued, "We became friends, remember? I know his travel patterns because we correspond."

Well hell, I thought, scrubbing a hand down my face. *Maybe I should write letters more often.* Mal-Yin's eyes twinkled and he gave Aewna one of his rare smiles. Or maybe it was the kind he saved only for her.

"Are you serious?" I asked. "Can you find him?"

Aewna thought for a few seconds, then nodded. "Yes, as

long as he sticks to his routine, I know where he'll be about now."

"Then it's settled," Lazlian announced. Standing, he rested his palms on the table in a commanding manner that did not go unnoticed. "I will write to every clan I spent time with during my years on the mainland," he waved a hand, "and Aewna will write to this Farip man."

THANKS TO AEWNA'S FRIENDSHIPS, we'd found a way forward twice now. She managed to locate Fabroni, bid him come, and a week later, he did.

I imagined the traveler would have done so even without the promise of gold, having grown so fond of Aewna. Not that he'd decline any coin we offered.

Farip hadn't aged much since I'd last seen him, but his traveler's clothes were clean and he smelled like he'd bathed, unlike the last time. On the other hand, he frequently flashed a toothy grin, seemingly at nothing, and I swore his eye occasionally twitched. It gave me the feeling that he'd descended further into... if not madness, then peculiarity, at least.

We tried to present him with our offer, but he immediately waved us off.

"Before we speak, might you bring out your best bottle of red? And what game you got? Deer? Duck? Something tender and juicy would help replenish me from such a long journey."

I folded my arms. Farip hadn't been particularly far -- he'd reached us in mere days.

The Spades had kept a small farm, from which Aewna

arranged for one of the rabbits to be roasted. The livestock wasn't plentiful enough to be a real boon to our food stores, considering the numbers we expected, but we immediately began breeding what remained, and supplemented our rations with hunting excursions. Zaria had claimed one tiny bunny as a companion for Sanda, effectively saving it. Her sad eyes told me she didn't like slaughtering the fuzzy animals, but she was practical enough to eat them just the same. Wasting nothing, the meager pelts would be tanned and sewn into jackets for extra warmth, or turned into fingerless gloves. Anything to help the fighters we expected to join our ranks.

Once Fabroni had his fill, patting his soft stomach to let us know he enjoyed the meal, we finally got down to business.

Unnervingly, our satellite wasn't far from Spade City. It would take several days to march an army there, but only one or two for a single rider to make it.

Fabroni scratched his beard and made several protests I knew were only in service of upping his payment. It took a chiding look from Aewna for Fabroni to end his game and agree on an amount.

"How is it you're managing to sneak in and out of Spade City?" I questioned him.

"Can't tell you that," Fabroni replied.

"Well, then how do you intend to get close to Jori?"

"It's not important," he said.

"Okay, so who do you know in Spade City?" I tried.

"You don't need to know that either," Farip said, smiling.

I ran a hand through my hair and groaned. "We need to trust you and you're not giving us very much! This entire scheme is held together with string and tape. One mistake and it all comes undone," I said, voice raising with frustration. "You don't know the High Twelve the way I do, you don't know the complexities of their political allegiances, the intricate web of spies. I need to know where you're going, who you're seeing, how long it will take, and every detail of your plan. I can see that you don't think I'm being logical, you just think I'm paranoid!"

Fabroni furrowed his brow and replied, "I don't think you're paranoid, you're paranoid."

I opened my mouth, then froze. Zaria and Lazlian chuckled. I scowled and crossed my arms.

"You're just gonna have to trust me," Fabroni said with a shrug.

I didn't. But I trusted his love of gold and we had no better option. Farip took his leave with a very light step for such a heavy purse. I fell into a chair, grumbling.

Zaria swooped beside me and kissed my cheek. "You worry, but how could you not, given what we've been through?" she asked, rhetorically. "I love you for it. It keeps us safe. Only, you don't have to carry that burden alone. You know that, right?"

I looked at her and at Lazlian, relaxing my shoulders.

"I know," I said. I meant it.

THE PLAN WENT off without a hitch and I admitted that it hadn't been necessary for us to know Farip's secret for him to succeed. Though we tried to persuade him to fight with us -- the traveler certainly had his assets -- Fabroni returned to his wandering. Still, I wondered if it was truly the last time we'd see him. The man had a way of popping up when we didn't expect it.

A short fortnight after we'd sent him to Spade City, I walked to the meeting point Fabroni had coordinated for Jori and me, deep within the woods. But with every step forward, I had to wonder whether I should turn back. By doing this, I was putting my trust in a madman and a schemer. I hoped the risk was worth the reward, but I insisted on taking it alone. Zaria and Lazlian remained far back in the forest.

Spying Jori waiting alone under the forest canopy, I exhaled deeply. He could have ambushed me by now, if he wanted to.

With his soft hands and perfectly coiffed hair, Jori looked out of place, despite wearing simple attire. No guards accompanied him, though I knew they hid in the trees, whether I could see them or not. They'd watch, and possibly hear, everything we said.

I hoped Jori's men were completely loyal. I hoped he wasn't.

"And here you are," Jori declared, upon seeing me. "Aligned with Mal-Yin and having captured satellite eleven. Poised for an invasion and stirring up the clans to join you. I can hardly imagine what else you've been up to since leaving Spade City, but your exploits are always impressive, as is the way you *rise*."

"I could say the same about you," I returned with a genuine smile. I had no idea how the man rose from slave to High Twelve, but I'd bet it was an interesting story. "Which is why we're here."

"We're here because you want to turn the tables," Jori stated, eyeing his thick ring as he spun it around his finger.

"To persuade me to your side as I'd tried to persuade you to ours."

"But it's not your side," I reminded. "The Spades are not your kin, your clan, or even your friend. We have an actual shot at winning this war if you'll take the soldiers under your command and fight with us. Think of what we can give you if we succeed. You'll rise higher than you've ever dreamed in a new world we create."

"You presume to know my dreams?" Jori asked. His blue eyes sharpened, making me feel as if he might know mine.

"I misspoke," I said firmly. "What I mean is, we can offer you a position of power greater than the one you have now, if we win."

"If."

My heart beat faster, knowing this didn't look good yet still holding onto hope. "If we win, we can guarantee you an elevated position, something akin to being number one amongst the High Twelve. Will you join us with that promise?"

"No," Jori replied, and my heart sank. "I might climb that high on my own, in time."

"It could take decades or you might not make it at all," I countered, reminding him that he wasn't getting any younger.

Jori shrugged and I scrambled. I thought I was good at reading people, but he was a difficult man to understand. Jori didn't seem to enjoy the Spade spectacles in the Bowl, yet when I'd once spoken of punishing and degrading Lazlian as a slave, Jori's eyes had gleamed at the vengeance.

An idea sparked. It wasn't entirely ethical, but neither was anything the Spades did.

"Larius Mikaster," I said quickly, remembering how Jori's

family had been captured, how his father had mercy-killed his mother and then shot himself, rather than let any Spade atrocities befall them. Perhaps Jori had a more personal vendetta again the man in charge? "We can see to it that Larius is a casualty of this war. He dies. Or perhaps he takes his own life, while awaiting trial," I suggested, shrugging at the implication.

Jori's eyes flashed and I couldn't hold back a small grin.

Got you.

Yet his next words made my stomach sink.

"I will not lead my company to fight against our own," Jori said slowly. *"But,"* he began, and my heart beat with hope, "I will abstain."

Abstain?

"What does that mean?" I asked in a rush.

"I will neither fight you nor the Spades, but I will order the men and women under my command not to engage. I will take those in the twelfth sector and remove our soldiers from the city before the battle. You will not attack us when we march, and we will not attack you."

Confused, I searched his face for understanding. "But... won't this endanger your life if we lose? And certainly your status. You'll be executed or labeled a coward or..." I cut myself off. "I'm grateful for anything you'll do. But won't you lose everything for doing it?"

"Let me worry about me. The men and women who follow my orders will be pardoned, should the Spades win. They'll have not taken arms against them and they were simply loyal to my command. But, should you win, I'll still demand a position of the highest rank. As you said, if you were to recreate a governing body similar to the High Twelve, I'll be number one." Jori's nose twitched as if he fought a snarl before his face quickly relaxed once more.

"And Larius Mikaster is wiped from the face of the earth. No trial, no pardons, no prison."

I studied Jori. Was he similar to his father, underneath it all? Trying to save his men while bearing the brunt of any consequences himself? Did he truly care about others, more than himself, beneath that cold and calculating façade? Or had he a trick up his sleeves? If there was a way for Jori to escape persecution from the Aureum, I was sure he'd find it.

"That is my offer," Jori concluded.

It was a pittance. It sounded like it might entail little risk and all reward for Jori, but it was the best we could do. Despite being number twelve, Jori had a powerful slice of the pie and removing it from play would significantly weaken the Spades.

"I have your word?" I asked.

"I have nothing to gain from deceiving you," Jori replied, plainly.

I laughed. He didn't say, *"You can trust me,"* or *"I'm not a liar."* And perhaps, there was more honesty in this statement.

I agreed with a nod. We shook hands, then departed in different directions beneath the leafy trees.

"IT'S NO SMALL THING," Lazlian assured me when I returned. "It could be the difference between winning and losing. You said it yourself, Jori might be number twelve, but he commands a large faction in Spade City. Isolating his sector, removing those men and women who follow him first and foremost, is a boon."

"The support of his army fighting *with us* would be the

difference," I insisted. "This might just be the difference between losing quickly and losing slowly."

"By your own account Jori is a clever man," Lazlian insisted. "He wouldn't be doing this if he didn't think we had a chance."

True.

We had the army of Rythas. Mal-Yin and his weaponry. The mainland clans, hopefully. And Jori's abstaining. We'd amassed considerable assets. But I still didn't see how they'd be enough against the Spades' silo of doom. I felt like we were instead giving our enemy what they wanted. The more people who joined us, the more they'd slaughter in one swoop.

While I'd been preparing for my meeting with Jori, Lazlian had sent Mal's scouts to locate the Rythasian army as they marched. He sent them the shocking news that their king lived, along with the keylord and Princess Zaria. Now messengers reported back that our army would arrive within the next few days.

I wished I could have been there to see Navere's face when he learned that Lazlian was alive. Any glory the Commander thought to achieve in this war would be wiped out in an instant as Navere would have to know that he'd been supplanted in command. Lazlian was not the king Juls was -- he wasn't even a king like Grahar.

Laz had something to prove, and he'd get his hands dirty doing it.

I supposed we had that in common.

I smiled to myself, imagining Navere's ire. *One silver lining in this sky of gray.*

"When the army arrives, I'll need to formally and publicly claim Sanda as heir to the throne," Lazlian said, over a breakfast of crackers and a wedge of hard, nutty cheese. His voice was tentative, testing. He wasn't requesting my permission, but he was asking for my understanding.

By now, he knew he didn't need to. By now, he knew that I appreciated it anyway.

I nodded.

Zaria's eyes darted back and forth between the two of us, brow furrowed with questions.

But to those I had no answers.

IN RYTHAS, EVERYONE FIGHTS
Zaria

Anxiously awaiting the arrival of the Rythasian army, I watched Lazlian transform himself into a king. I wondered if, in some small part of his mind, he'd permitted himself the fantasy or if, in the past, he'd considered it a betrayal of his brother's sovereignty.

Or maybe... somewhere in the dark confines of their captivity, Kirwyn had a role in what I saw happening. Perhaps that is why they relied on each other like brothers now.

The changes in us seemed to develop like the earth itself. It'd seen it in a book once -- new land formed, malleable as it first took shape, then solidifying as it cooled. The three of us had morphed and molded into new versions of ourselves as we'd matured, and I thought we might have reached an age where this form strongly resembled our final. My only wish was to be whoever we were back in Rythas.

Home.

"Even after all these years, it's still difficult to believe all this is real. It's like something from a night terror," I said one evening, sliding my fingertips up the hard metal wall of the angular bedroom Kirwyn and I shared. Why were there so many sharp edges in these designs? In Rythas, our buildings reached for the sky with intricate, lofty turrets. Corners were softened by graceful arches. Beauty abounded in the many terraces exploding with flora, lush and leafy as it cascaded from one balcony down to the next. "Everything in this world is cold. Cold lines, cold weather, cold choices."

"I long for home," I whispered, nuzzling Kirwyn's chest. "I miss Teddy so much. I know I can't do anything until it's over. But, god, Kirwyn, it *hurts*."

With Sanda asleep in the adjoining chamber, Kirwyn and I climbed into bed together. We kissed, and I nestled into the comfort of his arms around me.

We hadn't been intimate since Sanda's birth and I couldn't decide if I was grateful for the necessary waiting period after labor, or if I resented the fact. Had Kirwyn not made any sexual advances toward me because he respected my body's need to heal, or because he'd changed how he felt, given I'd borne another man's child and this entire situation was entirely messed up?

Questions burned on the tip of my tongue and I bit them back. I told myself I didn't want to pry or push, but I knew there was cowardice in my restraint. Or was it wisdom to cultivate patience and allow Kirwyn to lead? Was *that* the mature thing to do?

I guess we haven't fully formed yet, I thought, stroking his arm and inhaling his woodsy scent.

Once again, I mused at simplicity of physical battles over affairs of the heart, especially when three people were entangled. In war, one either succeeded in an attack, or failed. But moves here led to infinite outcomes. I wanted one where we were all happy.

Somehow.

~

A FEW DAYS later the compound was abuzz with news, beginning by the doors and spreading inward.

The Rythasian army is here, someone shouted, cries carrying from one person to the next, until everyone had jumped to their feet and nearly jammed the doorway in an effort to push outside.

Frosty air whipped at my face and hair as I, too, joined the gathering crowd. When I saw the banners -- a flag bearing the crown and key of Rythas -- my heart soared. Proudly, they marched, a mix of riders and foot soldiers. It was almost the full force of our army.

Navere rode at the front the company and Jesi, as First, to his left.

She was glorious in full Rythasian armor and intimidating as well. Ready to fight at any moment, Jesi had pulled her curls back in a tight twist against her neck. Beside her, Navere was equally terrifying on his mount, which gave rise to mixed feelings inside me.

Let's hope all that aggression is pointed toward defeating the Spades, I thought. Now was not the time for petty squabbles or power plays.

"Jesi!" I cried, weaving through the crowd, but she didn't hear or see me above the clamor of men and horses.

"Jesmoré Tash!" I called, using her full name to catch her attention. She snapped her head in my direction, grinned, and dismounted her black stallion in one smooth move.

"You're alive," she breathed, wrapping me in a tight hug.

Laughing, I replied, "I'm hard to kill."

"I always knew you were alive," she said. "But it's good to be *sure.*"

Navere gave me a tight nod, hard face unreadable, then he carried on to find Lazlian, I guessed. I suspected the Commander wanted to confirm, with his own eyes, that the king lived.

Erisio slid off his mount and bowed to me, shyly. Having fought beside him at the Battle of the Glass Gardens, I was relieved by his presence. He'd helped Lazlian construct the explosives when I bombed the Oxholde ships, so I knew he brought a plethora of skills we could use.

As Jesi was called away to attend her work, a wagon at the rear of the company caught my eye. It was important enough to be guarded, but not so much that it traveled centrally amongst the soldiers. Instead, it trailed behind, like an afterthought or a reluctant member of the party.

I made a note to ask about it, but my attention was pulled by a tightly braided head of light brown hair, bobbing through the crowd and into my direction.

Lida?

"What are you doing here?" I gushed, happy to see her though it set my nerves aflutter.

Lida looked at me as if I'd asked what the sun was doing in the sky.

Eyebrow cocked, she replied, "You have no counselor, no one to advise or manage any internal aspect of this campaign. Raoul stayed in High Spire to help Juls, and I elected to come here, as counterpart abroad."

Looking around I asked, "Are Tomé-"

Lida cut me off with a shake of her head. "Tomé and Marcin stayed to defend Rythas." Lida wrinkled her thoroughly Elowan nose and declared in a perfectly Elowan manner, "My god it's cold here!"

I laughed, ushering her into the warmth of the compound.

LIDA WASTED no time in coordinating between Lazlian and the army to organize all that needed managing. She arranged everyone's accommodations, meal schedules, and sorted out what required guarding and when. She also brought general news from High Spire, which, sadly, would be our last. We were cut off from Rythas until the war was over.

There would be no going home again. Not unless we won.

Though the warriors of Rythas had already received the news that we lived, they cast awe-filled glances at Kirwyn, Laz, and I to confirm it. Every time we turned, we met with astonished faces, as if we'd risen from the dead, like gods.

But I blinked with my own astonishment when, amidst the chaos of the central hall, an elegant figure glided my way.

If Aewna, delicately-boned and adverse to warfaring, and I, middling with a blade and holding a newborn, looked out of place in this underground lair -- Kelody did even more so.

The Commander's new bride entered our headquarters as if she'd waltzed into High Spire's throne room. Her hair was twisted and pinned with ornamentation shaped like golden coins. If a few strands had fallen in their journey, it didn't lessen the beauty of that shining chestnut mane. Kels wore a *dress,* and the nicest thing I could say about it was that at least it was dark, and not a more eye-catching cherry or blood orange. She'd finished off her look with black, sensible boots, at least.

Coming to greet me, Kelody said, "The queen -- the acting queen -- insisted that I leave High Spire for my own safety... in such a condition."

One hand on her belly immediately indicated the condition.

She's pregnant and Merie ordered Kelody to come here? I puzzled. Sending Kels out of Rythas before the impending blockade made sense. But if Merie wanted Kelody ensconced somewhere safe, our headquarters was the last place to ensure it. *Was Merie hoping something bad would happen to Kelody or her baby?*

No, Merie didn't have a cruel bone in her body, especially not where children were concerned. I was shamed the idea even occurred to me. There was a time, back in Elowa, when I'd been as innocent as Merie.

But Kelody's arrival made *no sense.* Her presence was purposeful, I was sure. Only, I didn't know the purpose. Merie and I never really saw eye-to-eye.

Navere himself was absent, but Kels didn't appear to be searching for him. I assumed he was busy leading his men and thus, unable to escort her. Kelody scrutinized our headquarters with a discerning eye. Her face remained schooled, but I didn't think the noble lady, raised in luxury, was keen to spend an unknown number of months in a Spade compound. I didn't blame her.

As the silence between Kels and I stretched awkwardly, I studied Navere's new wife. Under closer inspection, I caught the appearance of dark circles beneath her eyes. Newly pregnant, the journey must have been hard on her. Or perhaps the wasting affected her too.

"The accommodations here are quite different from High Spire," Kels said with a light smile.

At the mention of High Spire, I couldn't help but repeat my heart's desire, though I'd already had reassurance from Jesi and Lida both. "Have you been in the castle much? Is my son safe?" I was unsure how far to trust Kels, but I trusted her answer in this.

"Very much so," she replied, then added softly, "For now."

I understood the implication and the pain made my face crumple. Nothing in our future was guaranteed and I hated myself for being here and not there, just as much as I knew I'd hate myself if it were the reverse. I was divided and there would be no whole until Rythas was safe.

Telling myself this didn't lessen the guilt.

Reading the distress on my face, Kels tried to assuage it by saying, "Teddy is the delight of the kingdom. He's claimed all of High Spire as his playground, as well as your aunt's lands. I have seen him tottering into the kitchens to steal fruit and cake. The servants pretend not to notice and he's always thrilled at having captured a treat. Juls and Merie keep him endlessly entertained."

To keep myself from crying, I focused on the happy bits Kelody told me. Though imagining Juls -- the strange boy I'd once been sent to marry and had divorced -- doting on my son, was hard to picture.

Kelody glanced down at Sanda, squirming in my arms, but she did not ask about her sire.

I suspected there was nothing I could tell Kels that she didn't already know.

Any guesses the new bride might have would be confirmed soon enough, because Lazlian had called the first assembly for the following day, and attendance was mandatory.

With the entire Rythasian army to witness, I was to present the king with our baby, and he would claim her as his heir.

~

INSIDE MY CHEST, my heart pounded erratically when I entered the crowded, central hall of the Spade compound. Everyone thought I handled the attention so well, having been raised on it. But the truth was, I never felt comfortable with so many eyes on me. Not the way Aewna did. I'd just grown used to hiding it, oftentimes mimicking the poise I thought a royal should possess, rather than feeling I truly carried it in my bones.

No. I am of the sea and of Elowa, I reminded myself. *My bones are made of bedrock, my will as firm as wood.*

Thinking of the Elowan saying, I reminded myself, *just as trees make the best boats, the best bodies follow their form.* I expanded my shoulders wide and strong, like branches. I straightened my back, hard and proud, like a trunk.

And then, as I walked, I added my own little touch to the metaphor. I let myself bloom from within, imagining flowers blossoming on my boughs.

Lazlian sat in a chair that had been placed upon a dais, serving as a makeshift throne. But when I entered the room, he rose.

Carrying Sanda in my arms, thousands of eyes were upon me as I crossed the central aisle. Rythasians and Mal's men crammed either side, with a few Elowans sprinkled in between. Thankfully, Sanda remained blissfully asleep. I didn't think I'd look very regal if she howled as I walked.

When I reached the king, I knelt, placing our newborn at Lazlian's feet. Then I rose and stepped back.

My mouth grew curiously dry. Lazlian and I had been enemies so long that in some dark corner of my mind, I couldn't help but brace for a trick. With animosity having lasted for years, I realized, that tiny hint of suspicion might take years to *completely* dissipate. Trusting Lazlian to keep me safe from all others, I did without question. Trusting him to keep me safe from himself...

We had some work to do.

Lazlian looked down on me and I saw, with relief, no trickery behind his eyes.

Only pride.

Laz knelt, gently lifted Sanda, and held her high in the air.

"I proclaim this babe, Fersanda Doreste, as mine own daughter," he called, "and heir to the throne of Rythas."

Cheers erupted, enough to startle me and to shock Sanda awake and bawling. I took her from Laz and dashed out of the deafening hall.

But as I hurried, I wondered... how many of the men and women were genuinely rejoicing to have an heir, and how many were secretly seething? Scheming?

A MOON CYCLE waxed and waned and the clans trickled into our compound. Lazlian welcomed them as he had his own army, establishing himself as the unquestioned leader of this war.

Apparently, many friendships were fostered during

Laz's mainland years. The Copperheads and Swamp Lords came first. I didn't know what I imagined for the latter -- perhaps long-haired men all in green with crests or jewels indicating a noble status.

But the Swamp Lords were a clan like any other. What *did* distinguish them was the spiky armor they wore, apparently, as everyday attire. Metal braces Lazlian called vambraces protected their forearms, but their primary purpose wasn't for hand-to-hand combat. At least, not with a human. From this armor a protracted dagger could extend, handy to pierce the roof of a mouth, in case one was caught in the jaws of swamp beast.

"Gators and 'diles, as they call them, are their biggest threat," Lazlian informed me.

"What's that?" I asked, indicating a vial dangling from the neck of every man, woman, and child.

"Gators, 'diles, and *snakes* are their biggest threat," Laz amended. "That vial contains anti-venom for the most prolific snakes inhabiting their territory. One of the reasons we connected was that I was able to barter a deal at the Ex for more of the concoction, after I'd intercepted a Spade shipment to the people of Shreelos."

Catching a glimpse of a man chewing something thin, dark, and tough, Lazlian spoke before I could even ask, "Gators, 'diles, snakes, and *mosquitos* are their biggest threats. They eat a sort of jerky. As best I can tell, it's made from a combination of cinchona bark and several medicinal plants to stave off diseases carried by the insects. It's not so necessary here," he said, shrugging, "but habits are hard to break."

I exhaled slowly. Growing up in Elowa, I'd thought Black Titans were frightening. I had no idea how many beasts existed on the mainland, marauding up and down the coast and hiding in forests, all in tight proximity to humans.

Another reason the high walls of Spade City are so beloved by their people, I thought.

Days later, a lowland clan called Wolf Wrath arrived. They were joined by friends Lazlian had never even met, a cousin clan named Winged Wrath, who lived deeper in the forest.

Word of our war is spreading, I thought, with hope broadening equally in my breast.

Unfortunately, the Spade satellite wasn't large enough to accommodate entire armies. I thought everyone would freeze to death if they slept outside, but Lazlian said winters were mild here and snows infrequent, so it wasn't too great an inconvenience to those camping beside the stronghold.

From the Swamp Lords' nervous twitching I could tell they didn't enjoy the captivity of the compound, and they quickly set up tents outside our doors. The move worked out for everyone because they apparently had a quarrel with the Winged Wrath clan.

"At least no fights have broken out yet," Lazlian whispered to Kirwyn and I. "But they will."

I believed him, though never did I imagine the first would be ours.

It was late in the evening when I returned to our chambers to check on Sanda. She should have been sleeping and it wasn't even time to feed her, but something drew me to our bedroom.

Maybe it was a mother's intuition.

But it was faulty or I, too slow.

When I arrived, the door to Sanda's antechamber was open wide.

A horrifying image was forever seared into my brain, ready to drive me to madness if I looked at it too closely, too long.

Navere stood above Sanda's bed.

His sword was raised for a killing blow.

CHAPTER 49

ODERINT DUM METUANT
Lazlian

Kirwyn patted his body, looking for the extra round of ammunition he always carried, along with his guns. I thought he was overly cautious -- perhaps a bit paranoid -- but couldn't blame him, given everything we'd been through. He'd forgotten the spare clip, and that mistake was the only reason we were in the corridor, a fact I thought back on repeatedly, with gratitude.

Halfway down the hall leading to our rooms, I heard a scream and the unmistakable sound of combat coming from Zaria and Kirwyn's bedroom. The clash was brief, contained, and horrifically heart-stopping. I felt as if my stomach had been ripped from my body.

Kirwyn and I bolted the rest of the way down the hall. Just before we entered the bedroom, I heard the fight end with a *thud* I knew to be the sound of a fallen man.

Woman?

My blood iced and for half a heartbeat, I struggled not to freeze. Only seconds had passed between when I heard the scream and before we careened into the room. I couldn't take in the sight fast enough.

Relief flooded my entire being, so great it nearly knocked me off my feet.

In the main bedroom, Zaria held Sanda tight to her breast while in the doorway to the adjacent chamber, Jesi crouched above Navere's dead body. The blade in her hand made it clear she'd slain him. Breathing heavily, Jesi shot to her feet and sheathed her sword.

"He tried to murder Sanda in her bed. I tried to keep his death quiet."

For a moment, I almost couldn't believe the Commander had been so careless. Then I remembered how Kirwyn had taunted him that day in our war tower, saying whoever was behind the failed weapons deal shouldn't have sent an underling to do his dirty work. I thought of how Navere had tried to use Jesi for eavesdropping on our conversation, and of how she'd failed to report anything useful, as he'd hoped.

The Commander had finally decided to take matters into his own hands.

Jesi's were more capable.

I thanked all the gods for that.

"The two men who were guarding Sanda have disappeared," Jesi reported. "Bribed or tricked or lured away and killed, I don't know. Navere's path had been cleared."

Before I could let rage consume my entire being, I snapped my attention to Zaria, pressed against the wall, pale and shaking.

"Are you in shock?" I asked. It wasn't the keenest question to ask as a person who, in such a state, likely couldn't give an accurate reply, but I wasn't at my sharpest either. My eyes darted between Zaria and Navere's corpse. I had questions for Jesi too, but they would have to wait.

"No. Yes. A little," Zaria breathed. The contradictory answer mimicked her face as it dashed from one emotion to the next, unable to settle on any expression.

Kirwyn crossed to where she huddled, taking her face in his hands and examining it. He smoothed her hair from her brow and whispered words meant to soothe.

Clutching Sanda to her chest and anchoring on Navere's corpse, Zaria asked no one in particular, "What will you do with him?"

Kirwyn made a sound of fury, like grunt turned growl. "Throw him to the wild beasts in the forest. Let them devour his corpse."

"No," I said sharply. Thinking quickly, I closed the door behind me. "The word *traitor* will be carved across his brow and that disloyal head will be severed from his traitorous body. Call an assembly," I told Jesi. "We'll show whoever may have conspired with Navere what happens to those who betray us."

"For Mal's men and all the clans or-" Jesi began.

"Just the Rythasian soldiers," I said, waving a hand. "I'll keep our army in line, Mal can do the same with his. Although I'm sure word will spread and many will gather regardless. Which is just as well. I want them to see who their true leader is, and what becomes of anyone who dares go against me."

I knew Zaria didn't like this, but she was too shocked to protest. Or maybe she'd come around to understanding. Times like these called for such measures. There could be no room for dissent; not the slightest inch to question my rule.

Nodding in Kirwyn's direction, I asked "Do you want to do the honors?"

Kirwyn withdrew the dagger strapped to his waist. "With pleasure."

I filled the space he left at Zaria's side, bringing her and Sanda into my arms. The embrace would allow Zaria to turn her head to my chest, should she want to look away, or provide the comfort she needed, should she endeavor to observe. I declared the edict, but it was her choice whether or not to watch.

I, however, viewed with satisfaction as Kirwyn straddled Navere's corpse and carved the word into the flesh on his forehead. When he finished, Kirwyn drew his sword and hacked the Commander's head from his body. Trying to stay quiet, it took a few grisly swings to finish the job.

Zaria couldn't seem to look away but, frozen and speechless, she paled further, clutching Sanda as if one of us might rip our baby from her arms. Though Zaria stared, her eyes glazed, like she'd mentally transported herself elsewhere to avoid seeing the severed head before her.

"Zaria," Kirwyn said, standing in front of her to draw her attention away from the satisfyingly gruesome scene. "You have to go with Lazlian."

"Go?" she whispered, not understanding.

"You have to stand beside the king and show them your strength. Show them you've won. That it wasn't even a contest and you're not even affected."

"But I am affected," she breathed.

"I know," he said, rubbing her left arm, the one that wasn't pressed against my side. "But you need to fake it."

"Kirwyn's right," Jesi piped up. "I will find you the nicest clothing I can, and quickly. You must put on a gown, and jewels if you can find them," Jesi instructed, scanning the room for anything she might employ. "You need to dry your tears, make up your face, and face them all. Stand strong before anyone who would stand against you."

"I need time to breathe," Zaria protested, sucking in great gulps of air. "Why is it never enough? Can't I have a minute to breathe?"

"No," I told her. Gently but firmly, I turned her to me and cupped both her cheeks. "You can breathe after. We'll breathe with you, for you, whatever you need. But I need you now, we need you now, *our daughter* needs you now."

I knew the last part would help snap her out of her haze. Zaria began nodding. It was a bit manic and her eyes still glazed, but it was a start.

"Fetch the finest attire you can find, please," I said to Jesi. She gave a quick nod and hurried from the room.

"We show a strong, united front," I instructed. "I'll take the traitor's head, you hold our heir. Let them see, let them all see."

Jesi returned a moment later, bearing what looked to be a white, fringed throw. It was the kind of light blanket one would toss on a sofa, nearly as thin as a sheet. I supposed it was too much to hope the compound contained gowns. But somehow, with a clever, knotted twist at her shoulder and a belt just above the small round of her recently-pregnant belly, Jesi managed to drape the material onto Zaria as if it had been constructed for her body specifically. She nicked a rare bit of silver molding from a lamp, snapping it off in one quick pull. Impressed, I stared at the transformation taking place before my eyes. In mere seconds, Jesi worked a regal knot of some kind atop Zaria's head and adorned it with Spade metalwork, passing as Rythasian ornamentation.

Slipping into the makeshift dress and dipping low to allow Jesi to work on her hair, Zaria's movements were thick and slow, a counter to Jesi's quick fluttering. Zaria's limbs worked as if she trudged through mud. Her mind seemed equally sluggish, as if she'd awakened from a dream -- a nightmare, really -- and struggled to return to reality. But she *was* returning.

It helped when, without warning, Jesi pinched her cheeks. A tad harder than necessary, I suspected.

"Ouch!" Zaria exclaimed.

"You need color," Jesi replied, all-business. It was the same single-minded efficiency she applied to battle, applied now to beautification. "We haven't the time to raid the kitchens or I'd have found some beets or berries... something else to stain. Press your lips together, hard."

Zaria, growing more cognizant, rubbed and bit her lips until they too pinkened like her cheeks.

The entire transformation was complete in minutes, and I had to admit I was surprised at the efficiency and the effect. It helped that Zaria was naturally beautiful, but Jesi managed to make it look effortless, like an Elowan goddess stood before us. It was exactly the curated casualness we required.

Now we just needed Zaria's carriage to match her costuming. I winced, imagining Zaria fainting -- or worse -- crying on the dais.

Come 'round, little queen, I thought, willing her to strengthen. *The stubborn braenese I know wouldn't let others knock her down so easily.*

"Breathe," Jesi said, holding her friend's hands. "Be bold. You save me, I save you, remember? You and Sanda are safe and I'll be out there with you."

Something in her words caught Zaria's attention.

"It's us," she whispered, staring back at Jesi. Then more firmly, she insisted, *"It's us."*

I realized Zaria was echoing my words from the fealty ceremony and Kirwyn's from the compound, right before we departed. No one was coming to save us, to guide us, to tell us how to proceed in a battle so big it would determine the fate of the world. We had no one but each other to count upon.

Looking over the three of them, I realized I couldn't have chosen anyone better.

"It's always been us," Zaria stared at us intensely, eyes no longer glazing with shock, but shining with something else.

I wasn't sure Jesi understood her fully, but she nodded encouragingly and squeezed her friend's body in a tight hug.

"Are you ready?" I asked, and without waiting for a reply, I announced, "Jesi, find Lida and Erisio and tell them to assemble the army. Then return, and we'll ascend the dais together."

To Zaria, I said, "The mother of the young queen."

Approaching Kirwyn, I lightly grasped his bicep as I proclaimed, "The keylord."

Finally, I stood before Jesi.

"And the new Commander of the Rythasian Army," I pronounced, tipping my head.

Jesi sucked in an awed breath.

"I wish your promotion came under better circumstances," I said quickly. "And it's not just a token of my gratitude -- which is incalculable and impossible to put into words -- but because you deserve it. You've earned it. There is no one better and no one else I would have even considered."

Jesi bowed low, then hurried from our rooms.

SOLDIERS STOOD IN DISCIPLINED ROWS, but many shifted their weight from foot to foot in nervous anticipation. The king calling an assembly this late could mean anything.

Surveying them with slow command, I let my eyes linger, let any would-be traitors know that I would ferret them out and kill them.

Others had gathered once word spread. There wasn't much to do, crammed in our compound, and the mystery of this meeting caught everyone's interest, from the Rythasians -- who'd assembled in the central rows -- to the various clans, leaning against the walls or lounging on the sidelines. Everyone watched, tense, expectant.

Good. Let them see. Let them all see.

Zaria and I stood central on the dais. Kirwyn was to her right and Jesi, my left. Sanda watched quietly in Zaria's arms.

"Navere, once Commander of the Rythasian Army, was caught this evening attempting to murder the heir to Rythas," I announced, wasting no time. "Your young queen, an infant in her bundling, and *my daughter.*"

I growled the two words and jerked my head to Erisio, who stood with Lida in the shadows, awaiting my signal. Swiftly, he transferred to me what I needed.

Disgust immediately curled my lips to even touch the thing, but triumph swelled in my chest. No one would harm my family, no one would ever threaten my reign.

Fisting the hair on Navere's severed head, I spun on my heel and held it aloft for all to see.

Gasps echoed from the grotesque shock, then total silence filled the hall.

"Look upon the traitor's head," I shouted, and my

words echoed off the metal walls. "And know my only regret is that his death could not last longer. Here, far from proper Rythasian justice, this excuse for a man could not be sent to the Isle of Walking Corpses, as he deserved."

Pride and protectiveness were like drugs pumping through my veins. In that moment, I pitied anyone not on our side. Kirwyn and I scanned the faces of our soldiers, paying attention to who looked scared, nervous, or vengeful. I took special note of those whose eyes gleamed with the same sense of justice I felt.

With a roar of rage, I hurled Navere's head straight down the center aisle of the crowd, causing the few who'd moved into the pathway to jump back to avoid it. Luck was on my side as the gory head rolled to a stop facing upward, the word *traitor* prominently displayed and dead eyes staring blankly into the gathered assembly.

"Would anyone else like to step forward and join your friend in treason?" I called out to the crowd. "I promise a swift death. But if I find out the late Commander had conspirators, I swear you will be given a sentence here that makes the Isle of Walking Corpses look blissful. Step forward now, traitors, or step back in line. For if I root you out, I will cut you up and feed you to the backland beasts, one piece at a time."

Times like these call for kings like this, I told myself, watching to see if anyone would volunteer, rather than be caught later and face a worse fate.

Or perhaps they'd been swayed.

"Long live King Lazlian!" someone shouted. I noted that first woman, remembering to reward her loyalty later.

"King Lazlian!" came another cry.

"Lazlian!" echoed a third.

A chorus broke out, falling into a chant of my name.

"Lazlian, Lazlian, Lazlian," they shouted, punctuating the cry with a fist or a sword in the air. Some bent to a knee in fealty, some bowed, some stood on their tippy-toes or jumped with enthusiasm.

In the ecstatic frenzy to shout out their loyalty, Navere's severed head was inadvertently kicked and swept aside until it was forgotten, lost in the crowd.

WHEN THE FOUR of us returned to Zaria and Kirwyn's bedchambers, I was shocked to find Kels waiting, one hand resting gently on the small swell of her belly.

For the first time that evening, I felt a twinge of regret. I'd neglected to even inform her that her husband had been executed before I'd paraded his head for all to see. Failing to send her word wasn't my finest move. But at least I didn't see her as complicit in some way, condemning her along with her husband, as some kings of the past might have done.

I planned to offer my condolences, but before I could speak, Jesi announced, "It was Kelody who warned me."

Surprised, I paused.

"I didn't get a chance to explain before we had to move, and quickly," Jesi said. "The reason I knew what Navere planned was because Kelody told me of her suspicions. She overheard her husband plotting Sanda's murder, though she does not know with whom."

Likely the missing guards, I thought.

"Kels is the reason I raced down the hall and hid in the shadows to await what might happen," Jesi declared. "She's the reason your daughter lives."

"She is not the only reason," I told my new commander, with equal appreciation.

I turned to Kelody, who'd been watching quietly, and bowed deep to the young widow. I didn't need to press for answers. I could guess why she'd done it; easily imagining how poorly her marriage turned out. Likely Kels had caught Navere in bed with another. Perhaps multiple times. Perhaps he'd sworn to change and had done it again. Perhaps it made Kelody the subject of gossip in High Spire. However it occurred, I knew that Navere wasn't faithful just as I knew that Kelody was not the type of woman to suffer humiliation. Arrangements all parties agreed upon were one thing to Kels, being made a fool, quite another.

"You have my ever-lasting gratitude and will be given a permanent position of power in my court," I told her. "I regret that you are without a husband, but I can strike another match for you, if that is your wish. I do not have the means to skirt the blockade and return you to Rythas, but I can find you sanctuary elsewhere. We can arrange someplace safe for you to have your baby, if that is your desire. Tell me your wish, whatever it is, and if it is within my means, I will grant it."

Kels studied our faces carefully. "You have proclaimed Prince Theo to wed one of the noble daughters of Rythas," she reminded. "Should my child be a girl, I want his betrothal announced to my daughter. Should I bear a son, I want my baby betrothed to Sanda, your heir."

I heard Zaria suck in a breath and her eyes widened as if to say, *oh, what a play.* Kirwyn frowned, but other than an angry snort, said nothing. I could tell he was biding his time.

"You want me to betroth my daughter, the young queen, to the son of the man who just tried to murder her?"

I scoffed, waving an angry hand. "It is out of the question. Ask for something else."

"You have decreed that if my request is within your means, you will grant it." Kelody's chin rose higher. Though they looked nothing alike, the move reminded me a little of Zaria's stubborn stance. "This qualifies."

Sighing heavily, I let my eyelids flutter shut.

I didn't know how far back her family had been working to maneuver into the royal family, but this made three generations at least. Kels' mother, who'd been my father's mistress, Kelody herself, who'd angled to be my queen or my HRM, and now, with her son or daughter, Kels thought to finally achieve that goal.

Dammit, I cannot, in good conscience, deny her request. How could I refuse? Without her information, there would *be* no heir.

On the other hand, it wasn't my choice alone. One glance at their clenched jaws told me neither Kirwyn nor Zaria had any positive feelings about this reward.

That was putting it lightly. Both eyed me with a warning that they'd wring my neck if I granted it.

I scrubbed a hand down my face.

Most importantly, the match might not be a beneficial one. If we survived the war, who knew what alliances might need solidifying? I couldn't be shortsighted. Whether anyone liked it or not, Sanda was a key piece in the future of Rythas. We were all players on this board, even me.

"I refuse your request," I told Kels with finality. "Ask another."

Propriety out the window, Kelody's temper flared and she gestured angrily as she began arguing. Kels spoke with too much familiarity, owing to our past, and I, ready to snap from the exhaustion of the day's events, allowed my voice to rise as well.

"Stop!" Zaria called out, coming to stand between us and glowering at everyone. "As we are discussing the future of *my* children, I will be the one to have the final say."

My eyes darted to Kirwyn, but he'd relaxed, trusting whatever Zaria was about to do. I clenched my teeth and waited.

"As someone who was forced to marry with no voice in the matter, I cannot agree to your request," Zaria told Kels, softly. "My son and my daughter must have some say in the selection of their partner, and I cannot make a promise that that choice will be your offspring."

Kelody's lips turned down and her eyes narrowed, but she said nothing.

"But I can promise you this," Zaria hastened to add. "We will not betroth either Theo or Sanda to anyone else, and we will do our best to foster a... friendship. We vow not to hinder any affection that might develop between our children. And, should romance blossom on its own, we will do our best to create a smooth pathway toward a union between them."

For several seconds Kels searched Zaria's face. Then a grin lifted one side of her mouth.

Oh, I know that smile. It wasn't just for her trust in Zaria's honor, although that was there. It was that Kelody had no shortage of faith in herself, in her ability to mold any son or daughter of hers into as desirable a partner as possible.

"I accept," Kelody agreed.

The two women looked at us and Kirwyn and I nodded our agreement.

It was done.

Selfishly, I hoped the child would be a girl, and thus, Kirwyn's problem. Not that I wished him ill but the queen's consort, the king of Rythas, needed to be chosen with more care than by some backroom deal in an underground bunker, and on the brink of war no less.

Although, I had to admit, many an alliance was made in such a manner. It was in Kirwyn and Zaria's own back parlor, after all, that we'd begun our discussions about siring the heir.

I rubbed my forehead wearily. In case I needed a reminder, I'd been re-handed one of the key lessons in court politics.

Every move has a countermove.

This one held ramifications we wouldn't know until years in the future.

But seeing as how we all might not live for many months longer, there was no use wasting time overthinking it. Instead, I thanked and dismissed Kelody and Jesi, kissed Sanda on her soft, baby cheeks, and took myself to bed.

Before I departed, I caught the pained look on Zaria's face and the furrowed brow on Kirwyn's. I didn't want to think what my own face revealed, but leaving Sanda now, after what just happened, felt more wrong than ever.

My footsteps were heavy as I walked back to my room.

CHAPTER 50

NO EASY CHOICES
Zaria

A few days later, I eyed Kirwyn and Laz as we took breakfast on the floor in our chambers -- mine and Kirwyn's -- thinking about the odd scene we made. Beside us, Sanda played with her bunny. She was Lazlian's daughter... Lazlian, who slept in an antechamber beside his mistress and her husband.

Too weird, ponder something else.

We ate a breakfast of canned beans and crackers, rations better than the dried, powdery substance that formed Spade bricks and made up the dietary centerpiece for most of the soldiers in our camp. After the past few months, it was hard for the three of us to face a brick without retching. Crews were sent to hunt and forage daily, with Lida equitably distributing the boon to ensure everyone had enough nutrients.

Although, I thought, nervously squirming, *we're running low on game in our range, and the forest will soon be picked over.* We couldn't indefinitely sustain all our forces *plus* the many clans continually joining our effort.

Beside us, I turned Sanda onto her stomach. She hadn't begun crawling yet, but her features had developed early.

For some reason, I'd always pictured a babe with Lazlian's dark hair and my light eyes, but Sanda was the opposite. Whisps of honied hair adorned her head and her eyes were the sharp, striking hazel of her father -- though her brown and green seemed more amber and jade in the light. I swore I could tell, even from a few months old, that she was going to be fierce. Wild, perhaps. My little moon princess with a heart of fiery stars.

Though he'd inherited my long lashes and the shape of my nose, Teddy had turned out closer to a miniature version of Kirwyn, with dark hair, green eyes, and a mischievous grin. Sanda looked like balanced a mix of Lazlian and I, her face combining our features. I wasn't sure if it was because she was female or if it was just the luck of the draw.

I was scooping up the last of my bean sauce with a cracker, fantasizing about the feast we'd had the night of The Divine Slumber, when Erisio poked his head of sandy hair into our room.

Politely, he asked, "Ready to go?"

Erisio and Laz had spent a lot of time together working on explosives and other Spade technology back in High Spire, so the king had no qualms when Jesi named Erisio as First. I also thought the easy-going soldier was the closest thing Laz ever had to a friend, outside of his own family.

Until Kirwyn, I realized with bemusement.

We shot to our feet and I prepared Sanda in her warmest bundling. Despite the chill, I welcomed a respite from the confines of the compound. Air cold and fresh was better than warm and stale. At least, temporarily.

The four of us took our turn in the clearing outside the satellite and stayed overlong, stretching our legs and conversing under the brown, bare trees. For exercise, we raced one another and tried to be useful by hunting for any edible shoots in a fruitless attempt to find more food. I let Sanda feel the patchy grass and hard-packed dirt beneath her baby hands, while Kirwyn visited with different clans who camped beside the building. Giddy with fresh air, I watched Laz and Erisio mock-battle with tree branches for Sanda's amusement. She laughed whenever Erisio fake-stabbed daddy and he fell dramatically.

I swallowed thickly, not enjoying the sight myself.

Dusk fell and we still hadn't our fill, when Jesi raced up to our group.

"Mal-Yin has had a breakthrough and he can read the data cube," she reported. "He's called for us to meet in the war room." With an apologetic look at Erisio, she added, "Just us."

Erisio flashed a genial grin and shrugged, wandering off to amuse himself.

Together, the rest of us scurried toward the satellite doors, leaving behind the gray, wintry sky and heading back into the gray, wintry compound.

TO MY SURPRISE, Mal had invited Aewna and Lida to our meeting as well. With nervous excitement coursing through us, no one took a seat. Mal-Yin strode to the Spade monitor with its coastal map and began vaguely.

"With each passing year the Spades only become more

difficult to defeat. We might not get another chance in our lifetime, or any thereafter."

The screen moved, focusing on Spade City itself, an irregular circle ringed with high walls.

Mal-Yin turned to us and said, "The first problem we face is that the thousands of slaves will be shepherded *into* the outer walls whenever conflict is on the horizon. That is one of the reasons the walls are so thick. For days, weeks, or however long necessary, they are forced to live in these cramped quarters. Any attempt to blast through results in the death of innocents, and it won't end there. The Spades will use the other half of their slave population as human barricades. They'll become living defenses all throughout Spade City. It's violently horrific as there is no way to get to the enemy without first going through an innocent."

I sucked in a breath. We'd heard rumors of the latter, but never suspected the former, and certainly not the extent of either.

Mal rocked back on his heels, hands in his pockets. "It's been a long time since anyone mounted an attack against the Spades, but I believe where most have failed is in trying to free the slaves or in attempting to avoid harming them."

Mal cast an appreciative glance in my direction.

"But what we have provides us with a potential advantage. With the use of that golden data cube, we can hack their system and protect the innocents. We can't free them, exactly, but we can contain them. Lock them within the walls and away from the Spades. If we hack the system several hours before we attack, but before their soldiers start grabbing slaves to use in their defenses, we keep them in one place until the battle is over."

"But that's good," I said, confused at Mal-Yin's qualifying tone. "What's the problem? Let's do that."

Mal-Yin held up a hand. "There's two problems. First, it obviously limits us to blasting through the gates to attack the city. There are four. However, we'll be limited to funneling through those four, and they're stronger than the walls."

Kirwyn looked aghast at the idea. I was sure he imagined soldiers being picked off like flies in that scenario, as he'd predicted.

Lazlian, who didn't seem any more approving, stroked his lips and asked, "What's the second problem?"

"My men believe they can successfully hack their systems and corrupt the locks on the outer ring, so that the Spades can't use slaves as cannon fodder. But we can't *hide* an electronic invasion. Once we start attempting to shut it down, the Spades will be alerted to the fact that we're in their network. We risk losing the chance to secure anything else."

Mal-Yin gave us a look both sympathetic and serious. "Meaning we risk not being able to lock down the weapons silo. It might be one or the other if we run out of time, leaving their armory wide open."

My eyes rounded, but I clung to one word. *If.*

Mal nodded his head in Kirwyn's direction. "We cannot beat the Spades if they pull out the big guns; it's suicide. Either way, their armies will still have access to whatever they've got on hand outside the silo, but with *only* those weapons it will be a more evenly-matched battle. If we use what might be our one shot at hacking the system to protect the slaves over locking down the silo, we risk the Spades getting the weapons that mean our defeat."

Heavy silence descended upon the room as his words sunk in. My mind went all the way back to when Kirwyn and I were on the mainland years ago, and we'd been unable to save that wagon of children. I remembered the pleading in the little girl's eyes.

So many children. Just like Teddy and Sanda and all the kids at our camp.

The horror was unimaginable. Yet the risk was foolish.

If.

I clung to the word again.

"All of this is theoretical because we don't know for sure until we're in the system," Mal said, complicating the issue. "But whatever the odds are, we decrease them significantly if we don't go straight for the artillery."

If, I repeated.

The same word that haunted me after Ollier's death.

Dreadful silence returned, making the air feel thick, as if I'd choke on it. I realized we hadn't even begun fighting physically yet, and I was already sweating.

"As the leader of this war, I say we vote on it," Lazlian declared, turning to face us. "The seven of us." Looking at the makeshift war table, he said, "Everyone takes a seat to vote. Here, if you think we should go for the silo first," Laz said, pointing to a row of chairs, "and this side for the slaves."

It didn't take more than a moment for Kirwyn to stride forth first, choosing the silo.

No, I mentally screamed, heart sinking. Though I didn't entirely blame him. The regret on Kirwyn's face seemed to say, *you haven't seen what I've seen.*

I gaped as Jesi followed, choosing a chair beside Kirwyn.

"As Commander of the army, I have to do what's best to protect my soldiers," Jesi announced, "to give them a fighting chance."

It was already two against one. I hurried to the chair

opposite Kirwyn and Jesi. *How could I be on an opposing side?* But my heart said no. Maybe that made me the weaker one here. I didn't know; I just knew I what I couldn't do.

Hope sprung in my chest when Aewna sat beside me. "I vote to protect the innocents first," she said. "It is a risk, but it's one worth taking."

Lida looked from side to side and I felt my gut twist when she took a seat with Jesi. At my pleading gaze she said, "I'm sorry, Zaria. I have to choose what's logical and this is the more rational decision. One that, ultimately, leads to a likelier outcome of saving more lives."

I couldn't argue her logic. I hated it anyway.

I was defeated, because only Mal-Yin and Lazlian were left standing and Mal looked ready to speak. I wasn't sure what Laz would do, but it no longer mattered. Mal would declare for logic as well. He'd side with Kirwyn, who'd been his friend in many endeavors and whose wisdom he respected. Most importantly, Mal didn't care about the cost of lives in getting what he wanted.

My mouth fell when Mal-Yin strode to my side and wordlessly slid into the chair beside Aewna.

Still gaping, I leaned down the table and asked, "Why are you voting with me? I'm pleased but..." Uncaring who listened and utterly baffled, I asked, "Do you love Aewna that much that you're here for her sake? Because I do not believe for a second that you care about those people."

"They're not people," Kirwyn said in a low, dangerous voice. He leveled a calculating glare at Mal. "They're votes."

Votes? I scrambled to put together whatever Kirwyn had worked out and scoffed with disbelief. "Oh my god... You're willing to accept this risk for the reward. Whatever becomes of the city if we win..."

"No one is going to support a ruler who doesn't support them," Mal said, shrugging.

Oh my god. Mal didn't want the slaves protected because he valued their lives. He valued their vote. If we won, we'd create a power vacuum, and somebody had to fill it.

Might as well be me, Mal-Yin had once said, when speaking of ruling in Rythas. As it stood, we had no solid plan in place for post-war leadership. Yet. Mal was laying the groundwork for it to be him, *democratically.*

I threw Aewna a look that cried, *this* is the man you love? Her soft smile seemed to say, *he's on our side, don't worry too much about how he got here.*

Plopping back in my chair, I realized we were evenly divided. Kirwyn, Jesi, and Lida sat to one side of the table, Mal, Aewna, and I on the other...

...Leaving the deciding vote up to the king, who strode to the head of the table and surveyed us.

Oh no.

Sighing, Lazlian met Kirwyn's eyes. My heart hammered in my chest as the king's gaze next fell upon Jesi. There it remained.

"Kirwyn is the only one who's seen the weapons inside the silo. But as the only true Rythasian here and the Commander of our army, Jesi's opinion carries more weight than anyone else's. As such-"

"No!" I cried, frantically wracking my brain for a way to stop this. "She is your Commander?"

"Yes."

"She is your Commander?" I repeated, desperate. "And I am your *queen!*"

A FATE WORSE THAN DEATH
Zaria

I'd sprung to my feet as I finished, leveling the room into stunned silence, though I wasn't even sure what I was saying. I had Lazlian's full attention. But he looked both hungry at the meaning of my words and ready to whip me for insubordination at the same time.

Come to think of it, it wasn't the first time I'd seen that look on his face, though it was the most pronounced.

"Maybe not by marriage but in practice," I hedged. Save Kirwyn, I didn't care who listened or what they thought as I continued breathlessly. "I have lain with you again and again and given you an heir, *the* heir to all of Rythas. If that doesn't make me your queen or... the closest you have to it... then I don't know what does. As such, *my* word counts more than anyone else's at this table."

I couldn't meet Kirwyn or Jesi's gaze. I felt bad for overruling them, but not bad enough to take it back. Besides, I was too terrified to break eye contact with Lazlian as I wasn't sure what he read in my declaration. Had I made promises I couldn't keep? Was I offering him myself as he'd always wanted, to protect the slaves? Would he extract that from me later? Or would he be contented with some sort of compromise, as we seemed to be working toward?

Jaw clenched, Lazlian regarded me darkly with those scorched-earth eyes.

"Mal-Yin has never lost a battle in this life," I whispered, seeking to strengthen my argument. "Jesi is your most competent commander in ages, maybe ever. Kirwyn knows the inner workings of Spade City. And you've assembled the clans here, more than have ever gathered, some who've been waiting a lifetime for this chance."

Lazlian licked his lips. His eyelids briefly fluttered.

"Alright. We try to protect the slaves first."

I was so relieved, my entire body sagged with the gasp I made.

"But we're going to need all the help we can get, and what we have now isn't enough," Lazlian said.

I'd relaxed too soon. Laz nearly knocked me over with his next words.

"I'm sending an emissary to the Biohazards to ask them to join us. They are rumored to have advanced technology as well, smaller in scale but similar to the Spades. I know for a fact they wear contacts to color their eyes and have heard they've developed some remarkable advancements in medicine. But most importantly, they possess weapons and know how to use them."

"Wait, no-" I protested, panicked and disoriented with this unexpected turn. I briefly met Kirwyn's eyes to see he was equally alarmed at the idea of inviting the Biohazards to join us. In this matter, he and I were united.

"Zaria, sit down," Lazlian commanded impatiently.

"I'll go to the Biohazards," Lida piped up. "I can offer little assistance in battle plans and I'm not valuable enough for them to use as a hostage, should they turn hostile. I've read up on their clan and believe I can negotiate between us."

"But wait," I pled. Lazlian knew what Kirwyn and I had endured at the Hazard's hands, what we'd *lost*.

"I have made my decision and there is nothing more to discuss," Lazlian declared, tone clipped. I didn't like that he seemed to be concluding the meeting and in desperation, I sat, hoping for an opportunity to speak again.

"Lida, you will go to the Hazards," Lazlian commanded. "Mal, let's meet in the morning to review what we know from the data cube. You are all dismissed."

Lazlian spun on his heel and walked briskly from the room.

In unison, Kirwyn and I sprang from our chairs to follow him. Halfway down the hall, we caught up to the king and began speaking at once, trying to convince Laz that we shouldn't allow the Hazards anywhere *near* our war camp.

Lazlian held up one arrogant hand to silence us. "We don't have enough guns to defeat the Spades, especially not with this risky plan. Do either of you have a suggestion that solves the problem? Anything other than *not* requesting the Biohazards to join us?"

Kirwyn clenched his jaw. I chewed my lip. Lazlian straightened. He had an inch or two on Kirwyn and several on me.

"I appreciate your not showing flagrant insubordination in the middle of our meeting -- a lesson she needs to learn," Laz hurled, speaking to Kirwyn and pointing angrily at me. "But it doesn't change the fact that I have laid down my rule and it is *my* rule. That I granted this pieced-together assembly a chance to weigh in on the decision is a courtesy. I have heard your counsel and I have made my decision. That is the end of it," Lazlian declared. "Do as you please in your home, but the two of you cannot play wild freeborns in my court."

Lazlian's words hit us with the rough power of a storm wave, though he did not shout them. Nothing he said was untrue. But, ego bruised, I was sure the heat in my cheeks glowed in the dim hallway.

"I will hear you," Lazlian said, soft, but firm. "But if we are going to do... whatever this is... then we must present a united front at all times."

What *were* we doing, exactly? I couldn't ask the question aloud. Instead, I temporarily ignored my oath of fealty and bit out with resentment, "With you at the head?"

Lazlian's dark eyes pinned me. "Yes. Out there."

"I don't like—"

"Zaria," Kirwyn cut me off. He sighed heavily, then said, "He's right. Once a decision has been made, it doesn't help any of us to voice doubt or defiance in front of others."

I blinked, taken aback by Kirwyn's agreement and by being overruled by them both.

"But he's wrong about the plan," Kirwyn added, turning hard green eyes back to Laz. "You're making a bad move involving the Biohazards. We won't undermine your rule by not supporting it. But I want it noted that I'm *telling* you, it's a bad decision."

Lazlian lifted his chin and quipped, "Noted." Then he looked at me, eyebrows raised expectantly.

I huffed and replied, "Fine. But I also want it noted that

I'm telling you you're wrong. Bringing the Biohazards here is a terribly dangerous idea."

Lazlian cocked a half-grin. "Duly noted."

I was glad the secrets between us had finally ended, but this -- this ever-shifting power dynamic -- might be eternal. I was surprised to realize I wasn't truly upset. If, in a given scenario, Lazlian held the cards or Kirwyn came out on top or if I brought them both to heel, who cared? As long as it wasn't utterly unfair, I didn't terribly mind the way it changed. Stasis wasn't necessary to my being -- our being. It was like shifting ocean currents or changes in the wind. Without such movement, life would cease to exist.

If I were honest, the idea excited me a little.

Or I thought it might, someday. Now, I mostly felt nervous about what would happen next.

As we stood in our own, private musings, Aewna crept into the hall. She had an expression of regret or sympathy on her face, raising gullflesh on my neck.

Softly, she said, "Kirwyn. I have to show you something. Please, come with me now."

The three of us shared a look, immediately unnerved by her tone, and quickly followed her back into the monitor room.

Something clicked in my head and I knew the look Aewna wore. It was the same one she'd given me when I first met her, when I learned the truth about my family.

Aewna licked her lips, as if stalling, which was something Aewna never did.

"It was what Lazlian said about the Biohazards having advanced capabilities, like the Spades, that got me thinking. If they have weapons and medical technology they don't readily show to outsiders, I thought it might be possible..." she trailed off, her face crumpling with grief. "I'm so sorry, Kirwyn."

Mal-Yin flicked a switch and an image of two slaves appeared on the screen before us. The first thing I noticed was that it obvious they were slaves from the black X's tattooed on their backs and the corresponding data to the left. The second thing I put together were the names and faces.

We were looking at Theodos, Kirwyn's uncle, and Mackenzie, the girl who'd helped us escape the Biohazards.

I had the sudden sensation of falling. It reminded me of the expression about a rug being ripped out from beneath a person. I didn't hit the ground, but I knew I swayed.

Oh dear god. No, no, no.

I brought my hand to my mouth, stifling the gasp of pain.

Kirwyn's face paled and he fell to his knees, eyes riveted on the screen above him.

"It is my belief that the Hazards managed to extract the bullets and stave the bleeding," Aewna said gently. "They saved your uncle's life that night, and they never killed Mackenzie. Instead, as punishment, the Hazards sold them both to the Spades."

Kirwyn's whole body shook and the look of abject horror on his face said what we were all feeling. We'd thought Theo's death that night was the worst possible outcome. But this... this was a fate *worse* than death. Especially to a man who'd lived as a freeborn.

Tears spilled over my cheeks. I could barely handle looking at the images of Theo and Mack, backs marred with large x's they'd bear forever. Imagining what they'd endured for the past six years was too much to handle. *Years in which we all thought they were dead.*

"Turn it off!" Lazlian roared, deep and sharp, storming over to Kirwyn and kneeling.

Kneeling.

I blinked at the image. Lazlian didn't comfort Kirwyn in a way I would, embracing him or stroking his cheeks, but Laz laid his hands on Kirwyn's shoulders and got right up in his face, trying to distract him and block his view of the screen.

"All that time in the cellar you knew we'd escape and I didn't believe you and I was wrong. Listen to me now -- *hey, hey, look at me,*" Laz commanded. "I'm swearing to you that we'll get him out of there and if you think we won't, *you're* wrong. I don't care what it takes, it doesn't matter if we win or lose, live or die. We'll get him out."

The screen had darkened and Kirwyn now looked everywhere, his gaze as untethered as his thoughts.

"Six years." Kirwyn choked out the words. "My father's been enslaved while I've been living like royalty for the past six years, not lifting a finger to save him!"

By the time Kirwyn finished, I'd come to kneel beside him as well.

"Kirwyn, listen to me, you couldn't have known," I whispered gently, cupping his cheek to hold his head steady, to bring his gaze to mine. "Theo moved on when he thought you were dead. You did the same."

"But I was fine in that time and he's been-" Kirwyn couldn't even finish, covering his eyes with his hand.

"You *couldn't* have known," I repeated.

"We assumed!" he cried, biting his fist between words. "We assumed he was dead, just as we assumed the Hazards would kill Mack. We didn't even try to save either of them."

I pulled Kirwyn's fist from his mouth. Clasping both his

hands in mine, I brought them to my own lips and kissed them.

Lazlian squeezed Kirwyn's shoulder. "I swear that we'll save them," he declared. "That's a vow. And I always keep my vows."

CHAPTER 52

CHALLENGES
Zaria

It took almost two days before Kirwyn left our bed.

"We'll get them out," Lazlian swore, again and again. It was still a little odd seeing the king stand at Kirwyn's bedside, but it did funny things to my heart. The lines between us were blurring as Laz spent more time in our chambers. It was simply easier.

"We'll bring Mack and Theo to Rythas. Your father can meet his namesake," I said. Kirwyn had not referred to Theo as his uncle any longer and neither did I. "We'll ride together in the surf every day and dine on the beach at sunset. We'll show Theo how Teddy squeals with delight whenever we make a cup from the pitcher plants in the garden and let him sip a little guava juice right from the flower. He'll love it."

I hoped Lazlian and I helped, but in the end, I couldn't be sure it wasn't Kirwyn's own well of inner strength that pulled him out of his anguish. Once he healed, he hardened

-- not against any of us, but against despair. Kirwyn seemingly put up a wall between himself and any thoughts other than saving Theodos and Mackenzie. Had I any doubts about his commitment to the war, this would have dispelled them. Hyper focused, once Kirwyn left the bed, he worked tirelessly, strategizing until late in the night. Before Lida departed, we held a final meeting.

"I hate to admit it, but the Hazards might provide an advantage in more than just bolstering our weaponry," I announced. "If Lida can persuade them to join our cause, they may, in turn, persuade their sons. They certainly won't want to fight against them."

"Sons?" Lazlian and Kirwyn asked in unison, and I nodded.

"You probably don't remember as you were, well, you'd just reconnected with your father," I said softly. "But when they want to repopulate, the Hazards bear their own children. Only, if it's a son, they send him into the Spade army when he turns eleven and he's placed high in the ranks. No mother will want to fight against her son. Just as Kirwyn won some ground with Jori, those Biohazards with sons amongst the Spade forces might be able to persuade them to abstain or even switch the allegiance of their children."

At what should have been good news, Kirwyn wore an expression of grim frustration.

"So you're saying they have a way to sneak past the walls?" he asked. "Meaning there was no need to give Fabroni a wagonful of gold?"

"I don't know that they could have reached Jori, nor that they could be trusted to do so," I said honestly, and not just to make him feel better. "But I'd bet my crown that, whether they are supposed to or not, those mothers are in some way communicating with their sons. I don't believe for a minute that they kissed their little ones goodbye, never to speak again. No matter what Lysette might have commanded."

The next day, we sent Lida on her journey, accompanied by only female guards.

I couldn't help but have some mixed feelings when she returned in less than a fortnight, with almost the entire Biohazard clan and their sworn allegiance.

More than anything she'd said the chance to kill Spades had persuaded them, it seemed.

At the clan's arrival, Kirwyn hardened like stone. That was the other side of his earthen quality. With me he was akin to the soft, welcoming grass or the forests that delighted me, that beckoned exploration. But when he shut down, when faced with someone or something he did not like, he was like solid rockface, an impenetrable mountain none could move.

My blood ran cold at the sight of Lysette and I did not engage the yellow-eyed woman. Lazlian and Mal-Yin handled most communication, but it wasn't as if the tension went unnoticed.

The Hazards, it was decided, would not be a part of our initial attack, instead coming in as a fresh wave of reinforcements to surprise the Spades. When they joined the battle, it would serve as a signal to their sons. Having held back until that moment, those men would turn, joining to fight with their full effort, now on our side.

The vague scheme didn't sit right in my stomach and my worries weren't assuaged by the fact that Aewna weighed in with an uncertain verdict. According to her, the Biohazards had mixed feelings about our war and she couldn't get a clear read on what was true or false. I didn't feel any better until Kirwyn and I had a surprise encounter with Nalice and Frayde. As they'd been the ones who'd initially captured and marched us at gunpoint to the Biohazard hideout, I liked them the least.

But one evening, the duo materialized from the shadows, blocking our path as Kirwyn and I retired to our room. When they spoke, I didn't need Aewna to read the sincerity in their words.

Well, Nalice's words. The dark-skinned swordswoman seemed to speak on behalf of them both.

"I want you to know Frayde and I weren't there the night you escaped and Lysette chased you. We were on patrol in the front and we'd never..." Nalice's face hardened. "We wouldn't..." She clenched her teeth, clearly struggling -- if you knew what to look for. "We're sorry for what happened to your uncle and Mack."

I sucked in a breath as it dawned on me.

They want to tell us what happened to Mack and Theo, I gleaned. *And they can't.*

Despite the frightening red contacts, Nalice's eyes were remorseful. Beside her, Frayde watched quietly. The pale woman wasn't particularly tall, but her muscles were long and lean, more like a dancer's than a fighter's. With those white contacts obscuring even her irises, and her head crowned with flaming red waves, she reminded me of a candle.

With a nod of acknowledgement from Kirwyn, Nalice and Frayde departed, practically disappearing into the shadows.

Kirwyn and I still didn't trust the Hazards, but we were left with a better opinion of those two.

～

THE NEXT DAY, Mal-Yin called us to the war table. "I have good news and bad news," he announced. "The good news is, we've been able to get communicators working between this satellite and what will be the front line. Aewna will remain here, giving us the signal when the weapon silo is locked down and we can begin our attack."

"And the bad news?" Kirwyn asked.

"We don't have enough food to carry us through to the warmer weather," Mal-Yin informed us. "We risk snow if we attack now, but we might not be able to wait."

Everyone fell silent.

"There's food to be had," I pointed out, voicing an idea I'd been thinking about. "You just need to expand your definition of what's edible."

Kirwyn and Lazlian both frowned with disgust. I shrugged.

"Jesi, can you make me beautiful again?" I asked. "I have a plan."

I ASCENDED the dais with the full regality of my draped blanket-dress and a filigree lamp accent posing as a tiny tiara. It passed as elegance, if one didn't look too closely.

A table had been placed upon the stage and I took a central seat. Then, keeping my head high, I ate the worm which had been set before me, slowly and in plain sight of those we'd crowded into the hall.

It was my job to convince everyone that if the princess of Rythas thought it a worthy meal, they should too.

Mirkah, the bearded leader of the Swamp Lords, picked up his worm and swallowed it in one sensible bite. A few others from his clan followed suit, and I realized I was growing quite fond of their practicality. The Hazards, not wanting to be outdone, quickly gulped down their worms next, before any other clan could complete the task as a whole.

The rest of the hall was a mix. Some were spurred to competitive action and some refused. Some made their task more difficult by taking little bites and others got it over with as fast as possible. More than a few gagged and quickly washed the worm down with a cup of wine.

I sighed with relief. *It's a start.* We needed to incorporate an Elowan diet if we wanted to have enough food, and that included insects.

Aewna was nowhere to be found and I guessed she skipped the meal. I wouldn't have been surprised to learn that Mal had sweets tucked away, just for her. Out of sheer pride, Kirwyn and Laz ate their worms without any fuss, but I knew they were fighting to keep their stomachs settled. Some grumbled about the coming change in rations, but once the meal was complete, everyone scattered back to their work. As Kirwyn and I crossed the hall, however, we met with a surprise.

He froze, and I followed his gaze to see a petite woman with soft brown hair coming directly towards us. She wore a tan tank top, a brown skirt with an uneven hem, and tall brown boots. Slung around her waist was a thick belt, laden with little bags and flasks.

"Grethen," Kirwyn said her name and it took a second before it clicked in my head.

My mouth fell as I studied the woman Kirwyn told me about -- the one he had saved by pretending to assault and thus, chasing the other men away.

At Kirwyn's stricken look, Grethen smiled warmly.

"Don't worry," she told him. "You're not the demon from my nightmares, you're the angel from my dreams."

I was surprised at her perceptiveness.

"Oh, you smell good," Grethen gushed, before her gaze quickly darted to me. "I'm sorry, I didn't mean to sound flirtatious. It's just, well," she looked back at Kirwyn, "you absolutely *stank* the only other time I met you."

I looked nervously at Kirwyn, worried that the reminder of what he'd endured would upset him. But he only seemed relieved to learn that he hadn't scarred Grethen.

The petite brunette stilled, eyes widening slightly, and I glanced over my shoulder to realize she now stared at Jesi, who crossed the hall with a trail of soldiers behind her. I'd forgotten what a formidable sight our Commander made, especially bedecked in armor. Or perhaps the sight of a female commander was unusual where she came from.

Slowly looking back to us, Grethen said, "I came because I'm a healer. I can be of use in this war."

Kirwyn smiled appreciatively. "We're grateful for your help. Though if we do this right, it won't be a prolonged war, only a single battle... albeit one with heavy casualties on both sides. We'll definitely have use for those who can tend the wounded."

If we do it wrong, it will only be one battle as well, I couldn't help but think, chewing my lip.

We were interrupted by a commotion coming from one end of the hall as a fight broke out and quickly grew. Tables and chairs scraped as they were hastily pushed out of the way. Kirwyn, Laz, Jesi and I rushed over, relieved to see no one had yet come to blows. But several of the Hazards were shouting at once.

"He groped Nalice," Lysette accused a man standing nearby, and one look at Nalice's snarl confirmed it. The swordswoman's rage-filled gaze was locked on a short, dark-haired man from a clan I did not know.

"She's lying!" the man shouted. "Who you gonna believe, me or her?"

"We demand his immediate death!" Lysette ordered, stomping across the circle to face Lazlian. "It is our law."

Oh no. I shifted my weight nervously. Not only was it impossible for Lazlian to sentence a man to immediate death for something he couldn't verify -- no matter how much he believed it -- he couldn't allow the Biohazard rules and laws to supersede any others. On the other hand, he couldn't let the deed go unpunished, diminishing his power in the eyes of anyone watching. A sentence other than death might be viewed as weak to the Biohazards and anyone siding with them.

"I am in charge of this war," Lazalian announced, commanding attention with his tone and his height, "and thus, it is governed by the laws of Rythas and not your own."

In Rythas, the man would have been given a trial. It was a lengthy process no one had the time or resources for here -- nor could we drag the man back to our kingdom as he wasn't even Rythasian to begin with. I'd begun to sweat a little, when Kirwyn's voice called out, interrupting the scene.

"Everyone, listen up!" Kirwyn ordered, shoving men and women out of the way to stand in the middle of the circle. "In times of war, we can settle our differences quickly through trial by combat, if both parties agree. That is how it was done in the clans I've lived amongst."

No, it wasn't, I thought, narrowing my eyes. Kirwyn never lived with any clan.

The keylord and the king shared a conspiratorial look. Intrigued, I patiently waited to see what they were doing.

Nalice flashed a wide, hungry grin and stroked the pummel of her sword. The dark-haired man hesitated. He looked strong, toned -- but not as muscled as Nalice.

"As leader here, I cannot allow this," Lazlian said loudly. He angled himself protectively in front of the man. "The Biohazards are battle-tested regularly, but many of my soldiers and those of other clans have rarely seen combat."

"I've seen combat," the short man piped up in defense.

"But it still wouldn't be a fair fight for her to challenge you," Lazlian cautioned, brow furrowed with concern.

Oh, my little double-talkers.

"Whatcha mean not fair?" the man asked, lip curled in disgust. "You mean I could take her so easily it's not fair for *her?*"

Lazlian's flustered look was one I'd never seen before and was sure he'd never affect again... unless it was useful.

"No, I didn't mean to suggest that you personally couldn't take her, I simply meant that her daily exposure to danger might create an uneven match for other warriors who've been... trained differently."

With so many eyes glued to him, the man sneered, "Well it's your fault then. If you'da let me at her, you'da seen how I could take her. If she's stupid enough to risk her life, I woulda quickly ended it."

Lazlian showed nothing on his face, but I was sure that disrespect did not go unnoted.

"I couldn't let Nalice fight," Frayde gushed, stepping forward. Her sweet, earnest tone also did not match anything I'd ever heard before. Turning to her friend, she laid a hand on her shoulder and said wistfully, "I'll be your champion."

I watched the man's eyes flash as he sized up Frayde, who was much less physically intimidating than Nalice. Even if her ghostly irises creeped him out, the cascade of red curls, paired with her lithe form, probably gave her a doll-like appearance in his eyes.

"Let me fight," the short man growled to Lazlian. "What kinda king are you to interfere with justice?"

Lazlian pretended to be taken aback. "Well, if you insist... I suppose I shouldn't prevent you. To the death?" Lazlian asked, rhetorically. "No guns, just blades."

"That's right," the man said, nearly pushing the king back as he stepped forward.

Frayde puffed her chest, as if summoning courage, and moved to the circle's center. At Lazlian's orders we all stepped back, widening the ring around the two combatants.

I wrinkled my brow in confusion when Frayde awkwardly grasped her sword with her left hand. I'd thought she was right-handed, and the position of her scabbard seemed to confirm it. Frayde also didn't have an encouragingly strong grip on the weapon. Perhaps she'd rely on those eerie white eyes making it difficult to see where she looked, and thus, to predict her moves.

With a cocky grin, the dark-haired man rubbed saliva from the sides of his open mouth and firmed the grip on his own sword.

Lazlian gave a nod to Jesi, who stepped into the circle and announced, "No one may intervene. The fight is over when one participant is dead or declares defeat."

I felt my pulse and heart pick up speed, worried for Frayde. I shouldn't, considering what her clan had done to Mack and Theo... but she and Nalice seemed genuinely remorseful over it.

Jesi stepped back into the crowd and declared, "On three! One... two... three!"

The last number was barely out of her mouth by the time Frayde's sword hit the ground. The Hazard simply loosened her grip and let it fall. For a second, my stomach seemed to drop with it.

Then, in a flash, Frayde grabbed a dagger strapped to her waist. In one smooth move, she threw it across the circle and it embedded directly into the man's heart.

Everyone -- myself included -- was stunned silent. The dark-haired man dropped, dead on the floor. Half a second later, cheers and laughter broke out. I gasped my relief.

He died by a blade, fair and square, I thought.

Kirwyn and Lazlian's eyes gleamed, quite pleased with themselves. While that smug little twinkle made me roll my eyes, I had to admit their joint cunning was kind of sexy.

"Clever," I whispered, once we were pressed tight together again. "But I don't think it was enough to appease Lysette."

"Nothing appeases her," Lazlian replied, with a dismissive wave. "Nothing but her own will."

"I told you," Kirwyn reminded.

Mal-Yin joined us, a smile tugging at his lips. I wondered if he'd been watching from a safe distance throughout.

"Well done," he said.

"I think we need to relieve some stress before these clans tear one another apart," Lazlian remarked. "Can you break out whatever wine and ale remain? Tomorrow night, we'll have a celebration. It might be the last chance many will ever have to enjoy themselves."

~

THE NEXT EVENING, Kirwyn, Laz, and I drank in that crowded hall, like any other soldier who could fit in the room. Others lined the hallways or gathered by the doors outside the satellite building. Ale continually spilled at our feet and if we put a cup down, we risked losing it forever in the riotous celebration. Sergei, the man Mal-Yin had spared, played upbeat music on his piano. Whenever he chose a familiar tune, others sang along.

I knew this stirring of the blood that came before a battle. Adrenaline and fear mixed, goading one another like opponents squaring off in a match. But instead of taking one another down, their tussle only spiked passions.

Or rather, the only taking down anyone wanted was to take another flat against a bed. I glimpsed soldiers pairing off and scurrying into darkened corners. *Though with limited space and privacy, it looks like any alcove will do.*

We all knew it, *felt* it. This might be the last time our lives would be normal enough to enjoy what pleasures remained. Once we geared up to fight, once we marched, who would have a thought in the world for sex?

Take pleasure while you can, for soon we all may die.

I could sense the flirtations and tensions amidst the revelry, but I was focused on my own.

Our own.

Kirwyn, Lazlian, and I drank. Not to excess, but with purpose. Of that I was sure, even though I was unsure about what would happen as the night progressed.

The glances we shared were heavy. A feeling gathered, like coming rain -- but to my surprise it wasn't booming and wild like a thunderstorm. The change in weather was more subdued, more tentative, though no less desired. It felt like the earth thirsting so long for a drink and antici-pating its arrival.

Kirwyn's strong hand found mine, and he led me from the hall. I could feel Lazlian's dark eyes following us as we walked back to our chambers. Sanda remained guarded in her alcove, but Kirwyn dismissed the soldiers to the end of the hall for the rest of the evening. He returned to find me standing in the middle of the room, breathing heavily and unsure what was happening.

Kirwyn took my mouth in his and drew my makeshift dress down and over my hips. It pooled at my feet and my undergarments followed. Between stripping my clothing, Kirwyn sealed our mouths with deep kisses. Yet he hadn't removed his own attire and I pressed against him, frustrated.

I heard a door handle click, followed by the sound of a door swinging open.

Lazlian stepped into the room.

CHAPTER 53

ONE LAST HURRAH, ONE FIRST
Zaria

The silence was absolute. What room was left for noise when pressure sucked it out of our chambers, like a whirlpool creating a vacuum of space right down to the seabed? And like that whirling siphon, focus was funneled upon the small opening, spotlighting the three of us in the middle of the spin.

I realized I'd pressed myself a little closer against Kirwyn, covering my nudity. I was completely bare and yet another man had entered the room. I'd known on some level that *something* was happening and this was *Laz,* with whom we were both very familiar. But his presence in this scenario was not.

Kirwyn held my chin in his hands, lifting my gaze to his. But I didn't know what he was telling me with his eyes because nerves ruled my mind. He took me by my biceps and turned me around. I was still pressed to him, held by him, but I was... presented to Lazlian?

Once again, I felt a step behind as they communicated without words. Or maybe they were telling it all to me and I was too panicked to understand.

My heart had never pounded so hard. Did they hear it?

Lazlian's eyes raked over my naked body. From the wasting, I was a little thinner than I was used to and I hadn't fully regained my muscles yet. My stomach was soft and round, not having snapped back into shape without laps in the sea. I bore scars -- a few red lines on my abdomen I hoped would silver and fade, but they weren't my only ones. I carried scars from battles, scars from even Lazlian himself.

So did they. Beneath the clothing they now wore, Kirwyn and Laz, I knew, had picked up a few more marks from the clanless to add to what they already bore.

Of all the scenarios I'd imagined happening between the three of us, what quietly unfolded wasn't one of them.

I shook and in response, Lazlian crossed to where I stood. His hungry eyes found my mouth and he took it. While I was naked and Kirwyn held me in his arms, Lazlian kissed me. Hands roamed my bare body, though no one else had yet removed their clothing. I clenched and unclenched my fists, somehow sure Kirwyn and Lazlian didn't yet want to undress, power dynamics in play.

Kirwyn guided me to the bed and, still fully clothed, laid down. He positioned me lying back against his body and between his legs. Boldly, Kirwyn's hands found my thighs and guided them apart.

For Lazlian?

If being spun naked to face Laz spiked my heartrate, being opened for him made my heart pound so fiercely I grew lightheaded. My mouth felt as if I'd gargled with sand; it was dry, cottony, and incapable of forming words or producing saliva. I licked my lips repeatedly as Lazlian climbed onto the bed and kneeled between my open legs, his intention clear.

The sound of my frantic breathing filled the room. Lazlian had licked me in our time together, but with his fixation on making the heir, he'd only brought me to climax once between my legs, and it had been when I was out of my mind and remembered little. I never imagined him doing it a second time while Kirwyn held me. It was leagues stranger the first, and that time I'd been hooked to his ceiling.

Slowly, Lazlian lowered his head...

...and then his tongue touched my center.

Kirwyn was ready, holding me down when I jumped. The scruff of Lazlian's beard tickled my sensitive areas. As he tasted me, I trembled in Kirwyn's grip, and Kirwyn whispered words of reassurance, so softy I could only make out a few. The moment Lazlian fully dove into me, it felt like I'd been jolted out of my mind. Lying on Kirwyn, embraced in his warmth... while Lazlian licked me to climax, made me buck. As my arousal rose, Kirwyn's grip tightened with it.

I came, so lost in my orgasm I did not know if I shouted or swallowed my cries.

While my heart rate slowed, double sets of skilled hands fluidly lifted me into a sitting position and spun me to face Kirwyn.

My love, I thought, waves of adoration washing over me as he stripped off his pants. Kirwyn slipped inside me as Lazlian pressed to my back, grasping my chin and turning my face for a kiss. Laz's other arm wrapped around my torso and his hand slid to my clit, rubbing as I rolled my hips against Kirwyn. There was no direction I could move without meeting new pleasure; ecstasy enveloped me.

Kirwyn's cock filled me while Lazlian's tongue stroked mine and his long fingers teased me. Both men kept me safely enclosed between them, a pearl in a protective shell of love and longing.

I'd be a liar if I said I hadn't fantasized about it. But it was always rough, urgent, loud. There'd be groping and wild moans -- and maybe even some fighting -- as bodies slammed. Perhaps that might happen in the future. What unfolded was slower than I'd imagined and with an unexpected, quiet intensity. Needy on a soul level. I wondered if, like me, they'd suffered too many horrors and now, once again staring annihilation in the face, such passion became a defiance of death. Every caress was a desperate joining, every moan a declaration that *I am here. I am connected. I live.*

I lost my fear in the two of them, in their hungry kisses and possessive caresses. I whimpered into Lazlian's mouth and his grip on my face tightened. The sensations sent me to a second climax so fast, Kirwyn had to quicken his thrusts to catch up. I marveled at the surreal experience of him emptying his seed into me while I filled Lazlian's mouth with my cries. I trembled on, even after the pleasure had peaked.

I didn't remember removing myself from Kirwyn but somehow, I kneeled on the bed, facing Lazlian. His neglected cock strained for attention and my mouth watered to provide it. He was large, rock hard, and so damn sexy. I bent to take care of him as he'd so often guided my head back in High Spire. But now I did so because I wanted to finally taste him -- to devour and swallow as I'd never been permitted with his previous rules.

Lazlian looked every inch the king as he knelt on the bed, and I hoped he understood that his power did not diminish in my eyes because he shared that bed with Kirwyn. It only made me adore him more.

When I felt my hair gently pulled from my face, it wasn't Lazlian's hands. Kirwyn held it back and I sensed his hot gaze on me, despite my attention to Lazlian's cock. Or because of it? Kirwyn's other hand traced a trail down my spine and dipped into my wet sex, dripping with our combined juices. I took Lazlian into my throat as deeply as I could go, fighting to breathe through it, yearning to please them both as they'd pleased me. When Lazlian came, so much of his seed burst into my mouth that I could hardly contain it. I swallowed Lazlian's come while I finished riding out my pleasure on Kirwyn's fingers.

Yet I was disappointed to find that as the excitement faded and the pleasant buzz of alcohol ebbed, the flow of shame slowly crept forward, like an incoming tide.

People didn't do this. Or they *did,* but they didn't do it in the open, and with our positions nothing could be hidden for very long.

We can. I insisted. *We can do... whatever this is.*

No one had said a word the entire time, other than Kirwyn's soft murmuring of encouragement when Lazlian was between my legs. We'd connected so silently it made the entire evening feel otherworldly. The only noise had been soft cries of pleasure, mostly at its peak.

Kirwyn collapsed on the pillow to my left and Lazlian to my right.

The drinks and orgasms lulled me into a fast slumber, before too much doubt could darken my thoughts.

I awoke missing something I didn't understand, until my searching fingers felt the space beside me. I shot up in the bed to find Lazlian dressed and halfway across the room. My stomach sank, seeing the refusal in his sneaking.

We'd come so far.

Lazlian heard me and stopped, guilty. He was running or hiding or... doing whatever he'd done the night he snuck out of my bedroom all those years ago when I'd captured High Spire.

I slid off the bed, careful not to wake Kirwyn.

"You're leaving," I whispered, standing before him.

He said nothing.

I knew some of how Lazlian felt because I'd experienced the same hesitations in the morning light after he'd whipped me. The cloak of darkness shaded my unease, but the sun illuminated it. Maybe in his version of masculinity two women were an ego boost and two men, a blow.

"What happened to the flippant, cocksure man who said, *'we can show them whatever they want to see and behind closed doors, do whatever we want?'*"

I'd referenced the words he'd said upon first persuading me to make the heir. He'd alluded to this outcome. Why turn cowardly now?

Lazlian clenched his jaw but still said nothing.

"You told me you wouldn't lie any longer," I said. "So stop."

I raised my hand to Lazlian's cheek and he flinched but did not pull away. My heart teetered on a tightrope, beating with desperate hope not to plummet to the ground far below. I searched for the words to carry us both across the ravine.

"Everything you've ever wanted is on *this* side of *that* door."

Lazlian did not meet my eyes. I didn't want him to be this version of himself. I wanted the king who cared more about his own desires than court opinions.

"Not just what we shared last night, but friendship and family," I implored. "Love, Lazlian. And a reign benefitting from all our talents."

I hadn't actually said *I love you.* For some reason, I'd never said it. But this was the same thing, pretty much.

"You think it's so easy?" Lazlian bit out the words in an angry whisper, eyes darting to the bed to ensure Kirwyn slept. "How can I sell it to them when I have trouble convincing myself?"

I licked my lips, stalling, then answered, "There is only one way. The same way I made myself untouchable after we exploded Oxholde's ships. We must win this war. And then you will be utterly irreproachable. We all will. You can do whatever you want once you are the king who saves Rythas and the world." My shoulders fell as I added, "And if we fail... well then we'll all be dead and it won't matter anyway."

Lazlian averted his eyes again, staring at the door but unmoving.

"If you want to leave because this isn't what you want, then go," I whispered. "But if it is... then please don't put the opinions and desires of others above your own. Above our own."

My heart thumped faster, hoping Laz wouldn't touch the door handle. I could stroke him, kiss him, whisper promises of pleasure. But instead of pushing forward, I pulled back.

I had the best intentions in my *heart* when I did what I did next, but I couldn't deny that in the back of my *mind,* I knew I played with some darker emotions too.

Gently, I climbed onto the bed. Kirwyn would not refuse me if he were to awaken with my lips around him. I quietly drew back the sheet, exposing his nakedness, and knelt between his legs. As I took him in my mouth, I spread and arched obscenely, offering Lazlian whatever he wanted.

I could sway Kirwyn with seduction, but I could only satisfy Lazlian with submission.

Kirwyn stirred and though he jumped a little, I heard his soft moan and felt him relax into the pleasure I gave.

For long, painful moments there was no sound behind me. I dreaded hearing the slam of the door, indicating Lazlian had left.

Take me. However you want.

I spread wider and arched further, trying not to blush at the view I provided. Hoping he found it enticing.

My heart thudded and a jolt ran through my stomach when I the felt the rough grip of Lazlian's hands on my hips, repositioning and pinning me.

Yes. Controlling fingers encircled my waist.

He sunk into me in one thrust.

My world felt complete.

LAZLIAN LEFT TO gather his meager belongings and to move them into our room. I lounged in bed with Kirwyn, soaking up every last moment we'd have to be languorous.

"Did you embrace the ways of Rythasian royals?" I asked softly, half-joking. Then more seriously, I probed, "or was it what happened before you found me?"

"I guess both," Kirwyn replied. Absent-mindedly he stroked my sides, his front pressed to my back. "But also, the likely possibility of imminent death puts things into perspective. It's so monumentally mind-altering that I don't think it's possible for anyone to understand unless they've faced it. Our chances of survival aren't good, Zaria. It's hard worry about losing you to him when we'll all lose our lives in the next few moon cycles."

I flipped to face Kirwyn and laid a hand upon his hard chest. "What can I say to make you believe that you will not lose me, that you will never?"

"I misspoke," he corrected, tucking my hair behind my ear. "What I mean is, that worry is past. My only concern now is for all three of us to survive the war."

"All three?" I asked, still disbelieving just a little.

Kirwyn cocked a half-grin. "You before him."

Then his eyes glazed over and I knew he was back in the dark cellar.

"But yes," he said, voice deep. "Him too."

I wanted words to define what we were, to lay out the rules so that I could understand what was expected of me and what to expect in return. It seemed the sensible thing to do. But neither Kirwyn nor Lazlian offered anything specific, and I was afraid that asking questions would break whatever spell had been cast. *Who leads? How? Am I to touch you both whenever? Do you take turns? What is permitted and what goes too far?*

Perhaps they offered no information because they did not know either. Perhaps words came later, when we figured it out. Perhaps they never came at all because we were feeling it through, wordlessly.

Whatever the reason, Kirwyn and Lazlian did not want or need them right now, and I put my trust in them, over words.

Above anything else in this world, I put my trust in us.

∿

As the days passed and battle plans intensified, meetings lasted late into the night. One evening, exhausted and irritable, everyone broke for a midnight snack. Before I could return to the war table, however, Lazlian and Kirwyn pulled me aside and prevented me.

"You wanted to be here and I agree," Kirwyn said, pointing to the floor to indicate the compound. "But Zaria, when it comes to the attack, you have no place in it. I don't want you on the battlefield. Laz and I are in agreement. You can join the Biohazards with Lida to watch from the hill above. But there you must remain, even when they charge."

My mind spun. Before I argued, I shrugged and lied, "There's no harm in me hearing specific plans of attack."

"You think I don't know how your mind works?" Kirwyn said, smiling and revealing those sharp canines. "You'll listen and find some way to sneak into the fight later. I don't want you tempted. If not for your own life, then for Teddy and Sanda. Someone has to stay safe for them. Please, go get some sleep."

I hated that Kirwyn wasn't wrong about my fighting skills and his logic wasn't flawed either. One of us three needed to remain safe. As the worst combatant, I was the best choice.

But my ego bruised at the insult and worse, my heart couldn't bear the idea of being separated.

"No." I tossed my head back and squared my shoulders.

"Lazlian." Kirwyn said his name in a tone somewhere between a hopeful question and a resigned request. Veiled layers of meaning were communicated in one word and as I stood trying to parse out the intention, Lazlian grabbed and hoisted me over his shoulder. I immediately flailed but I

couldn't shriek my protests without alerting others to my predicament -- which became increasingly humiliating for the fact that my dress slid upwards, revealing my undergarments. I was sure Lazlian had counted on that.

"You're going to your room," he said.

"Kirwyn," I whisper-shouted. "This isn't fair, listen to me, please."

"Wait," Kirwyn said. Lazlian halted and turned around. My head now pointed in Kirwyn's direction, but it didn't do much good as Laz didn't release me from my upside-down position. I dangled awkwardly, waiting for Kirwyn to speak.

"Tell me, Zaria, what about this do you find unfair?" he asked.

"You can't lock me away just because you don't want me endangered in battle," I explained. "I'm my own person, capable of making my own decisions." Though no one saw, I lifted my chin.

"I'm sure you'll recall what you did to me on Mal's ship before we attacked High Spire?" Kirwyn prompted. I couldn't see him but could practically feel him crossing his arms as he adopted his instructor-mode voice. "When *you* didn't want *me* to endanger my own life, and you handcuffed me to the boat. Pray tell, how is this different? Oh right, I'm not tricking you as you tried to trick me."

I scrambled to find weak points in Kirwyn's reasoning and couldn't. I simply dangled in my undignified position with my backside in the air, trying to salvage some pride by not pouting... and trying *not* to say something that would have Kirwyn cuffing me at the last moment, as I'd done to him.

Trying to work the bitter taste of my own medicine out of my mouth.

After a silent pause, Lazlian continued walking.

In the past and one on one, I'd managed to outma-neuver Kirwyn or Laz. But when they teamed up it was just... *unfair.* Quietly, I beat Lazlian's back and tried to push myself from his shoulders without calling attention to my struggle. It was a wasted effort. When we reached the bedroom door, I was unceremoniously deposited on my feet.

"So what if I want to fight?" I said, scowling up at him, hands balled into fists. "I'm not helpless. I've fought before."

Lazlian shook his head. "Not in a battle like this."

"You can't-"

"Save your life?" he interrupted. "It's likely we are all going to die. Don't you dare make me the bad guy for wanting one of us to live."

I gave a little start when, out of the darkness, Nalice emerged to my right. At the same time, the tip of her sword rose menacingly to Lazlian's throat.

I reddened, wondering if she'd witnessed the whole scene.

"If a lady wants to fight, she fights. We don't hold women back," Nalice announced. As she spoke, I spied Frayde over Lazlian's shoulder, a dagger of her own poised to his neck.

My god, they are stealthy. Excitement fluttered in my chest to have them on my side, defending my wishes. Lazlian froze, his posture perfectly straight. Though he appeared calm, the fire behind his eyes told me he wouldn't hesitate to send the Hazards to the Isle of Walking Corpses for threatening him.

With casual arrogance, Laz declared, "I could cut off your hand for raising it to your king."

"You're not our king," Nalice proclaimed.

"Maybe not, but I am hers. And she's taken vows to do as I say."

Nalice and Frayde exchanged a look. My palms sweated in the prolonged silence.

"It doesn't matter," Nalice argued. "In times of war, her will to fight supersedes your desire that she not."

"Perhaps that is the way of your laws, not ours."

"We are in this war *together,*" Nalice reminded.

"Under *my* command," Lazlian grit out, baring his teeth. "Zaria is no warrior and she will endanger everyone who is worried about protecting her, which is a long list. Sanda is the future of Rythas and *she* must protect *her.* Now lower your weapon or I'll make an example of you by gutting you with it myself, in the hall for everyone to see."

"Try it and the Hazards will gut as many of your men as we can before we take our army and leave, or die in the process," Frayde hissed from his back. "Either way you come out weaker."

"Stop," I commanded, before the next words left Lazlian's mouth. What he'd said, and the emotion with which he'd spoken, struck a nerve. For Sanda and for Teddy, I had to stay safe. Angling myself in front of Laz, I laid my hand on Nalice's blade and gently guided it down.

"Thank you for defending me. I will not forget it. But he's right. I'm a middling fighter at best," I admitted softly. "With all of our clans together, there is little I can do to help our efforts in the battle itself, and much my presence can do to harm them. I will stay back with your forces where I can watch as you are called. I will remain there with Lida and the other non-combatants who keep to the hillside."

Nalice blinked, then shrugged. I turned to Lazlian.

"If anything happens..." I trailed off, swallowing thickly.

"I'll take Sanda and run. You are right. I don't belong in this battle."

"I know. Next time I'd appreciate it if you do as I say without swords being raised."

"You've won this round," I said, crossing my arms with irritation. "Don't push your luck."

"Don't push my patience," he countered. "That goes for all of you," Lazlian said pointedly, dismissing the Hazards with an arrogant jerk of his chin.

Behind him, Frayde sheathed her dagger with reluctance.

"I don't know what he's got in his pants to make you put up with him, but no man is worth it, not even a king," Frayde advised as she backed away. "Slit his throat in the night and take the crown yourself. Whatever desires he fulfills, we've got devices to replace it," she said with a half-grin.

Before I could reply, Frayde and Nalice took off down the hall, disappearing into the darkness once more.

Alone with Lazlian, I frowned. "What devices is she talking about?"

Laz chuckled and, ignoring me, grabbed my elbow to escort me into our room.

"It's late. I need to return to our plans and you need rest."

I huffed. "Lazlian. What devices?"

He shook his head. "Somehow I'm sure you'll blame me, but it's your own fault for never picking up a book."

"Oh, like you do?"

"I don't need to. Boys talk, growing up."

"Well no one in Elowa talked to me," I cried, "and we certainly didn't possess devices."

"I know. Isn't it lovely how innocent you can be sometimes?"

I nearly decked him. "Are you trying to provoke me into punching you? Because I'm about to."

"You are the last of your kind," Lazlian sighed, surprisingly reverent. He kissed my forehead and stroked my cheek with the backs of his knuckles. I stilled at his tenderness. "The last chosen braenese. There will never be another like you, and you're mine. Let me corrupt you at my own pace."

I stared into Lazlian's scorched-earth eyes, considering. So pleased at having ended the horrible tradition, it never occurred to me that in some twisted way, I'd only increased my own prize value as the last that would ever exist. I wanted to rage against Lazlian for the offensive idea and to tell him where to shove his insulting objectification, but I paused. Because I knew how much I asked of him. Because Laz had made astounding compromises. Because it wasn't really *"you're mine,"* it was *"you're ours."*

So I bit my tongue and conceded in allowing him to decide when I was ready for... whatever we were talking about.

"Yes, your majesty," I teased, batting my lashes and smiling sweetly. "I am yours. Corrupt at your leisure."

"There's a good little queen," he teased back, although with Lazlian I couldn't be sure it was teasing. "We'll return later, but I expect to find you long asleep and let me remind you that I don't like it when my expectations are not met."

Laz slid a finger against my mouth to quiet it, purposefully being an ass to frustrate me. I shot him a look of annoyance. He grinned.

"No more arguing. Go to bed. Now."

Some things do change, I thought, half-rolling my eyes. *But some never will.*

CHAPTER 54

A TIME FOR WAR
Zaria

In the days leading up to our departure we sought one another with quiet need, though we did not couple. Thoughts of that kind of intimacy were far from our minds.

Mal-Yin theorized that we'd trigger the ships encircling Rythas to attack when we invaded Spade City, and the information he could glean from their systems seemed to corroborate it. That knowledge was both a blessing and a curse, and Lazlian especially clung to the hope and dreaded it equally.

Two days before our departure, we sat together in our chambers. Lazlian, with his height, seemed too big for the small chair at the table. His elbow rested upon the tabletop, his head in his hand. Dark waves of hair fell to obscure his eyes, though I could see enough to note his strain. He nursed the last of our wine, taking small sips every now and again. Kirwyn and I sat on the bed nearby, watching Laz, and it was as if he suddenly became cognizant of our concern and looked up.

"Sorry, I'm... distracted," Laz said, and it was still jarring to hear those kinds of words from his lips. "I know you're worried about Teddy. And your friends. It's just that I feel responsible for everyone. They swore vows to me at the fealty ceremony and I vowed to protect them in return. And I'm not even there."

It didn't matter that Lazlian was hunched over with distress and not sprawled arrogantly in the small chair. To me, he looked like a king. That protectiveness Laz always felt for his brother and for his family had grown to encompass all of Rythas.

He would be a good king, I thought, *if he ever gets a real chance.* A little rash, a little scary, but worthy of the role.

Well, a lot scary, I mentally corrected, remembering Navere's severed head. *But skilled nonetheless.*

"It's okay," I assured Lazlian. "It's not a competition of who gets to worry more."

"We're with you," Kirwyn added. "Any way we can be."

It was also still strange to hear Kirwyn's words of comfort to Lazlian, though the oddity was an insignificant consideration at the moment.

"Merie couldn't have known exactly what would unfold, but I think she hoped Kelody's presence might somehow interrupt Navere's plans," I said, wanting to encourage Laz. "She's smarter than we give her credit for it's just... a different kind of intelligence. She'll help your brother defend High Spire. As will Raoul and Saos and Tomé and Marcin."

Alette, I knew, would protect Teddy. Whatever happened, she'd keep him safe.

There was nothing the three of us could do *there*. The best thing for everyone was to fight our hardest *here*.

~

THE NIGHT BEFORE WE DEPARTED, I paced the compound, biting my nails to stubs, and I bumped into Jesi in a corridor near my bedroom.

"I came to see if you wanted me to battle-bind your hair," Jesi said.

I shook my head. "I'll just tie it back. There's no need for anything to last through a battle as I'm not fighting."

Noticing the tightly-woven style of Jesi's braids, I knit my brow. Jesi excelled at all forms of plaiting, but this didn't look like something she could accomplish alone, as it was so meticulously smoothed against the back of her head. I suddenly felt like I'd failed her as a friend for not being able to assist her the way she always could when it came to my hair.

"Did you do that yourself?" I asked, half expecting her to tell me Lida had done it, though I knew Lida had been busy with other preparations in the hall. Jesi had to have washed her hair in order to work it like that, so maybe they'd done it together earlier.

Patting the back of her head where her dark curls had been immaculately braided, Jesi averted her eyes and said, "Nalice helped me with it."

"Oh," I replied. "Well, she's really good at it."

Jesi gave me a hug and I squeezed her tightly, more afraid for her than I was for myself. I was staying on the hill, and she was leading one of the four primary charges.

"I wish I could tell you to hold back," I said, blinking away tears. "To not do anything risky or daring. But I could no more tell the earth not to spin or the stars not to shine."

I could hear the grin in her voice when she said, "Don't worry. I'm hard to kill."

You save me, I save you, I wanted to say, but couldn't. I wouldn't be there to help save anyone at all.

That night I barely slept, despite being securely wedged between Kirwyn and Lazlian. As nervous as the compound made me, leaving its security amplified that fear, encompassing me until I seemed to choke on it. Our plan was to travel for three days, then to camp a few miles outside Spade City in a location Kirwyn had chosen. We'd attack on the fourth morning.

Once we marched, there'd be no turning back.

The sooner we move, the sooner I might hold Teddy again, I told myself. I tried not to worry that he'd forgotten me or to think overlong about all the ways he'd suffered, being apart from his mother and father. *He's resilient and Saos and Alette love him.* Still, in the darkness especially, my heart seemed to scream with longing to hold him once more.

I must have dozed off at some point, because I awoke with a jolt to an empty bed. Kirwyn and Lazlian were quietly dressing in battle gear, and the compound outside my door had come to life with the movement of people.

It was time to go.

THE BOOTS I'd worn when leaving the other satellite didn't properly fit, so Kirwyn procured new ones for me from somewhere within our base. I didn't see many scruff marks, but I couldn't be sure they hadn't come off a dead woman. When he'd conquered the base, Mal-Yin's soldiers had stripped the corpses of anything we could use -- tokens, jewelry, weapons, even clothing. Those who'd been given warmer pants or jackets didn't complain, even if they were blood-stained, and neither did I.

Kissing Sanda goodbye made me weep, but I knew she'd be safest with Aewna, who would remain in the compound.

When I departed, I left a part of my heart in that satellite with her.

The morning air was chilly and our march, slow-moving -- though on the plus side this was because we had so many bodies to move. At night I slept in a tent with Kirwyn and Lazlian. If anyone cared, they didn't bother to raise concerns in the middle of what may be a march to their doom.

Aewna kept contact with Mal-Yin through his electronic communicator, continually assuring us the Spades hadn't yet unleashed their advanced weaponry. Our plan of locking everything down relied on both the skill of Mal-Yin's technical men *and* timing. If we were correct, the window of opportunity for an electronic attack would open *after* the Spades had sequestered their slaves into the walls but *before* they unleashed the silo of weaponry. If we struck too soon, the slaves wouldn't be safe and too late... none of us would.

Once we received the signal from Aewna, we'd attack, bombing the gates to Spade City with Mal's explosives and the use of his APATs -- alternatively-powered armored tanks.

I considered those nimble little vehicles key in our battle. Mal, however, did not possess as many as I'd imagined. A mere six APATs rolled alongside us as we marched.

Jesi would head the charge on the East gate, Mal-Yin to

the West, Kirwyn and Lazlian at the Southmost, and the bulk of the clans coming from the North under the command of a woman from Wolf Wrath whom Lazlian knew and appointed. Our plan was to overwhelm and encircle the Spades from all four directions, much like Mal-Yin and I had once done to High Spire when we flooded the castle from two sides.

Over the course of three days and nights our march was steady and blissfully uneventful. But it was as if I scaled a mountain of anxiety as we rode, peaking the final night we camped.

I'd only once experienced the pre-battle anxiety of a planned attack, and that was but a taste of what I now endured. My stomach roiled and when I ran out of nails, I bit the surrounding skin.

Evening fell upon our camp, enveloping it in an eerie darkness. I knew I'd never get used to mainland nights. They weren't balmy and sultry; the air perfumed with jasmine and the sweet lull of the surf carried by the breeze. These nights were cold, still, and broken only by the occasional cry of strange birds or beasts.

Jittery, I paced the camp. *If we win...* I made bargains to Keroe but I did not know what the Sea God truly desired. A shrine built in his honor, somewhere high on the cliffs? An offering of jewels to his waters, as the Rythasians practiced?

On a lap near my tent, I spied a head of wild red hair, still unbound. Frayde sat in the shadows, watching Nalice converse with Lysette, some distance away.

Wanting to distract myself and giving the Biohazard leader wide berth, I sat beside Frayde. She said nothing to acknowledge my presence and I wondered what her people customarily did before battle.

"Do you believe in any gods?" I asked her, after a long silence. "The one or many?"

"I have to," she replied, without turning. Her mane of copper curls partially obscured her face. I wondered if she'd take the time to pin her hair for the attack.

I nodded. "It's a comfort to think there's something more-"

"Comfort?" Frayde asked, scoffing with such venom I froze. "This world has been no comfort and I do not believe any being who created it would bring me any *comfort* either." Frayde jutted her chin. "No, I have to believe in a higher power for the only consolation I can hope to have -- the chance to demand of this being why they made a world in which one half wants to hurt and kill the other?" Frayde spat the question to which I had no answer, but I well understood which half of the population she referenced.

"What possessed this creator to weave a fundamentally hateful and horrific flaw into its design?" Frayde turned to look at me with her eerie, white eyes set amidst her pale skin. It was like looking into the face of a spirit, causing gullbumps to rise on my skin. "No, I do not wish for god's existence to alleviate my fear, I want to demand its accountability." Her hand tightened around her dagger's hilt. "I want the reckoning I'm owed."

In the weighty silence, I fumbled for the right words, pondering what terrors Frayde had endured in this world but not wanting to ask. I thought of Aewna and wished I knew what she would say. I had to curl my fingers to stop my hands from reaching for Frayde, the way I would if she were Jesi.

Softly, I whispered, "I'm sorry that you've experienced so much pain."

Frayde's nostrils flared and her grip tightened on her dagger once more.

"Not. Me," she said, shifting her gaze to Nalice. Frayde suddenly huffed and sprang to her feet. Without another glance, she strode off, leaving me alone.

I blinked, staring at Nalice. *Oh...*

If Frayde, with her pillar-like form and fiery hair is akin to a candle, I realized, *then she burns for Nalice.*

Alone, I retired to our tent, but didn't know what to do with myself. I had no need to practice drills like the soldiers around me, yet my hands itched to hold a weapon, if only to put them to some use. I wished I could occupy my mind, yet there seemed no final tasks to attend for which I was equipped, either. I didn't trust my sewing to mend clothing needed for something as serious as battle, my cooking skills were abysmal, and Lida had already organized every aspect of our camp.

No one needed me... which allowed me to ask the question, *what do I need?*

The sea. It always came back to the ocean, for me.

In desperation, I flung a blanket around me like a cloak, and headed out the tent to seek the stream running through the boundaries of our camp perimeter.

"Where are you going?"

Lida's voice stopped me in my tracks. She wasn't fighting either, but she'd braided her hair in her usual style and dressed in practical clothing of black Spade pants, boots, and a combat jacket with Spade buttons.

I was too nervous to blush at the confession. "The stream. There's no sea here, but it's the next best thing."

Lida studied me for a moment, then nodded. "I'll come with you."

Even if Lida didn't believe in much of anything -- save herself -- she was Elowan and thus, she understood.

Weaving through the encampment, we were hit with a blast of cold wind and a cacophony of noise as soldiers made final preparations. Some were helpful -- those more skilled instructed those with less experience in how to wield a blade or reload a gun. Others were less so... I saw a few arguments break out as men fought over arms, armor, and even food.

The Spades are less united than they seem, I thought, heart sinking, *but so are we.* Rythasians would stay together, I knew, as well as the few Elowans scattered amongst the ranks. Mal's men would never disobey a command. But the other clans? Who would hold their ground and who would turn and flee when we needed them?

After a few minutes, Lida and I reached our destination and knelt together on the rocky banks of the stream. Inhaling deeply, I rejoiced in the scent of water, despite the cold. Away from the smell of so many people, I could almost taste the loamy earth and the crispness of the tree bark. A thick forest canopy blocked the moon's light, so I couldn't see beyond a nearby bend where the stream curved into darkness.

I hoped it flowed to the sea.

After a few seconds of hesitation, I could feel Lida's gaze on me, prompting an explanation.

"I don't know if the Sea God hears me anymore, after what I did," I said, thinking of Ollier and Breyline and chewing my lip.

"Whatever it was, you did it on land," Lida replied sensibly. "He didn't see."

I barked a laugh. Finally, I drew a deep breath and

dipped my hand into the stream. *All water is connected,* I told myself. Whispering prayers in my mind, I let the cold stream run through my fingers.

Please let us win, I concluded simply, eyes closed.

I took the soft tinkling of the waves rushing over rocks as a reply.

Finished, I watched the water swoop and gurgle downstream, feeling both silly and hopeless at the same time. I could mitigate self-consciousness by arguing that praying to the Sea God did no harm, but I couldn't help my feelings of despair that it did no good either.

I don't want to go to war, I want to go home. My mind looped the fruitless protest and I was both mad at myself for its childishness and also angry that I thought I should feel this way.

"There's an ancient saying," Lida said, studying me with one eyebrow raised. "The stars incline us, they do not bind us."

"I've never known you to be one for mysticisms."

"When they encourage free will I'm all for it," she said, flicking her braid.

The stars incline us, they do not bind us. I ran it over in my head, alternatively liking and disliking it. Or rather, I liked the idea of charting my own course but was unsettled by the notion that it might be entirely incorrect. What was the point of stars inclining us if we ignored their heeding? And it wasn't as if we'd had a bevy of earthly role models in the form of our parents or elders to guide us either. Or even anyone to have helped prevent this chaos from unfolding in the first place.

An image of Lazlian's tattoo, of the smattering of stars surrounding the wound above his heart, popped into my head. I thought of Kirwyn's marking and my own as well. Beneath my blanket-cape, I slid my hand to it.

There haven't been stars to guide us for a long time, I reminded myself. *It's us. We have to look to each other.*

I rose, thanking Lida and finding my way back to my tent. This time it was occupied with two men very displeased at my not having told the guards where I was going.

Seeing them both, I burst into the tears I'd been holding back the past three days of our march. Kirwyn had me in his arms so immediately I didn't even know how I got there. *My love,* I thought, staring up at him with bare need as my eyes fell to lips so beautiful it was cruel.

Kirwyn leaned down and kissed me, his tongue sweeping my mouth with as much desperation as my own. Desire and fear mingled in that kiss and showed themselves in the way our hands gripped one another. The desperation wasn't for just ourselves -- it was for Teddy too. Our one hope was that throughout the fighting and after, Alette would keep our son safe.

For the hundredth time I asked Kirwyn, "Are you sure the Spades won't attack us in the night? While we're sleeping?"

He shook his head. "There's no reason for them to risk anything when we're delivering ourselves to their door. They've got tall walls and piles of weapons just as high, right at their fingertips. They *want* us encouraged, want us to have hope. If they attack and we scatter, they'll have to hunt us down and attack again."

I nodded, knowing all this but needing the reassurance. *His* reassurance.

Kirwyn released me and Lazlian took me in his arms,

also leaning down to kiss me. His hair had grown and without any smoothing potion, waves formed once more. I clung to those dark waves as fiercely now as I'd done the first time he'd kissed me, years ago. I remembered the frightening boy I once fought against and tried to take courage in how intimidating he could be, how good it was to have him on my side. Our side.

"If we lose, if anything goes wrong, take Sanda and run," Lazlian commanded, eyes hard. "Swear it."

"I swear I'll take Sanda and run." It came out a little breathlessly, but I did not allow my lip to quiver or the tears to flow again.

For her, for all of us, I'd be strong.

No matter what befalls us, I repeated the next morning. Beneath the pre-dawn sky, I buttoned the combat-jacket I wore and strapped my Rythasian dagger to my waist, the barest of essentials. Beside me, Kirwyn and Lazlian donned the more protective combat gear from Mal with tense, serious quietude.

We hadn't even moved and my heart was already galloping.

You're a royal, I scolded myself, lifting my chin. *You can't cry, you must lead by example.*

Refusing tears, I stared at the men I loved, memorizing every inch.

Stay alive, I willed.

Soon, the sky would lighten, and I remembered the vow I'd once made as a young girl. I'd been watching the dawn on a beach with Juls, back when I was his unwilling bride.

With its patience and tenacity, the rising sun, I'd reflected, was unbeatable.

No matter what happens, I swore, digging the stubs of my fingernails into my palms. *I vow to be like the sun, rising again and again.*

CHAPTER 55

FOR RYTHAS
Kirwyn

I could smell fear in the air and too much of it was coming from the men and women at my back. If I were outside this battle, looking down with a bird's eye view and having the choice of sides to join, it wouldn't be ours.

With all the clans combined, our numbers are greater, I reminded myself.

The thought was met with the depressing echo that *our casualties will be greater too.*

It was too early to tell what the winds would bring. The air was brisk in the shadows, yet warm on the open hill, where we gathered. By noon the skies could open to relentless rain, or the sun could beat down and have us sweltering as we fought. Late Spring in Spade territory the weather was unpredictable, with too many variables in play.

The way it mirrored our battle made me uneasy.

To my immense relief, Jori kept his word and led the combatants under his command out of the city and into the woods, abstaining from the coming battle. I couldn't imagine what he'd told his soldiers or how he'd save face with the Aureum, but I was sure he managed something clever. Loyal to Jori, I saw hundreds on both foot and horseback having removed themselves from the fight to remain neutral.

Citizens had left the walled city too. Our scouts reported the exodus began before we arrived, and people continued to trickle into the surrounding territories throughout the night. We let them pass, unharmed. Though I did not consider those who took slaves and laughed at the Bowl to be wholly innocent, there was no way to know who amongst the fleeing was exceptionally guilty.

The Aureum would wait within the walls, I knew, expecting a quick victory. Some non-combatants remained with them to have front row seats at what they too believed would be an easy win. To them, the show we put forth would be like a spectacle in the Bowl. I'd bet some even watched from their windows, cup of wine in hand and shrieking with glee if an explosion came too close, thinking themselves courageous for having braved it.

A few, unfortunately, had likely remained in their homes because they couldn't leave or had nowhere else to go, but there was nothing we could do about that.

And the slaves... at least they were within the walls and out of the way.

God, I couldn't imagine how those people felt, crammed atop one another and wondering if the army who would bring them freedom would bring them death first, exploding the walls of Spade City and indiscriminately killing whoever was unlucky enough to be in that section.

Was my father amongst them?

It would be worse to be chosen -- to be pulled from the thick perimeter and used as a human shield.

The children, I thought, imagining the screams of little ones yanked from a parent's arms for Spade slaughtering.

Teddy will be safe, I told the pain in my chest. *Alette will protect him with her life.*

Picturing the horrors made me grateful for Zaria's insistence, however foolish it might prove. We awaited word from Aewna back in the satellite to let us know if -- *when* -- Mal-Yin's men hacked the Spade system to permanently lock down both the slaves and the weapon's silo.

Riding from the east, a man headed straight to where I sat my horse at the front of the line. Beside me on their mounts were Lazlian, Jesi, Mal-Yin, and a woman named Tanina who was leading our fourth charge to the north gate.

I quickly dismissed my initial thought that this might be a Spade negotiator of some kind when I observed how the man sat a horse.

Farip Fabroni rode right to me, clearly having enjoyed a few cups of wine. He was armed with a hodgepodge of firearms and daggers, but his shoulder-length hair was untied and he hadn't proper armor.

"I will fight with you," he announced proudly, perhaps having rehearsed the line a few times, though this seemed a last-minute, alcohol-induced decision.

A goddamn wild card till the end.

Lazlian frowned and replied, "You're drunk."

Fabroni ignored the king and said to me, "You wanted to know how I sneak in and out of the city? My sister Evren lives there. She is the lover of Larius Mikaster, the highest of the High Twelve. One of his lovers, anyway."

"A... slave?" I asked, wondering how in the world his sister wound up in that position when it seemed she could easily escape the city.

Fabroni shook his head. "Not by name, but there are other ways to enchain just as heavily. Evren has two babes from Larius and she would die before she left those children. My sister has no power over the lives of her offspring, but she's acquired the coveted ability to sneak around the city, on account of her role as Larius's mistress. To the guards, I'm a traveler peddling exotic potions she buys to maintain her loveliness. Should she lose her beauty and Larius's favor, they'd lose the heavy tokens she drops into their eager palms."

I sighed at the reminder of myriad ways an innocent person might be stuck in this Spade web. Lazlian shrugged. We hadn't the time left to debate.

"Fight with us if you want to," Laz said to Fabroni, "just don't get in our way. And try not to shoot any of our own men."

Fabroni, already armed, steered his horse next to Erisio, who stood just behind us. At his nearness, I could confirm by smell that Fabroni had been drinking. A strange sense of protectiveness washed over me as I wanted to tell him to sit this one out. *How our roles have reversed since the day he captured Zaria and me.* But it seemed like whatever his sister endured motivated him to fight, and I didn't think he could be dissuaded from that.

Mal-Yin had only been half-listening to our conversation, tuned in to the communicator in his ear and awaiting Aewna's command. He snapped his gaze to us and I saw excitement dancing his in eyes.

"We've done it," he announced, grinning. "My men have done it. The slaves are locked down as is the weapons silo. Now is the time to attack."

My heart thumped and I met Lazlian's eyes. *Holy shit, we've done it.* It was a little early -- we weren't fully in position yet -- but better now than never.

"It's time," Mal commanded, loudly. "We must ride!"

Shouting, Tanina spirited away in the direction of her company, aiming to lead them around the city and to the northern gate. Mal-Yin rode toward his assembled clan, intending to lead them west. Jesi kicked her heels against her mount and rode to the other half of Rythasian soldiers, readying to attack the east gate.

All four leaders, plus Lysette, were connected by an earpiece, allowing us to keep in contact with one another.

"Warriors of Rythas!" Lazlian shouted, riding across the front line. His black mount, black clothing, and black hair were a dark contrast against the green hill as he moved. "We fight for Rythas! The Spade fleet encircling our kingdom *will* attack when we do, and our families will be massacred if we do not win." Lazlian rode harder and the slight breeze picked up, pushing the clouds faster across the sky. "Fight for freedom, fight for glory, but above all, fight for Rythas! For the love of our kingdom and for those who live there!"

Ear-splitting cheers began before the king even finished his rousing speech. I felt the war cries reverberate in my bones and my left hand tightened on the reins. In my right, I firmed my grip on my gun.

We were synced as Laz and I kicked our horses into action, racing toward the tall walls of Spade City with an army howling beside and behind us. The selected men and women who'd been tasked to attack the gate itself kept pace with Laz and I. Half those soldiers rode within the security of an APAT, armed with Mal's long-range weaponry. The other half were on horseback and equipped with explosives that were more reliable but required closer positioning.

My heart was in my throat as we neared the gate and the Spades atop their walls fired upon us...

...but to my relief, they did not do so nearly as heavily as I knew they could.

Fools.

For one, I believed they *wanted* us to knock down their doors and to funnel inside together, to hem us in from behind and deliver ourselves unto their intended slaughter en masse. For another, I liked to imagine the unexpected invasion into their systems had sent those high in the ranks scrambling to figure out what the hell was going on. Hopefully, we'd unleashed some chaos within their command.

I couldn't help but flinch when the first shot from the APAT fired on the gate. High atop the walls Spades fired back, and I winced to see the spray of bullets cause a swath of our men to fall.

Fuck. I didn't know what guns they used, but those they employed now were highly effective.

The APAT halted after a few unsuccessful attempts, and those on horseback rode forward with courage I admired. We couldn't effectively cover them as the Spades shooting down on us were well-protected behind metal and steel. I could only glimpse the ends of barrels peeking out to rain fire below.

I watched helplessly as two of the five riders went down, falling off their horses, and tumbling on the grass, dead.

Come on, I willed.

A third man went down -- though I couldn't tell if it had been the horse or the rider who was shot.

The two remaining reached the gate.

Yes. My heart leapt as I watched them quickly unload their explosives, remount, and ride out.

No.

One woman took a shot to the back and went down.

The last rider galloped back to us, clearing the necessary range as the bombs exploded and blew the gate wide enough for us to charge. Though it wasn't as large a space as I'd like, I was ecstatic that we'd done it at all.

The sound of our shouts *had* to frighten some of the Spades, I reasoned. There were thousands of us, wild clanspeople they feared, hopefully hemming in the city from all directions. Lazlian and I kicked our horses into a gallop and rode through the rubble of the gate before the smoke even cleared.

If a king and a keylord on the front lines didn't inspire others to fight, I didn't know what did.

We emerged into Spade City and immediately met with a row of soldiers, some standing and some kneeling, firearms I recognized trained on us.

My heart thundered in my chest.

Now we learn the truth.

"Hold," the commander of their army ordered.

Come on, I willed.

"Hold!" the leader repeated as we neared.

Come on...

"Fire!" he shouted.

Nothing happened.

"Fire!" he cried again.

I roared with laughter, licking my teeth and throwing my head back as we rode.

The weapons Mal-Yin provided the Spades -- the ones they deemed to name FLO for *First Line of Offense* -- did not fire. Not a single shot. Mal, never committing to anyone or anything without working an advantage for himself, had constructed those firearms with a kill-switch he now employed.

FLOP weapons, he privately joked.

Every gun those soldiers depended upon was rendered useless. Half the Spade soldiers broke position, screaming and scrambling. The other half searched for secondary weapons. Most were swordless, so those without back-up firearms were now wonderfully disadvantaged against us.

Spades who weren't fast enough to run met the first wave of our riders, who mercilessly trampled them.

I tuned out their screams, but I watched the chaos erupt around me. Laz and I rode straight, firing into the thickest groupings of soldiers. Beside us, warriors of Rythas did the same. But it wasn't long before Lazlian's horse was shot out, and I jumped off mine as well. It was easier this way, to chase our enemy into the alleyways and alcoves where they tried to hide. Surrounding me it was a mix of the same -- some sat a horse, others attacked on foot. Those who burned through their bullets too quickly attacked with swords and daggers and the sound of fighting rang out in the air. With adrenaline pumping through my veins, a bloodlust seized me, and I didn't even think I would feel it if I were shot.

Luckily, with every passing second the odds of that happening diminished. We decimated the first wave of Spades, cutting through them as if we'd sliced a red-hot Rythasian blade through a scoop of soft butter.

Spade reinforcements, however, quickly began to flood our position.

Where were the other prongs of our attack? We needed them now.

With a moment's respite, Lazlian and I ducked behind a wall and he panted into his earpiece, "Mal, check in! Where are you?" Sweat dripped from his dark hair, but he was whole, uninjured.

Watching Lazlian's eyes round made my stomach sink. After a pause, Laz looked at me and said, "Mal's stuck. The Spades are fighting back in some kind of electronic attack, trying to reclaim their systems. He's taking half his men to strike what he believes is the physical location of their technical workers and the other half to try and guard the silo, should they fail to keep it locked."

Shit. I let my eyes momentarily flutter shut.

"Is he playing us?" I couldn't help but ask.

Lazlian shook his head quickly. "I don't think so. It's the first time I ever heard him like that. I'd say panicked if I didn't know better."

The idea that Mal-Yin might be *panicked* was more unsettling than a betrayal.

Lazlian's earpiece must have sprung to life again because he stilled, listening, and agonizing seconds ticked by. The wind blew harder now, pushing clouds above that were helpless to its power. They flew past the sun, casting Lazlian in alternating light and shadow. I watched as he gritted his teeth, then cursed.

"Jesi is in, but Tanina can't explode her gate," he said, breathing heavily. "It's chaos on the north end. Seems like a quarter of Tanina's clans took it as a bad sign and fled to the trees. In the confusion, those remaining split, half running east and half west. But many of those heading toward Mal-Yin are now going to be running right to their death as he's not there. Only those backing up Jesi will have a fighting chance. She's pushing to meet us, but fuck!" Lazlian kicked at the ground. "We've lost the advantage of numbers."

My adrenaline spike wore off, quickly replaced by a horrible sinking feeling. *Oh fuck.* We were down to little more than half our forces now. *Not nearly enough.* The Hazards would come soon, I hoped, and maybe Mal would quickly neutralize the Spades he fought and join us...

I scrubbed a hand down my face, pushing away the fool's hope. As the sound of the gunfire came closer to where we stood, Lazlian met my eyes and I nodded. Whether hope was a help or a hinderance, there was nothing we could do but fight on. In unison, Laz and I took a deep breath and re-joined the fray.

Bodies littered the ground and as ammunition on both sides ran low, Rythasians and Spades alike swiped whatever weaponry they could from the fallen -- a sword, a gun, any dagger they had time to take. My stomach felt as if it were full of rocks as I watched wave after wave of our enemy funnel through the Spade streets to swarm us. There was nothing we could do but try to hold off until Jesi arrived, but that was unlikely as she was probably facing the same issue. Without a four-prong attack, her position and ours would be overwhelmed.

We were stuck. Ripe to be picked off, one by one.

Shit, no!

There was no glory and no bloodlust now, only the screams of the dying around me and the rise of our defeat.

I lost sight of Lazlian when I was pushed to my knees and then quickly, my back. It happened in the span of two seconds. One moment, I was swinging my own blade, the next, I was down. Above me, a giant of a man raised his sword for the killing blow. It happened so fast that I hadn't the time to avoid his strike. Though this man was bald, his sheer size reminded me of Craigory, and I wondered if it was poetic irony to finally meet my end this way.

Zaria, I thought, bracing. It was as I'd read -- in that one second, flashes of our life together ran through my mind at impossible speeds, accompanied by an unbearable ache in my heart. Seeing her for the first time in her cave back in Elowa. When she was ripped away from me on a rain-soaked boat at sea. Finally finding her again on a sunny beach in the mainland.

Our wedding in the surf.

Our son, born in that same surf.

Her bright smile. Always, her smile.

I hoped she'd be able to smile again. For our son. For herself.

The face of the soldier above me twisted in gleeful rage and I knew the killing blow was coming. His arm swung downward and I said her name one last time in my mind.

Zaria --

To my astonishment, another hand abruptly reached out and blocked the swing. At the same time, a sword pierced my attacker's exposed abdomen, slaying him. The fast turn of events left me gaping and unable to speak as Lazlian, heaving and remorseless, kicked the dying man to the ground with a sneer of disgust.

Still breathing heavily, he stretched out his hand, offering me a lift to my feet.

Lazlian just saved me from certain death. Holy fuck.

Oh, fuck.

I clasped Laz's hand, as sweaty and dirt-encrusted as my own, and asked, "You're going to boast about this every day for the rest of our lives, aren't you?"

"Oh, absolutely," he gloated, pulling me up. Laz smiled but there was no joy in it as he nodded toward the thickest part of the fighting. His voice rang with bitterness as he added, "Fortunately for you, the rest of our lives don't look to be very long."

Lazlian was right -- we couldn't beat this many Spades pummeling us relentlessly. The only upside I could see was that none of the weapons from the silo appeared and thus, we wouldn't be killed in mere minutes. Mal-Yin must have either had some success in preventing the Spade techs from unlocking the silo, or he was physically guarding it, because the Spades hadn't yet unleashed the big guns.

It will be a slower defeat as they overwhelm us, I thought, heart sinking, *but still a defeat.* Perhaps we could last half an hour, if we were lucky. But men were screaming and falling all around me. We would die here without fresh fighters, that was a certainty.

Jori, I suddenly thought. *Jori has men.*

My eyes fell upon the nearest horse.

"Find Jori!" I shouted, grabbing Lazlian by his biceps. "Ride out, promise him anything he wants if he'll join us! Anything!"

Lazlian's eyes blew wide, considering. "You have to do it, you know him," he countered.

"You go!" I shouted. Sweat dripped from my forehead and into my eyes as I jerked backward at the sound of approaching gunfire. "Promise him anything, everything. I'll cover you, I'm a better shot."

Laz shook his head and protested, "They won't hold the line for you."

No. I thought. *I'm not their king.*

Quickly, I glanced at our men and then back at the horse, cursing. Laz was right. Before running, I paused, clenching my jaw.

"If I die..."

"I know," he finished for me. "And if I die, tell her she was heart-breakingly beautiful in that dress the night of my coronation," Laz said quickly. "I don't know why I never told her."

"I will," I promised.

"Go!" Laz ordered. "I'll cover you."

Crouching low to the ground, I crept toward the edge of our men.

Then I bolted at full speed for the horse.

CHAPTER 56

WHAT WE'RE MADE FOR
Merie

Standing between the scarlet hibiscus plants on the wide veranda, Juls and I anxiously watched the Spade fleet for Raoul's return. We clasped hands but didn't speak much, partially because I kept holding my breath and not realizing I was doing it. Then I'd gasp for air, only to repeat the process minutes later.

If anyone can make peace, it's Raoul, I comforted myself.

Our enemy had positioned closer to High Spire the night before. For weeks they'd set fire to homes as soldiers marched from the lowland territories, seemingly corralling those who hadn't evacuated on Juls's orders. But as the Spades pushed further up the coast, we'd run out of room to fall back. At the same time, their ships had moved nearer as well.

Yet something was happening we couldn't understand, because our enemy had paused and it didn't make sense.

What were they waiting for? Some kind of signal? Or did it mean we had hope?

There wasn't enough space to protect so many people within the castle itself, and the city below wasn't fortified. Every able body would fight -- it was our way. But the old and the young? The sick?

I screwed my eyes shut. *They'd be the first to die.*

Our only hope was that Raoul had somehow negotiated, if not peace, then at least more time. Not that we could do much with it. We'd been living under the blockade for months, going about our lives in the ominous shadow of the Spade ships, our food and other vital provisions diminishing. Their leaders had refused our previous attempts to meet. It was only now, as their army marched close to our fortress, that they'd agreed to speak with Raoul.

I clutched my skirts with my free hand, crushing the silk as I fisted it.

If anyone has hope of negotiating anything, it's Raoul.

At the sight of a small boat breaking away from the Spade fleet, Juls and I spun in unison, hurrying down the castle steps and toward the Garden Gate. Flanked by many guards, we wove our way through the towering palm trees and onto the royal beach.

As the boat neared our shore, I spied the four guards who had accompanied our advisor.

Where was Raoul?

I swallowed thickly as my heart beat a nervous pace.

The boat did not head toward the dock, instead moving quickly and directly to the beach. Juls and I hurried to the water's edge to meet it. When it was near enough, all four guards jumped into the surf and retrieved something from the hull.

A wretched cry escaped my lips and I brought my hand to my mouth to stifle anything louder.

Raoul's lifeless body was lifted from the small boat, carried the few steps onto the sand, and held before us.

His cause of death was obvious from the dagger pierced deep into his heart, pinning a note to his chest.

Surrender or you die like him

Why? My mind screamed. *Why were the Spades so cruel? What did they want from us?*

I shook the question from my head. Conquerors always wanted the same thing: to conquer. And, when it came to the Spades, death would be kinder than capture.

A guard by Raoul's right shoulder met Juls's eyes and said the two words I'd been dreading.

"They attack."

There was no time to mourn our beloved advisor as Juls and I looked up to see hundreds of Spades jumping from their ships and loading into smaller boats.

"Back to the castle!" Juls shouted, corralling the guards. "Defend our home!"

This is it, I thought as I ran. *The moment we'd been dreading for months.*

"They can destroy us from a distance, but they don't," I cried, lifting my skirts as we sprinted back to the castle. Though we'd discussed this outcome many times in the assembly, it was still difficult to believe.

"They want Rythas intact," Juls agreed, keeping a pace

that was hard for me to match. "It's the same reason they didn't burn most of the older homes. They want all of this for their own."

My heart pounded wildly by the time we'd retreated into the safety of the castle. All around us we were joined by those who could fight.

A queen is calm, I told my racing heart. *We can hold out here. For a while, at least.*

We'd been forced into a defensive position, as I'd once teased Juls, but my husband playing defense was deadly.

The Black Passage was too narrow for the Spades to amass a larger attack. It was also now heavily defended, thanks to Juls learning from Zaria's ploy years ago. The King's Gate would be a disadvantage for anyone foolish enough to charge it, because it was a steep, uphill battle.

That left the Bone Gate and the Garden Gate.

Once again, perhaps we had Zaria to thank for testing our weaknesses, I thought, surveying the soldiers shouting and positioning all around me.

We'd rigged a trap beneath the Bone Gate, and those who attacked that passageway would now find themselves facing a heavily-reinforced door. Before an enemy had the time to explode it or to retreat, we'd rigged a solid, secondary gate to shut behind any invading party. As the Bone Gate abutted the sea, it had been easy enough for us to construct a hidden dam beside it. Once we trapped our enemy, we'd open the dam to release the ocean unto those unlucky souls within.

It was a trick we could only pull once, but they'd die, and we'd render that passageway useless for attack.

On the other side of the castle, we had a plan in place for the Garden Gate as well. The area was ringed with trees and market stalls, highly flammable even before we'd hidden *hundreds* of firestarters throughout. Once the Spades fanned out over that swath of land to press the attack, we'd set it ablaze, burning them all and smoking out the lucky ones who were fast enough to run.

War was nasty business, and I didn't want to see or hear any of that when it happened. Many would die in the flames and others, the waves. Those who remained would meet our bullets, steel, and if it came down to it, we even had boulders to toss from the ramparts. There was no point in hiding our weaponry any longer, and when it ran out we'd use whatever we had, holding them off until...

...until we no longer could.

Helpless, I stood beside Juls as he barked orders and the Spade army marched nearer. I'd never felt so out of my depth and utterly useless as I watched armored men and women scurry into battle positions. I wasn't a commander or a warrior. I was just me, Merie.

In truth, I'd been raised to be ornamental, another jewel in the crown. My parents had groomed Navere to be Commander and, despite Juls's betrothal, they'd raised me with the hope I'd be queen. My brother and I had done what we were trained to do; I'd fulfilled my purpose. I tried my best to be a just and wise queen, but wisdom wasn't a weapon I could wield in this battle. What could I possibly do to help us fight?

Nothing.

I thought of Zaria, who wasn't much of a warrior either but always seemed to have a ready trick up her sleeve or some unusual scheme she'd employ -- even if it was shocking. I was scandalized the time she'd thrown Kirwyn a birthday celebration in the brothels, hoping to improve business. *A prince's party in an establishment for whores.* I'd thought she was out of her mind, but I had to admit that the royal couple's presence did draw attention and the architecture was stunning. The gleaming, white stone fountains and pretty little bathing pools made a lovely backdrop.

I gasped, audibly.

"The brothels!" I exclaimed, racing over to Juls and grabbing his hand.

He halted in his frantic preparation and furrowed his brow at me.

"The buildings are historical," I said in a rush. "The Spades won't want to destroy them. I'll take the children there, and the elderly, and anyone else who can't fight."

Juls searched my face, eyes wide.

"No," he protested. "It's a good idea, but we'll send someone else. I can't let you go."

"It must be me," I cried. "Many will be too frightened to follow anyone else across the city. I will show them that it's safe by being with them."

Juls clenched his teeth and frowned. "No," he repeated. "I can't let you go."

I laid a hand on his cheek, failing as I tried not to cry. My heart already ached terribly.

"This is what we were made for," I said. "You will stay with those who can fight. Defend our kingdom. I will stay with those who cannot. I will protect our people."

That is what it means to be king and queen, I said with my eyes.

Juls released a pained moan. Then he cupped the back of my head and pulled me to him for a deep kiss. When it ended, he held me, his forehead pressed to mine.

"I love you," Juls said, tears gathering on his thick lashes. "I have always loved you, since we were little children."

"And I you," I replied, breathlessly. "I have loved you since before I can remember, as I cannot recall when I first laid eyes on you. I have only ever known a life of loving you. If we... die... my last thoughts will be of you."

Juls winced as he attempted to keep his composure in front of his men. "And mine of you."

We broke apart with reluctance and I tried to remember him like this. He looked so gallant, dressed for combat. Juls was unquestionably the most beautiful king Rythas had ever known. He possessed a charming, boyish smile, kind brown eyes, and a good heart to match. He'd always been a handsome and honorable boy, but Juls had grown into a man I was so proud to call husband.

At the sound of the Spade army drawing nearer the castle, I jumped. Juls called Tomé and Marcin to his side, the Elowans who'd been prepping defenses with us the last few months.

Marcin was a little taller and possessed a slightly less muscular frame than his partner. He'd tied his hair back for battle in what Elowans called a *goat's tail*. Tomé, with shorter locks, had no need. But besides those differences, the two Elowans were so similar to me they could have been kin. Both Tomé and Marcin had striking manes of light blonde hair, blue eyes, and typical Elowan features.

"Guard the queen," Juls ordered. "Take ten men and escort the party she assembles to the brothels. Both of you," he said, referring to Tomé and Marcin, "are to return to defend High Spire once they are safely delivered. But leave the remaining soldiers to protect those who can't fight."

Juls gritted his teeth and I knew it was because he couldn't spare more guards. I wished I could tell him that I understood.

It didn't matter if he provided one or one hundred

soldiers to protect us. It was ultimately a waste of men if we were attacked.

I kissed Juls hungrily one last time, then tore away before I lost the nerve to do so.

Tomé and Marcin called out sharply, gathering the necessary guards, then quickly led me out of the castle and into the city.

"I mean no offense, your majesty, but I didn't think you knew of the tunnels," Tomé said as we hurried through the streets. "It's a very good idea though."

"Tunnels?" I echoed, bewildered and nearly tripping on my skirts.

The Elowan scrutinized my face. "Isn't that why you want to hide the children in the brothels?" he asked.

"I believe the Spades won't bombard the buildings because they want to preserve them. Of what tunnels do you speak?"

Tomé looked taken aback. Never breaking our rapid pace, he explained, "Not every nobleman -- or woman -- wants to be observed pursuing a dalliance. The tunnels beneath the brothels are used by patrons who seek discretion."

For a moment, I couldn't find my tongue. I'd never heard of this before and I supposed Juls wasn't aware of these passageways either.

"I will take you and the children there," Tomé said, firmly. "They're not exceptionally well-hidden but they're not obvious if you don't know what to look for. It will buy you time in case..." he trailed off. "And it will keep some of the fighting from the children's ears."

"They're dark," Marcin added. "We'll bring many candles."

I nodded as my heart swelled with gratitude. "Thank you."

"If you're discovered, you can exit the tunnels from the far end..." Marcin trailed off, shaking his head with frustration. "You can run, scatter. Some may escape..."

Which, again, would only buy time. Should a child slip through the hands of Spades, where would he or she ultimately go? Our island was surrounded. Little Teddy had the best chance of survival, but that was only a matter of time as well. Days ago, Alette had taken him to a safehouse hidden deep within the woods.

There weren't enough of those to protect us all.

Together, the guards and I shouted to collect anyone who lingered, unable to fight. We mostly met with little ones and a few grandmothers who held the hands of these frightened children. The city was deserted as most people had already rushed to defend the castle. I was frustrated as we made painfully slow progress, since neither the young ones nor the elderly could move quickly.

"Come with us!" I shouted to the empty streets, beckoning those who were hiding. "We're taking you to safety!" The guards around me echoed my cries, but our party paused in unison when black smoke billowed horrifically across the clear blue sky.

My heart seemed to stop and for a few dazed moments, our group stared.

Juls has set the markets ablaze, I thought, stomach sinking in terror as the reality set in. I wasn't even sure Tomé and Marcin could make it back to the castle now, though I knew they'd try. From our distance, I couldn't hear the Spades scream, but I imagined many were dead or dying.

"Let's go!" Tomé ordered, jarring us back into action.

We moved faster now, fear nipping at our heels. By the

time we passed under the gleaming stone archways marking our destination, we'd collected dozens of children. Entering the brothel district, I heard the gurgle of many fountains beneath the sleepy shade of palm trees, and the scents from various houses carried on the air. Rose and sandalwood, jasmine and leather, a heavy bouquet of white flowers. Something sharp, like the air before a storm or the fire in a hearth, emanated from one direction.

Too lovely to destroy, I hoped.

Tomé and Marcin were a godsend, flying through the brothels and ferreting out those in hiding who might help us. Several had already fled to the tunnels themselves. With many terrified children pressed close behind me, the two Elowan warriors escorted us down into the concealed passageways, illuminating our way with candles held aloft.

We made an odd scene, collectively. Huddled in the dim light stood the ten well-armored guards, a few elders, many children, and our hosts... the men and women of pleasure... who wore almost no clothing at all. Neither my guards nor anyone else seemed disciplined enough not to steal curious glances.

But all I could think about was Juls and his defense of High Spire. My stomach rioted as I wondered what was happening back in the castle. Though I had eaten nothing, I fought not to be sick.

"We must go," Tomé announced, once everyone was settled.

"Stay safe," Marcin said, bowing his head.

"Stay safe," I echoed, with courage I pretended.

"Rythas has long been our home," Marcin reminded. "We'll do our best to defend her."

I thanked the Elowans and bid them a hasty goodbye. I was reluctant to let them leave, but not only did the battle need these two for their strength and skill, it wouldn't have been fair to hold them back. They weren't Rythasian-born, but they'd integrated themselves into our kingdom. Both Elowans, I knew, were close to Zaria and had been witnesses for the heir's conception.

I also had no guarantee they'd be any safer here, with me. Not in the end.

Feeling alone, I resisted the urge to clutch my skirts or to wring my hands. Instead, I stood perfectly still with my head held high.

A queen is calm.

Whatever happened, I would make my king, my husband, proud to the last. Just as he would endeavor to make me proud.

We'd be strong for each other, and for Rythas.

But god, I wish I knew how they fared back in the castle. Was Juls still alive? Please let him be alive.

As painfully tense minutes passed, I had to admire the pleasure-ladies. Skilled in amusing others, I supposed, they smiled effortlessly as we huddled, playing games and singing songs with the children. I almost laughed as an elderly woman covered her grandson's eyes when a girl waltzed by in a sheer gown, distributing slices of mango to distract the little ones.

Such silliness! How can anyone worry about seeing too much flesh when we all might not live to see another day?

Noticing the hesitation in some of the more pious women, I made a show of profusely thanking the... courtesan... and taking a slice of mango for myself.

When no one was looking, however, I passed it to a boy about five years of age, who was crouched in a corner, knees to his chest.

I couldn't possibly eat a bite as the first sounds of the Spade army reached our ears. Distant, but drawing nearer.

Please keep us safe, I prayed. Over and over I chanted the simple plea in my mind. Minutes passed, and I heard the dreaded sound of our enemy close enough that the clamor of their many footfalls echoed through the tunnels.

Would they find the doorways leading to our hiding spot?

As a child burst out crying, I quickly scooped her into my arms and rocked her. Then I ripped the modest tiara from my head and presented it to another girl, hoping to distract her with the shiny object. Desperate for anything that might help, I unfastened my necklace and shoved it into the hands of a little boy so that he could play with it. When the child I bounced finally hushed, I put her down and went so far as to rip some of the silks of my gown. I waved the swaths I'd torn and presented them to boys and girls as scarfs they too might wave, or tie into knots, or around their hair or... I didn't know what! But I'd try anything to distract the children from our enemy, coming closer.

It seemed inevitable when I heard the Spades burst directly into the brothels above and just beyond our door. The noise was quickly followed by the sound of soldiers fanning out.

Will they find the hidden door?

I gulped, standing barefoot in the middle of the stone passageway, having given my sandals to a child as well. My hair was a mess, my gown torn, and I bore no jewels or finery to distinguish my status. It might have been hysteria that made a giggle escape my lips. I realized that, should we be discovered, I would likely be mistaken for a lady of pleasure. Perhaps a commoner. Certainly no queen.

I found courage in the knowledge that, if this was it, at least I'd acted as a queen should act, right up until the end. Everything that truly mattered was within me and no Spade could take that away.

The footfalls grew more frantic.

I took a deep breath and held it.

Please.

I squeezed my eyes tight and prayed for a miracle.

THE POWER OF THE OCEAN
Zaria

My stomach churned as, from the hillside, I looked upon a disaster that would soon be a massacre.

I didn't know what happened exactly, but Mal's army had been diverted to another section of the city, removing a quarter of our forces from the main attack. We received worse news when Lysette announced that the northernmost gate didn't explode, leaving another quarter of the army to scatter. They rode east and west in a disorganized attempt to find passage into the city from the other gates.

Some clans, however, seemed to take the failure as a bad sign and abandoned the battle entirely, turning tail and running for the trees.

Within the forest, Jori's army stood. I wondered if his soldiers would slay the deserters as they fled or let them pass, keeping to neutrality.

Standing on the hillside and watching it unfold was like

watching my world come to an end. I couldn't see into the city entirely, but from what Lysette reported through her earpiece, I understood our situation was desperate. The boom of gunfire was ceaseless, echoing throughout the surrounding farms, and my heart screamed with every shot. For all I knew, one of those bullets could have taken down Kirwyn, Laz, or Jesi.

"You have to ride, it's time!" I shouted to Lysette. What was she waiting for? She hadn't mounted her horse, yet she was armed and ready for battle, so she clearly intended to fight. Which was good because we *needed* her force. Now.

Lysette turned her yellow eyes on me and coquina clams raced up my spine.

"Hazards," Lysette called, slowly looking away from me. "These weak clans are losing this battle and we must fight... not with Rythas but against her!" Lysette announced, turning to address the Biohazards as they encircled her. Her words stole my breath and the ocean roared in my ears. "I have made a deal that grants us the kingdom of Rythas when this war is over. We'll have our own island, fortified and isolated for safety, and large enough to grow and flourish like never before!"

My stomach twisted and I clutched it as if I'd been punched. *That's why Aewna couldn't get a read on Lysette,* I realized. The Hazard leader was probably waiting to see how the battle shaped up before truly committing to a side. I squeezed my eyes shut. Kirwyn and I had tried to warn Lazlian that she couldn't be trusted. *And now we'll all die for this betrayal.*

"Our children are down there," Nalice yelled as she stepped forward, eyes round with horror. The switching of sides was news to her too. "Our sons."

"They will quickly fall in line or they will die," Lysette

declared, "They are soldiers, Nalice. They know what it means to fight."

No, my mind screamed. Those boys were going to be confused as hell at what was happening.

Desperate, I scanned the eyes of the Hazards. I could tell from their anxious looks and fidgeting that Lysette's move wasn't supported by most of the clan. At least, not fully. Yet no one wanted to go against their formidable leader either.

"We'll have our own island," Lysette announced. "And I will be queen."

"My daughter will be queen," I shouted at her back.

Lysette turned her sickly eyes to me. "She can be next. I have no wish to make my own heir."

Snarling, I spat, "You mean you'll buy the allegiance from the remaining people of Rythas with her succession. I will never let you take my baby from me."

Lysette shrugged. "You can stay as her wet nurse or we can find another. I have no other use for you. Think carefully as the other side of the deal is death."

"Rythas is our kingdom. She will never be yours!" I screamed.

I wasn't even aware I made the decision before I attacked Lysette, but my effort was pathetic. The Biohazard leader threw me off her like I was nothing more than a troublesome child. To my shock, Frayde followed, but Lysette tossed her to the ground just as easily. Much like me, Frayde was too angry to think clearly and our position on the bright hillside offered no chance for her usual stealth. The redhead landed hard on the dirt, emitting a cry and cradling her ankle.

Seeing her friend shoved to the ground, Nalice roared and drew her large sword. Trailing only half a second behind, Lysette followed suit.

Nearly in unison other Hazards stepped back to widen the circle as the two women prepared to fight. Nalice, strong and skilled, advanced hard, putting the Biohazard leader on the defense and pushing her back. There was a clattering of swords and grunts from both women as they sparred.

My heart soared watching Nalice's prowess. She would win. She was better.

Lysette seemed to realize the same -- she couldn't beat the expert swordswoman. The Biohazard ruler hesitated, and then, to my disbelief, lowered her weapon.

Nalice, breathing heavily, stopped her attack, though her eyes glistened with rage. She seemed divided as she forced herself to halt.

I released a cry of joy. It was over, and it had only taken a few seconds.

Before Nalice could speak, Lysette, head bowed, lifted only her gaze as she smiled. In a flash, she kicked the dirt, sending it swirling up around Nalice and into her eyes. Immediately, Lysette lunged to attack while Nalice struggled to see.

Cheater, I thought -- or maybe I cried it. Or maybe it was the other women around me. Yet no one moved to intervene. Even Frayde, who would do anything to protect Nalice, had no entry into this wild dance of swinging blades. Nalice was forced back, struggling to block the blows from Lysette.

Shoot her, my mind screamed. *Someone take a gun and shoot Lysette.* Most of the weapons hadn't yet been distributed but surely *someone* had *something.* Was this their way, to not interfere? But couldn't the rules be broken, when Lysette had already cheated? Or perhaps throwing dirt was considered permissible?

Trying to rub her eyes and hold a sword at the same time, Nalice was unfairly outmatched. Lysette knocked Nalice onto her back and I heard the gasp echo throughout the Hazards.

Either Lysette was going to kill Nalice, or we'd lose the war with Lysette's continued command, or both.

Mere seconds had passed since I was first thrown to the ground, and I was still on that grassy patch in the circle of women. Present, but forgotten. My hands tightened on the hilt of my dagger and I remembered Kirwyn's long ago words from the day I'd confronted him in our safe. *Position here,* he'd instructed, moving my hand higher on the neck as I playfully held my dagger to his throat. *Don't hesitate.*

If I moved, I'd risk my life. But if I didn't, I'd risk everyone's. Everyone I loved. Maybe the world.

I licked my lips and blinked the sweat from my eyes. I made no sound.

On three, I told myself. The count seemed to beat in my head, the rhythm of an Elowan drum. It was deafening, but no one else could hear it. I was the only Elowan in sight. Ignored on the ground, I'd been dismissed -- a nursemaid, a nanny goat, a vehicle for milk, no more.

One...

But I had been the chosen braenese of Elowa. I had been the queen of Rythas. And I knew who and what I was now.

Two...

Lysette did not know. And she'd die for it. Or I'd die to prove it.

Three.

I did not roar, shout, or make a single sound. I was not clunky or careless. My limbs moved with a grace I'd only previously known in the ocean. Fluidly, as if a wave bore me, I rose, carried on its back until the swell crested at Lysette. I lifted my arm as I would for a stroke in the sea --

-- and quick as a sharp-toothed predator from the depths, I sliced my blade across her throat.

Lysette made a gargling, choking noise that did not sound horrific to my ears. It sounded like victory.

The Biohazard leader fell to her knees, then collapsed in a heap on the ground. I stood above her, not with rage, but with quiet command. Triumph swelled in my breast, yet I did not gloat over her corpse to my awe-filled audience, who gathered closer around me with stunned and admiring eyes. Like the ocean sending a destructive wave upon the shore and receding into calm once more, I'd proven my power and let the stillness wash over me.

After a moment, I realized that everyone was looking to me for orders, as if by besting their leader I'd taken her role. Perhaps this was the way of their clan, but I had no claim to command it.

I bent, drawing Lysette's dagger from its sheath, and crossed the grass to where Nalice stood, helping Frayde to her feet. I bowed before the two women and held the dagger aloft as a sign of power transfer I hoped was universal.

"I have slain your tyrant for you," I announced, a bit breathlessly. "Will you fight for me?"

Please. And fast. We're running out of time.

I tried not to picture what was happening below, tried not to wonder if Kirwyn, Laz, and Jesi were still alive...

"We will fight for you," Nalice shouted the words for all to hear. She took the dagger I'd presented and held it high in the air. "And we will *win*."

Roars broke out all around us and I gasped with relief.

Frayde struck out her hand for me and I shook it as I straightened.

"It's likely our position has been compromised by Lysette," Nalice warned amongst a rush of frenzied preparations. "You and Lida must return to the base."

I froze, realizing I could not. Kirwyn and Lazlian fought below. I could no more walk away now and continue to live, than I could cleave my own heart from my chest and continue to breathe. There was only one thing in the entire world worse than not running to Sanda and Teddy, and it was abandoning Kirwyn and Laz on that field of destruction. I couldn't do it.

"No," I breathed. "If a lady wants to fight, she fights, yes?"

Nalice flashed a wide, toothy grin. She pulled me to her and used her other hand to clap me on the back.

"Get this tricky island queen a horse!" Nalice barked to a tall brunette.

I spun on my heel and pushed my way through the women until I reached Lida, who'd been standing at the edge of the circle.

"Go to Sanda," I shouted, straining to be heard over the clamor of everyone hastening to ride. "Protect her. Take her far away if you have to, if we..." *Lose.* I couldn't say the word. "Help Teddy if you can make it back to Rythas. Tell them I love them," I begged. *"Please."*

Lida laid a confident hand on my shoulder. "I know what to do."

I closed my eyes and nodded. She did. There was no one better to trust with the safety of my children than Lida, wise and clever. If we all fell, if the kingdom fell... she'd know what to do to survive.

My heart was in my throat. I hadn't enough armor. Still,

I swung myself onto the horse Nalice had ordered and tucked the two guns I was handed into the waistband of my pants. Across my chest, a band with extra clips was strung. To my left and right, Hazards were equally equipped with firearms, ammunition, and explosive devices, as well as swords and daggers.

We're coming, I thought. *Please be alive. Stay alive.*

"Hazards!" Nalice cried, cantering across our front line. I was central amongst them, grasping the reins and sweating astride a dappled gray steed. He pawed the earth and whinnied, eager to move.

There was no time for elongated speeches. Nalice simply shouted, "We give no mercy to these men! Coat your swords in the blood of as many Spade devils as you can, so that they may never again use their swords to bleed our kind."

I'm coming. I will save you. Or I will die by your side.

"Destroy the Spades, once and for all!" Nalice roared, turning her steed forward and punching one hand in the air. "Hazards, with me!"

Hollering and howling, we took off at full speed down the hillside.

Thump-thump, thump-thump.

The rhythm of hundreds of hoofbeats thundered our arrival as we headed straight for the southernmost gate.

CHAPTER 58

SAVIOR
Lazlian

Glancing at our men, my chest tightened. I needed more than to hold position, I needed a charge to distract the Spades. It was most likely suicide for anyone rushing forth, but it had to be done because we'd *all* die if Kirwyn couldn't get out and convince Jori to help us.

Erisio met my eyes.

No. Not you.

His sharp nod told me he wasn't listening. Erisio was no fool; he knew what we needed and the risk it entailed. A bullet whizzing past my head reinforced that there was no time for any of us to feel bad about it. No time to think, only to act.

Kirwyn swung onto the horse. I crawled into position behind a steel container of some kind and aimed my gun, eyes on Kirwyn's path.

Erisio shouted something encouraging to our soldiers. Over my pounding heart I heard my name. Rythas. Erisio gave a loud, rallying cry. I caught a glimpse of his raised sword and then he charged forward with the men. I quickly refocused on Kirwyn. Pressed low to his steed, Kirwyn kicked its flanks and galloped in the opposite direction.

His life was in my hands and the fate of Rythas sat on both our shoulders in these next few seconds.

My heart pumped in time with the rapid hoofbeats against the Spade street. Sweat ran in rivers down my back. I steadied my aim, cursing my sweaty hands and the obstructed view. I could only shoot those I could see.

A rider came straight for Kirwyn and I shot him off his horse. Another popped out from behind a wall. *Bam, bam.* Two down. I missed the third, but Kirwyn quickly steered his horse in another direction, avoiding the blow of that man's sword.

As Kirwyn put more distance between us, I frantically scanned the city blocks and spied one Spade, low to the ground like me. His gun was focused on Kirwyn.

Rapidly, I fired, sacrificing accuracy for a flurry of bullets I hoped would make the shooter take cover or at least, distract him. *One, two, three...* It took me at least eight shots -- I'd lost count and emptied my clip -- before the man vanished. I didn't know if he rolled away injured or I'd had any luck and he died.

Fuck. I was out of firepower, but Kirwyn was out of range now anyway, disappearing down the wide road. A quick glance around proved fruitless for me to find another gun. I drew my sword just as I heard a cry of pain that seemed to physically rip through me. I turned and roared, seeing Erisio with a sword through his gut.

No, not him.

Like a madman, I lunged at his attacker and stabbed the

Spade through the neck before he even had a chance to see me.

"Erisio!" I shouted as he fell to the ground.

"Erisio!" I cried again, shaking him.

It was no use. I knew my friend was dead, but it didn't stop me from cursing and bargaining. Memories flooded my mind, evenings we'd spent in the war tower, tinkering with contraband. Mornings we rode side by side. Erisio was always genial, always helpful, often quiet. I think that was what first drew us together -- working quietly on the technology I swiped from our secret stores.

But if I spared any time to mourn or to move him, I'd quickly join him. Cursing again, I ran, folding into my men as the Spades pressed us back.

This was it -- we were outnumbered and outgunned. Many Rythasians, like me, were left to fight bullets with steel. Spade soldiers seemed to fall upon us from every direction, although they were light at our rear.

At least it will be quick. Death by gunshot is usually quick.

"Hold!" I screamed, every now and again. If their own king fighting at their sides couldn't encourage them, nothing could. "Hold your position!"

My heart thundered and my adrenaline spiked, knowing I neared my end. It was as much luck as it was skill to stay alive at this point. Like an animal, I shouted and howled as I slashed at my enemy. But I sweated like a man, and I'd die like one.

Someone shoved a gun into my hand and I fired at the Spades, quickly running out of ammo and leaving me without firepower once again. My shots weren't very accurate this time, but it was better than nothing. More Spades attacked our disadvantaged position and our numbers dwindled. Our enemy began spreading toward our rear, blocking any possible retreat -- not that I ever would have ordered it.

I hated that I'd die not knowing if we saved Rythas. I'd never learn if I left a kingdom for Sanda or an empire of sand.

He'll sweet talk Jori or he'll get Sanda somewhere safe. And if not, Zaria still lives. She'll flee with our baby.

At the thought of Zaria, I felt a renewed vigor to attack. We'd never battled like this in Rythas. The sheer size of the fighting was hard to wrap my head around, as was the destruction. Gunshots rang out like some infernal staccato beat, and the cries of the wounded and the dying were like a melody from hell. In the distance, explosions from bombs and the Spades' tank-like vehicles gave a particularly horrific flourish to this living composition.

I can't choose to live, I thought, taking a deep breath. *But I can choose how I die. And I will go down fighting.*

My muscles tensed, I raised my sword, and I charged forth once more --

-- But I immediately halted at the sound of a war cry. It was loud, female, and fearsome. Spades and Rythasians alike paused, eyes wide as we took in the sight of the Biohazards barreling down on us.

I laughed, and then my breath caught when I saw her. She rode, advancing like a beam of golden sunlight focused directly on me.

Zaria was neither properly dressed for combat, nor was her hair correctly bound. Long strands fanned out around her head as she rode, like rays of the sun. She headed straight to where I stood. Somehow, in the midst of battle, she'd found me.

Dear god, she shouldn't be here.

I ran toward her recklessly, and bullets flew past my

head. Between ducking and running, I fell, skidding across the street and rolling to protect myself from the horses flying past our warriors and attacking the Spades.

"Lazlian!" Zaria cried, and suddenly she was above me. For a moment, I didn't respond, both trying to clear my head and reveling in her kisses, which she planted all over my face. "I love you, I love you. Don't be dead, please," she begged, weeping over me. "I've loved you for so long, I just couldn't tell you."

I opened my eyes. "I know."

Zaria gasped.

"What I didn't know is what would finally make you say it."

Zaria covered me in more salty, dirty kisses, the tears streaking her face and mixing with the sweat soaking mine.

"That it takes nothing short of me nearly dying doesn't surprise me," I rasped. "You're impossibly stubborn."

She laugh-cried, "Live and I'll let you do anything you want. Whip it out of me, I don't care."

"I plan to." I sat up quickly and it hit me how was sore I was all over. "If we live and Kirwyn finds you here, he might whip you harder."

"Where is he?" Zaria cried.

"He's safe," I told her. "Rode off to get reinforcements, we hope."

Zaria sighed and thrust a gun into my hands.

"You swore you wouldn't come," I growled through clenched teeth, finding my feet to re-join the fray. We'd been granted a temporary reprieve by the Biohazards pushing the fighting back, but it wouldn't last long. All around me I could hear the dying on both sides.

"Yeah, well, I'm shit at keeping promises," Zaria said, still laugh-crying as she echoed words Kirwyn once spoke to me. God, the two of them were so alike sometimes. "Not when they no longer serve. I'd tell you to kill me for it, but you've already tried that and it didn't work."

"Whipping then," I said, pulling her against me and kissing her. "Works wonders on you."

I was livid and terrified and grateful to see her. My thoughts warred as I took stock of Zaria's weaponry and cocked my own gun.

"You can shoot but stay behind me!" I ordered, shouting as the noise increased.

She nodded, and we took a sort of tandem position where I shielded her and she crouched behind me, firing at Spades. Her accuracy rate was average but having me in front afforded her the opportunity to improve her aim.

Unfortunately, it was only a matter of time before we both ran out of ammunition. With the Biohazards reinforcing our ranks, we initially pushed the Spades back. A fresh volley of gunfire had the tendency to do that, as did the sight of the formidable horsewomen charging forth and knocking down the many Spades who'd been on their feet.

But from their rear, our enemy was constantly bolstered by new men and women funneling through the city blocks. It only took minutes for Zaria and me to empty our clips in a battle of this size.

To my right, I glimpsed Nalice. The red-eyed swordswoman had been knocked from her mount and now fought on foot with her pale companion by her side. A Spade soldier charged forward with a sword raised to Nalice's chest, but the Biohazard lunged and was lucky to have the blade pierce her upper arm instead.

The one with the flaming hair screamed -- I didn't think I'd ever heard her speak above a whisper before -- and lunged in front of Nalice.

Frayde, I remembered her name. She was a little hellion, spinning, screaming, and slashing. She took down four men, five...

An arrow flew, piercing Frayde's neck. For a moment, I was taken aback at the sight of such weaponry, as it wasn't plentiful here. Without access to the silo, I guessed the Spades grabbed whatever they could get their hands on. The redhead fell, sputtering and choking. Nalice howled and knelt beside her, but it was clearly too late.

I moved back, pushing Zaria with me so fast that we tripped over two fallen men. Death was all around us, but we had to look away and fight our own battles or we'd join the dead.

It's not enough. The addition of the Hazards had bought us precious time, but it still wasn't enough to defeat the Spades completely, who overwhelmed our position with sheer numbers.

Goddammit, we'd been so close!

Zaria met my eyes. She knew. It was hopeless.

I clasped her hand, desperately seeking a way to get her out of this or to shield her.

And then, I saw them filtering into the city from the direction of the northernmost gate.

Kirwyn did it, he persuaded Jori. The mainland rat had actually done it.

I laughed, triumphant, as Jori's men attacked the Spades from the rear. The twelfth company was fresh and their weaponry abundant. It was more than enough to turn the tide in our favor.

We've won, I thought, still grinning widely.

And yet... I frowned at the enemy directly before me.

What was this?

HE'LL PROTECT HER
Zaria

A laugh burst from my lips and tears streaked down my face, recognizing Jori's army.

We were saved!

At the clamor of so many horses and quite a few tanks, the Spades turned and saw their defeat.

It's over. Thank Keroe, it's over.

I took great gulps of air, rejoicing and catching my breath.

Yet... I cocked my head, confused, as the enemy directly before us slowly turned *back* to where we stood, death in their eyes.

Why...

No.... *No!* My heart sank.

Reinforcements came by multitudes, a wave of victory...

But not for us, I realized.

It was obvious to the Spades at our front that they could not beat the vast company of men and women barreling down the city streets behind them. But instead of surrendering or turning to fight, the Spade soldiers nearest Laz and I charged *forward*, engaging our rapidly-dwindling flanks to triumph in the smaller battle at which they *could* succeed. The company nearest our position was neither surrendering, nor joining the battle at their backs. Perhaps they were tougher than I'd judged or perhaps they wanted to take out the king. Whatever the reason, to my utter shock, the soldiers *re-engaged* for a final strike.

I grasped the heart shattering truth as the Spades advanced.

They'd die, but they'd take us with them.

With the vast force funneling into the city, I realized with relief that we'd ultimately win this war, but our division wouldn't live long enough to see it. We hadn't the numbers to hold this Spade attack at bay until the full strength of Jori's reinforcements crushed them.

Reaching the same conclusion, Lazlian squeezed my hand. A lump the size of the world formed in my throat.

I tried to picture the future of Rythas, once my prison, now a kingdom I'd die to protect. She'd thrive, ruled by Sanda under Kirwyn's safeguarding and his tutelage. *Kirwyn and Juls, Lida and Jesi, Tomé and Marcin. Saos and Alette. Raoul, Aewna, Merie... and maybe even Mal-Yin.* So many people I trusted would protect Rythas and usher in a new era for our island.

I choked on the devastating knowledge that I wouldn't live to see Teddy and Sanda grow. The yearning to hold my babies and the ache to touch Kirwyn one last time was pure agony. I whimpered aloud, like a dying animal of some kind.

"We'll lose this battle but win the war."

Lazlian said what I already knew. His voice cracked as

he tried to be encouraging, here at the end. "Though I suppose it hasn't the same triumphant glee when you're amongst the lost."

"I don't want to die," I whispered. Tears fell into my mouth as I spoke. I needed to stop their stinging flow if I had any hope of putting up a fight. This wasn't the first time I'd faced death, but in my youth, I'd had much less to lose. Older now, it didn't feel at all like the last time I'd been through a battle. "But if we both must..." My voice cracked too. I struggled to form the right words and squeezed Lazlian's hand. "Then I'm grateful we'll face it together."

Lazlian tore his gaze from our doom to look at me. Tears dampened the flames in those scorched-earth eyes and the sight broke my heart. The clash of swords drew closer on both sides, ringing out our end.

"He'll protect her," Laz said in a rush, and I wasn't sure if he meant Sanda or Rythas or both, but I knew who *he* was. How strange it was for us both. As the kingdom I'd once hated became my paradise, the man Lazlian once despised became the one he depended upon.

The lump in my throat prevented speech; I could only nod.

"And I'll protect you," Lazlian shouted above the nearing roar. "For as long as I can. Get behind me. Don't argue."

I didn't argue, but I didn't intend on listening either. At least, not once we were overwhelmed, which would be soon.

It was a hideous thing, hearing the sound of my death coming to me. Watching it happen. Had I not already sweated out all my moisture, I wasn't sure I could have held onto my bladder. The sheer terror could not be put into words, nor the anguish of not being able to see my children again.

But a warrior cornered fights like a lion to survive, and I did, ignoring the cries and screams all around me to focus on keeping alive. As our soldiers circled to protect their king, we were shielded from the heaviest of fighting, engaging only when an enemy broke through the line. Each time a Spade ran wildly, hoping to be the one to slay the king -- or myself -- either Lazlian or I were lucky enough to swing the death blow instead. Lazlian had done as he'd sworn and blocked me with his body and with his sword for as long as he was able. But too many Spades crowded our position, and soon I had to engage or die.

I spun, and Lazlian and I fought back-to-back. He quickly turned if he was able, positioning himself to face the stronger opponent. It was hard to distinguish friend from foe in the chaos. At one point I faced the death-blow from a Spade's sword, when a bullet from his own companion took him down. I assumed the gunman had been aiming at my head. In the shooter's pause of stunned horror, Lazlian slew the Spade with a quick thrust of his sword and quickly swiped the dead man's gun for himself.

Lazlian had the same problem, however. In the tangle of our close combat, it was hard to get a clear shot at the enemy. He saved the bullets for those charging us, firing until he'd emptied the clip, then tucking the gun into the waistband of his pants.

I re-firmed my grip on my sword, but my swings grew sluggish. Slow reflexes were a death sentence, and mine were never great to begin with. I wasn't a natural swordswoman and only the repeated strokes of my daily swims had given me the strength I needed to survive this far.

This is the end, I thought. *A gradual winding down as I grow increasingly weaker, unable to fend off an attack.*

A mountain of muscle charged Lazlian and I, seemingly keying in on the king and wanting to make quick work of eliminating him. I had to tilt my head back just to take in the attacker's height.

Oh god, no.

Lazlian, quickly assessing that he had no hope of beating this beast of a soldier in hand-to-hand combat, drew his gun and aimed it at the Spade's head.

The man halted, but I cringed, knowing Laz bluffed. There were no bullets left.

"I'd hate to kill such a fine specimen of man." Lazlian had to shout to be heard above the clanging of swords. "Run!" he cried. "Leave this battle and I'll spare your life."

The enormous Spade soldier took a moment to decide and then, to my astonishment, turned on his heel and fled. Lazlian let out a gasp of a laugh but it was short-lived. Several men and women to our left dropped dead to the ground, opening the way for more Spades to flood our position.

There were just too many of them. In the end, it came down to numbers and we were overwhelmed.

Lazlian shoved me back -- hard -- and ran forward to fight them off... or maybe he'd put distance between us to draw away our enemy's attention. He pushed me so forcefully I stumbled and fell, taking painfully long seconds to regain my feet. In that time, Lazlian had moved several yards away.

We were going to die, and I wouldn't even be beside him when it happened.

I quickly looked around, intending to sprint to Laz, but I

blinked to see someone running through the battle and heading directly toward us.

Kirwyn.

At the same time my heart soared, my stomach sank. *My love, my beautiful, foolish love.* He'd die with us. Of course he'd choose to do so. But he was supposed to stay alive for our children. He was supposed to accomplish what I'd failed.

I could tell by the formation of Kirwyn's mouth that he shouted something, but I couldn't hear it above the fighting. Between dodging a blow or abruptly stopping to fire his gun at someone, Kirwyn waved his arms wildly. Charging forth, he maneuvered through an opening in the flanks, screaming all the while.

I could finally make out his words when he neared.

"Get down!" he shouted. My gaze rose over his shoulder and to the rolling tank behind him, but I was confused, because it wasn't coming for us and it was a *good* thing to finally see one of the APATs nearby. Also... a man sat within the metal machine and... was that Fabroni?

I didn't have time to think any further, let alone move, because the tank barreled forth and when it reached the thickest tangle of Spades, it exploded. At the same time, Kirwyn leapt, shoving me to the ground and covering me with his body.

I momentarily lost consciousness. My head spun and my ears rang, drowning out all other sound for several long, dizzying seconds. Smoke stung my eyes and I gasped for air as I realized the wind had been knocked from me.

Above me, I felt Kirwyn's weight. Below me, the hard Spade street.

When my senses began to restore themselves, I heard *tremendous* celebrating. It was distant at first but grew closer and louder as it spread. It took me several long seconds to piece together what was happening -- the tank explosion had wiped out the Spade division attacking us, saving the lives of our people and expediting our victory.

The Spades were surrendering.

We'd won. Oh my god, we'd actually won.

But it was all so separate from me it might as well have not happened at all. My world narrowed to nothing but Kirwyn, unresponsive as Lazlian hauled him off me and shouted for assistance.

Kirwyn!

Shrapnel and other debris had embedded in Kirwyn's back, metal shredded his shirt and buried itself grotesquely in his flesh. Aside from giving me a once-over, Lazlian did not focus on my physical well-being and I did not need him to. Other people came to help me, directing my attention to something metal poking out of my arm. I was too concerned with Kirwyn to feel it, and my heart howled too loudly for me to hear their words.

"Kirwyn, Kirwyn," I cried. "Stay with me, please. Please don't leave me."

He didn't respond. Everywhere, the cheers rose higher, spreading as more Spades surrendered. I ignored them.

Please, god, don't let him be dead, I prayed. *Take me. Not him. He's the best of us.*

"Where is the nearest hospital? Get him to the hospital!" Lazlian ordered. "Find anyone with medical training!"

"Get off me!" I screamed, pushing back whoever tried to help me.

He never even wanted to fight this war. Don't let him die for it.

On my hands and knees, I prayed next to Kirwyn's body. Above me, Lazlian shouted orders, pointing, commanding.

It wasn't fair. We'd *won*. He shouldn't be dead when we won.

Me not him. Me not him, I begged.

Abruptly, Kirwyn's eyes snapped open and my heart sputtered. His eyes were wide, unseeing... lifeless. My mouth opened in a silent scream.

Then Kirwyn's gaze seemed to focus on me and my heart skipped several beats.

"Shiiit," he groaned so breathlessly it was barely audible. "This really fucking hurts."

Alive!

Laughing and sobbing, I kissed Kirwyn all over his face.

CHAPTER 60

HISTORY REPEATS ITSELF
Zaria

"You're alive! Stay with me, we're getting help. You have to stay alive because we love you and we've won!"

Kirwyn unleashed a string of expletives including some colorful mainland ones I'd never heard before, before quickly morphing back into groans of pain.

"Find Theo and Mack," Kirwyn moaned.

"We will. We're getting you to their doctors, wherever they are," Lazlian said, crouching beside me. "Hang on."

Kirwyn gave a barely-perceptible nod, eyes closed.

We won. We're safe.

I wanted to shout the words and to join in with those celebrating around me, but my focus remained on Kirwyn.

"Fabroni," he rasped. "He's dead. Got in that tank and couldn't figure out how to shoot it. He loaded it with explosives and drove it forward and..." Kirwyn trailed off.

Set it off himself? I wondered. *Let one bomb detonate another?*

He saved our lives with his own, I realized, which brought forth a wave of fresh tears. *Although he almost killed us in the process.*

Someone produced a stretcher and Lazlian helped to lift and position Kirwyn face-down on the cot-like bed.

"Find my father!" he cried as he was carried. "Find Mack."

Amidst the surrender, we raced Kirwyn to the Spades' medical building, finding it already crowding with injured soldiers. Spade civilians who hadn't fought were tasked, willingly or not, to tend to the wounded under the command of both our army and Mal-Yin's. At Lazlian's urging, Kirwyn was carried to a more private room, which, to my surprise, was already occupied by someone with a familiar head of dark curls.

Jesi.

As soon as I saw her, I ran to hug her.

"I told you I'm hard to kill," she said, giving a light laugh.

She lived. We lived. How lucky we all were.

"You are and you did it. I don't know what happened wherever you fought, but I know none of this would have been possible without you."

"Without *us,*" Jesi returned.

"Without us," I repeated, clutching her.

Jesi's injuries were superficial; she'd only briefly stopped by to bandage a few cuts and then return to where she was needed. Grethen, who must have been tending the wounded, rushed into our room and fussed over Jesi. She treated the Commander with special healer's potions despite the fact that Jesi sustained no serious injuries. Our commander was quickly released, and with Lazlian's support, she left to oversee the surrender.

I needed minor surgery to remove the metal from my arm and to stitch the cut. I must have still been high on adrenaline as it didn't hurt too much. Lazlian had taken a sword to his side and the wound was deeper than he'd let on. Yet as they worked on him, he managed to bark orders, ensuring Mal-Yin took over the Spade communicators and demanded their ships to cease any attack on High Spire.

It was Kirwyn who'd sustained the most wounds, requiring long hours of surgery to extract all the shrapnel in his back and to sew him together again. The Spade drugs dulled his pain enough for him to converse with us, and when the doctors finished, we three needed to talk. But Jesi unexpectedly poked her head back into our room.

"I found someone eager to see you," she announced.

At her words, Theodos stepped into view and I gasped. Ill-fitting clothing hung off his thinned frame and the little creases around his eyes had deepened, but he was alive and *whole.* Kirwyn's face couldn't seem to settle on an emotion and Lazlian and I quickly vacated the room to give him and his father privacy.

I heard them both crying before I managed to exit, nearly smacking into Mackenzie on my way out. The mainland girl threw her arms around me, weeping.

"I'm so sorry," I said, voice quaking as I tried not to cry. Mack wasn't the sturdy girl I remembered. Like Theo, she'd lost mass at the hands of the Spades. Mack's hair had dulled and her eyes were dark-rimmed and sunken. *But she's alive.* I tried not to think too much about how she and Theo had suffered, how they all suffered.

"We should never have assumed you were dead. We're going to take care of you now," I swore. If the guilt I felt was crushing, I couldn't imagine how Kirwyn was handling it. "You'll come to Rythas and live with us."

Over Mack's shoulder, I met Lazlian's eyes and he nodded.

~

It was late when Theo and Mack departed and Kirwyn, Laz and I were finally alone in the small room. One glance and I could see that Kirwyn was both physically and emotionally exhausted.

"What did you promise Jori to persuade him to join us?" Lazlian whispered.

Kirwyn shifted his gaze behind Laz, doubly ensuring no one was listening, though we'd closed the door.

"I don't think it was my promises that did it," Kirwyn replied. "I think it was that, at that point, Jori could literally *see* that his own men would be the deciding factor, and, by joining us he'd rise higher. But I still had to promise him two things."

Lazlian and I cocked our heads in unison.

"As we'd originally negotiated, Larius will have taken his own life in shame at his defeat." Kirwyn whispered and his face darkened. "Publicly."

Lazlian arched a brow. "And privately?"

"We're handing him over to Jori to do whatever he wants and not asking any questions."

I sucked in a breath, wondering what horrors the Spade leader might suffer at Jori's hands. Before I could think too long, Kirwyn's next words nearly stole all my air.

"And I'm sorry, but I had to promise Jori what might be... an Elowan of his own."

"What?" A laugh of disbelief escaped my lips. I hadn't heard him correctly.

"Listen, it happened really fast and I had no time to debate. Jori said he wanted to preside over the establishment of new relations with Elowa, but since he'd be too busy with the work rebuilding here, he instead requested one or two Elowans be sent to him. He claimed it would foster friendship and help build a relationship between the clans."

A chilling sense of foreboding raced up my spine and my mind raced with possibilities.

"What does that *mean?*" I asked, panic rising in my chest as I searched Kirwyn's face. "Why is he interested in my people? Could this turn into sending an Elowan as a bride or for some kind of experimentation or... *why* this constant fascination? It's happening all over again, isn't it?" I cried. "What do they want from us?"

"Your people are beautiful, they don't have fertility issues, and you don't know for sure all the secrets of your DNA," Lazlian reminded, matter-of-factly. "It might hold keys for them to unlock greater potential in themselves or their offspring."

Or it might hold absolutely nothing.

I fell into a chair and clutched the armrests, my stomach twisting with writhing eels. What did Jori mean by the demand? Was it history repeating itself? After all I'd done to stop the custom of sending the chosen braenese to Rythas, I couldn't believe that I might be witnessing the practice beginning *again,* now with Spade City. I couldn't believe that I might have a part in starting it.

I was going to be sick.

"The truth is, I don't know for sure what Jori's intentions are." Kirwyn's dark green eyes seemed to pierce me as he spoke. "There wasn't time for discussions."

"Can't we question him?" Lazlian asked.

"I don't think Jori is one to give full, honest answers," Kirwyn said. "On the other hand, I don't dislike him and we wouldn't be here without him. It could be an innocent request."

"On the other hand, even if he has less malicious intentions, this is *exactly* how it started before," I moaned, holding my head in my hands. "At least, that's how Aewna and I think it began. And if the idea is so innocent, why demand it?"

Kirwyn and Lazlian exchanged a dark look.

Not again, I pled. *Not all over again.*

"I had to agree at the time, but I hope you know I wouldn't let him hurt you or your people," Kirwyn said in a low, ominous tone. His eyes flicked to the door again before he continued. "If you'd like, we can eliminate Jori entirely before we leave the city. But it has to be now as we might not get another chance. They're your people; it's your decision."

I glanced up at Lazlian. "It's your decision," he agreed with a nod, "but I know who to trust if we need to send someone into his house-"

"No," I said, waving my hand as I cut Lazlian off. "I don't... I don't know what's right." I groaned softly before declaring, "But if I decide something needs to be done about him... then I think... I have to be the one to do it."

I didn't know how to explain my insistence to Kirwyn and Laz, as I didn't even understand it myself. I didn't want the burden of this decision; it felt too big and too murky. After all I'd been through, I would much rather have run away and not thought about it at all. But Kirwyn was right -

- I had to be the one to decide. And if I made a choice to... eliminate Jori, and tasked someone else to follow through with the act, it felt cowardly.

To my relief, Kirwyn and Laz nodded in silent understanding. But that didn't help me figure anything out.

~

I KNEW Kirwyn was feeling better -- or at least that the pain meds were working -- when he complained that evening, "I'd take another hit if it meant I could get a hot shower."

The doctor overseeing his care tsked, "You'll be sponge-bathing for the foreseeable future. If you can convince me you're rested enough, I'll give you instructions for your release tomorrow morning."

The woman looked between Lazlian and I, unsure.

"I am the king of Rythas," Lazlian scoffed, exasperated. To Kirwyn, he raised a brow and said, "I'm not sponge-bathing you. She's got this."

Lazlian shifted his weight, restless. We'd received word hours ago that Mal-Yin had rounded up members of the Aureum and negotiated some kind of surrender back in High Spire. I assumed he'd done it upon the threat of death and destruction, here. Most importantly, Mal had reported that Teddy was safe, as was everyone else we loved...

...Except, I grieved to hear, Raoul, who'd been killed before the fighting even began.

But other than some rather high-level information, the three of us were woefully in the dark, and I knew Laz wanted to speak with his brother if it could be arranged.

"I need to oversee command and connect with Juls," Laz said, echoing my thoughts.

I kissed his cheek. "Go take care of what's necessary, out

there," I said, inclining my head to the door. God only knew what was happening with Mal-Yin in charge. "I'll take care of what's necessary, in here."

Before he left, Lazlian paused and searched my face. "It will be a few days before we can return to Rythas," he said, holding my gaze meaningfully.

I understood what he was telling me, what he couldn't say with the doctor in the room.

I had a few days to decide what to do about Jori.

OUR BURDEN TO BEAR
Zaria

I surveyed the hellscape of Spade City as we left the medical facilities. The streets were lined with rubble from the ruination of buildings. Shell casings and a variety of discarded weaponry littered the ground. There were bodies, too, and I couldn't imagine how many had covered the streets the day before. Not a corner of the city was quiet, but the conflicting noise was almost too disparate to be believed. We passed clans celebrating, Spades and Rythasians weeping, soldiers barking orders, and civilians simply engaged in idle chatter, like any other day.

I pursed my lips to hold back a cry. The aftermath of war was different for everyone, so what was it to me? My head felt like it might explode, trying to process what I saw. I thought that might be why, in an effort to protect itself, my mind raced back to the simplicity of Elowa, to the solitude on Queen's Beach, or the quietude of our forests.

And yet... I wouldn't take it back. Everyone would have fared far worse, had we not fought. I tried to focus on that -- on the slaves who were freed and the clans who were saved. But the realities of the price we paid were all around me.

Jesi escorted us to a modest house, where Lida awaited with Sanda in her arms. A little white bunny hopped around her feet, who I guessed was coming back to Rythas with us. I burst into tears and for a long time, I sat in a chair and wrapped my body around Sanda's, smelling her sweet baby scent. The battle had exhausted and depleted me, but Sanda giggled and played, blissfully unaware of what was happening outside our door.

Unaware of how close she'd come to losing her whole family and her entire kingdom.

"We saved your throne for you, my baby," I whispered, kissing her soft, pink cheeks.

That night, I was bone-weary, yet I couldn't sit still. Once Sanda and Kirwyn were asleep, I left our well-guarded house and sought out Jesi so that she could put me to work. Anyone else might have refused to task me, but I knew that Jesi wouldn't hesitate to tell me what to do. For a while, I lost myself in the mindlessness of clearing streets, sorting food, or bringing water to the injured.

I let people see me as I worked, hoping it would inspire others to roll up their sleeves, and for the most part, it was effective. I'd earned respect, now more than ever, as the tale of Kirwyn, Lazlian, and I holding off the last of the Spade forces spread throughout our people.

There were a few men and women, however, who cast admonishing glances my way or whispered when I walked by. I heard the pointedly emphasized words and knew what they did not like about me.

Two men. Whore.

I walked on and forgot their faces.

Shame is a weapon, I thought, *a blade an aggressor thrusts against the neck of a would-be victim.* But those who whispered did not know what I knew. The secret of that dirty little shame-blade was this: the attacker could draw no blood. A cut could only be made if the target themselves leaned into the knife and accepted the wound.

Whether I was a princess or a queen or bore no title at all, it mattered not. I would always be Zaria, and I would not bend or bow for anyone ever again.

Well, I reminded myself, as I thought of the two men who loved me and of all the things we would do together. Things that would set those tongues wagging even more. *Almost no one.*

THE SPEED at which the Biohazards departed Spade City surprised me. They helped themselves to generous quantities of weapons and medicine, then retreated into the woods before significant progress at organizing the city or the spoils began. Only a few clanswomen stayed behind to report what was happening.

Nalice was one of them.

I was not surprised to learn that while Kirwyn, Laz, and I were in the hospital, Mal-Yin had been busy. He visited each section of the city walls, individually freeing the slaves, block by block. Cheered by both the clans whom he'd armed and the people he so *personally* liberated, Mal became the face of our victory, along with Jori, who was clever enough to never be far from Mal's side.

I didn't like how quickly Jori positioned himself there

and my stomach roiled whenever I thought about the decision I needed to make.

One thing I was sure of, however, was exactly where Spade City headed in its restructuring. Whatever title the newly-elected leader might hold, Mal-Yin would be the one to possess it. Perhaps that was why he never minded Lazlian leading the attack. Should we have failed, the blame would have fallen on the king's head. Should we succeed, Lazlian posed no threat, as he was always going to return to his own throne.

A few days after we won, Aewna came by our little house, and I already missed her.

"You wish to stay," I said, part of me hoping she'd refute the statement.

"We'll visit Rythas often," she promised. "You're our strongest ally."

"What should we do with our parents now?" I asked. It was a question that always unsettled my stomach. I could never know for sure if my mother had hastened my father's death. I could never know what went through her head when she'd tossed me, her baby, into the sea. It was difficult to forgive her for all the lies about the world and for my arranged marriage, but it was *impossible* to trust her. "Do you plan to pardon them? End their exile?"

Aewna considered, surveying the plain-looking room in which we sat. It wasn't an opulent manor, Kirwyn preferred we convalesce in a more modest home toward the outer rim of the city. The house was easy enough to guard and we didn't plan on staying long.

"I don't know," Aewna sighed. "I may leave the choice to my mother. I intend for Enith to rule as regent until Jona comes of age. Perhaps the Fire Maidens will have a say. I believe they're poised to do more, politically, now that Mal-

Yin is leaving." Aewna smoothed her dress and concluded, "For my part, I don't intend to keep them guarded at the estate any longer. But I don't have the authority to permit your mother or my father to live in Elowa. My place is here now."

And my place was in Rythas.

I wondered if my mother was happy with the way things were. I knew Jona, Gereth, and Naseroson visited her at Volmar's estate. Pama had always wanted Volmar, and now that she had him to herself, maybe that was enough for her.

Or maybe she reviled Volmar for trying to have me killed. Or maybe she was pleased to know that I, in some way, ruled Rythas as she'd always wanted.

I'd never know.

So much of my mother would forever remain a mystery.

SPADE CITIZENS TRICKLED BACK into their city. It was not the swift victory the High Twelve had hoped for, it was a devasting loss and a mess. The Aureum needed to be dealt with, along with other high-ranking officials.

But that was for Mal-Yin to decide.

My responsibility was another decision entirely and I was running out of time to make it.

There wouldn't be an easy opportunity to strike again if I waited to see what Jori's intentions were with the Elowans -- if it set off another cycle of stolen brides or something even worse. Now was the soft, malleable period when policies were forming. I knew first-hand that once matters settled they hardened as they cooled, and it would be more difficult to change any customs created.

I could ask Aewna to sit with Jori and to use her skills to read the truth in his heart. But that still wouldn't show me the future. She couldn't tell me if Jori might change his mind or if sending my people as supposed emissaries or personal ambassadors or whatever he wanted to call it, set off a practice of something darker.

Watching Sanda play on the floor, I thought of all the innocent girls who'd come before me as the chosen braenese, and of how many would have come after me if I hadn't changed the rule. I thought about how I had protected Sanda in the Spade satellite, even at the cost of Ollier and Breyline's lives. And, sitting alone with her in that dark, quiet room of the little house, I knew the decision I'd make.

I think I'd always known, I just didn't like it. Didn't like what it made me.

I would do the same for Elowa as I had done for my daughter; I would protect her and eliminate any potential threats. I couldn't know with certainty if I did the right thing. But that was my burden to bear and no one else's.

It helped assuage my conscience that Kirwyn and Lazlian shared my reservations and yet they were also in agreement. In a complete reversal of my struggle to decide, the act itself was surprisingly simple. Switching sides created many enemies for Jori within Spade City, and thus, many suspects to a murder.

We three, of course, had no known motive.

Lazlian whispered something in Mal-Yin's ear and procured for us a poison that would painlessly end Jori's life. I was grateful for that part. Then, two days before we departed, Kirwyn charmed his way into a dinner invite at Jori's manor for the three of us.

As a final step, I sat next to the man who had been our critical ally, intending to poison his cup.

Jori seemed very distracted by my presence, making my amateur sleight-of-hand fairly easy. Many years ago, I'd twice slipped a potion into Juls's cup, and the basic steps were the same.

My intentions this time, however, were a world apart.

Once I poured the liquid, I knew I'd emerge changed yet again. But the curious, lingering looks Jori gave me in his last hour of life firmed my resolve.

Once, a long time ago, my destiny had been to purchase a temporary peace for Elowa with my submission to some Rythasian nobleman or a king.

Instead, I tipped the poison into Jori's cup and purchased a more permanent security with his life and another piece of my soul.

I would carry the weight of my decision for the rest of my life and it would haunt me, along with countless other heart-aching choices I'd made.

But later that night, when I turned into Kirwyn's chest to feign distress at the news of Jori's death and for show, Lazlian angrily ordered a thorough investigation as he placed a comforting hand on my shoulder... I remembered in that moment that I never truly carried any burden alone any longer.

We three understood each other in a way no one else could.

ON OUR FINAL night in Spade City, we ate dinner crammed together in the little house. Our spirits were not as solemn as they'd been the past few days; it was like a fog slowly being lifted to reveal the sun. Nalice, Jesi, and Lida joined us and for the first time, we allowed our talk to turn hopeful, discussing what the future might look like now that the Spades were no longer a threat. I felt the first twinges of excitement for what that meant for my family and the way Rythas would flourish, going forward.

The wine helped.

When the evening ended, I slipped into Sanda's room and realized Nalice and Jesi had not departed. They lingered in the small passage between houses, and I could hear their conversation through the open window. I didn't want to move fast for fear of waking Sanda, so I backed out of the room slowly, catching a bit of their conversation.

"I loved her more than anyone in the entire world," Nalice said softly. "And still, it was not the way she wanted me to love her."

Was she talking about Frayde?

"Come to Rythas," Jesi implored. "Come with me. We'll have such a life together."

"I cannot," Nalice protested, voice heavy. "My place is with my people. I shouldn't even be here now. Lysette is gone. I just..." she trailed off, then finished, "wanted more time with you."

My heart beat faster, hating everything I heard. We'd won the war. If Jesi wanted to be with Nalice, there should be no reason she couldn't.

"Come with *me*," Nalice pled. "You cannot imagine the joys of our clan, the paradise we've cultivated, deep within the forest. Food is abundant, learning is plentiful, and plea-sures abound. We want for nothing."

"I cannot," Jesi echoed Nalice's words. "My place is with my people."

No. I wanted to scream my protest as my fingernails dug into my palms.

"I will never forget you," Jesi swore, breathlessly.

That was the last I heard before I made myself quietly exit the room. I wondered if Jesi would speak on it or if she preferred to keep the secret to herself. I decided I wouldn't bring it up unless she did.

Returning to Kirwyn and Laz, I found they still sat at the table, finishing their wine and chatting with subdued, but mounting, excitement.

"Rythas remains unconquered," I said, taking a seat and a sip from Lazlian's glass. He gave me a chastising look at my theft but said nothing. "Elowans will never be captured for Spade use. Mainland clans will no longer live in fear. And the slaves have been freed. We actually did what we set out to do," I concluded, almost disbelieving. "We did it all. Together."

"You always do what you set out to," Kirwyn said. "I never doubted it for a moment."

I snorted. "Liar."

"Maybe there was a little doubt," he joked. "But I won't make that mistake again."

We won, I repeated in my mind. *And we'll soon be home again.* Going home was all I wanted. The agony in my heart wouldn't stop until I held Teddy in my arms.

"You know," Lazlian said, considering Kirwyn, "You weren't in attendance when I was crowned, and you're retuning as the keylord and a war hero," he reminded. "Every single Rythasian noble has knelt and sworn an oath to me, their king. Even my brother. Even her." Lazlian pointed out, tilting his head in my direction. "Every single person of note. But you."

"It would be a lie," Kirwyn replied, holding Lazlian's eyes. "I won't put you above her."

Lazlian paused a long while, then leaned back and nodded. "The only exemption I'll accept."

~

As we readied for a temporary goodbye, Theo kissed Kirwyn's forehead and hugged him tightly.

"My son, my son," Theodos repeated, and Kirwyn held onto his father for a long time, speechless in his gratitude.

While our army had prepared to leave, I almost never glimpsed Theodos and Mackenzie not holding hands, and often, Kirwyn's father would protectively angle his body ever so slightly in front of Mack's. I wondered if they'd worked together in whatever roles they were forced to play under their Spade masters. I wondered if Theo had sheltered Mack from harm or helped by bringing her extra food... maybe even giving her his own. I couldn't fathom what they'd endured. But, like Kirwyn, Laz, and I, it seemed the ordeal had diminished the importance of other, minor matters. Any misgivings Theo had about the difference in their ages was an insignificant consideration against surviving the hell they'd suffered together.

Mack and Theo sailed in a ship alongside ours as we crossed the God Sea, but they would turn and head directly to special healers in High Spire, while Kirwyn, Laz and I instead moved up the coast to survey the damage to Rythas. The detour wouldn't cost too much time and Theo's ship was safe under Jesi's command.

In that same boat, Grethen sailed. I noticed she never seemed to be far from Jesi's side, and I wondered if Jesi would eventually notice it, too.

As I watched Kirwyn's father sail away from us, I had the odd realization that, if a romance had indeed blossomed between Theo and Mack and they married as a result... that would make Mackenzie my mother-in-law.

If the notion was strange to me, it must have been even stranger to Kirwyn, who was once intimate with the mainland freeborn.

Well, it's not like Rythas doesn't have its fair share of unusual conventions and arrangements I thought.

Other ships sailed along with us, several of whose hulls carried too many bodies as the dead were to be returned home and buried.

Erisio was among them.

We had a special funeral planned for the First and for Raoul, long-time advisor to the Dorestes. In my head I understood that war wasn't fair, but it ached my heart just the same that two of the kindest people I knew were casualties of it. We planned to mourn Fabroni as an honorary Rythasian, as well, with Lazlian erecting a statue over an empty grave.

I did not know how Frayde would be put to rest, back with her people, but I hoped the fiery warrior found some of the answers she sought. If not, I hoped she found peace anyway.

Reaching Rythas, other ships sailed alongside us as we made our way up the coast. But the passengers aboard those boats didn't know of my manor with its cheerful, yellow garden, and they had no reason to stop. They didn't know of the flowers Kirwyn and I had planted and tended with our own hands. They didn't know of that burst of sunny flora I always looked for when I was at sea.

Instinctively, I scanned the coastline as we passed, looking for our happy garden...

...only to be met with ash.

"Dock the boat!" I cried to the captain, shaking as I stared at the hole in the world where our manor should be.

Everything that happened next seemed to occur under a veil of fog in my mind. I heard Kirwyn and Lazlian's voices, but I couldn't understand their words over the screaming in my heart. One minute I was on the boat and the next, I was standing on the ground of what was once our house -- burned to nothing by the Spades.

Hot tears streamed down my cheeks as I fell onto my hands and knees, sifting wildly through the ashes, hoping I might find something precious the fire left untouched. My hands groped at burning, twisted bits of metal. The flaming sun beat onto the back of my neck, scorching it. My eyes stung as if phantom smoke filled the air. The more I rubbed, the more my vision seemed to cloud.

Kirwyn gathered me in his arms, stopping my mad shuffling. "We're okay, it's going to be okay," he soothed. "We're alive. This -- it's just stuff, it can be replaced."

"Everything's gone," I wept. "All our memories. Teddy's blanket and your books and my flowers... our lives, Kirwyn. Gone."

Why hadn't I thought about this before? We knew the Spades burned at random, to spread terror and for their own enjoyment. Yet I'd never imagined it would be our house. Maybe this was punishment for all the death I'd caused, all the blood on my hands.

I sobbed and Kirwyn rocked me, eventually pulling back to examine my face. "You're covered in soot," he said, wiping my cheeks with his hands and the hem of his shirt. "Little ash girl, like the fairy tale."

I didn't know what story he was talking about and continued to weep. My heart was broken because it *wasn't* just stuff, it was the tangible memories of our lives together, gone in an instant and never to be recovered. I understood that it was infinitely more important that we were all alive and that none of us had been harmed beyond physical repair, but it still felt like I'd lost a piece of myself.

Eventually, I got my crying under control and simply surveyed the devastation quietly. With Kirwyn beside me, stroking my hair, we were both still on our knees when I finally spoke.

"Our home is gone," I murmured, as another tear slid down my cheeks, "Where will we go?"

A hand fell upon my shoulder. Lazlian had been quiet while I wept and Kirwyn consoled me.

"You'll come and live at High Spire," Laz said, "Of course."

From the corner of my eye, I could see he'd laid a hand on Kirwyn's shoulder too.

High Spire. Yes, of course. There was nothing we could do to bring back our old home. We could only rebuild it here... or we could make new memories in the castle.

I nodded, wiping my tears with the back of my hand. "Take me to Teddy, please," I asked of both men. "And take us home."

CHAPTER 62

HOME, ETERNAL
Zaria

For speed we journeyed to Saos and Alette's manor by boat and met my aunt, my uncle, and Mazriah outside their house. I immediately ran to Teddy, who laughed and jumped as I swept him into my arms.

How he'd grown.

I couldn't stop nuzzling and smelling him, bursting into tears once more. I had to hold Teddy aloft as Finley, leaping and tail wagging, nearly knocked me over in her exuberance. Kirwyn folded himself onto the other side of our son, wrapping him in a cocoon between us.

A year. We'd been apart for one year.

I'd never get that year back with Teddy, but I reminded myself that I'd have lost *all* the years, had I not done what I did.

Happy and resilient, Theo didn't seem upset, on the surface at least. I hoped this would hold true under closer observation, but only time would tell. Kirwyn shifted Teddy into his own arms, and I stood alongside Lazlian as he held out Sanda for Teddy's inspection.

"This is your sister," I told Theo, gently. I wondered if he'd ask questions about where the baby had come from, especially considering the king beheld her.

"Sister?" Teddy repeated, looking down as he searched Sanda with wide, curious eyes. Then he wriggled to free himself from Kirwyn's arms as he asked, "Can I have snack?"

We all laughed, and I felt sure my heart would burst.

Kirwyn and I gave Saos and Alette our deepest gratitude and requested they visit us at High Spire, bringing Mazriah along with them, as soon as we were rested. Our elderly nanny couldn't sit a horse, but we borrowed three steeds from the stables and rode to the castle. Finley raced alongside us, and I nearly wept again as we traveled. Despite losing our manor and all of our belongings, the fact the three of us made it back to Rythas felt like a dream. A part of me feared that when I fell asleep that night, I'd awaken to find it all not true. I feared I'd open my eyes to see that I was back in one of the Spade satellites, possibly awaiting death.

When we arrived, I was shocked at the devastation ringing the Garden Gate but elated to see Juls and Merie in the castle doorway, their arms *literally* wide open.

It made my heart thump when Juls hugged his brother, clutching his back tightly.

Teddy, having spent plenty of time in the castle with Juls and Merie, immediately raced around in what he'd *already* determined was one of his homes, or at least one of his playgrounds. He tugged our clothing to show us his favorite hiding places and was thrilled to be presented with his own bed in the royal tower. A room of dark greens and bright blues had been waiting for him, it seemed, just in case.

Merie had set up a bedroom for Sanda in the kindery, as well.

"Is it too much?" she asked me, gently.

"No, it's perfect," I said, looking over the beautiful sage walls and melon trimmings, the regal gold and silver accents fit for a young queen. Merie's skillful design was better than anything I could have achieved, and I had no idea when she'd found the time to do this.

"We live in castle now?" Teddy asked, eyes glittering with excitement. "Mommy and Daddy too?"

"Yes, baby," I said, laying kisses all over his sweet face and wetting it with my tears. "We all live together now."

I didn't know the way to best explain to Theo how the king fit into our lives. But since he'd already grown accustomed to an extended family of both kin and friends without blood ties, I hoped it wouldn't be too strange for him.

Whatever unfolds, I thought with a sigh, *he'll likely handle it better than the rest of the kingdom.*

It was a long day and it took even longer to get Teddy and Sanda to sleep, excited by their new surroundings and, in Teddy's case, all of us being together. By the time we'd accomplished the task, the fortress had fallen quiet.

When I was first held at High Spire, I hadn't fully appreciated the beauty of the castle when the moon was high and the commotion, low. The night-blooming flowers unfurled their petals, scenting the air, and the waves could be heard gently crashing against the rocks below. Within the royal courtyard fairy lights glowed, and now, beyond the King's Stair, Kirwyn's bioluminescent trees lit up the gardens like magic.

There was a weighty moment when Lazlian, Kirwyn, and I approached the threshold of Laz's bedroom door -- a pause in which it was as if we wondered, *are we really doing this?*

I stepped into the room and began peeling off my clothing.

"What are you doing?" Kirwyn asked, looking over his shoulder to make sure no guards stood nearby and angling his body to protect me from the threat of an empty hallway.

"I'm exhausted and I'm filthy. I'm taking a bath and going to bed. You can both stand there in the doorway or you can join me." Nearly bare, I said, "I should mention I have no clean clothes here, so I will be naked all night."

Lazlian and Kirwyn shared a look. Springing into action, I was surprised neither of them tripped and fell as they shouldered each other to be the first into the room.

I bit back a smile.

OVER THE NEXT FEW WEEKS, Juls and Merie re-commenced arrangements for relocating to Low Spire. I was thrilled to hear that, freed from royal duties, they planned to run a camp, similar to the one Kirwyn and I had lost in the fire. They had chosen to do so in the more elegant region of Low Spire, but it was a blessing for all the children who'd attend...

...and maybe for themselves, as well. Still unsure if they could have children of their own, I wondered if this would perhaps give them the opportunity to be like a mother and father to many.

Shortly before they departed the castle, I was in one of the formal, shared chambers of the royal tower, when Juls excitedly pulled Merie into the room. He spoke immediately, and before I had a chance to reveal myself. Trapped, I ducked down in the high-backed, heavily-upholstered chair in which I sat, not wanting to intrude.

"I have a gift for you," Juls said softly.

Neither Juls nor Merie were looking in my direction, and the chair wings hid most of my head, yet I could see them both.

Merie smiled prettily and her eyes gleamed.

From his pocket, Juls withdrew a small black box and held it out for Merie. After a slight hesitation, she lifted and opened the box, revealing a magnificent ring. For a moment, I was transported back several years, to when Juls gave me a ruby ring of engagement before my Presentation Party. But this stone was even more brilliant, it glowed as if a fire caught the light and refracted it.

"It's a red diamond," Juls said, slipping the ring onto Merie's finger where it fit without struggle.

"Did you steal this from Spade City?" Merie asked, brow furrowed, "Is it... the spoils of war?"

"No," Juls replied, quick and firm. "This ring belongs to the Crown of Rythas. Or it did, once."

"The Spades stole it," Merie said, frowning.

"Not exactly," Juls hedged. "But they might as well have. Keeping the Spades at bay required more than just diverting them with our amusements. Gifts, which were nothing more than forced bribes, were necessary throughout the years. My great, great, grandmother gave this ring to the Aureum in an attempt to buy peace. Before that, it had always belonged to the Queen of Rythas and now it shall again."

"But," Merie protested, "I'm not the queen."

Juls took her face in his hands.

"You're my queen."

I quickly averted my eyes as he leaned in to kiss her, wishing I could give them privacy and hoping they'd leave before escalating onto other activities.

I had no use for more rings as my fingers were already claimed by all that I needed. I only hoped Merie understood that, as I was sure Juls did, and never felt the need to hide her jewel from me. Merie had saved the children when the Spades attacked. If marrying Juls didn't make her a queen in her own right -- which it did, to me -- then protecting those who needed it certainly had to persuade anyone who doubted it.

That ring, I knew, was on the hand it was meant for.

PUBLIC REACTION to Kirwyn and I residing in the castle was quiet, at first. Initial gossip had already spread in the Spade satellite before our attack and I was right -- the aftermath of war was a curious time. Most people were too busy mourning, celebrating, or rebuilding to care too much about who was sleeping in whose bed at night somewhere up in the royal tower.

Eventually, however, something formal needed to be declared. Lazlian had created a new Assembly of Elites, consisting of both the noblemen and women who'd previously served, as well as the addition of Lida, Jesi, Tomé, and Juls. It was with the Assembly that Lazlian had to discuss what could be legally permitted between the three of us.

Having Kirwyn's consent, I hoped some sort of exception might be made, wherein a union might consist of two husbands and one wife. Considering we were war heroes and Rythas had all sorts of clandestine arrangements anyway, it wasn't so alarming. Curiously, however, Kirwyn and Laz were almost... ambivalent. I'd expected Lazlian to push harder, especially remembering that I'd all but promised him whatever he wanted of me, in exchange for agreeing to protect the slaves before locking down the weapons.

It was late one morning when Kirwyn and I waited for Lazlian's critical meeting to conclude. With our children occupied and the two of us idling in bed for so long, we found ourselves basking in the afterglow of sex. Despite the years and frequency, I never tired of coupling with Kirwyn and it sometimes made me wonder if what Tomé had said about Elowans and our supposed lust was true, or if it was just *us*, Kirwyn and me. When I looked at him, I wanted to be as physically close to him as possible. That hadn't diminished since we first met; growing with him, seeing the man he had turned into, only increased my desire.

My favorite times were when he manhandled me, picking me up and moving us from a wall to a table or the bed, and then forcefully rolling and positioning our bodies one way and then another. I knew Kirwyn's back was fully healed when we recommenced with such playful roughness. But his scars were still treatable, and so, after an enthusiastic and literal tumble, I bid Kirwyn to lay on his stomach and rubbed a special healing ointment Grethen had created onto the marks.

I always concluded my task by kissing each one of his scars. They weren't so bad -- in fact, they reminded me of his love and his daring, and I found that beautiful. I wanted to make sure Kirwyn knew that.

He was lying face-down on the bed, reading a book and letting the ointment dry, when Lazlian finally returned.

"What did the Assembly say?" I asked, leaping off the

bed. While Kirwyn and I were also members, we'd sat this one out at Lazlian's advisement.

"They're not keen on the proposal," Laz announced, shrugging off his formal jacket. Half-rolling his eyes he added, "They're more inclined to let Kirwyn and I marry."

My mouth fell. "What?"

"Some don't know quite what to make of us," he said, flashing a crooked grin. "If Kirwyn and I are lovers, it makes more sense to need you, the mother, to produce heirs. That's an arrangement they feel they can sell."

"I see," I whispered, looking at the floor. "And... what did you say?"

"I said I'm not interested in making Kirwyn my queen," Lazlian snapped with disbelief.

"I'm not interested in being your queen," Kirwyn called out from the bed, not bothering to look up from his book. "But you would have been lucky to have me."

"So, where does that leave us?" I asked with impatience. Kirwyn and Laz seemed very nonchalant about the matter. "What's the plan to-"

"Zaria, listen to me," Lazlian cut me off. With a sigh, he said, "It's probably best if we never marry. Not anymore. I tried to tell you this before Sanda was born."

"Oh? Why is that?" I asked, nervous for his next words.

"Because I want more children with you," Lazlian declared, surprising me. "Don't you see? The day you gave birth to Sanda was the day it became impossible for us to marry. Any future children we'd have, born in wedlock, would become a threat to her."

I blinked rapidly as his words sank in.

Her birth sealed our fate. Even if another son or daughter didn't *want* the crown, others might push for it, using the illegitimacy of Sanda as an excuse to overthrow her. And she was already disadvantaged by the sexist attitude many held toward her for being a girl.

"I – I do want more children someday," I admitted. "Maybe one or two. But not now and no more than that."

"And I think, by that time, we should keep things as they are," Lazlian said, cupping his hand against my cheek.

Kirwyn had been relatively quiet throughout. I got the feeling he'd already worked out what I hadn't realized.

"Are you... do you feel like they see you as a lesser king for sharing a woman with another man?" I asked the question gently, looking up through my lashes and treading lightly around Lazlian's ego.

He barked a laugh so sharp that I jumped a little. "From what I gleaned at the meeting they don't look at it that way at all. They believe me to be the most selfish king ever to sit the throne. Don't you see? How greedy I must be in refusing to take *just* a wife... just one partner of any sex... when with you both I can claim a woman *and* a man, a prince and a princess. A matched set, if you will."

I was stunned into open-mouthed silence. Kirwyn let out an agonized cry, half-genuine, half-dramatic.

"Aw, come on," he moaned, throwing his arms in the air and accidentally knocking his book to the floor. "You're saying that's how I go down in history? I might as well be your damn queen. They'll whisper what? That I'm keylord-consort?"

Lazlian shrugged, his mouth losing the battle not to grin. I supposed it didn't bother him what people thought of his preferences, so long as they always thought him commanding every situation he constructed.

"You come from nothing," Lazlian reminded, haughtily. "You should be glad for any place in history at all."

I gave Laz an exasperated look for rubbing salt in the wound.

"You'd *have* no kingdom, your history would end here if it weren't for me," Kirwyn shot back the cold, hard truth. He jumped from the bed, glowering. Then he swiped a shirt from the floor and pulled it onto his head. "I'm going for a ride."

"Don't ride too far," Lazlian taunted. "Or I'll have to send guards to find and return my little consort."

My eyes bulged and I nearly slapped Laz.

"Fuck you," Kirwyn returned, letting the door slam behind him.

"What? He's fine," Lazlian said, shrugging.

I knew that, deep down, that was probably an accurate statement. Because the truth was, Kirwyn had never been very concerned with what other people thought.

Because the truth was, he and Laz not only enjoyed each other's company, they'd come to depend on it.

That didn't mean I condoned Lazlian's instigation.

"What does this make us?" I asked him, frowning a little.

"What does this make *you*," Lazlian corrected. "I am still everyone's king, no matter what. Perhaps you could say that I'm also your lover, as you are still officially HRM. Though I suppose you could call me your master as this makes you forever the king's mistress."

I shot Laz a look of displeasure.

"It's rather amusing, you must admit," Lazlian goaded as he stroked my cheek condescendingly, eyes glittering, "to know you will be my eternal whore."

I was pretty sure my bulging eyes twitched at his provocation. I knew Laz was saying such things just to get a rise out of me. He'd take no wife and no queen... meaning in all the ways that mattered, I'd fill that role. However unofficially it may be. I also knew that what happened on the surface wasn't the whole truth. When push came to shove, Lazlian deferred to Kirwyn's counsel more often than not.

Yet I couldn't stop myself from lunging at Laz. He caught my wrists and pinned me down on the bed.

And then, he did all the things he could to remind me that I was, in fact, the mistress who belonged to him.

〜

THE NEXT MORNING, Lazlian awoke with a loud grunt, startling Kirwyn and me.

Kirwyn had returned for dinner the night before, not only having forgotten about what people might think, but entirely distracted by another project having something to do with better preserving the books in the royal library. It was all he could talk about as I rubbed that special ointment on his back to help with the marks from the shrapnel.

Lazlian shouted again, fully waking me, and I caught the tail end of Finley's exuberance as she jumped off the bed. I guessed she must have leapt onto Lazlian, hopped around a bit, then bolted back to the floor.

She seemed to delight in antagonizing the king. We had that in common.

"I hate this dog," Lazlian complained, grumpily. "I never planned on sharing my bed with two people, let alone an animal. She stinks."

"She knows you don't like her and it only makes her torment you more," I said, stretching. I didn't mind being awoken early. Though the sun was only starting to rise, it was one of my favorite times to swim. I'd take Finley down to the royal beach with me.

"Besides," I chided, "you two come back to bed stinking like horses whenever you go riding at dawn."

Lazlian frowned and protested, "We bathe before we wake you."

"Liar. Last week you literally raced each other back to High Spire, naming dibs on where to take me as the prize. And after sending your testosterone levels sky high with some boyish competition, you attacked me while I was still asleep and without cleaning up first. I reevaluated my choice of bedmates then and there."

"We had to," Kirwyn countered, now awake as well and running a hand through his hair. "You don't like waking up alone."

"I don't like waking up with one man sliding into my mouth and another thrusting between my legs without warning."

"Yes, you do. You love it," Kirwyn said.

"The only thing keeping the entire castle from hearing your screams as you came was that cock stuffing your mouth," Lazlian added.

My face heated at the memory, only cooling when Lazlian frowned, brow knit. "We didn't really stink though, did we?"

I smiled dismissively at his worry. "No. I just can smell things better than anyone else and I knew you came straight from a ride."

Lazlian had always been prone to tidiness, but since his ordeal in that hellish cellar he felt the need to keep the space around him more pristine than ever. We three had emerged from the past year with ticks and tendencies no one else could understand.

"The two of you together can be too much to handle sometimes," I teased, crawling off the bed to find my seasuit. "Though I suppose every warrior maiden needs both a sword... and a shield."

I purposely avoided eye contact with either of them as I finished.

"I'm the sword," they both said in unison.

I laughed, stepping into my seasuit.

We weren't quite there yet -- dark shadows still receded and might always haunt the corners of our minds. But I had a feeling that, in our future, laughter would be a hallmark of our unusual union. After all we'd endured, we needed it. We earned it.

Just as we needed, and earned, each other.

PART IV

EVER AFTER

EPILOGUE
Zaria

As the years passed, joy seemed to perfume the air in High Spire as much as the abundance of flowers cascading down our royal balconies. With peace, open trade, and the leadership of dedicated rulers, Rythas flourished.

Just as Lazlian predicted when he'd come to our manor to first discuss making the heir, Kirwyn's talents were advantageous. I'd heard of various spells and soothsaying some practiced, but never money magic before. Yet Kirwyn seemed to possess it, because it was as if he could conjure coins from thin air. With the power of the crown behind him, Kirwyn did the same thing for the kingdom as he'd done for our family, creating wealth through dizzying designs I didn't always follow.

He always claimed he'd read about it somewhere, and my favorite idea came from a text about an ancient society. Kirwyn implemented a system that cultivated the competitive spirit amongst the nobles by tasking them with specific projects and lessening tax burdens on the commoners. The noble families of Rythas were given rotating responsibilities to create and maintain things like our public buildings, roads, and services. Doing it better than the previous family nearly grew into a sport, and in this manner we decreased taxes and helped the people recover after recent losses.

Lazlian, as he'd once stated, had no desire to sit the throne and hear every boring dispute and petition in the kingdom. He transferred some power to a separate assembly to dispense judgement on less important cases, an endeavor overseen by Lida, his royal advisor. When he did make decisions, however, they were almost always unquestioned. Challenges to his reign and to Sanda's succession were long past.

No one wanted to cross a king like Laz.

Of course, one change Lazlian did not make was to end the custom of prostrating and kissing the king's feet when given an audience. He claimed it was more important than ever to enforce such traditions.

Kirwyn and I rolled our eyes but didn't fight him.

And after years of stepping back, I rolled up my sleeves to pitch in with *everything* -- planning fêtes, hosting ambassadors, running our charities, managing castle staff and wages, weighing in on new laws, and contributing anywhere else I could spare the time. I enjoyed it, and though I technically did not hold the title, I sat the throne as queen when the occasion called for it.

What I loved most of all, however, was watching Teddy and Sanda grow and play.

❋

IT WAS LESS than two years after the Battle of Spade City when Lazlian brought up the idea of having more children. I was on the fence about carrying *two* more pregnancies, however, especially considering how difficult they were. I knew the crown needed more than one offspring in the line of succession, yet I wanted Teddy to have a full-blooded sibling. It was something Kirwyn had always felt he'd missed out on as a child, and something he and I had talked about for years.

Somehow, as the three of us discussed the issue, it became a little competitive *and* daring. I shouldn't have been surprised -- competing was something Kirwyn and Laz never seemed to tire of doing.

They came to a gentleman's agreement that if *I* agreed, they'd fight it out... inside me.

The plan was for Teddy and Sanda to spend the weekend at Saos and Alette's, and to make it more interesting, I'd take a dose of the Eroska. Then we'd close the bedroom door for three days with all three of us, together, on the other side.

May the best man win.

I thought they'd lost their minds but seeing as how they were no longer arguing about it, I agreed.

Lazlian *loved* the Eroska. More specifically, he loved me on it. The full dose, combined with whatever my hormones were naturally doing as I matured, and capped off by being in close, confined proximity to the two men I loved, made it feel like the medicine hit a hundred times harder. He made me say and do things I'd never say and do under normal circumstances, teasing and withholding pleasure until I complied. Kirwyn wasn't nearly as sadistic, or his desire overrode any control. That first day, anytime I moaned and spread, he'd groan and spear me. We'd lock eyes, thread our fingers, and climax at the same time, if we could manage it. We'd always had good sex, but the way he and I coupled during those three days was an experience I'd never forget.

The strange drug made me feel like an animal in heat -- I was always a little too warm and I couldn't get enough pleasure. It had an upside, though. If any awkwardness or inhibitions remained between the three of us, they burned away that weekend in my needy heat. Atop the table, in the garden, on both verandas... there was nowhere we didn't couple.

After thirty-some hours of debauchery, Kirwyn and Laz were limp and exhausted on the bed, but I was still aroused. I straddled Lazlian's lap, grinding to bring him to attention. But he only grunted, and, to my shock, groggily plucked me up and placed me on Kirwyn's lap.

Kirwyn, exhausted, didn't even realize I'd just been re-positioned, and without opening his eyes, he lifted and deposited me *back* on Lazlian.

Stunned, I blinked. I never thought I'd wear them both out.

Well, then.

With a frustrated huff, I declared, "Fine. I'll pleasure myself."

I touched myself openly, but despite my somewhat theatrical noises, neither man stirred. Indigent, I pouted for no one to see.

"Fine," I sighed, jumping up and loudly crossing to the bedroom door, completely naked. "I'll just see if any of the guards want to please me."

Two accompanying thuds sounded behind me as Laz and Kirwyn shot out of bed and half fell onto the floor in their efforts to drag me back.

I smiled.

"I'll make you sorry you said that when I have more energy," Kirwyn said sleepily, hauling me onto the bedcovers.

"Do your worst," I challenged, rubbing my naked body against his. "Just help me climax first. One more time before bed, please?"

"Hearing you beg *is* one of my favorite things in the world," Lazlian sighed. He crossed to the vanity and discarded his rings. Before heading into the bathing room -- to clean his teeth, I presumed -- he cocked a brow at Kirwyn.

"Warm her up for me, will you?"

Kirwyn's devilish eyes met mine as he yanked me flat on my back, making me squeal.

To my utter shock and Kirwyn's dejection, it became clear that there were two sets of arms and legs moving around inside me.

Twins.

Lazlian was overjoyed since twins seemed to run in his family. If, indeed, his family had an accurate accounting of their lineage to begin with. Now that I knew what went on behind the scenes, I couldn't pass the statues of his supposed ancestors without raising one suspicious brow.

I tried to console Kirwyn -- with the medicine increasing the odds of multiples, they could just as easily be his.

As overjoyed as I was, I had no idea how hard a pregnancy could be until I doubled it. Most days, I couldn't leave the bed. But this time, I had *two* men making sure I had water, bringing Theo and Sanda to me, and propping me up to read them stories.

When the first baby was delivered, I was pretty sure he was Lazlian's son, as his tan coloring matched Sanda's and he looked more like a mix of Lazlian and me. But I gasped and shot a look at Kirwyn when a girl came out next, several long minutes later, and she looked more like a combination of Kirwyn and me. Volleying my gaze back and forth between my two babies seemed to confirm it.

That's not possible.

"You took the Eroska?" The doctor asked, and I nodded.

"Then you likely ovulated more than one egg," he explained rather clinically. "It's entirely possible that both the king and the keylord fathered one child. They're technically twins, but with different paternal DNA. It's rare, but it happens, even without the Eroska."

The doctor sounded less judgmental and more fascinated by the unusual occurrence. Kirwyn, Lazlian, and I were at a loss for words, turning the twins over in our arms and marveling at our little ones.

So much had gone wrong in our past that it felt like we deserved this blessing; that we'd earned finally having something go better than expected.

I named our boy Devlin and our girl Daphina. To our amazement, it didn't take long at all for the doctor's explanation to be proven accurate. As the twins grew, it was obvious from Devlin's facial features that he was entirely Lazlian's son, and from those same markers I knew that Daphina was Kirwyn's daughter. Devlin's hair was darker, but both twins possessed a thick, brown mane. Daphina had light, piercing blue eyes, and Devlin's were blue as well, but they were a deep marine blue.

As they grew, I saw how twins possessed a bond outside of their parents, a connection that predated it. In some ways, Devlin and Daphina belonged more to each other than they ever belonged to us. They whispered, excluding others from the conversation. They laughed at jokes none of us were privy to. And if, god forbid, we tried to separate them for lessons or grooming, the fits of temper made it not worth the struggle.

Royal twins with separate sires was, understandably, the talk of High Spire. Perhaps sensing everyone's scrutiny and feeling like oddities, Devlin and Daphina sometimes shied away from public duties. They preferred playing together in the gardens -- indeed, they did everything together, and woe betide anyone who thought to insult or bully one of them. Initially, it seemed Devlin was overprotective of his sister -- and he was. But Daphina was just as likely to enact revenge on any perceived slight against her brother. She was just quieter about it.

As Sanda grew, I wasn't surprised when she turned out to be what Lazlian christened *our hellion princess*. If I had taken the rules of royalty and thrown them into the ocean, then Sanda fished them out, set them aflame, and danced on the ashes.

She wanted to do anything we told her not to and it took Kirwyn, Lazlian, and I combined to have any hope at reining her in. We were often unsuccessful. Theo, ever a voice of reason and nearer her age, seemed best at getting through to her. By ten, Sanda liked to sneak out of the castle and steal a horse from the stables. She'd ride off without a guard to god-only-knew-where, in boots and trousers with a sword strapped to her waist, all the while proclaiming that she was her *own* guard.

I think she picked that up from Jesi.

When she was older, Sanda still preferred the comforts of men's attire for her physical activities, but, surprising us all, she didn't eschew gowns and finery, either. On the contrary, whenever the occasion called for it, Sanda would appear bedecked in Rythasian silks and jewels, laughing and flirting with eager nobles she'd tease with the prospect of her hand.

I think she picked that up from Jesi, too.

It only made the nobles want her more, the legendary moon princess who couldn't be tamed and would inherit a kingdom. It didn't hurt that she'd grown up glittering, with bronzed skin and golden hair and amber eyes.

They called her the Jewel of Rythas, and she truly was.

LAZLIAN HAD BEEN IMMENSELY RELIEVED when Kels gave birth to a girl she named Filiana. Kirwyn said he'd reserve judgement on the whole situation until she came of age, but I knew Theo wasn't going to be pleased to learn we'd promised him to any noblewoman at all.

In the customary way of Rythas, Kelody's daughter was often called by her nickname, Liana, but Theo alone insisted on calling her Filly. *Little Filly* when he was feeling particularly in the mood to taunt. Close in age, Fersanda and Filiana grew to be best friends, but Theo often tormented them both, setting up mischievous pranks and rolling his eyes when his baby sister and Liana followed him around.

It didn't escape our notice that little Liana followed

Theo around with *particularly* adoring eyes. It seemed a happy coincidence, but as the years passed and we reminded Theo of his need to choose a noblewoman to marry, he grew to resent the proclamation. If we pushed too hard, he'd shut down and shut us out.

He reminded me of a young Kirwyn whenever he brooded like that.

Unfortunately, the idea that the prince of Rythas might never choose a bride as he was required became an increasing worry as Theo grew into a man. Heated arguments ensued and during the worst one Theo shot to his feet and uncharacteristically told Lazlian that he wasn't his real father.

Lazlian shrugged and replied, "But I am your king," at the same time Kirwyn said, "Well I am."

I groaned and dropped my head into my hands.

We reached a tense stalemate that was going to have to come to a head, when, a few moon cycles later, Liana returned from a mainland trip abroad. Kelody's daughter had spent time in Spade City and we'd had no notice of her journey back to Rythas. One day, Filiana simply entered the throne room, bedecked in a scarlet gown with gold accents.

Every head turned -- including Theo's.

In the year she'd spent on the mainland, little Liana had grown up to be as gorgeous as her mother.

It was almost comical how Theo's mouth dropped.

But oh, Filiana did not forget the prince who'd tormented her in her youth. She was no longer a gangly girl, tripping over herself in an attempt to chase after her best friend's older brother.

Liana was utterly *merciless.*

I was sure she'd inherited that from her mother, too.

Kirwyn, Laz and I had not expected such a turning of

tables, Teddy having ranted so long and loud about how he'd never marry, just to spite us. Suddenly, our son was only too eager to make a fool of himself for Liana's delight.

I don't think Theo slept more than four hours a night the first few weeks after the young noblewoman's reappearance. He brought her flowers he picked himself, wrote poetry he'd slip under her bedroom door, and showed up each morning with horses ready for rides she'd only grant him half the time. It was Theo's turn to chase Liana while she spun away with a tinkling laugh, giving another eager nobleman her hand for a dance and driving Theo wild with jealousy he poorly concealed.

Eventually, Filiana put Theo out of his exquisite, and perhaps deserved misery, when she agreed to marry him.

In the end, it worked out better than we'd ever hoped.

I RECALLED a simple day as one of my finest memories. It wasn't particularly unusual -- Kirwyn, Laz, and I had many happy days together. But this one held a special place in my heart as it was when I realized I had everything I wanted.

What happened in my life and the choices I'd made carved scars inside me, the kind I'd forever bear. But I wouldn't change my decisions in the past, and I didn't carry the pain alone.

In my memory, Kirwyn worked beside a small tree before our guests arrived, tying the trunk to a piece of wood to stabilize it. Lazlian, nearby, stirred a passionfruit cocktail he'd created to welcome everyone. The fairy lights in our royal courtyard had just begun twinkling to life. Aewna and Mal-Yin had traveled to High Spire for a visit and our planned, smaller supper had somehow turned into a larger, more celebratory gathering.

Jesi and Grethen entered first, with Jesi giving Kirwyn her usual greeting of wink and a "thanks for saving my wife," reminder. Awkwardness long forgotten, it always made them both smile. The couple laughed together as they sat our table and sipped the passionfruit drink, with Grethen resting her head on Jesi's shoulder.

Tomé and Marcin followed shortly thereafter, carrying an artful dessert Marcin had made. Saos and Alette arrived next, with Saos lifting me off the ground in the exuberance of his bear hug, and Alette cooing over the children. Lida, Mack, and Theo arrived at the same time, with Kirwyn's father holding Mack's hand firmly in his grip. The couple lived just outside the castle and visited almost daily, with Theo especially liking to spend time in the royal library.

Aewna and Mal-Yin descended from the guest chambers together. At the time of my memory, they were married but did not yet have their son, and Aewna hadn't yet been voted in for her terms leading Spade City.

Last to arrive, I was pleased that even Juls and Merie rode from Low Spire to attend our impromptu party.

Kirwyn, Lazlian and I sat at the long wooden table next to the mango tree and with everyone we loved beside us. In the grassy patch nearby, Teddy and Sanda played with Devlin and Daphina, who were still little at the time. Teddy, as eldest, kept an extra, brotherly eye on the twins, whose curiosity about the pool had them crawling in that direction.

They'd grow to be swimmers too. I'd make sure of it.

Surveying our chattering guests that evening, I couldn't help but think of how lucky I was -- how lucky we all were -- to be here.

Years ago, when I met Kirwyn on Queen's beach, I'd been running to escape the confines of my room. It was far from the first time I'd snuck out, but that day determined the course of my life and my world.

In this cherished memory of mine the sun was setting, and although I couldn't glimpse that glory from our inner, royal courtyard, everything I wanted was there with me.

Once, a long time ago, everything I'd wanted was somewhere else, somewhere far away. I'd been running to that something else the morning I'd met Kirwyn. Back then, what I wanted was elsewhere.

Now it was here with me.

I didn't need to run to or from anything anymore, but gratitude washed over me whenever I thought about how lucky I was to have done so that day. *All those years ago.* Looking over everyone I loved as they laughed together in our courtyard made my heart swell with so much joy I struggled not to weep.

It was only because I'd once been determinedly running elsewhere and seeking *without,* that I now possessed all this abundance here, *within.*

THE SEA QUEEN'S LAST SWIM
Zaria

*Y*ou made up for it, I told Keroe, waves lapping my feet. I didn't quite believe in the Sea God the same way as I had when I was younger, but I believed in the power of the ocean and giving a name to it felt easier. *You had me going there for a while. Made me believe I was fated to a life of suffering. But look at all you gave me instead.*

More than I could have imagined, and I had a pretty good imagination.

Thank you.

Kirwyn and Lazlian watched over me as if a sudden surge might sweep me away. I almost couldn't blame them -- they had to support my weight to make the journey down the tiresome castle stairs and across the royal beach.

It would be the final time I touched the sea in my mortal body. I knew this in my bones.

The sun had recently set but the sky held onto the last of the pink light. For a few more moments, at least. The men I loved brought me down when it was cooler, easier for me.

Seeing Kirwyn and Lazlian together was so natural it was almost hard to believe there was a time when they hadn't stood side by side. The three of us could communicate in wordless glances, as if we'd developed a secret language apart from the rest of the world. But sometimes I thought that the two of them had their own, hidden from even me, often because it was about me.

But not always.

I was a bond, but there were others. That which had cemented us together went beyond me. If anything, Kirwyn was the key, but it wasn't that simple. His ties with Lazlian had first forged somewhere in that dark dungeon and over the years, we'd evolved into something stronger.

I remembered the day I met Kirwyn, my betrothal day, when I was so young and the world was filled with endless possibility -- all of it simple and happy, I'd thought. I was annoyed that the sun seemed too slow and stubborn to rise, holding me back from my morning swim.

I was stubbornly annoyed now that we wouldn't all die together. It wasn't fair that one should outlive the other two. But I supposed, with all the blessings we'd been given, I couldn't complain too much.

Instead, I decided to make the next best thing happen.

I would wait for them. It was only fair. They'd each spent time waiting for me.

I let the waves play with my wrinkled, sun-spotted hands, remembering when they were strong, swimmer's hands. I'd be a liar if I said I didn't miss my youthful beauty, at times, but I missed my physical strength more.

My children are safe and grew up to be so very happy.

I repeated that fact whenever I needed a reminder. Love

and happiness were all I ever wanted for them. All I ever wanted for myself. Lazlian, Kirwyn, and I had safeguarded our kingdom and our children enjoyed an amazing life we'd been lucky enough to share.

The three of us didn't over speak. When I grew weak, there had been a rush to say so many things we all knew anyway, and then it grew too difficult and long silences drawled between us.

I swallowed and broke the quiet. "There has never been a day, not one, where I haven't been grateful for you both," I said. Even after all these years, looking at Kirwyn and Laz made my heart thump. "I love you and it will bind us. Do you believe me? Together, in the next life."

Kirwyn's eyes fluttered shut and he clenched his teeth, fighting not to weep as he sat down beside me.

"Zaria," he choked out the word and kissed my forehead. "Without question I believe anything you say you can do. Only a fool would bet against you and as you've once told me, I'm a wise man. Far wiser than him," he said, jutting his chin in Lazlian's direction and making the jab to make me smile. Of course I smiled, because he wanted me to.

I watched Lazlian's throat bob as he swallowed. He'd been staring at the ocean instead of me, and when he finally turned and sat on my other side, tears dampened those brutal flames in his scorched-earth eyes.

"And you will find me, Lazlian?" I asked.

"My little queen," Lazlian said, and I believed he could still see me that way -- lithe and young, though I was frail and wrinkled now. As was he. For years gray had threaded the hair at Lazlian's temples and the stubble of his beard, giving him a distinguished look. But now, like Kirwyn, gray coated all the thinned remains.

It was a gift, our age. I knew that.

Lazlian looked at me with the determined eyes of a boy who'd cornered me on a balcony one night, a lifetime ago.

"I will find you. That's a vow."

Together, we waded in the waves to just past where my feet could touch the sand below. I kicked my legs and glided in small circles. It was all I could manage, but it was enough.

How I love the sea, I thought as I swam. *How I love our land and most of all, our family.*

It was a love beyond any words I knew.

After a several minutes we returned to the beach. For a long time we sat together, holding each other and staring at the dark and mysterious ocean; just as, in another sense, we stared at the unknowing abyss gaping before us.

I didn't want to go. I missed our children and grandchildren already, so badly it burned in my heart. But as long as I knew Kirwyn and Lazlian would find their way to me, it would be alright.

Elowa, Rythas... not even the Earth was my home. They were and always would be. So it would be okay.

And hopefully, just as this life had proved, it would turn out to be so much more than we could dream.

THE KING'S ULTIMATE REFLECTION
Lazlian

I grew old, like all who are lucky enough.

Somehow, like all who are lucky enough, I didn't think it would happen to me.

If my regrets were bigger than most, so were my blessings. Only a handful of men and women throughout the history of the world could say they lived a life like mine.

Fewer still could claim to have enjoyed it in *quite* the same manner.

The regret I came back to again and again, now, at the end, was my wish for more time with her at the beginning. To have told her sooner... told myself, allowed myself. When we were young and new. The incalculable idiocy of my formative years could only be appreciated at an age such as mine.

But even that regret could not be a true wish. Because had I the ability to change it, I wouldn't.

It had to have happened as it did.

She had to leave. She had to return. With him.

I had to leave. I had to return. Alone.

I had to leave with him and return with them both.

Did she know, at her end, how I regretted so much from our beginning?

The hateful sight of her empty bed made me want to rage.

Once more, once more... let me have another day with her. Just one, please.

Instinctively, she looked to Kirwyn first, when in need. When she'd scraped her leg on coral or awoken from a nightmare. It used to flare a twitch of jealousy in my chest when we were younger. I understood why when we were older.

I relied upon that steadfastness more times than I could count and would continue to do so at the end.

When I crossed our chambers and my knee gave out, I looked too.

No, Kirwyn was already there before I hit the ground, arm around my back, supporting it. The mainland rat would outlive us both, though who knew for how long.

He helped me to my bed. We'd had our own since she fell ill and needed it. The desire to use the bed for activities other than rest had passed years ago. I did not mourn that change, I counted myself lucky to have experienced it. *Lucky* was a word I came back to again and again. Our lives and our entire world could have turned out in incalculably different ways with only the slightest change setting a new course in motion.

We'd shaped this world, created it. We'd live on in our legacy. Our children. A part of us was immortal. Through the war and our reign, we'd made legend of our legacy.

"I'm going to die soon. We both know it, don't bother

with your false comforts," I said, waving my hand before Kirwyn could open his mouth. "I need you to watch over Sanda."

"She has a husband to help her," he pointed out, ever practical. "And it's been decades since she's needed watching."

"Yes, but she'll be crowned. You need to assist with her transition-"

A fit of coughing cut me off. I didn't bother to continue. I trusted what Kirwyn already knew and didn't doubt his competency.

I was glad to be the next to go, selfish bastard that I was. He'd had everything first with her in this world, the least he could do was let me reach her first in the afterlife.

I told him so when I found the strength to speak.

He snorted. "Tricky bastard. Just like the times you'd trip me after a race, or use a secret passage up to our room, or order a guard to hold me back. I think you're busying me with need here so that I'm distracted from too quickly reaching you there."

I grinned, but it faded. I didn't envy Kirwyn being left alone. We had never been alone.

"Fuck," he swore, wiping his nose with the back of his hand.

I looked at the man I'd shared a life with. Shared the woman I loved.

"It doesn't matter if it takes ten days or ten years. We'll be waiting for you," I vowed.

I swallowed an annoying lump.

"And I always keep my vows."

THE HERO'S FINAL STAND
Kirwyn

They left me. Both of them.

Servants busied in and out of our quarters, but they were like ghosts. Or maybe I was the ghost. I did what I needed to do and never faltered, never complained when my joints screamed in protest as I made the trek down the stairs of the royal tower, or when crown business ran late and I fought sleep in order to keep a seat at the table as I watched over the transition.

But I always returned to these empty rooms and shuffled around, haunting them. Wishing they'd return to haunt me. Talking aloud to them as if they had.

The mad mutterings of an old man.

I wasn't alone in the world; I had the kids. But they'd made families of their own long ago.

I could see us when I stared down from our balcony and into the lush courtyard. I'd thought the end would be more poetic, but all those damn clichés about time were true. It had passed so quickly. Like I was a young man down there by the pool and I'd only blinked… just one blink… and it was gone. All of it.

Now I stood alone.

I held onto the balcony rail at twilight, gazing downward. I saw us in that courtyard, under the bright sun, picking fruit for the kids. Sugar apples, oversweet and custardy, would drizzle down Sanda's chin and she'd giggle. Her tongue would circle around in a comical attempt to lap it up. Devlin and Daphina were little in my memory, rolling together on the grass. I saw us older, as well, when we'd dine as one big family by candlelight, right next to the mango tree. We'd listen to Theo excitedly tell us what he'd learned from the stablemaster or his tutors. I was so proud of him. His sense of honor and optimism reminded me of my father, his namesake.

In my mind I could so clearly picture Zaria swimming in the morning. God, she was beautiful with the sun shining on her hair and the water glistening on her skin. I could see Lazlian and I set up a game of senorok, poolside. We'd make wagers on who'd win and tease Zaria about the ever creative ways in which she'd be the prize. The more shocking they became, the more she'd blush. But she loved it.

She was blissfully happy.

What more could I ask for?

What more could anyone ever ask for than the life the three of us had been given?

No. We weren't given it. We'd grabbed it, fought for it, held on to it screaming and bleeding. Dared. We bore the scars but we were rewarded with splendor.

I closed my eyes, wishing that when I reopened them, I could see them in the courtyard below, even as ghosts.

But it was only emptiness and night birds chirping and a slight breeze rustling the foliage.

I'm coming soon. Wherever you are. Wait for me. You're both so impulsive. Wait.

When Zaria died, Lazlian and I wept over her body. But when Lazlian died, it was only me.

I wouldn't have wanted her to be the last. And he couldn't suffer it either. It had to be me.

But goddammit these empty days and nights were unbearable purgatory. After everything the three of us had done, I wondered if there was a hell and if we were all destined for it. But I couldn't imagine anything worse than my endless isolation as I waited.

Given the option, I knew each of us would choose hell together over heaven apart.

Zaria was explicit on how she wanted our funeral to proceed. *No land burial,* she'd demanded. We agreed to her wishes, of course.

Lazlian never grew to like the ocean. But he'd suffer his fear for eternity in order to spend it by her side.

Zaria never liked the idea of fire consuming her at the end. But she'd burn for him.

"And I'm the dirt," I told her, trying to make her smile in those last days, when we planned how it would happen. She didn't like the idea of being locked to the land any more than fire, but she'd mesh her remains with the earth, for me.

"You're everything," she said, voice shaking as she tried not to cry. "Everything solid and sure. I'm not afraid when you're with me. Stay with me now," she pled, clinging to my hand as she laid upon her bed and I sat above her, not knowing I'd repeat the same scene with Lazlian only a few short months later.

There was no one left to hold my hand.

How could you both leave me? You were always the rash ones.

I was the durable one and it was my curse. My healthy body was a cage, trapping me here.

Robust, Zaria had often called me, when her joints ached and Lazlian developed a cough and I raced to fetch wet cloths to cool them down and medicine that no longer worked.

She should have outlived Lazlian and me, our Elowan. Then again, she was the most impulsive, the most curious out of the three of us. Zaria was the one kept in isolation from this world for so long, perhaps she wanted to be the first to see the next world, to be the one to show it to us, as we had shown her this one.

I grew tired more frequently now and I was glad for it. I laid down in my bed, in the chambers we shared for most of our lives.

The last of our trio.

What are you two up to on the other side? I wondered. *Don't do anything foolish.*

Who was I kidding? I pictured Zaria disapproving of however things were structured in the next life and conspiring to change it. I imagined Lazlian stirring up trouble of some kind.

I'm coming soon. My wife. My brother.

I've missed you more than you can imagine.

I closed my eyes, hoping that they would not reopen to this world. Hoping when I next raised my eyelids, I'd see the two of them laughing and holding out their arms for me.

CHAPTER 67

FAREWELL
Fersanda

Whatever god watched over my parents was here at their end, sending them off in a spectacle.

The sky was impossibly golden -- not just the sunset, but the entire firmament. As far as I could see, that vibrant shade of yellow-orange glowed across the heavens. I knew I'd never forget it; it was the kind of sunset people talked about for years.

They had been the kind of rulers people talked about for centuries.

I only hoped I could do a fraction of what they did. *With a smidge less scandal,* I thought, smiling and biting my lip to keep from crying.

Standing aboard our royal ship, I gave the command. Standing beside me, Theo shot the arrow.

He had his father's aim. I had my father's crown.

We both had our mother's heart.

Princess, mistress, savior, queen. She was always something different, depending on the tale and person telling it. She had never truly wanted any of those roles, she'd only wanted love, and the safety to enjoy it.

Even at his advanced age and through his tears, Theo's aim was perfect. The flaming arrow caught, sending the small boat into a blaze of fire upon the water. The wood had been doused in so much oil the sea didn't dampen the pyre. Silently and with a terrible ache in my heart, I watched as the bodies of our three parents burned.

When she died, my mother had been temporarily held in an earth-packed casket above ground, awaiting the death of my father and her husband, both to be enclosed within, beside her. They were determined to depart this life as they'd lived it -- together. And since the timing wouldn't magically work out, my mother, stubborn as ever, made it happen anyway. I wouldn't have expected anything less from her.

Sometimes I wondered if the entire world had been reborn through her sheer will, her iron determination alone.

I reached for my brother's hand as he silently wept. My half-sibling, raised as my whole.

Prince Theo was so like his father. He possessed the same arch of his brow, the strong cut of his jaw, and the tears he was not ashamed to show. Around his neck he wore the keylord's necklace, once his father's and before that, my father's. Theo rode a horse as well as Kirwyn and loved just as faithfully. He could be relied upon at court as a man who honored his word and served as my most trusted advisor. He'd been a prankster all his life too -- far more mischievous than his father though much less dangerous, having inherited a moral code more like our mother's. Kirwyn often told Theo he'd grown to be the man he'd always wished he himself could be.

Growing up in a time of peace enabled that goodness to flourish in a way it had not, in our parents' time.

Yet look at what they'd done, what they'd built together.

The world didn't allow them what they wanted to be, but I hoped our parents knew that what they became was something even better. They became what the world needed, and what they needed from each other. My parents left our corner of the world a better place than they found it, on a magnitude that would likely not be matched for centuries, if ever.

"We couldn't have asked to be given a better life than the one they gave us, and they lived longer than most," I whispered to Theo. Providing comfort wasn't my best asset, especially not when I was struggling myself. I was like my father in that regard.

He nodded, once, curt. "I know."

"They were extraordinarily happy," I said, squeezing his hand. It wasn't a lie, though I knew that sometimes, the ordeals of their past crept forth like sentient shadows, casting them each into darkness, in turn. They always looked to each other to return to the light.

Theo faltered a moment, swallowing back a lump perhaps. At least, I did.

"I know."

I glanced behind me, wondering if I should say something to the twins. But Devlin was already whispering to Daphina, providing his sister comfort in a way I knew no one else could. Eyes watery, Daphina rested her head on his shoulder, drawing from her brother's strength.

I turned back around as the last of that gilded, molten sun dipped below the horizon. In those final seconds, the most astounding array of sparkles glistened off the waves, silver and gold and glittering as it coated the sea in all directions. It looked as if coins had been scattered across the ocean or as if tiny fish had swum to the surface, flitting about in farewell.

The shining silver and gold reminded me of the colors of a Rythasian wedding, or some sign from the sea kingdom my mother believed in, far below.

Of course they couldn't depart this world without one last display, I thought, feeling the tears wet my lips.

I tried to hold myself together before our ship returned to port, but I didn't make it. Once back in the castle, Theo, Devlin, Daphina and I shared a supper in the royal tower as we shared one beloved memory after the next, toasting our parents until the sun rose the next morning.

A few weeks after their funeral, I moved into the king's chambers -- though it was now known as the queen's, even though my husband shared it with me and had taken the title of king.

The servants often whispered about ghosts in the tower and other places throughout High Spire, but I never believed them.

Not until I heard the laughter in the royal courtyard.

It was always just out of reach, carried on a breeze and quickly gone when the wind died down. Or in the throne room after a celebration ended, and for a moment it was as if I heard the three of them dancing on in the dark and quiet hall.

I liked to think of my parents contented together, somewhere in another world. But it also felt as if they returned to their earthly home for visits, to frolic and play.

They are everywhere, I thought, jutting my chin as I surveyed the kingdom from one of the terraces that faced both the city and the sea. *With me, beside me.* I couldn't escape their memory if I wanted to, and I never wanted to.

They'd etched a place in our history, and in our hearts.

The End

ALSO BY ELORA MORGAN

<u>Beyond the God Sea Series</u>

Beyond the God Sea (Betrothed)

Bound by Dark Waters (Wed)

Borne to Salt and Sin (Fated)

Crowned in Shattered Stars